GRIT & GLAMOUR
LEIGHTONSHIRE LOVERS
BOOK ONE

JONI HARPER

Copyright © 2024 Joni Harper

The right of Joni Harper to be identified as the author of this work has been asserted in accordance with the Copyright, Designs and Patents Act 1988. All rights reserved.

No part of this publication may be reproduced, stored in or transmitted into any retrieval system, in any form, or by any means (electronic, mechanical, photocopying, recording or otherwise) without the prior written permission of the publisher. Any person who does any unauthorised act in relation to this publication may be liable to criminal prosecution and civil claims for damages.

This is a work of fiction. Names, characters, businesses, places, events and incidents are either the products of the author's imagination or used in a fictitious manner. Any resemblance to actual persons, living or dead, or actual events is purely coincidental.

Cover design by Louise Brown.

Cover images @[Pexels] via Canva.com @[Annet Debar] via Canva.com

Please note: cover images are models and are not related to any characters in the story.

ALSO BY JONI HARPER

Leightonshire Lovers

1. Grit & Glamour
2. Envy & Elegance
3. Tinsel & Temptation

Also available is The Chase, a short story set in the world of the Leightonshire Lovers, exclusive digitally to members of the Joni Harper Readers Club – sign up at joniharperwriter.com

CAST

The Humans
In alphabetical order by last name

Tony Alton
British husband of Willa. Mobile phone billionaire. Lover of golf and Hawaiian shirts. Lives at Palisade Heights.

Willa Alton
Aspiring American dressage rider. Loves gossip and #RoséAllDay.

Bradley Alton
Tony and Willa's oldest son. A wild one.

Chandler Alton
Tony and Willa's youngest son. An angel.

Aaron Andrews
Aging eventer and ex-investment banker. Always looking for some action.

Bunnie Andrews
Aaron's Barbour-wearing wife of thirty years. Loves a good gossip.

Lady Patricia Babbington
Eccentric aunt of Robert. Recently widowed. Jolly good sort.

Sir Harold 'Harry' Babbington
Lady Patricia's late husband.

Bartholomew Babbington
Deceased son of Sir Harry and Lady Patricia.

Robert Babbington
Banker and polo-playing party-boy nephew of Lady Patricia.

Gareth Baker
Journalist with the *Leightonshire Chronicle*. Indiscreet. Provocative. Always after a good scoop.

Fergus Bingley
Show jumper turned event rider. Known for absolute precision.

Doctor Rowland 'Rolly' Bonner
Plastic surgeon extraordinaire.

Ryan Donaldson
Works for Blake Mentmore in the USA. Hattie's jealous ex-boyfriend.

Liberty Edwards
Runs a homemade luxury vegan candle company from the kitchen of her home, Badger's End. Neighbour of Hattie Kimble.

Eddie Flint
Daniel Templeton-Smith's kind-hearted head groom.

Bill Hodges
Local gardener and maintenance guy. Keeps watch for Robert Babbington.

Tyler Jacobs
Successful businessman, now semi-retired. Owns Dewberry (ridden by Daniel Templeton-Smith).

Jenny Jackson
Local vet and amateur eventer. Friend of Daniel Templeton-Smith.

JaXX
Reclusive singer-songwriter. Frontman of the Deciders. Lover of hats. Patron of My Last Wish charity. High Drayton Horse Trials takes place on his land.

Harriet 'Hattie' Kimble
Horseless horse whisperer. Aspiring event rider.

Melanie Kimble
Hattie's late mother. A talented woman across country.

Dexter Marchfield-Wright
Property tycoon and drink-fuelled sex party thrower.

Lexi Marchfield-Wright
Sexually dominant wife of Dexter. Used to having her own way.

Jean-Luc Malmond
French businessman. Event horse owner. Oral specialist.

Blake Mentmore
World-famous horse whisperer. US-based.

Marco
Gorgeous Italian beachgoer.

Helga Neilson
Greta's blonde head groom.

Mike Reynolds
Jovial owner of the Dog and Duck pub.

Bunty Saunderton
Daniel Templeton-Smith's shy yard hand and working pupil.

Jonathan Scott
Medal-winning Australian rider. Known for vigorous pursuits.

Marcy Sommerville
Yoga enthusiast and teacher at her husband's luxury retreat resort. Joint-owner of Novices Uptown and Knightime, ridden by Daniel Templeton-Smith.

Teddy Sommerville
Ex-banker now luxury retreat resort owner. Owns Uptown and Knightime with his wife, Marcy.

Grenville Stanton-Bassett
Inherited wealth but not grace. Loves the finer things. Chauvinist.

Hugh Stewkley
Chairman of Compass Electronics. Honourable fellow and jolly good chap.

Penelope Stockley
Accident-prone event rider. Part-time criminal lawyer.

Gerald Talbot
Private secretary to Lady Patricia. Loyal in every way.

Daniel Templeton-Smith
Gorgeous and talented event rider. Broke. Owns Templeton Manor.

Daphne Wainscoat
Stalwart of the eventing scene. Knows everything about everyone.

George Waterstock
Retail king, now retired. Always on the lookout for a new investment.

Alan Winkler
Organiser of High Drayton Horse Trials. Husband of Gerry Winkler.

Gerry Winkler
CEO of Michman Auto. Husband of Alan.

Greta Wolfe
Medal-winning German rider. Likes to be on top.

The Animals
In alphabetical order

Banana
Robert Babbington's golden Labrador. Chaser of geese. Lover of cheese.

Dinky
Jenny Jackson's pint-sized event horse.

Dewberry
Promising grey gelding. Owned by Tyler Jacobs (on behalf of his little granddaughter, Sophia). Ridden by Daniel Templeton-Smith.

Dodger
Fergus Bingley's less-experienced Advanced horse.

Gertrude
Daniel Templeton-Smith's small black cat. Chief mouser of Templeton Manor.

Gladys
Brown pygmy goat. Nervous disposition. Lives at Clover Hill House.

Knightime
Daniel Templeton-Smith's home-raised young gelding. Green but talented.

Mabel
Black-and-white pygmy goat. Fond of headbutting. Lives at Clover Hill House.

McQueen
Eddie Flint's swift three-legged collie. Proud rescue. Partial to pork scratchings.

Mermaid's Gold
A gift horse. 100% firecracker.

Peanut
Robert Babbington's wire-haired terrier. Lover of cheese.

Pink Fizz
Flighty roan gelding with talent and attitude in spades. Ridden by Daniel Templeton-Smith. Owned by Lexi Marchfield-Wright.

Pornstar Martini
Lemon-and-white skewbald mare. A real little speedster. Ridden by Daniel Templeton-Smith. Owned by Lexi Marchfield-Wright.

Rocket Fuel
Daniel Templeton-Smith's up-and-coming event horse. Dislikes getting his feet wet. Owned by Lexi Marchfield-Wright.

Rosalind
Fergus Bingley's championship-winning bay mare.

Sheridan
Daphne Wainscoat's cake-loving terrier.

Tiktac
Young bay gelding. Highly sensitive with bags of scope. Belongs to Jonathan Scott.

Top Cat
Talented and bold Advanced ride of Greta Wolfe.

The Rogue
Daniel Templeton-Smith's top horse. Bold over fences. Fan of ginger biscuits.

Westworlder
Ridden by Greta Wolfe. Owned by Mrs Clifford.

PROLOGUE

BEFORE: 24TH AUGUST 1989

The farewell disco at Leightonshire Pony Club's annual summer camp is the stuff of legend. After a week of riding lessons and proficiency tests, competitions and team selection, the kids can relax and the instructors, and the army of mums and dads who've pulled together to make the week run smoothly, can have a few drinks and let loose on the dance floor. The huge tent where meals have been served all week has been transformed: tables and chairs pushed to the edge of the space, a temporary dance floor and DJ booth erected, and a huge glitter-ball and set of flashing, multi-coloured disco lights hung from the ceiling poles.

As lead instructor, this is usually her favourite moment – her job teaching is done and there's a glass of red in her hand – but this year things are different. Glancing across the tented dance floor, she sees him. Tall and athletic, he fills out his jeans and Ralph Lauren polo shirt in all the right places. He's laughing with some of the other dads, and as he does he turns and she catches a glimpse of his strong jaw with just a shadow of stubble, and his blond hair flopping over his forehead. For a brief moment, their eyes meet. He gives her a smile and she knows for sure what will happen again tonight. Her stomach flips and the warmth between her legs intensifies. For the first time ever, she wishes the disco would hurry up and finish.

'Isn't this fun?' Rosemary Marsh, an enthusiastic mother of four, bustles over and clinks her glass against hers. She gestures towards the throng of kids jumping around on the dance floor to the latest Madonna track. 'You must be knackered after herding this lot about all week.'

Smiling, she goes into 'talking with the parents' mode. 'It's been fun, but I could do with a long sleep.'

'I wanted to thank you again for putting Tilly through for the show jumping team. She's so excited. And we'll get her out practising each week like you said, and make sure we get some brightly coloured fillers to practice with under our jumps at home.'

She's nodding. Agreeing with Rosemary Marsh. But she can't concentrate.

Rosemary doesn't seem to notice. 'We'll do everything we can to help her and Sparky be the best they can be.'

She smiles. She's used to pushy Pony Club mothers whose ambitions about winning team and individual trophies are far greater than their children's abilities, but Rosemary isn't one of them. Rosemary works two jobs as well as looking after her brood, and Tilly is a talented and ambitious girl who has done really well on Sparky, a pony she's trained herself. 'Tilly deserves her place. Keep up the practice and she'll do great.'

'Thanks, I just—'

The DJ cuts Rosemary off, announcing the end of the night and encouraging couples to get together on the floor for the last dance. The gentle rhythm of Chris de Burgh's 'Lady in Red' fills the tent.

'This is my favourite,' squeals Rosemary. She waves at her husband, who's standing over by the buffet making short work of the remaining sausage rolls.

At Rosemary's beckoning, he drops a half-eaten sausage roll, which is quickly scoffed by an appreciative Jack Russell lurking beneath the trestle table, and scuttles over to them.

'Have fun,' she says, watching Rosemary and her portly husband join the crowded dance floor.

Chris de Burgh has reached the chorus now. On the dance floor, parents and kids alike are dancing, some lovingly, some awkwardly, some blatantly taking the piss out of the song. She stands alone and for a moment it seems like everyone is dancing except for her.

Then he's standing in front of her. He holds out his hand. 'Can I have this dance?'

Her stomach gives another flip. The naughty twinkle in his eye gets her every time. Smiling, she takes his hand. 'Of course.'

They dance.

The heat of the summer night, and the heat from the crowd on the dance floor, makes her feel warm, and the red wine makes her feel pleasantly fuzzy. The multi-coloured disco lights flicker across the tent, making lazy patterns across their faces in time with the music. Chris de Burgh keeps singing.

'I thought we were keeping this a secret,' she says.

'I could hardly leave you standing on the sidelines.' His lips brush her cheek. His breath is warm against her ear. 'You're the lady in red.'

She smiles at the corniness. After all, the red jersey dress with black belt she's wearing is one of her favourites; fitted but stretchy, it shows off her curves in the right way and contrasts with her long, black hair. Working with horses, she tends to spend most of her time in jodhpurs and dirt. It's nice to get to dress up. 'Very true.'

She's conscious a few of the parents are watching as they slow dance past. Some of the older kids are side-eyeing them too, but right here, in this moment, she doesn't care.

Pressing herself tighter to him, she inhales his citrusy aftershave. Feels the warmth of his chest against hers. And fights the urge to kiss him, for now.

While the kids get ready for lights out, she heads across the field to the temporary stables – home to the kids' horses and ponies during camp. It's strange to think that tomorrow afternoon, once everyone has left, these wooden-sided stables with their canvas roof will be dismantled and taken away, only to return in a year's time to do it all again.

She walks between the rows of stables, checking inside that each pony has enough water and hay. The sweet aroma of meadow hay, and the steady, rhythmic munching of contented ponies in their stables, is one of the most relaxing combinations. In previous years she'd have stayed here longer, but tonight she's in a hurry.

Glancing across the field, she sees the queue for the toilet and shower block is down to the last few, and that most of the lights are out in the kids' caravans, horseboxes and tents. She looks at her watch – it's two minutes to eleven. In a couple of minutes, the 'fathers of the night' – the three or four dads assigned to sleep in the parents' caravans to keep an eye on the kids and watch out for intruders – will start to do their rounds, checking everyone is in the correct sleeping accommodation, with the right people, and their lights are out. It's futile, of course. As soon as rounds are done, the older kids will sneak out for illicit rendezvous in other caravans or horseboxes.

She tops up the water of Jester, the tiny bay Shetland pony who belongs to the youngest child in camp, and throws an extra section of hay into the net of a huge skewbald mare. One of the instructors' horses has managed to knock their water bucket over, so she quickly refills it and gets rid of the sodden straw.

Checking her watch again, she sees it's nearly eleven fifteen. She bites her lip. Anticipation fizzes in her belly. It's nearly time.

She hurries back across the field towards the camp. All the kids' accommodation is in darkness now; the only lights are in the fathers of the night caravans and the campfire smouldering in the centre of the encampment circle. As she gets closer, she sees the four fathers of the night sitting outside one of their caravans, and hears the clink of beer bottles being knocked together. She hears him laugh, and her stomach clenches as the memory of how he tastes, and how he feels inside her, replays in her mind.

What they're doing is wrong. She knows that. But being in camp is like a bubble; the outside world doesn't exist. It'll be over tomorrow, she knows that, so she swallows down the guilt fretting on the edge of her desire. She's going to make the most of tonight.

She hears him tell the other fathers that he'll do another last check. They don't offer to help. Probably they suspect that he's doing something else, someone else, her. But it's Chatham House Rules here, and they won't tell. Moments later she sees him flit, shadow-like, across the camp circle and disappear inside her caravan.

Hurrying, she loops around the horseboxes and tents to the far side of the circle. She hears muted laughter from a horsebox; voices – a boy and a girl – trying, and failing, to stay quiet in a nearby tent; the splash of liquid, forbidden alcohol no doubt, into glasses in another. She ignores it all. Reaches her caravan.

There's a soft clunk as she opens the door. Her heart is banging in her chest. She feels lightheaded with lust.

He steps towards her. He's already naked.

She pulls him to her. They kiss, urgent and wanting. She runs her hands down his chest, across the fine scattering of hair and over his toned abs. Sliding her hand lower, she feels him hard against her touch. Desire pulses between her legs. She's so wet.

Removing her belt, she unfastens her dress and lets it drop to the floor.

'Spectacular,' he whispers. 'I need to—'

She presses a finger to his lips and pushes him down onto the bed. Straddling him, she wraps her belt around his wrists, looping it up over the window handle.

There's lust in his eyes. His erection grows harder.

She guides him inside her. Rides him slow and deep. She feels powerful, in control. Kissing him hard, she whispers, 'Tonight, we're doing this my way.'

CHAPTER ONE

HATTIE

NOW

*H*attie is having the worst day.

'Dammit.' Exhaling hard, she switches the wipers of her clapped-out Ford Focus onto super-fast, but it doesn't make much of a difference. It's pouring and the wipers are losing the fight to clear the windscreen. Typical. She's moving home, again, so of course it's bloody raining. No. Not moving home. Hattie bites her lip as the grief hits her like a twelve-foot wave. She doesn't have a real home, or proper roots, anymore. Not since Mum died.

As a competition groom, she's always 'lived in' – sharing basic, communal accommodation with the other yard staff. But since getting fired last week for the umpteenth time, she hasn't even had that. She's had five days in a budget hotel, and now she's moving again, this time to look after someone else's home.

She crawls the car along the lane, peering through the glass, trying to find the right address. The wipers are struggling out of sync – whanging away but not clearing the screen. Hattie wills them to keep working until she finds the place she's looking for: Clover Hill House.

It's got to be around here somewhere. The sat nav told her she'd arrived at her destination over five minutes ago and she's very late, half an hour and counting. The owner – Robert Babbington – has already sent her two messages demanding to know where she is. Hattie grips the steering wheel tighter. She can't afford to be sacked before she's even arrived.

In her lap, her mobile pings. Glancing down at it, she reads the message.

WHERE ARE YOU?? I'M ON A TIME LIMIT HERE

A horn blasts. Flinching, Hattie looks up and sees the blurry outline of a white Range Rover flashing its lights as it hurtles towards her. Cursing, she yanks the wheel left. Hits the high grass verge and jolts to an abrupt halt. The Range Rover speeds past with its horn still blaring, showering Hattie's windscreen in dirty brown water. Her Ford's engine splutters out. Her phone pings with another message.

I'M LEAVING FOR HEATHROW IN 15. HURRY UP!!

Heart racing, Hattie turns the key in the ignition. Nothing. She tries again, but the Focus isn't playing ball. Turning it off, she waits a few seconds then tries again. Hoping for third time lucky, she presses hard on the accelerator as she turns the key, trying to coax the engine back to life. 'Come on, come on.'

The Ford's engine gives a few spluttery coughs and conks out.

'Shit, shit, shit.' Hattie smacks her palms against the steering wheel. Fights the urge to cry. She can't give up. She's nowhere else to go and she's almost out of cash. She needs this job. She'll have to find the place on foot.

Grabbing her phone, she climbs out of the car, slamming the door behind her. The Ford's parked at a pretty jaunty angle, half the front end up on the verge with its rear hanging into the road. But there's enough room for cars to get through, maybe a lorry at a squeeze, and it's not as if she can move the bloody thing anyway. Hattie taps out a quick message.

ALMOST THERE!

She hopes it's true. Shoving her phone into her pocket, she hurries up the lane towards the crest of the hill. Clover Hill House has to be around here somewhere.

The rain is relentless and she's drenched in seconds. Muttering, Hattie pushes on faster. There's no sight of the house yet, just high hedges around a pink-rendered mansion called Palisade Heights on one side of the lane and open pastureland filled with soggy-looking sheep and their lambs on the other. Hattie feels her phone vibrate in her pocket. She stops for a moment, hardly able to bear looking at the message.

BLOODY WELL HURRY!

She's out of time and she knows she should give it up, but she just can't. She needs this job and Robert Babbington still needs a house sitter, even if he's angry as hell. Phone in hand, she starts to run.

At the top of the hill, she sees another property. She feels a surge of hope as she recognises the charming Victorian house with the chequerboard brickwork from the pictures Robert Babbington emailed her with the job offer. This has to be it. Sprinting her way down the lane, trying to avoid the water-filled potholes and loose stones on the failing tarmac, she reaches the entrance. There's a sign on the ancient brick wall: *Clover Hill House*. Relief courses through her. She's found it.

The gates are open so she hurries up the driveway, wet gravel crunching beneath her feet. There's a massive Porsche four-by-four with a personalised number plate parked in front of the house. Hopefully that means Robert Babbington is still here. Because, wow, even in the rain the place looks gorgeous – the square frontage, original sash windows, and flowering red roses climbing up the chequerboard brickwork on either side of the front door make it look like a dream.

The rain eases off to a light drizzle. Maybe this is a good omen, thinks Hattie. Perhaps my luck is about to change. Then the front door opens.

'Are you Hattie?'

She looks up at him. Hesitates for just a fraction of a second. 'Yes, I'm sorry I—'

'Well finally! Where the bloody hell have you been?' The man striding towards her is nothing like she'd imagined. For a start, he doesn't look like a country person – everything about him is clean and shiny. Beneath the large, black umbrella he's holding, he's impeccably dressed in a navy suit, brown brogues and a stripy blue-and-white shirt. He's handsome, in rather haughty way, and his dark hair is cropped short and neat. A suit is not how she'd have dressed for a long-haul flight; it's glamorous but not practical for being cramped in a seat for hours on end. Then again, she thinks, he's bound to be flying first class. He's probably never seen what economy looks like.

Shit. Hattie runs a hand through her shoulder-length brown hair that's more dripping rat's tails than glamorous, pushing it back from her face. She glances down at her faded Joules polo shirt, old jeans and battered Ariat yard boots – all are drenched. She wishes she'd taken the time to grab her waterproof jacket from the car before sprinting up the hill. This is not the way to make a good first impression. 'I had—'

'Never mind. It doesn't matter.' He holds his hand up to stop her talking. 'I'm leaving in ten minutes.' He looks at his watch. 'Scratch that, eight minutes. Fetch your bags later. First let me give you the tour. We'll start outside given you're...' He gestures towards her.

Hattie knows she looks a right state. Stay strong, she tells herself. She just has to tough it out for eight minutes and then he'll go. 'Lead the way.'

Robert marches around the side of the house. He punches a

code into the keypad beside a wooden five-bar gate. Glances back at her as the gate swings open. 'The code's 69, 69, 69.'

'Got it,' says Hattie, keeping her expression deadpan. She's heard the rumours about Robert Babbington. He's got a big reputation for playing fast on the polo field, making fast deals in the City and going fast and hard on the party circuit. There's a glint in his eye as he tells her the code, and she can well believe the rumours. He's got that look about him. Dangerous.

'There's about five acres here. Not too much for you to do – my polo ponies are all liveried over at Kelsworth Polo Club until I'm back, and there's a local guy, Bill Hodges, who comes in once a week to do the maintenance on the place. His number is on the chalkboard in the kitchen. If anything critical breaks between visits, give him a call, yes? He offers an emergency service.'

'Okay, no problem.' Hattie follows Robert across a perfectly swept yard with ten stables, five on either side, and what looks like a hay barn, feed store and tack room either side of an archway with a clock tower above. Through the archway she can see a perfectly harrowed all-weather riding arena. 'Wow.'

'Basically everything's shut up until I get back, but I need you to look after the goats. Bloody things are a damn nuisance really but my Aunt Patricia sent them over a few months ago. They were her latest impulse save, and she seems set on them staying here.' He turns to look at Hattie. 'Aunt Patricia has a thing for lame ducks and sob stories. She saved them from slaughter apparently, which is fine, but why she can't have them at her place, I've no idea.'

Hattie lets him talk. His arrogant swagger grates on her, but there's something sensual about him as well that she can't put her finger on. She knows plenty of grooms who'd jump on him like a shot, but he doesn't do it for her; too self-absorbed, and far too overbearing. She likes her men more rugged and less self-important.

Hattie shakes her head. Who is she kidding? She hasn't had a relationship for over a year and can't be bothered with the whole Tinder, hook-ups or dating thing.

'Problem?' Robert raises an eyebrow.

'No, it's fine. I like goats, they're funny.'

'If you say so,' he says, looking at her like she must be bonkers. He gestures to the door to the right of the archway. 'That's the hay barn. You'll find hay and straw in there.' He gestures to the door on the other side of the archway. 'That's the feed store. The goats get a quarter scoop of pasture mix each evening. Once the colder weather in autumn sets in, they'll need hay overnight in their shelter, yes?'

'Of course,' says Hattie. Seeing a yard like this all shut up and unused makes her sad. It's a perfect training facility. If only she had a horse.

'They live in the closest field. Follow me.'

She hurries alongside Robert as he strides under the archway and along the side of the arena to the fields beyond. The land is split into small paddocks. In the one nearest are two tiny goats. Hattie smiles. 'They're so cute.'

Robert raises an eyebrow. 'The brown one is Gladys. Mabel is the black-and-white. Watch Mabel: she'll give you an evil headbutt if you don't feed her fast enough.'

'Will do.'

Robert checks his watch. Swears under his breath. 'I've got two minutes and then I must get going. Let me show you the house.'

He leads her back around to the house and in through the open back door. Pausing, Hattie takes off her boots and leaves them on the mat in the boot room. Padding across the stone floor, she grimaces as she realises she's leaving damp sock prints across the floor. Luckily Robert doesn't seem to notice as he hurries on ahead.

The house is as spotless as the unused yard and as classically stylish as something in *Homes and Gardens* magazine. 'This is beautiful.'

'Aunt Patricia's favourite interior designer did it.' He frowns. 'It's a bit overly twee for me, but it does the job. I'll probably redo it when I get back. It'll be a couple of years old by then so time for a change.'

Hattie can't imagine anyone thinking this place is twee, or changing their kitchen design every two years, and anyway, this place is perfect. The kitchen has pale green units and oak countertops, and there's a grey four-door Aga. The floors are oak, and the walls are muted off-white shades. It's classy, peaceful and so neat, it looks more like a show home than as if it's lived in. Hattie's glad Robert's not going to be here – she could never keep up with this level of tidiness.

Robert rushes her through the house. 'That's the sitting room.'

Hattie glances in as he hurries past her and is relieved there's a big telly. She'll be able to watch the Badminton Horse Trials highlights on iPlayer later, maybe even catch the end of the live action if she's lucky. Today is the cross-country day. She can't miss it.

'This is my study. Brace yourself,' says Robert, opening the door.

A golden Labrador and wire-haired terrier hurtle out of the room, wriggling around Robert's legs and then bounding over to see her. Hattie laughs. 'Aren't you both fabulous.'

'Banana is the lab, and she is bananas. The terrier is Peanut. He's usually the more sensible one.'

Hattie kneels down, fussing the two dogs. 'They're great.'

'They love food so you can easily bribe them if they're being naughty. I'm afraid they sleep wherever they like, and pretty much do as they please, but they're house-trained and have fairly good manners, for dogs anyway.'

Hattie smiles at him. His love for the dogs is clear. 'I'll take good care of them for you.'

He stares at her for a moment and it feels like he's deciding whether or not to trust her with them. Then, mind seemingly made up, he continues. 'They have meals at breakfast and dinner, and a chew at lunchtime. If you're cooking, Banana is fond of sugar snap peas, Peanut prefers a piece of courgette, they both enjoy steak.'

'I'll make sure I remember.'

'I wrote it all down. There's a note beside the sink explaining their routine.'

Robert checks his watch. 'I'm late. Shit.' He gives the dogs a scratch behind their ears. 'I've got to get going. Can you look around the rest on your own?'

'No problem.'

'Great.' Robert hurries along the hallway. 'You can have the blue bedroom; you'll see which one it is – the name gives it away.'

They reach the front door. Robert opens it and steps outside towards the huge Porsche four-by-four parked outside. The dogs swarm around him, thinking they're going on the trip. As he opens the driver's door, Peanut jumps up onto the seat. 'Sorry, guys, not this time.' Robert points back towards the house. 'Go back inside.'

Reluctantly, the dogs obey. Peanut starts to whine. Banana looks soulful.

'I hate leaving them,' says Robert. 'Especially this long.'

He looks so sad, she starts to feel sorry for him.

'Look, come out here, yes? And pull the door to, or they'll make another run for it.'

She does as he asks, even though her old Ariats are back in the boot room and she has to step across the gravel in just her socks. It doesn't really matter; it's not like they can get much wetter.

'Keys to the castle.' Robert holds out a set of keys.

'Thanks,' she says, taking them. 'And don't worry, everything will be fine.'

'I won't be back until the New Year, but I'll check in before that.' Robert looks around. Frowns. 'Where's your stuff? Didn't you say you had a car?'

'Yes, it—'

'Doesn't matter, I don't care.' He waves at her to stop speaking. 'Just look after the place properly. No throwing wild parties. And don't feed the dogs cheese. They love it but it'll make them fat and farty. And no trying any of that horse whispering nonsense I hear you're into with the goats, yes?'

'Sure.' Hattie feels herself blush. She's always been a blusher, it's super annoying. Extra annoying now because it makes it look like she's embarrassed about being a horse whisperer. She isn't embarrassed. She's bloody not.

'Perfect.' Robert climbs into the driver's seat of the black Porsche Cayenne S. 'That natural horsemanship crap doesn't go down well round here. We like the traditional ways, tried-and-tested methods. You don't win championships by rope-wiggling and pony-patting, yes?' He laughs. It makes him sound like a braying donkey.

Hattie clenches her fists and stays silent. Swallowing down the indignation building inside her as she watches Robert fire up the four-by-four and speed out of the driveway in a shower of gravel. He's wrong. They're all bloody wrong. Natural horsemanship does work.

She just needs a horse, and then she'll prove it.

CHAPTER TWO

DANIEL

'Twenty seconds on the clock,' says the tweed-jacketed, flat-cap-wearing chief starter, stepping out of the timing booth and standing, stopwatch and clipboard in hand, in front of the white-railed starting box.

'Thank you,' says Daniel, touching the peak of his jockey skull cap. In twenty seconds, he'll be setting out on the legendary cross-country course at Badminton Horse Trials, a track of just over four miles across the Badminton House parkland, with thirty-three solid fences, and a time to hit of just under twelve minutes.

All the eyes of the crowd seated in the grandstand here in the main arena, and those watching at home via the livestream on Badminton TV, are on him now and he feels the familiar fizz of nerves. He walks The Rogue in a circle once more and leans forward to give his neck a reassuring rub. The horse blows out hard. Jigs a little. They're both as ready as they can be.

'Fifteen seconds,' says the starter, not looking up from the stopwatch in his hand. There's a younger guy next to the starter now, operating a second stopwatch, the backup in case the main timer fails. There's no tweed for the second guy; he sports brown cords and a Badminton-logoed polo shirt instead.

Daniel gets his mind back on the job. He runs through his final checks: making sure The Rogue's girth is tight enough, and his breastplate straight, and that the cord connecting his body-protector to The Rogue's saddle is fixed correctly, so it'll inflate if they have a fall and the connection is broken. He shudders. Pushes any negative thoughts out of his mind. They can't fall. This has to go well.

It's been a hard season so far. After retiring Gossip Guy, his crowd-pleasing old campaigner last autumn, he then lost one of his younger four-star horses to lameness over the winter. The Sommervilles having to sell Match Point, Daniel's recently upgraded five-star ride, due to cash flow issues, came out of the blue, and meant The Rogue is his only competition-fit top-level horse this year.

The Novice and Intermediate horses have done well during the spring season, but it's the big prizes that attract owners, and Daniel badly needs at least one more if he's going to be able to stay in this game. It means The Rogue has had to run in more than his fair share of competitions already this season, and Daniel feels bad about that. But they've got to eat, and keeping an event yard in the black is almost impossible these days.

The Rogue blows out again and gives an impatient shake of his head. Daniel smiles. Despite the extra runs, the horse feels good – on top form, in fact, according to *Horse & Hound*'s competition preview of Badminton Horse Trials in last week's edition. 'You can have a month off after this, boy, and as many ginger biscuits as you can eat,' Daniel tells him, circling them back towards the start box. Ginger biscuits are The Rogue's absolute favourite.

The Rogue's ears prick up and he jigs again. He loves competition, and the cross-country is his favourite phase of a three-day event. He loves the crowds too and there's always a great atmosphere here at Badminton. Daniel glances up towards the stands around the main arena. There are so many people: adults and kids. They're all hunkered down against the weather in waterproofs and hats, but still laughing and smiling. Watching to see what happens next. The atmosphere feels electric. The crowd's excited anticipation matches his own.

'Ten seconds,' says the starter.

Daniel walks The Rogue towards the start box – a three-sided pen made of white rails and flanked by potted conifers. Behind them, he spots the owners' and riders' enclosure, and the event sponsor's flags flapping vigorously in the wind from the flagpoles either side of the VIP pavilion. Eddie, his ginger-haired head groom, stands by the barrier between the enclosure and the start. He smiles and gives a thumbs up, but Daniel can see the worry behind his expression. The course has been causing a lot of problems; even Olympic medal winners have ended up in the mud, and several previous winners have retired partway around. Now, towards the end of the day, the best ground has all been churned up. Badminton is always a true test of talent and stamina. This year, it's even tougher.

At least the downpour of earlier has eased to a light drizzle which means there'll be better visibility on the course, but the going out there is still going to be heavy. Daniel strokes The Rogue's neck again. Hopes the horse will manage okay; he's always preferred firmer ground.

'Five.'

Daniel's nerves jangle. The Rogue gives a loud exhale as they enter the box. Daniel sees the track of hoof prints in the turf. They need to walk one circle, timed perfectly with the countdown, so they start bang on the money. Getting within the optimum time can be the difference between winning and losing.

The starter counts them down. 'Four. Three. Two. One. Good luck.'

The Rogue leaps out of the box into a gallop, cruising towards the first fence, an ascending spread planted with flowers – the year emblazoned across it in crimson geraniums. The crowd in the stands hold their breath. The Rogue accelerates towards the fence and hops over like it's a cavaletti.

The crowd cheers. Daniel's nerves disappear.

They gallop out of the main arena and towards the second fence.

CHAPTER THREE

HATTIE

*H*aving coaxed the Focus back into life and kangaroo-hopped it up the hill into the driveway of Clover Hill House, it's time to move her stuff inside. Opening the boot, Hattie looks at the small red suitcase, battered rucksack and two plastic storage crates. She doesn't have much. Being a jobbing groom has taught her to keep personal possessions to a minimum and always travel light. Recently her luck holding onto jobs has been so bad she's stopped unpacking and lived out of her suitcase. It's easier to leave that way. And she's learnt that whether it's in the first week or the first month, they'll eventually ask her to go.

It's not that she doesn't work hard or do a good job; in fact, it's the opposite. She cares too much and gets too invested in the horses. She wants to help them, so she uses the horse whispering methods she learnt working out in the States with one of the world's top horse whisperers. She learnt so much in those two blissful years – how to calm an anxious horse, how to load and travel a claustrophobic horse in a trailer or lorry, how to gain a horse's trust, how to make them confident. She would have stayed longer in the States, but last autumn her mum got sick and despite her mum's protests that she'd be fine and there was no need to worry, Hattie came home to visit her. It wasn't until she saw her mum at Heathrow airport that she realised just how bad things were. She knew in that moment that her week-long vacation was going to be far more permanent.

Standing in the rain, the drizzle leaching through her already-wet-through clothes and onto her skin, Hattie relives the moment again and again. How she'd rushed along the green customs lane. Hurried through the doors into arrivals, scanning the waiting crowd for her mum. How she'd stopped when she couldn't see her, and one of her fellow passengers had almost cannoned into her, their own eyes fixed on the person they were meeting. How maybe twenty seconds later a woman had rushed up to her: stick thin, yellow-tinged skin stretched gaunt across her cheekbones, dark hair cropped close to her scalp, but bright, sharp eyes. Eyes filled with love. The woman was familiar but for a split second Hattie couldn't place her – and then when she did, Hattie remembers how she'd tried to hide her shock, and suppress her fear, as she'd hugged the woman, her wonderful mum, tight. Clinging on as if she'd never be able to let her go. But of course she'd had to, in the end.

The guilt sucker-punches her in the chest. If she'd known how ill Mum had been for months, if she'd realised the cancer was terminal, she'd have flown home much earlier. But her mum had played it down – told her she was 'a bit under the weather' or 'just feeling a bit tired' rather than that she was having chemo drugs pumped into her, or that the cancer in her breast had spread to her bones. Hattie swallows hard. Blinks back tears. It's been five months now but she still feels just as alone, as lost, as the moment after her mum took her final breath.

There's water running down her face – tears mingling with rain. Swallowing back her emotion, Hattie grabs the rucksack and suitcase, and carries them over to the porch. Then returns for the two crates. She shuts the boot and glances through the window at the wooden trunk that's sitting on the back seat – the newest addition to her possessions: her mum's memory box. Biting her lip, she opens the door and removes the trunk, adding it to the pile of luggage in the porch.

Letting herself back into the house, she moves her stuff into the hallway and then picks up her suitcase and heads upstairs to find the blue bedroom. Banana and Peanut hurtle up the stairs ahead of her and bound along the landing, leading the way. The ceilings are lower on the first floor but it's just as clean and neat as downstairs – all whitewashed wooden floors, light-painted walls and tasteful, neutral fabric curtains. The first door she opens reveals a huge bedroom with a decidedly masculine smell to it. The dogs charge into the room and hurl themselves onto the bed. From the creaseless black duvet on the four-poster bed, the neatly lined up hats on the shelves, and the male grooming products in the en-suite, Hattie is pretty sure this is Robert's room. Leaving the dogs on the bed, she exits the room and continues along the landing.

Next she finds what seem to be two guest bedrooms, one with pale pink walls and a smaller four-poster with white frilly bed linen, and the other with pale yellow walls and twin beds made up with matching grey linens. Then a massive bathroom with the most beautiful claw-footed roll-top bath she's ever seen. Reaching the end of the landing, she opens the last door.

Her eyes widen as she takes in the room. It's twice the size of anywhere she's lived before. She can see why it's called the blue bedroom; it has pale cream walls and white wooden furniture – bedside tables, a wardrobe and a chest of drawers – but the soft furnishings are all accented in blue. A waffle-weave blue rug, a quilted blue-and-white chequered bedspread, cream curtains with pale blue flowers, and a cornflower blue velvet headboard on the bed. The blue theme continues into a small en-suite with fluffy blue towels hanging over the towel rail in an otherwise white shower room. Robert Babbington might have been an arse earlier, but she is grateful to him for letting her have this room.

Hattie fetches the rucksack and two crates from downstairs and sets them down in the corner of the room alongside her suitcase. The dogs thunder along the landing to join her, leaping onto the bed and quickly making themselves at home on the quilted bedspread. She laughs. 'I guess you guys might be sleeping with me then.'

Sitting on the bed beside them, she strokes their silky heads and looks out of the window, past the stables to the paddocks. Mabel and Gladys are grazing happily despite the rain. Hattie's sure she read somewhere that goats weren't very waterproof but it seems like nobody's told Gladys and Mable that. As she watches, a bunch of geese land a few metres from the goats and get busy looking for grubs. That's interesting, thinks Hattie. It's wet but not *that* wet in the paddocks. She wonders if there's a stream behind the hedgerow, or a pond in the spinney on the far side of the fields that's attracted the birds here.

As if reading her mind, Peanut sits up on the bed, ears pricked. Next moment, something startles the geese and they rise as one into the air. Peanut sees them, and launching himself off the bed, he stands on his hind legs with his front paws scrabbling on the windowsill and barks like crazy.

Hattie laughs. 'And you're supposed to be the sensible one.'

With Peanut still barking, even though the geese are long gone, Hattie gets up and peels off her wet clothes. Rummaging in her suitcase, she finds a Harry Hall sweatshirt and another pair of jeans. She ties her hair up into a bun, then heads back downstairs. It's almost three thirty. If she's lucky, she'll be able to catch the last hour or so of the cross-country at Badminton Horse Trials.

Switching on the telly, she settles back onto the sofa with the dogs sprawled out alongside her, and switches over to the livestream. The familiar voices of the eventing commentators start up, and a wiry grey horse with a female rider in the German team colours leaps over a fearsome-looking steeplechase fence and gallops out of shot. Hattie recognises the rider – Greta Wolfe – silver medallist at the last Olympics and fearless woman across the country. The commentators are suggesting she could be one of the few riders going inside the time.

The camera picks up another rider – Fergus Bingley and his bay mare, Rosalind. The commentators are calling him the 'king of cool' and saying he's incapable of seeing a bad line to a fence. Hattie watches as Fergus gallops across the old parkland and in front of Badminton House. Her heart flutters. Riding at Badminton has been her dream ever since she was a child.

She still remembers the first time her mum took her there. They'd stayed in a tent in the Badminton camping field and watched the whole thing – from the trot-up at the first horse inspection on the Wednesday through to the prize-giving ceremony on the Sunday. As a single mother, Hattie's mum didn't have much money for holidays and she'd taken an extra cleaning job in the evenings to save up for it. For Hattie, the whole thing was more magical than any beach trip could have been. The glamour of the dressage phase with the gleaming horses and their plaited manes, and the riders decked out in black jackets and white breeches, then the speed and excitement of the cross-country phase as horses and riders galloped around the course of solid fences trying to get inside the optimum time, and then the precision test of the show jumping phase, where the horses and riders had to shrug off the adrenaline of the day before and remain calm and clean-jumping to leave the poles up if they were to be in with a chance of the prizes.

When she was older, Mum told her how on that first visit, when they'd walked around the cross-country course looking at the fences, little Hattie had stood in front of the yawning ditch at the famous Vicarage V and told all the other people walking the course that she could easily jump the fence on her pony. She was six years old at the time, and the pony she was referring to had belonged to the local farmer's son. The son didn't have much interest in his pony, so Hattie had been allowed to exercise him on the days the boy didn't want to ride, which luckily for her was most of them. He'd taught her a lot, that pony, but mainly how to fall off and get back on again. It was a valuable lesson for an event rider.

On screen, a new starter on the course riding a big bay horse clears fence three. Hattie recognises the name – Daniel Templeton-Smith on The Rogue. She's pretty sure he lives around here somewhere. The commentators are chatting away, saying that 'Danny' is thirty-two and the British team selectors have had their eye on him for a while and will be taking a close interest in his round.

Hattie sighs. They're almost the same age and yet Daniel is galloping across country at Badminton – living her dream – while she's further from it than ever. It's as if when her mum died something inside her died too, and she can't find a way to bring herself out of the funk. This is the first year they've not watched Badminton together. Even when Hattie was in the States, they'd streamed it at the same time, texting back and forth about who was doing well and who'd got dunked in the lake. Hattie bites her lip as it starts to quiver.

She glances across the room at the wooden trunk she left there earlier. With its dark wooden panels adorned with carvings of leaping and prancing horses, it's beautiful. It's heavy too, so she's keeping it here in the lounge rather than lugging it up the stairs. It's typical of her mum to have done something so kind and thoughtful, and so planned. She'd already put together the memory box for Hattie to remember her by before Hattie arrived at Heathrow, but it was only when the will was read after her mum's death that Hattie found out about it. Her mum had left it with the solicitor for safekeeping. Hattie's kept it with her ever since – transporting it from place to place, job to job – but has never unlocked it.

She takes a breath then looks away from the trunk. She knows she's not ready.

Even after five months, she still can't bring herself to look inside.

CHAPTER FOUR

DANIEL

The hail starts as they're approaching fence four. It's the first big technical question on the course and the visibility is almost non-existent. Daniel shortens his reins and steadies The Rogue into a hand gallop, making sure the horse has enough power in his stride for the challenge to come.

Spectators, undeterred by the awful weather, are gathered along the edges of the white ropes that mark the course. Somewhere to his right a baby is crying. Up ahead he can hear a dog bark. Daniel pushes the distractions from his mind. Stays focused on the fence. He's walked the course multiple times and planned how to ride every challenge. He just needs to stick to his strategy.

The direction the course is run alternates each year – clockwise one year, anti-clockwise the next. This year, the Staircase comes early on the course. The first element is a sturdy tree trunk positioned on the lip of the hill, then a couple of strides to two big steps down with no stride between them, making the horses do the two jumps in quick succession, then a few strides downhill to a massive spread fence – parallel bars made from extra thick telegraph poles.

The heavy downpour and the fifty-plus horses that have

jumped the course before them has turned the ground into a muddy bog around the fences. The going is far too deep and heavy for The Rogue's taste, and Daniel knows it. The horse has always struggled with this type of ground. For a moment, Daniel thinks about pulling up and retiring from the competition, but then he thinks of the stack of final-demand bills sitting on his kitchen worktop, and the twelve horses in his stables that he needs to keep feeding, and his two grooms who rely on him for their wages, and he knows that he can't. He's in fourth position in the competition after the dressage phase and with over £100,000 to the winner, and significant cash for all who place in the top twenty, he can't afford to pull out. He needs to be able to pay those bills, and he needs to attract another sponsor. There's no choice. He has to finish this.

'Keep sharp, we've got this,' Daniel tells The Rogue.

The crowd fall silent as he approaches the first fence, the tree trunk.

The Rogue pops over it like it's nothing, rather than the 1.20m high obstacle that it is, and strides confidently towards the two steps down. Daniel stays upright in the saddle, keeping in balance with the horse.

The slope to the steps rides steeper than Daniel anticipated. The Rogue's hooves are slipping in the mud. Daniel tightens his grip on the reins. 'Steady.'

The Rogue doesn't want to steady. Rather than take an extra small stride to get closer to the first step, he takes off early. Daniel swears under his breath. Sitting back in the saddle, he tries to use his own weight to help the horse balance. The Rogue lands and immediately takes off down the next step.

The crowd gasp.

Daniel sits tight.

As he lands, The Rogue's front feet slip and the horse throws his head up, trying to stay upright. He's floundering, but the momentum pushes them forward towards the last element – the parallel bars.

'Steady, steady,' says Daniel. He can feel the horse is off-kilter, and he's got too much weight on his forehand. His strides are long and flat; he's got speed but not enough power for jumping such a big fence out of mud.

With an almighty effort, The Rogue leaps out of the quagmire over the parallel bars.

Daniel sits tight. Teeth gritted.

The crowd cheer. But it's not over yet.

The Rogue slips as he lands.

The crowd gasp.

Daniel lets his reins slide through his hands to give the horse his head. For a moment he thinks they're going down, but then The Rogue seems to find an extra leg and stays upright.

Daniel exhales hard. The crowd cheer. Dogs bark. The hail worsens.

As they gallop away from the fence and along the rope-lined course towards the next jump, Daniel hears the familiar tones of the commentator over the loudspeakers.

'Daniel Templeton-Smith and The Rogue are through the Staircase, with a huge leap out over the final element. This horse is looking full of running.'

But Daniel isn't sure about that. The Rogue feels different. Yes, he's still fired up and keen to gallop – pulling down the reins as hard as ever – but something has changed. The horse's stride doesn't feel quite so fluid. He wonders if he tweaked a muscle when they slipped.

Again he thinks about pulling up and retiring from the competition, saving the horse's energy for another day. Then he sees those final-demand bills in his mind's eye and knows that's not an option.

Squinting through the hail, he focuses on the next fence

looming on the horizon. Set on undulating ground among the trees, it's a wide table fence – designed to look like a huge kitchen table – with conifers filling the gap between the ground and the 'tabletop'.

Up ahead, the course stewards are blowing their whistles, warning spectators that a horse is coming and to clear the path. A loose dog runs across the course, its young owner sprinting after it.

Daniel sees his line to the fence. He loops around an oak tree and aims for the left side of the table. It's a slightly longer route that will add seconds to their course time, but the ground is better than on the right of the obstacle.

The Rogue's ears prick up as he sees the fence.

Daniel sees a good stride and urges The Rogue to gallop on. They accelerate.

On the last stride, The Rogue slips. It's too late to stop, and their momentum carries them forward to the jump. Heroically, the horse does everything he can to push off with his hind legs – trying to get into the air and clear of the solid obstacle.

It doesn't work. The Rogue doesn't jump high enough and collides with the timber fence, hitting it with his chest. Momentum pitches horse and rider forwards, somersaulting over the table. Daniel stays in the saddle until the horse is almost vertical. Then gravity forces them apart and throws them head-first down into the mud.

The ground rushes up to meet him. Daniel tastes mud and blood. A split second later, the breath is knocked out of him as The Rogue lands on him, pressing him further into the dirt. His air-jacket body-protector has inflated but it's no protection against the weight of the horse. Daniel can't breathe. His vision blurs.

Then The Rogue rolls off him.

Daniel fights the urge to vomit. Pushing himself up to standing, he turns to check the horse is okay. Relief floods through him as he sees The Rogue's up on his feet. There's no obvious damage – the special grease that Eddie had smeared across the horse's chest and legs to help him slide free if he hit a fence has worked.

'Are you okay?' asks a kind-looking woman in a headscarf. The badge on the lapel of her wax jacket says 'fence judge'. She takes hold of The Rogue's reins.

Daniel blinks. Feels lightheaded. 'I'm fine... I just...'

The movement brings more nausea. Black spots swirl across his vision.

Reaching out, Daniel takes The Rogue's reins from the fence judge's hand. He strokes the horse's nose. 'Are you okay?' he says, peering at the horse, looking for injuries.

As he scans the horse's body, every movement Daniel makes causes pain, as if someone's punching him in the ribs with a knuckleduster. He clenches his jaw. Thinks he's probably busted a couple of ribs. But that doesn't matter. It'll heal. What matters is The Rogue. Ignoring the pain, he limps forward and asks the horse to walk a few steps.

The Rogue tries to move. He steps forward with his front legs, then stops. He raises his off hind. Jumps forward with his near hind. Won't put his off hind leg to the ground.

Shit. Shit. Shit, thinks Daniel. He rubs the horse's neck. Presses his forehead against The Rogue's damp coat as guilt and fear rushes through him. Behind him, he hears the fence judge radioing for the on-site vet and a horse ambulance. There are whispers in the crowd: *This is awful. Is his leg broken? He was going so well. Not surprising on this ground. What did he do? Will they put him down?* And then louder, clearer, the tearful voice of a little girl: *Will the horsey die?*

Daniel tries to swallow back the fear and the guilt threatening to overwhelm him. All eyes are on them. He has to keep it together until they're away from here. The Rogue nestles his nose into the crook of Daniel's neck, his soft breath warm against his skin.

The horse has always been brave and loyal. Daniel knew the ground would be too soft for him. He knew the dangers, but he rode anyway and now The Rogue is injured.

He feels a hand on his shoulder. 'The vet's coming.'

Looking round, he sees the fence judge's grief-stricken expression and he knows what they're thinking.

It could be fatal.

Oh God, thinks Daniel. What the hell have I done?

CHAPTER FIVE

LEXI

*I*t's hardly the most glamorous location, thinks Lexi as she shifts her bottom back as far as she can on the narrow, faux-marble countertop behind the toilet, sending the complementary toiletries and tissues flying. Hitching up her skirt, she pushes the pretty blond-haired waiter down in front of her so he's kneeling on the closed loo seat.

Really, the VIP toilets are far too cramped for this. But the VIP enclosure is filled with the worst bores imaginable and you have to get your fun where you can. She spreads her legs and raises an eyebrow at the waiter. He gets the hint and pushes her thong aside. Lexi shudders in anticipation. Grabbing his head, she pulls him to her, encouraging his mouth to get to work.

It's always the same with horse sports; everyone is so fixated on the damn horses or talking about cricket or dogs or some other yawn-inducing topic. Personally, she hates the things, but her husband, Dexter Marchfield-Wright, does so love the horsey crowd and having worked his way through the racing set he's looking for a new sport to milk for investors. He's into his schmoozing big-time, is Dexter, always on the hunt for investors and 'making connections' – tunnel-visioned with his business goals. To her, it feels like he only really seems to notice her when she can be useful – to charm a new client or host a fun party.

That's why she has to get her kicks elsewhere. Not that she minds.

She's always been good at making her own connections.

Lexi looks down. The waiter – Paul or Simon or Jack or some such – is working away down there. Full marks for enthusiasm but the poor boy isn't very good.

'Faster… use your tongue more… now add your fingers… more than that.' She pulls his head closer. 'Faster… faster… harder.'

The waiter makes some muffled sounds that might be words but as his mouth is rammed up so tight against her pussy she can't hear him properly. She stifles a yawn. She'd thought this, whoever he is, would be a fun way to pass the time, but he's making such a bad job of it that it's almost as unsatisfying as having to tolerate her husband's small talk.

God, how she wishes she'd brought her glass of champagne with her. She feels dreadfully parched. As the waiter keeps at it, prodding and sucking in the most amateur way, her attention is drawn to the flat screen television on the back of the toilet door. Great, thinks Lexi. You can't even escape from the bloody horses in the loos. Now if they were streaming *Real Housewives* or something, that would be an improvement. At least the sound is muted.

Onscreen, she watches a big brown horse misjudge a solid-looking fence and somersault over the top. The rider disappears beneath the horse. The camera suddenly cuts away to the crowds. Lexi can see the shock on their faces. Must be a bad fall, she thinks. Everyone loves seeing the falls really – but not if one of the precious horses is damaged.

The screen shows more shots of the crowd – all looking worried about the horse and bedraggled from the rain – and then switches to a helicopter view of the park, giving a bird's eye view of the course, the crowd and a little way into the distance the shopping village trade stands. Maybe she'll go and do a bit of shopping. That might cheer her up.

She flinches as a loudspeaker outside the toilets crackles into life. The commentator announces that the riders have been stopped on the course due to an accident at fence six. Then they start waffling away about the history of Badminton Horse Trials.

Lexi tunes them out. Tries one last time to school the waiter. 'Another finger… better. Another. Yes… now your tongue on my clit.'

Maybe he's doing a passable job, but it's borderline. She's a way off coming and it's not like she's hard to get to climax. She can do it herself in less than a minute.

Her gaze goes back to the screen and that's when she sees him. The helicopter view has switched to a close-up on the rider of the fallen horse. The creature is on its feet but looks wobbly. The rider is stroking its neck and, ridiculously, seems to be talking to it.

Lexi inhales hard, and not because of the waiter's fumbling. She stares at the screen, at the rider. With the strong jaw, those soulful eyes and that athletic body, this one looks like a Greek god dressed in riding gear. And the poor boy looks so distraught. At the bottom of the screen is his competition number, his horse The Rogue and his name Daniel Templeton-Smith. Lexi licks her lips. Now *that* is a man it would be hard to get bored of.

Reaching down, she runs her fingers through the waiter's thick, blond hair, then grabs a handful in each fist and pulls him off her. 'That's enough.'

'Don't you want to…' He grabs himself. Looks hungrily at her.

Lexi shakes her head. Standing up, she pulls her dress down, smoothing out any creases. 'Not this time, darling.'

The hopeful leer disappears from the waiter's face. Crestfallen.

Unlocking the stall door, she's about to leave but then she has an idea. She turns back to the waiter. 'How old are you?'

'I'm twenty-two. I know I'm a few years younger than you but I can still—'

She waves his words away. Flattery won't get him anywhere with her, she knows who and what she is – cougar, man-eater, whatever – but it's nice that he tried. It shows good manners. A pretty boy like this might go down well at one of her and Dexter's special parties. And it's clear he's quite happy getting intimate with older women. After all, while she might not look it thanks to Doctor Rowland, she's more than thirty years this boy's senior.

Taking a card from her clutch bag, she hands it to him. 'If you're open-minded and like to party give me a call next week. I might have some… hospitality work… you'd be interested in.'

He grabs the card from her. Grins. 'Absolutely.'

'Good boy.' Lexi kisses him on the cheek and then pulls open the stall door and struts out.

~

Back in the VIP enclosure, she ignores Dexter's waves to come over and talk to whatever chinless bore he's trying to reel into investing now, and thrusts her way through the space towards her target. With the action on the course stopped, everyone's gassing away, pontificating about what this will do to the leaderboard and whether the course is jumping well or strong or fast or slow. Lexi doesn't give a crap about any of that. She pushes past a large group of Pony Club competition winners, all dressed in branded fleeces with their logo and branch name on the back, who are wolfing down finger sandwiches two at a time. Then ignores the inviting glances of several ruddy-faced, tweedy types. She's not interested in them.

'Drink, madam?' asks a cute waiter who has a striking resemblance to a young Colin Farrell. He offers her a tray with several pre-poured champagne flutes.

'Don't mind if I do,' says Lexi, taking a glass from the tray. Maybe she should have tried this waiter rather than the blond. She holds his gaze just a couple of seconds longer than necessary. 'Thank you so much.'

The waiter blushes. Cute.

She continues on her mission, weaving her way through the enclosure. Passing groupies and try-hards. Old money and new. As she nears her target, Lexi nearly trips over a pair of golden retrievers stretched out on the sisal-carpeted floor. She grimaces as one of them presses its nose against her leg and fights the urge to kick it away; horrid, slobbery thing. Recovering her balance, she fixes a concerned look on her face, and makes her approach.

Daphne Wainscoat is sitting at a table feeding chunks of carrot cake to a particularly unappealing terrier on the chair beside her. Lexi tries not to show her disgust. She knows an easy way to getting this sort of people onside is through paying attention to their stupid animals. Daphne knows everyone and everything in the world of eventing, and right now, Lexi needs some of her oracle-like insight.

'Oh, how sweet,' she gushes. She reaches out and pets the terrier. Forcing herself not to recoil as it licks her fingers. 'Is he yours? He's gorgeous. What's his name?'

Daphne grins. 'He's my pride and joy. He'll be five next month, won't you, Sheridan.' She makes kissing noises to the dog.

Lexi battles to keep the smile on her face. Really, these people are ridiculous. She moves closer to Daphne. Glances back towards the course, and with a serious expression and tone says, 'Daphne, please darling, tell me everything you know about Daniel Templeton-Smith. I just saw his fall onscreen. So awful.'

'Yes, such a dreadful shame,' says Daphne, following Lexi's gaze. 'He's so talented. The British team selectors have had their eye on him for a while.' She glances around, checking who might be in earshot. Lowers her voice. 'The word was that if he ran well here at Badminton, he was going to get the call to join the squad. That looks unlikely now of course.'

Lexi frowns. 'Because he fell?'

'Not just that.' She feeds another piece of cake to the terrier, who wolfs it down, leaving a sprinkling of icing around its whiskery mouth. 'If The Rogue is out of action for a bit, or permanently, poor Daniel's got no top-level horse to ride for this season. He retired Gossip Guy at the end of last year, and the Sommervilles sold Match Point to the States a couple of months ago so he lost the ride. There's nothing else at his yard ready for a team place.'

'Well, that's just so sad,' says Lexi, holding back a smile as a plan starts to form in her mind.

'Yes, very.' Daphne nods. 'He's got some promising Novices coming up through the ranks, but they're a few years off this level. He needs at least a couple of four-star horses if he's going to have any chance of making the team.'

'And he can't afford that himself?'

Daphne glances around again. 'He's got the name and the land but his parents weren't good with money, they left him with a lot of debt. The Rogue is his, and he buys and sells youngsters to make ends meet, but with the more advanced horses he's utterly reliant on owners and sponsors.'

'I see,' says Lexi, barely able to conceal her excitement. 'How very sad.'

Daphne tucks her grey, bobbed hair behind her ears and cocks her head to one side. She narrows her gaze. 'You know, I didn't peg you for someone who followed the sport.'

Lexi smiles. Daphne is totally right in her assumption of course, at least until about ten minutes ago, and Lexi has no illusions about what Daphne, and all the others, think about her. She isn't one of them. She knows that. She doesn't talk horse, and she doesn't wear the uniform: not breeches and polo shirt, or jeans and Joules, or cords and wax jacket.

She glances down at her burnt-orange Gucci rain jacket, her DKNY leopard-print dress and her white Hunter wellies; she's more Glastonbury glamper than horse trials supporter. She couldn't be dressed more differently to Daphne with her sensible paddock boots, jeans, striped shirt and gilet outfit. But although Lexi isn't one of them, and she doesn't have class or a title that would allow her some eccentricity, the horsey set have tolerated her. And she knows why. It's because she has something else that they recognise as important, and a lot of it – cold hard cash. In their world, money means horses, and horses are everything.

She won't ever be one of them, but she will beat them at their own game, and it will be so much fun. She's found her perfect candidate and now it's time to put her plan into action. Exhaling hard, Lexi puts her hand on Daphne's arm. 'I love this sport, darling. I'm just too much of an amateur to talk much about it around all you super-knowledgeable people.'

'Well, I'm sorry I got that wrong,' says Daphne, patting Lexi's hand. 'I know it can be jolly hard to learn the ropes and fit in. If I can ever help, just let me know.'

Lexi loves not fitting in. To fit in, you have to be conventional, and conventional is so incredibly dull. Still, she doesn't correct Daphne. She needs her support and this is the best way to get it. So instead she smiles sweetly. 'I really appreciate that, Daphne. Actually, I wondered if you could fill me in on something.'

'Absolutely, I'd be very happy to,' says Daphne, feeding another piece of cake to Sheridan the terrier, and then patting the empty chair next to her. 'Sit, please.'

Got you, thinks Lexi, her smile broadening as she takes a seat on the opposite side of the table to the disgusting dog. 'So tell me, Daphne darling, what does the owner of an event horse actually do?'

CHAPTER SIX

HATTIE

*H*attie turns off the telly. The riders on the Badminton Horse Trials cross-country course have been stopped for a while now, and that can only mean one thing – the fall is serious. She hopes the horse and rider are okay. The sport's much safer now than it was twenty years ago – most of the solid elements to fences are now built with quick-release frangible pins that will break if there's impact – but accidents do still happen.

Not wanting to think about it, Hattie stands up and moves towards the door. She claps her palm against her thigh. 'Banana, Peanut, come on. Walk time.'

The dogs don't need much encouragement. They leap from the sofa and scuttle through to the boot room. Hattie wishes she had that much energy. Pulling on her still-sodden Ariat boots and one of Robert's Barbours, she opens the door and heads out towards the fields. The rain has almost stopped now, but the grass is damp and the ground slippery underfoot.

The dogs don't care. They run on ahead, chasing after sniffs. The rain has made everything smell stronger, greener. Hattie loves the spring and its promise for the future as the plants and the young animals grow. As she walks, she starts to feel a bit better. More positive. Maybe being here – surrounded by nature but without the pressure to conform in a traditionally run yard – will help her to heal.

Over in their paddock, Mable and Gladys are watching. Mable gives a hungry bleat. Then Gladys joins in and the two of them trot over to see her. Smiling, Hattie scratches the top of their heads. Mable sticks her head and neck through the gap between the bottom and middle railings and tries to eat the laces of her boots. Hattie laughs. 'You're telling me you're hungry, huh?'

With the dogs at her heels, she heads towards the stables and lets herself into the feed room. It's as neat and clean as Robert's kitchen. Rectangular metal feed bins line both sides of the room, and along the back wall a long countertop supports an array of feed supplements. She reads the labels – cod liver oil, dried seaweed and rosehips, garlic granules, milk thistle and devil's claw. Beneath the counter are stacks of feed bowls. Hattie assumes the two small purple bowls on the counter belong to the goats. Moving inside, she opens the feed bins in turn, searching for the goat's pasture mix. She finds it in the end bin and puts a quarter scoop into each bowl before adding a bit of water.

When she steps out of the feed room and back towards the paddocks, the goats' bleating rises in crescendo. Hattie puts the bowls through the fence and Gladys and Mable shove their mouths into them greedily. She laughs. 'You're very small but you don't half make a lot of noise.'

There's a brief moment of peace as the goats munch their food. Then the geese land in the paddock beside the goat field. Peanut sees the birds first and races towards them, barking the alert. Moments later, Banana emerges from the hedge, round green sticky willy burrs stuck all across her coat, and legs it after Peanut. Hattie holds her breath, hoping the birds see the danger.

At the last moment, the geese take off, honking in irritation.

Peanut leaps into the air, snapping, but with no hope of catching them. Then he stands in the paddock looking skywards, still barking, while Banana scurries around, sniffing the grass where the birds were.

'Come on,' calls Hattie, laughing at the dog's antics now that the geese are safely airborne. She'll tidy the goats' bowls away later. 'Back to the house, you two.'

As she approaches the back door, Hattie sees there's a new car in the driveway – a grey Lexus. She frowns. Aside from the weekly handyman, Robert hadn't warned her to expect visitors, and she's pretty sure the note on the chalkboard in the kitchen said Bill Hodges worked on Tuesdays.

Unlocking the back door, she's barely got it open wide enough before the dogs hurtle through the gap and the boot room and disappear into the kitchen. As Hattie removes her boots, she can hear them scurrying around.

'Hello, sweethearts.' The voice is female, unmistakeably posh and coming from the kitchen.

Who the hell is that?

Hattie hurries into the kitchen. There's a woman sitting at the table. She's hard to age – somewhere in her sixties or seventies – tall, with upright posture, short white hair swept back off her forehead, and a handsome face. Her clothes are bright – a floaty shirt in a kaleidoscope of oranges, pinks and purples, dark jeans and red sandals despite the weather. Peanut is sitting on her lap and looking very pleased with himself.

Hattie frowns. Confused. 'Erm... hello?'

'He didn't tell you about me, did he?' The older woman tuts. 'That's so typical of Robert, but no matter. I'm perfectly capable of introducing myself. Hello, I'm Pat.' She holds out a hand.

Hattie shakes it. She wonders how this woman got inside – all the doors are locked. 'I'm Hattie, the house sitter.'

'Of course, I know that, dear.' Pat smiles. 'I'm the one who found you.'

'You found me?' says Hattie, confused.

'I did. It was at afternoon tea last week. Lindy Bradshaw was hosting.' Pat leans closer. 'She's frightfully annoying, but her help does an amazing carrot cake so it's worth going and tolerating the verbal diarrhoea.'

Hattie isn't any the wiser. She doesn't know Lindy Bradshaw or her help. 'Are you a friend of Robert?'

'A friend – well, that's up for debate.' The older woman laughs. 'No, I'm his Auntie Pat. Or Lady Patricia Babbington, if you want to be formal about it.'

Heat flushes across Hattie's cheeks. Robert told her about his aunt who rescued the goats – it's logical she might want to come over and see them. Now she feels like an idiot. 'I'm... I'm so sorry, I—'

'It's all fine.' Pat waves away her apologies. 'It was at Lindy's afternoon tea, in conversation, that I happened to mention about Robert needing a house sitter. He'd interviewed a bunch of girls, you see, but wasn't happy with any of them. They were all London types with no experience of rural life. He was worried they'd get bored or kill the dogs, or both. And, of course, the days were counting down until he flew off to the States. He'd been dithering over a decision for ages, and I told the ladies that. And that was when your name came up.' She closes her eyes, thinking. 'Yes, it was Melina Gavin who said about you – that you'd been doing some yard work for her husband, Lawrence, but he was going to have to let you go because you kept trying to use horse whispering malarkey on his event horses and he didn't like it. She felt sorry for you, you know. Said you were jolly hard working and she'd tried to persuade Lawrence to keep you but his mind was made up and he always could be awfully bullish. She recommended you for this job.'

Hattie understands. It all makes sense now. When Lawrence

fired her, he told her she didn't need to worry because he'd found her another job that would start in less than a week – that a friend of a friend needed a house sitter until the end of the year. All she needed to do was call the number he gave her. She needed cash and a place to live, and had no other options so she called Robert, did an interview over the phone, and accepted the job. 'I guess I should say thank you then.'

Patricia raises an eyebrow and Hattie notices she's wearing silver eyeshadow. 'I guess you should, dear. Yet you don't seem very happy about it?'

Hattie doesn't want to come across as ungrateful, but taking this job, as a house sitter rather than a professional groom, feels like a failure. She's experienced with horses, and good at what she does, even if the people she's worked for recently can't see that. So far people round here have been so bound by the traditional ways, they refuse to see the great results she gets with their horses. Instead, they fire her, dismissing her horse whispering techniques as rope-wiggling circus tricks. She shakes her head. Usually it isn't the horses that need fixing anyway, it's the people. They're the ones that cause the problems. 'I'm sorry, I really am happy to have the job.'

Pat tilts her head to one side. 'But?'

'Horses are my life. I trained in the States with a world-renowned horse whisperer but people around here seem to think it's either nonsense or witchcraft.'

'Of course they do, dear,' says Pat, getting up and walking over to the fridge. 'They don't understand what you're doing, and so they certainly don't want you doing it with their valuable horses.'

'And you do understand it?'

Pat laughs. 'Oh no, I hardly know one end of a horse from the other, but I'm not afraid of experimenting with new things.' She takes a block of cheese from the fridge and, after fishing around in the dishwasher, finds a knife and carves some into cubes.

Peanut and Banana rush across to her and sit, eyes on the

cheese, at her feet. Holding a cube in each hand, Pat says to the dogs, 'Ready?'

She throws the cubes of cheese into the air. Both dogs leap up in unison to catch a piece.

'Robert says they mustn't have cheese,' says Harriet. 'It's bad for them.'

'Nonsense,' says Pat, throwing two more cubes for the dogs to catch. 'See, they love it.'

Looking at Peanut and Banana's happy faces and wagging tails, it's hard for Hattie to argue.

Pat laughs. 'You must stop looking so worried, dear. You have to enjoy life's little pleasures, otherwise what's the point?' She gestures to the dogs. 'These two certainly agree.'

'It's not always that easy,' says Hattie, thinking about how she's been ridiculed in the last three jobs she's done. How each one has knocked her confidence and set her back further from her dream.

'Take it from me, dear, because it's the truth. When you get to my age, you realise there's no point in worrying about what people think. They don't know any better than you or I do, in fact many of them probably know much less. What's important is that you live your life your way, on your terms, doing what you think is important, and along the way try not to be an arsehole. It's really very liberating.'

Hattie looks at Pat and wishes she had half of her confidence.

Pat narrows her eyes at Hattie. 'If you could do anything, what would it be?'

Hattie doesn't even have to think about it. 'Win Badminton Horse Trials on a horse I've trained.'

'Good, dear, very good,' says Pat, nodding thoughtfully. She smiles. 'So what are you waiting for? Get going and make it happen.'

CHAPTER SEVEN

DEXTER

Heart pounding, and not in a good way, Dexter stares at the screen. The numbers aren't looking good. No, worse than that, they're looking dangerous – caught out, reputation-losing, not-enough-cash-to-meet-the-obligations dangerous.

He taps a few figures into the calculator on his desk. Inhales sharply. Maybe he'll just about be able to meet next month's payments if he's careful. He'll dial back the socialising and expensive dinners for a few weeks, and hold off on reserving any boxes for sporting events too. He takes a breath. Yes, he can make this work. It just needs a bit of imagination, and he has plenty of that.

He stares out of the window as he starts to formulate a plan. The open countryside stretches out beneath him. It's calming. Soothing. A far cry from the cramped two-bed terrace house in Birmingham that he grew up in with his parents and three brothers. His study is on the top floor of his six-bedroom house – a loft room with 360-degree views through the Velux windows that makes him feel like he's in the turret of a castle. This is his space – muted colours, pale wooden office furniture, a big desk with an old-fashioned green blotter. No pictures. No knickknacks. Nothing like the maximalist design Lexi insisted on for the rest of the house.

He's worked hard for this, erased everything that linked him to his old life – changed his tastes, his style and his accent. Cut all family ties, changed his first name and added the 'field-Wright' to his original last name of March. He gambled everything he had and he won. He can't lose now. And he won't.

He takes a few deep breaths. The plan is getting clearer. For the next month, he'll minimise spending and focus on reeling in a few more investors – proper players who can afford the big bucks. He picked up some good contacts in the VIP enclosure at Badminton Horse Trials last weekend. He'll get in touch with them. Start warming them up. That'll get things back on an upward trajectory. He can pull this back. It'll be okay.

'Baby, where are you?' Lexi's voice. He can hear her footsteps on the stairs.

Shit. When Lexi shows up in his study, it always means trouble.

'Well, here you are.' Lexi appears through the doorway. 'You are a naughty boy. I've been looking for you all over.'

'Jesus.' He drops the calculator. The vision of her takes his breath away. She's in full make-up, her hair is teased and tousled, and her body's poured into the tightest PVC catsuit he's ever seen. She's got a whip in one hand and handcuffs and a ball-gag in the other. The look on her face tells him the trouble he's in is serious.

'I'm bored,' says Lexi, crossing her arms and pouting. 'I need some fun, and you need telling off for leaving me alone for *so* long.'

'I'm sorry, honey, it's accounts time, I need to—'

Lexi presses the end of the whip against his lips. 'You don't get to say no, darling. You understand that, right?'

Dexter nods. This is part of the game – him reluctant, her dominant. He knows what's expected. He plays his part. 'Yes.'

'Well that's good.' She slips the handcuffs onto his wrists and encourages him to stand up. 'You'd better come with me.'

∼

The playroom is in the basement. It runs the full length of the house and cost over a million to install. Padded wall dividers section the space into zones: BDSM chamber, massage parlour, the orgy bed area that takes up to ten people at once, the heated pool with powerful jets and a sex swing. The chandeliers cost over ten grand each. The walls are decorated in Farrow & Ball's darkest paint colours. Everything is high end, including the sex toys. It's one of the reasons the parties they hold here are so popular.

Today is a party for two. Dexter's handcuffed inside the cage in the BDSM chamber, naked and spreadeagled with his wrists and ankles attached to the posts. Lexi is standing in front of him. She smacks the whip against her PVC-clad leg. Dexter flinches.

'So I've got a request.' Lexi keeps her eyes on him.

He feels a tightening in his chest. This isn't good. Requests always involve money, and he's nothing to spare this month. He stares back at her. Waiting.

'I don't need much,' says Lexi. 'Only half a million, maybe a little bit more.'

Dexter's breath catches in his throat. He tries to speak, but it's hard with the ball-gag strapped so tight. The word is muffled. 'Why?'

'I want to buy some horses.' Lexi smiles and tickles the whip across the back of his neck. 'You're always telling me I need a hobby, so I'm going to get one. You want to support me, don't you, baby?'

Dexter doesn't move or try to speak. He's thinking. Trying to work out a way to say no to her that won't end in pain. Lexi's always starting things and he's always paying – twice-weekly golf lessons with a pro, acting lessons with an Oscar winner, and so on and so on. She starts off enthusiastic and then a few months later she's done with it, and he's a few thousand poorer; a few thousand mind, not half a million. This ask is way higher than anything that's come before.

'So, baby.' She runs the whip across his face, over his clenched teeth and the ball-gag within them, and then down his chest and below. She taps the whip against his balls. 'Are you going to let me have the money?'

The panic tightens in his chest. He can't afford it. It's already going to be a struggle to make the next payments unless he can land a few more big fish investors.

The whip taps are getting harder. Stinging now. Dexter's eyes start to water.

'Baby?' There's an edge to Lexi's voice now. The purr has turned spikey. The whip spanks against his balls. 'The money, will you give it to me?'

Dexter says nothing. He tries to swallow but the gag makes it hard.

Whack. Whack.

He blinks the tears from his eyes. Bites down harder on the gag.

'You won't deny me this, will you, baby?' Lexi's voice is as hard and cold as granite. 'That would be risky, wouldn't it? Especially when I know so much about the *business*.'

She's got him. He can't refuse and risk her talking. It would ruin him. She knows that.

And so he nods, a small nod at first but the spanking doesn't stop and the pain shoots through his balls and into his core with every smack. So he makes the nods more exaggerated, faster.

'Oh baby, that's wonderful,' Lexi coos.

Finally the whip is stilled. She kneels in front of him and takes him in her mouth.

Dexter groans as Lexi sucks and licks and flicks her tongue

over him. His balls are still tingling. Pleasure and pain are mixing into one.

He cums. Yelling her name into the gag. Bucking against the restraints that hold him.

Standing, Lexi wipes her mouth with the back of her hand and grins.

She's going to ruin him, Dexter knows that, but what else can he do? She knows all his secrets – the bad and the bloody awful. He can't refuse to indulge her obsessions.

He's a slave to her.

Has been for thirty years.

Always will be.

CHAPTER EIGHT

DANIEL

Jenny's expression is hard to read. Crouching down beside The Rogue, she runs the handheld scanner over his off hind leg, watching the screen of the portable ultrasound machine as the images appear. It's the third scan the horse has had in as many days. At first there was too much swelling to let them assess the true extent of the injury, but now it's beginning to reduce, Jenny thinks they should be able to get a better idea of the damage.

Daniel tries not to let his nerves show as he breaks a ginger biscuit in half and gives a piece to The Rogue. The horse takes it and munches happily as Jenny continues the scan.

'He's such a dude,' says Eddie, the head groom, who's standing alongside Daniel, watching Jenny work. 'A real trooper.'

Daniel clenches his jaw. Doesn't trust himself to speak without getting emotional. Immediately after the accident, The Rogue was taken back to the Badminton stables in a horse ambulance and given painkillers and anti-inflammatory injections by the on-site vet. Since they got him home, he's been on two sachets of bute twice a day – in his breakfast and his dinner. But even with the strong painkillers and anti-inflammatories in his system, he's still hobbling around on three legs.

Daniel feels like total shit. The guilt about what happened and the fear that The Rogue won't recover are eating away at him – stopping him sleeping and sending his anxiety sky high. The vet bills from this are going to be well into the thousands, and although Daniel knows Jenny will let him work something out with her, he has no ideas for getting himself out of the red. The bills are mounting up. The wages are due to be paid next week. And he's already over his overdraft and at the top of his credit card limit.

Eddie's been a real star. He's kept the yard running, and schooled the youngsters himself – knowing that Daniel isn't up to it with his cracked ribs. Daniel knows he's going to have to find a way out of his current financial situation. But right now he just doesn't see any viable options aside from selling this place, and that's if anyone would buy it in the state it's in.

Pushing her red corkscrew curls from her face, Jenny looks up at Daniel and Eddie. 'So I think you're looking at a minimum of six weeks' box rest, then we'll scan again and if it's healing well he could do some light hand-walking and we'll build up from there.'

'And if it doesn't go well?' says Daniel.

Jenny gestures to the image on the ultrasound screen. 'There's a big hole in the tendon, Danny. It might never heal well enough to go back to top level.'

The Rogue nuzzles at Daniel's hand. Asking for the other half of the biscuit. Daniel feeds it to him on autopilot. 'But he'll be able to retire if that's the case? It's not a—'

'He'll be comfortable as a minimum. I'm confident we can get him to that point.' Jenny puts the handheld device into the slot at the side of the ultrasound and pushes the machine away from The Rogue. 'But any more than that, I don't know. We're going to have to wait and see.'

Daniel exhales hard. 'Okay, okay. I can handle that.'

Eddie nods. 'So worst-case scenario is he has to be retired at grass. Best case is he can go back to eventing next year?'

Standing up, Jenny brushes some dirt off her cargo pants. 'Yes. But, as I said, we have to take it day by day. With this type of injury there's never any guarantee he'll come one hundred percent sound again.' She puts her hand on Daniel's shoulder. 'It must be bloody tough for you, Danny. I know you love this horse.'

'We thought he was the one who'd get us into the big time,' says Eddie, scratching The Rogue's withers and smiling as the horse stretches out his neck and raises his top lip in appreciation. 'He's certainly got the character for it.'

'It's...' Daniel battles to keep the emotion out of his voice. 'Look, as long as I'm not going to lose him completely...'

The Rogue pushes his nose into Daniel's pocket, wiggling his top lip around, trying to get hold of the packet of biscuits.

Jenny smiles. 'He's still got his sense of humour.'

'For now, although I'm not sure how long it'll last if he's got to stay on box rest,' says Eddie. 'He'll have the water buckets thrown out over the door and the bedding churned up in no time.'

'I can give you something to help him chill out if you need it?' says Jenny.

'Worth us having just in case,' says Eddie. 'You got anything for Daniel, too?'

Jenny laughs. Daniel tries to join in but it feels forced.

'How are those ribs doing?' she asks, frowning.

'Okay,' says Daniel. Truth be told, his ribs hurt like a bitch even when strapped up, but compared to The Rogue he's got off lightly. 'They'll heal.'

She looks at him sympathetically. 'Well, if you're up to it, I'd really appreciate a cross-country lesson before I do my first Intermediate next month. We've had some good runs this year but Dinky's been feeling a bit sticky over the trickier questions, especially corner combinations. I'd appreciate your advice.'

'I can do that,' says Daniel, forcing a smile. Usually he enjoys teaching, but right now, with everything, he can't feel motivated to do it. He needs to earn money, though. He can't afford to turn down any opportunity.

'Excellent.' Jenny grins. She gestures to the ultrasound. 'I'll put this visit on your account and book The Rogue in again for six weeks' time.' She looks at Eddie. 'Give me a call if you need anything else in the meantime.'

'Always,' says Eddie.

Jenny leans down and picks up the ultrasound machine, but not before Daniel sees that she's blushing. Weird. Is it his imagination or is something going on between Jenny and his head groom?

'Right then,' says Jenny. 'I'd better be off.'

A magenta Bentley convertible hurtles into the parking area. Lady Gaga's 'Poker Face' is pounding out of the speakers, shattering the quiet calm of the yard. The Rogue startles. Eddie swears. Jenny and Daniel look round, surprised.

The engine stops and moments later the driver's door opens and a slim woman with far too much blonde hair to be natural jumps out. Her dark glasses seem to cover most of her face, and she's wearing some kind of jumpsuit.

She raises a hand and starts striding across the parking area towards the wooden gate into the yard.

Eddie's frowning. 'Isn't that Lexi Marchfield-Wright?'

'Shit,' says Daniel. 'She called me last night. Said she and her husband Dexter are thinking about buying an event horse. I'd totally forgotten she was coming.'

'Interesting.' Jenny raises her eyebrow. 'Have you heard the rumours about what goes on up at their place?'

'What rumours?' says Daniel.

'Sex parties,' whispers Jenny. 'Every kink catered for, apparently.'

'How do you know that?' says Eddie, a little too quickly.

Jenny taps the side of her nose and smiles. 'I've got clients who've been invited.' She winks at Daniel. 'Maybe if she buys one of the horses, you'll get on the guest list for the next party.'

Daniel grimaces. He's not a prude by any means but the idea of an orgy doesn't do it for him. 'Let's hope not.'

Lexi's at the gate now, trying to undo the latch but having trouble due to her ridiculously long red nails. Reluctantly, Daniel hands the rope attached to The Rogue's headcollar to Eddie and heads over to help her.

'Good morning,' he says, forcing a light-hearted tone he really isn't feeling. He undoes the gate. 'Please, come on in.'

Grinning, Lexi walks through into the yard. 'Daniel, darling, lovely to meet you. I'm so glad you could fit me in. I'm a hugger.' She pulls him into a hug.

Her perfume is overpowering. Daniel's eyes water and his throat feels scratchy. She squeezes him tighter and he winces as pain shoots through his ribs. Lexi doesn't seem to notice.

'Lovely to meet you too,' he says, politely, extracting himself from her clutches and taking a couple of steps back. 'Would you like me to show you around?'

'Most definitely,' says Lexi, smiling again. There's something predatory about her – like a shark or a wolf – and her teeth seem incredibly white against the bright red of her lips. 'I want to see everything.'

'No problem,' says Daniel. 'You mentioned on the phone that you're thinking about buying a—'

'Who's that?' asks Lexi, the warm tone of moments ago has turned ice cold. 'Does she work here or...'

Daniel follows her gaze over towards the stables. 'That's Jenny. Come over, I'll introduce you.'

'Alright,' says Lexi. She's still got her shades on, but Daniel's pretty sure she's frowning and there's a distinct chill to her manner.

Shit, thinks Daniel. Have I managed to mess up a sale already? He'd really hoped she'd be interested in a couple of his own youngsters – they're still green but have lots of talent. He hates selling any horse, but at the moment it's a needs must situation. And, if she and her husband didn't have a rider lined up, he'd hoped they might let him keep the ride on the horse they buy. He glances at her again. Her expression is like thunder. Any chance of a sale seems unlikely.

They reach Eddie and Jenny who are still chatting and making a fuss of The Rogue, who is nuzzling at the pockets in Jenny's cargo pants, looking for the polos she always has.

Daniel clears his throat. 'Lexi, this is Jenny Jackson, the vet who's overseeing The Rogue's treatment. Jenny, this is Lexi Marchfield-Wright; she's interested in buying a horse.'

Lexi visibly relaxes. 'Oh, the vet? How wonderful.'

'Hi,' says Jenny.

Lexi turns her attention to Eddie. 'And you are?'

'I'm head groom here,' says Eddie. 'I work with Daniel.'

'How lovely,' says Lexi, holding Eddie's gaze a moment too long. Then she turns to Daniel and loops her arm through his. 'Now, why don't you show me around, darling?'

It's not going well. Lexi doesn't seem interested in the horses. She doesn't even smile when The Rogue pulls the packet of ginger biscuits from Daniel's pocket, shakes them up and down, trying to get the biscuits out, then gobbles up the crumbs from the floor. Daniel has no idea why she's here. She'd said she was interested in buying an event horse but when he asked her if she'd like to see any of the youngsters ridden, she said no. She's shown no interest in any of the horses, and been frosty to his teenage stable hand, Bunty, when he introduced them. Poor Bunty – painfully shy at the best of times but a natural with the horses – scuttled away red-faced.

As he shows Lexi the stables, the outdoor all-weather riding arena and the jumping field, Daniel finds it increasingly hard to fake enthusiasm. Even with his cracked ribs, he'd much rather be mucking out than having to entertain this bloody woman in her white jumpsuit and unsuitable footwear. He stops, waiting for Lexi to pick her way along the path, avoiding anything that looks like horse muck.

He'd been surprised to get her call, but a potential sale is a potential sale. And with the costs of The Rogue's vet treatment to add to the towering pile of bills he already has, he can't afford to be picky. Now he's sorry he agreed to show her round. It's obviously a waste of time and all she's doing is upsetting his team.

'So that's pretty much everything,' Daniel says as they walk back up from the fields towards the yard, hoping he can get rid of her quickly. 'Have you seen anything you like?'

Lexi cocks her head to one side and bats her lashes. 'Perhaps.'

Daniel's surprised. 'Really? Which—'

'How much does a top event horse cost?'

The last of his hopes disappear. He doesn't have a top horse to sell. 'It depends. Anything from sixty thousand upwards.'

'I see.' Lexi looks thoughtful. She glances towards the house. 'Perhaps we can talk inside? You could make me a drink.'

Daniel has no desire to prolong the meeting, but he supposes one drink won't hurt. 'Sure, come in.'

'So you live here in the manor house?' says Lexi, looking up at the imposing old building as they walk around to the back entrance.

'I do.' With the climbing roses around the door starting to flower, their pale yellow petals a perfect contrast against the dark brick of the house, Daniel knows it looks nice. It's just a shame the upkeep of the place is so high. In an old property like this, things need fixing all the time. He barely manages to do the minimum to stop it falling down. Many of the rooms on the top floor are uninhabitable due to mould. 'The team all live here –

me, Eddie and Bunty. It's a big place so we've each got our own spaces.'

He opens the back door and leads her inside. A little black cat is sitting on a stack of *Horse & Hound*s on the kitchen table. She opens one eye to see what's going on, purring loudly when Daniel strokes her head. 'And this is Gertrude – she's chief mouser. And McQueen, Eddie's dog, is around somewhere.'

'Well this is all very sweet,' says Lexi, ignoring Gertrude and wrinkling her nose as she glances round the kitchen. 'And you all live here together? How lovely.' Her expression suggests she thinks the opposite.

'We muck in together to keep the place going,' says Daniel. Although right now he supposes the place isn't very clean – Bunty had the whole yard to look after while he and Eddie were at Badminton, so that didn't leave much time for tidying up, and in the few days they've been back, Eddie's been doing Daniel's share of the work as Daniel's been pretty much out of action with his ribs. As a result, the washing up is piled high beside the sink, the bin is overflowing and the recycling hasn't been taken out. Add that to the stacks of dog-eared *Horse & Hound*s on the kitchen table, the saddle cloths and bandages drying on the radiators and over the handles of the Aga, and the flakes of dried mud and horse hair on the flagstone floor, and he supposes this isn't the sort of place Lexi would choose to be. Maybe it'll encourage her to leave quickly, at least he hopes so.

'So, that drink?' says Lexi.

'Sure,' says Daniel. 'Tea, coffee?'

'I was thinking of something a bit stronger, darling. After all, the sun must be over the yardarm somewhere in the world.'

Daniel says nothing. It's not even noon. 'Whiskey?'

'Neat would be perfect.'

Taking the cleanest glasses from a kitchen cabinet, Daniel gives them a quick wipe with a tea towel and pours two fingers of single malt into each. He passes one to Lexi. 'What are we drinking to?'

'Well, darling, that rather depends on you.'

He frowns. 'How'd you mean?'

Lexi smiles. Her heavily made-up eyes are gleaming. She licks her lips.

She is a wolf, thinks Daniel. Definitely. A wolf in designer labels.

'So, the word is that you have all the talent but no top horses. If you had a top horse you could make it onto the British team, but The Rogue is out of action, and your other top ride has been sold overseas. You've got horses here but none are ready for the big time. So you're going to miss your shot. Is that about right?'

Daniel looks away. 'Pretty much.'

'And a top horse would cost a minimum of sixty grand. And to keep it on the road competing would cost, what?'

'Thirty thousand, at least, more if we targeted overseas internationals.'

'Okay,' says Lexi, tapping a few numbers into her diamond-encrusted phone. 'And then you'd need a wage for the work you're doing, and the value you're putting on the horse.'

Daniel frowns. He doesn't know where she's going with this. He thought she'd wanted to buy one of his young event horses; now she's talking about top horses and his wages. 'What do you—'

'I've got a proposition for you, Daniel,' Lexi says, smiling. She steps closer to him. That predatory intensity is in her eyes again. Her perfume is invading his senses. 'If we said a hundred grand per horse, with fifty grand running costs, and a fifty grand wage for the work you'd put in, that comes to two hundred grand for the first year.'

Daniel says silent. He's never paid more than ten grand for a horse – always bought them young with raw talent and trained them himself, rather than buying them with miles on the clock and wins under their belts. A hundred grand would buy a really talented, established horse. And fifty grand as a wage for a year – he's barely made that in profit during the whole time he's been in business – it's way over the going rate for riders. 'I…'

Lexi presses her fingers to his lips and steps even closer. Her breasts are pressing against his chest. Her flowery perfume mingles with his earthy, horse scent. 'And of course you really need two top horses, in case one is off work for a period of time.'

He nods. Words fail him. Is she offering to buy him two horses?

'So two horses, at a cost of two hundred grand each for the first year, makes four hundred grand in total. But, why don't we call it five hundred thousand; it has a better ring to it, doesn't it?' She moves her face closer to his. Her warm breath tickles against his mouth. 'If we have an agreement, I could transfer the first monthly payment to your account this afternoon. Do you want that, Daniel?'

He feels frozen to the spot. Five hundred grand would pay off all his debts, guarantee the wages of his team for a year or more, and get him a couple of horses that would put him firmly back on the radar of the British team selectors. 'What would you want in return? I can put your husband's company logo on the horsebox, the horses' gear – rugs, saddlecloths, and everything. I'd rather—'

Lexi presses her mouth against his. She kisses him hard, her tongue pushing into his mouth, her hands on the back of his head, stopping him from pulling away.

Nausea twists in his stomach as the realisation hits him. Now he understands.

She smiles, wolfishly. 'In return, darling, I want you – whenever I want, wherever I want, however I want. You're mine exclusively, until I say otherwise.'

Daniel tries not to recoil as Lexi runs her red nails, sharp as claws, across his cheek. 'What… what about your husband?' he stammers.

Lexi waves away his concerns. 'He'll not even notice. But even if he did, it won't matter. We have an open marriage, so it's fine for me to have fun.'

Daniel stares at her. Fun. That isn't what this is. It's a business deal – no money worries and a shot at the big time in exchange for being a paid lover. 'I won't compromise on the horses' schedule. I need to have full control over what the horses do, how I train them, where I run them, everything.'

'Done,' says Lexi, running her fingers down his chest to the top of his breeches.

'And you're sure this won't be a problem with your husband?'

Laughing, she undoes the top button of his breeches and sides her hand inside. 'Completely, darling.'

Daniel closes his eyes. He thinks of how close he got to being selected for the British team and how his dreams crashed and burned at Badminton. He thinks of the pile of final-reminder bills on the kitchen counter, of The Rogue's veterinary treatment, the wages that need paying in a couple of days' time, and his maxed-out overdraft and credit cards. He doesn't fancy Lexi. He doesn't even like her. But there are five hundred thousand reasons to do this.

CHAPTER NINE

HATTIE

Make it happen.

Lady Patricia's words have been echoing around Hattie's mind ever since she said them on Saturday afternoon. It's Tuesday morning now, but Hattie still has no idea how to make a step towards her dream. She's not even riding as part of her job now and it feels like she's further from where she wants to be than she's ever been. Over the weekend she looked at adverts for horses for sale – all too expensive, especially as she's broke – and studied the horses available for loan, but none of them looked a good fit for eventing.

Sitting at the kitchen table, with the dogs sprawled out on the floor at her feet, Hattie takes a sip of her coffee and, using the browser on her phone, searches for horse jobs in the local area. Most of them are full-time, live-in groom jobs – hours that won't be compatible with house sitting and looking after Robert's animals – but two have more potential. She decides to take the plunge and dials the first number.

'Larkton Stud,' says the gruff-sounding man who answers.

'I'm calling about your advert in *Horse & Hound* for a part-time groom? My name's Hattie Kimble and I—'

'Sorry, it's gone.'

Hattie frowns. 'What do you—?'

'The job – it's already gone. Filled it last week.'

'Okay, thanks,' says Hattie, and ends the call. It's only when she switches back to the browser and relooks at the job that she realises the advert was only listed yesterday.

Trying not to be put off, she dials the number for the other job.

It rings for ages and Hattie's about to end the call when a stressed-sounding woman answers. 'Yes?'

'Hi, is that Rosemount Equestrian Centre?' Down the line, Hattie can hear the clink of horseshoes against tarmac. She wonders if the woman is answering the phone while hacking along the road.

'Yep.'

'I'm calling about the groom/rider job you have listed in *Horse & Hound* online.'

'Oh great.' The woman's voice sounds slightly less irate. 'Have you got experience?'

'I've worked with horses for over ten years. I've worked with show jumpers, eventers and in livery and competition yards. I'm used to handling youngsters and brood mares. I'm a confident rider.'

'Well, that sounds good.' As the woman speaks, there's the sound of a car whooshing past, and the clinking hoof beats speed up briefly. 'Where did you work last and why did you leave?'

Hattie takes a breath. This is tricky. The horse world is a small place and her last job wasn't too far from Leightonshire. 'Most recently I worked for Gavin Lawrence at his competition yard over in—'

'Let me stop you there.' The woman sighs down the phone. 'Look, I know Gavin. And I'm sorry, but no.'

'Pardon?'

'I said no. I can't take you on. You're that horse whisperer, aren't you?'

Hattie clenches the phone tighter. Feels heat rise up her neck and across her cheeks. 'I am trained as a horse whisperer, yes, but I'm also very experienced as a—'

'Look, I get the natural horsemanship stuff personally, but we're a traditional yard and our liveries aren't into it, no offence. You start wiggling a rope at their horses and... well, you being here just wouldn't work.'

'Okay, but I could still...' Hattie stops, looks at the screen on her phone.

The woman has hung up.

Hattie bites her lip. It's hopeless – she hasn't got a horse, and she can't even get a job to work with them. There has to be a way. She taps 'horses for loan' into the search window. A list of available horses fills the screen. She scrolls through them. Most are the same as when she searched the site at the weekend, but there are a couple that have been added. One is too small – a thirteen-hands-high child's pony – but the other is possible. The horse is young, just four years old, but from the look of the picture it could have potential. Hattie reads the description: 'Bay gelding, 16 hands, warmblood X, lightly backed and turned away, ready to be schooled on but lack of rider. For loan for one year to an experienced rider.'

It's a possibility. Although she'd only have the horse for a year and then have to hand them back to the owner. When Hattie reads the location, her heart sinks. The horse is in Newport, Wales, which is a beautiful place but a long journey from Leightonshire. Her Ford Focus barely made the short trip to Clover Hill House; the chances of it making the drive to Wales and back are slim to zero. Maybe there's a route by train? She opens the Maps app, and is investigating when a loud banging at the back door startles her.

'Open up,' says a deep voice that's definitely male. 'I've got a problem with those bloody goats again.'

'It's open,' calls Hattie, standing up and moving across the kitchen towards the door.

As she reaches the boot room, the back door opens and an annoyed-looking man steps across the threshold. Dressed in beige trousers, a green sweatshirt with paint smears across it, and sturdy work boots, he's small and wiry, with wispy grey hair. 'Bloody goats,' he mutters under his breath. Then to Hattie, 'You the house sitter?'

'Yes, I'm Hattie.' If this is the handyman Robert mentioned, then he's very different to what she'd imagined. 'Bill?'

'Yep, that's me. Robert told me he'd lined up a young lass to look after the place while he was off in the States.' He narrows his eyes as he looks her up and down. 'How good are you at dealing with goats?'

Hattie stands up straight. Squares her shoulders. 'I can handle a seventeen-hand stallion getting frisky for a mare in season. A pygmy goat shouldn't be a problem.'

Bill chuckles to himself knowingly. 'If you say so.'

'So what's the problem?' says Hattie, keeping her tone no-nonsense.

'I went to move the bloody things, like I usually do if I'm doing work in the paddock – so they can't steal my tools like they did that first time – and, anyway, the blighters pushed past me and legged it off across the garden, didn't they.' He looks at Hattie expectantly. When she doesn't say anything immediately, he gestures across the lawn. 'You need to catch them. They were heading for the hippy neighbour at Badger's End again.'

Hattie frowns. 'Badger's End?'

'It's the place next door, the cottage. And the neighbour, well, she's...' Bill whistles through his teeth. 'She's a right one. From London, you know? Moved in about six months back and full of organic, hippy dippy, vegan nonsense. Got all upset when I took out some trees that bordered her garden. Didn't understand they were diseased and dying anyway. Bloody townies.'

Hattie doesn't think organic farming or veganism is nonsense but it seems she doesn't have time to argue about that with Bill right now. Pulling on her boots, she asks him, 'What's her name, the neighbour?'

'Liberty Edwards, now hurry – those goats can do real damage in a garden, and they do love her organic vegetables.' He chuckles.

Rushing outside, Hattie runs across the gravel to the goat's paddock. The gate is open and the goats are definitely gone. Bill didn't say which part of Robert's land the neighbour's garden backs onto. She's thinking she'll have to go back and ask him, but then she sees their tiny hoof prints in the soft mud alongside the outside of the paddock fencing. Following their tracks at a jog, she calls their names. 'Gladys? Mabel?'

There's no bleating. No sign of them anywhere – not the other paddocks, or the spinney beyond. 'Where are you?'

'Over here.' Bill's voice sounds irate and is coming from Robert's garden. 'They're in here.'

Shit. Hattie sprints back along the grass and across the gravel to the garden. That's when she sees them – over by the high hedge. Gladys and Mabel have their heads in the greenery. It's hard to say if they're eating or escaping.

Bill rushes forward, trying to shoo the goats away from the hedge. He has the opposite effect. Mable pushes herself further into the greenery. Only her bottom is visible now, her stumpy little tail thrashing back and forth. Gladys stands motionless beside her friend, her eyes wide and afraid.

'Stop,' shouts Hattie. 'You're scaring them.'

Bill ignores her and charges towards the goats. He grabs Mabel's backend and tries to yank her out of the hedge. Bleating, Mabel kicks at him. He lets go, swearing blue murder, when a blow from her back leg connects with his knee. She wriggles through the greenery and disappears. Bill bellows with rage. Gladys is distraught. Wide-eyed and bleating in terror, she launches herself into the hedge after Mabel.

'What the hell are you doing?' says Hattie, as she reaches Bill.

'Trying to catch the little blighters.' Red-faced, and rubbing his knee, he glares at her. 'If you'd helped me instead of being soft, we'd have stopped them.'

Hattie's not having him put the blame on her. He let them out. She didn't cause this. 'If you hadn't terrified the crap out of them, they wouldn't have run in the first place.'

Bill mutters something under his breath.

'What's that?' asks Hattie, refusing to let him intimidate her.

Bill gestures at her dismissively. 'I suppose you think you could have whispered in their fluffy ears and they'd have trotted back to the paddock all nice?' He raises his eyes to the heavens. 'Bloody stupid nonsense.'

'*You* were the one who let them escape in the first place,' says Hattie, her voice outwardly calm, and her tone stern, even though she's shaking with anger on the inside. 'And *you* scared them into going through that hedge. But don't worry, I'll go and sort *your* mess out. Because you obviously aren't capable.'

She leaves Bill red-faced, indignant and gulping air like a landed pike, and strides around the house and down the driveway towards Badger's End.

CHAPTER TEN

DEXTER

*H*e's been a member of the club for over a year, but he still gets a brief flash of imposter syndrome as he walks up the marble steps and through the imposing, double-sized front door. The reception room is lit by a couple of over-sized floor lamps and the glow of the fire in the grate of the huge fireplace, giving it a winter evening feel even though it's just before noon on a sunny day in mid-May. The walls are painted a deep green above the dark-stained oak panelling, which adds to the cosy ambience.

A smart, pretty girl in her twenties stands behind the oak desk. She looks him up and down and then smiles. 'Good morning, Mr Marchfield-Wright. Will you be joining us for lunch today?'

Dexter looks at the brass nametag that's affixed to her tailored black jacket. 'Hi, Josephine.' He gives her his most charming smile. 'Yes, lunch would be good. And I've got a guest joining me – Mr Stanten-Bassett.'

'Perfect.' Josephine taps something into the iPad she's holding, then looks back at him. 'That's all arranged for you, Mr Marchfield-Wright. Your usual table will be ready from 12.15 onwards.'

'Great. Thanks, Josephine. Can you let me know when my guest has arrived? I'll be...' He pauses as the front door swings open and a tall, distinguished-looking man in a tweed jacket steps inside. Dexter smiles warmly. 'Ah, Mr Stanten-Bassett, good to see you again.'

'Likewise,' says Stanten-Bassett, scanning the room haughtily. His gaze stops on Josephine. He licks his lips and smooths down his moustache.

Josephine doesn't react. Given her job is front-of-house at a gentleman's club, Dexter supposes she must be used to lechers and pervs ogling her, but that doesn't make it right anyway. He watches as she fixes a polite smile on her face and pushes an oversized, leather-bound book across the desk towards Stanten-Bassett. 'If you could do us the honour of signing in, please, sir.'

As Stanten-Bassett signs the guestbook, a second girl, dressed in the same black trouser suit as Josephine, with her white blonde hair swept up into a demure bun, joins her colleague at the reception desk. Josephine turns to Dexter. 'This is Elizabeth, she'll escort you to your table.'

After thanking Josephine, he follows Elizabeth along the wood-panelled corridor to the grand staircase, and up to the first-floor restaurant. The wooden boards beneath their feet creak as they ascend the stairs. Hanging on the wall are oil paintings of the five founder members of the club. Many thousands of men will have made the trip up these stairs since the club began in 1908. Dexter wonders how many were on the do-or-die knife-edge financially – and reputationally – as he is in this moment. He tries not to let it show.

'Nice place this,' says Stanten-Bassett, his clipped vowels and air of disinterest seemingly at odds with his comment. 'Been a member long?'

Dexter tries not to let the man's tone put him off. He knows he's trying to suss him out, test his strength of character and whether he's worth an investment. Usually Dexter lives for this –

the chase and the win – but today, with the threat of financial ruin so close he can hear it breathing, Dexter just wants the deal to be done. Still, he fights to retain a casual air, like a man on top of the world. 'For a while, yes. I've always found it very comfortable.'

Stanten-Bassett sniffs loudly but doesn't reply.

Dexter clenches his jaw. Feels the tension rising in his chest. He takes a breath and forces himself to relax. 'How was your journey?'

'Usual train nonsense,' says Stanten-Bassett. 'Never on time and always overcrowded. The country is going to the dogs, of course.'

'Your table, gentleman.'

Elizabeth's words stop Dexter from having to reply to the trains comment, and for that he's glad. He needs to shift Stanton-Bassett from his glass-half-empty mood towards the glass overflowing if he's to have any joy in getting the man to invest.

Dexter looks up at Elizabeth. 'A bottle of the Carruades De Lafite 2018, please.'

Stanten-Bassett nods approvingly. 'Nice choice.'

It bloody should be at over six hundred quid a bottle, thinks Dexter. But a man like Stanten-Bassett is going to be hard to win around; a display of wealth and success is important for his sort so Dexter knows he needs to put on a good show.

Invest to win. Win or it's all over.

As Elizabeth hands Dexter a menu, it feels like a hollow pit opens in his stomach. Food won't satisfy it, only cash will do. But in his mind, the nagging question echoes – *what if this doesn't work?*

Opposite him, Stanten-Bassett opens his menu and scans it greedily. 'Some oysters to start, I think,' he says to Elizabeth.

'Great choice,' says Dexter, inwardly cursing the sixty quid price tag on a single portion of oysters. He knows he has to match Stanten-Bassett or he risks looking cheap. 'I'll have the same.'

'Good man,' says Stanten-Bassett, approvingly.

Dexter hopes it's worth it. He decides to double down and pick the most expensive main on the menu. 'And I'll have the steak and lobster to follow.'

For the first time, a smile ticks up the corners of Stanten-Bassett's thin lips. 'Me as well.'

Dexter returns the smile. He checks his body language – leans back a little in his chair, stays relaxed. He plays the part of the wealthy and successful entrepreneur. After all, no one wants to invest in a desperate man. Investors need to see confidence, reassurance, and most of all almost guaranteed success. Dexter can deliver that; he's a master at the art of possibility. He's built his whole business on it, and he can pull this off too. He just needs to hold his nerve. He doesn't have the luxury of failure.

So, as the wine is poured and the food is served, Dexter bides his time. Waiting for the perfect moment to make his move. He needs Stanten-Bassett to ask the question.

∼

That moment comes when they've finished dessert, and are half done with the coffee and brandy. Dexter takes out a metal cigar tin from inside his jacket pocket. Opening it, he holds the tin out to Stanten-Bassett. 'These are the very best. Hand-rolled in Cuba. I recommend.'

Stanten-Bassett raises an eyebrow. He considers the cigars for a long moment before taking one. 'I promised the wife I'd given up. One can't hurt though.'

'Indeed,' says Dexter with a wink. 'Your secret's safe with me.'

He lights Stanten-Bassett's cigar first and then his own. Inhales deeply. Waits for the question he knows will come any moment. Counts the seconds; one, two, three…

'So tell me about this opportunity,' says Stanten-Bassett. His haughty stare has been softened with alcohol, his waspish edge more relaxed now he's eaten.

'It's luxury property rentals,' says Dexter. He makes his tone serious. Keeps strong eye contact, his body language open. 'Largely overseas and very exclusive – the Caribbean, Borneo, Mauritius and an island in the Maldives.'

Stanten-Bassett's nodding thoughtfully. He undoes his tie, loosens the top button of his shirt, and gestures for Dexter to continue.

'I've been doing this a while. I have people on the ground in all the countries where the investments are made, and it's proved very successful. More recently I've been able to extend some opportunities to an additional group of select investors. People I trust, with a good eye for a deal and a sharp instinct for business.' Dexter pauses to let the last sentence sink in. It's important to stroke the ego of a potential investor – make them feel special and smart. Gaining their trust and making them feel like they're joining something exclusive is all part of the game. 'The minimum investment for this particular opportunity is five hundred thousand, although as a rule people have invested more. Growth over the past two years has been twelve and fifteen percent, so way over the average. And from the data I have, I anticipate this upward trend will continue.'

Stanten-Bassett leans forward, mouth open like a fish on a line. He's looking so keen, he's practically salivating. 'Let's say I want to invest two million. How does it all work?'

Dexter swallows down his excitement. A sum like that would get him out of the shit and keep the company viable for at least another six months, maybe more. He needs to get this closed. So he goes into the full spiel – the most exclusive properties, the more exotic locations, the pros and cons of investment, the monthly and full year returns.

Within an hour, and a half bottle of the club's most expensive brandy, they shake hands and the deal is done. Another fifteen minutes and calls have been made and wire transfers agreed. The money will be in Dexter's account before the end of the week.

For now, his dirty secret is safe.

CHAPTER ELEVEN

HATTIE

*L*iberty Edwards is tall and gorgeous with her black hair in short braids and no make-up. She's wearing an old Faithless t-shirt, faded jeans and hot pink Birkenstocks. As the door opens and their eyes meet, the frown on the thirty-something woman's face changes to a curious smile.

Hattie's nerves disappear as she smiles back. 'I'm Hattie, from next door. I'm really sorry but the goats have escaped into your garden. I've come to—'

'They're fine. Don't worry,' says Liberty, waving Hattie's concerns away. 'When I heard the knock on the door, I thought it would be Bill coming to rant at me again.'

'No, I'm the house sitter,' says Hattie, wondering why Bill has felt the need to have a go at Liberty previously. 'I started at the weekend.'

Liberty frowns and cocks her head to one side. 'Robert's gone away?'

'Yes, until the end of the year.'

'Really?' says Liberty, shaking her head. 'Well that's interesting.'

Hattie isn't sure what to say.

Luckily, Liberty continues talking. 'So is it just you, or is Bill still around?'

Hattie can't help but pull a face. 'He's still very much around, but I left him back at Robert's.'

'Good,' says Liberty, anger clear in her tone. 'I've told him he's not welcome here. That man has no grace.'

'So true. If you heard yelling a few minutes ago, that was him. He was shouting at Gladys and Mabel. Bloody idiot terrified them.'

'Well, sod him,' says Liberty, beckoning Hattie inside. 'Come on, I'll show you where the girls are.'

The interior of Badger's End is a riot of colour. The walls are painted in dark hues, and the mismatched furniture is vibrant pinks, blues and greens. There's a large gilt-framed mirror on the wall in the hallway and through the open door into the lounge, Hattie glimpses a mustard corduroy sofa, a multi-coloured parrot-shaped lamp on a teal side table and lots of jewel-coloured tea lights lined up along the hearth and mantle of the fireplace.

'Come on through,' says Liberty, leading Hattie into the kitchen and towards the back door. 'Sorry about the mess. I'm in the middle of a batch so, you know, it's chaos.'

Liberty's not joking. The room looks more like a science lab than a kitchen. There are huge glass storage jars with brightly coloured soy flakes inside, trays of what looks like different lengths and thicknesses of string, and on the gas range are four large stainless steel bain-marie melting pots. On the island unit, around forty glass jars of different sizes are lined up across the counter. Beside the ceramic butler's sink are three wooden trugs filled with lavender, rose petals and oranges. 'What do you—?'

'The girls are out in the garden,' says Liberty pointing out through the French windows that are open onto a stone patio. 'It's totally enclosed and safe. There's chicken wire lining the fences aside from that hedge with Robert's, so if they go anywhere from here it'll only be back to your place.'

Across on the far side of the lawn, Hattie can see Gladys and Mabel are feasting on something in one of the borders. She clears her throat. 'I think they're eating your—'

'Carrots? Yes, I know, don't worry. I grew those for them – carrots are one of their favourite things, and as they often visit I thought I'd make them a pick-your-own treat.' Her expression clouds over. 'After all, it's not like Robert paid them much attention. Once they were here for two days before he noticed they were gone.'

Hattie wonders what the story is between Liberty and Robert. Liberty seems unsettled by the news Robert's gone away, and also a bit pissed off, too much so to be purely down to the escaping of the goats. Then she remembers how dismissive Robert was of her horse whispering and understands how quickly an issue with him could snowball into hostility.

Unlike the manicured gardens of Clover Hill House, Liberty's place has a wild, natural feel to it. Climbing roses mingle with honeysuckle, tulips light up the borders with their red, yellow and orange flowers, and lavender weaves throughout the beds. There are chickens and ducks ranging free, and a small cat sunning itself over by a lily-pad-covered pond.

Hattie turns to Liberty. 'Your garden's gorgeous.'

'Thanks. I try to keep the weeds at bay, but the rest is all nature.' She gestures towards the raised beds that are just visible through a wisteria-covered archway. 'Other than in that area; that's my experiment – I'm trying to see how self-sufficient I can be, and it's where I grow a lot of my fragrances.'

Hattie raises an eyebrow. She thinks about the laboratory-like equipment in the kitchen. 'You make perfume?'

'Not exactly. Bill didn't tell you about my "hippy dippy" ways?'

Hattie gives a wry smile. 'He did mention something like that.'

'I bet he did,' says Liberty, shaking her head. 'It's because of the candles. He used to be pleasant enough. Then he tried to get me to buy animal fat from some farmer friend of his and I refused – told him I make vegan candles. Since then, he's never spoken to me unless he's had to because of the goats, and then only in words of one syllable.'

'So you make candles?'

'I do now. I used to be a marketing exec at an agency in London – crazy hours, no social life, always "on" 24/7. One of my colleagues had a heart attack after working yet another sixteen-hour day. He was thirty-one years old.' Liberty exhales hard. 'His death was a real wake-up call. I quit my job that week. Sold my flat in Hackney and moved out here. I'd always wanted to do something creative and I love candles, so I started experimenting and here I am.'

'Sounds great.' Hattie can hear the passion in Liberty's voice. It's been a while since she's felt like that about her own work. The equestrian yards she's worked in these past few months have felt too constricting to allow her to relax.

'Yeah, it's fun, but building a business takes time, and financially there's no guarantees.' Liberty smiles. 'I don't regret it, though, and as well as the farmers and artisan markets, my online shop is doing pretty well. You've got to follow your dreams, haven't you? No one wants to look back and regret that they didn't.'

Hattie turns away, blinking, so Liberty can't see her eyes are watering. 'We should catch the goats.'

'No problem,' says Liberty, rummaging around in one of the cream Shaker-style kitchen cabinets. 'I've got some little goat halters in here. Makes it easier to lead them back to your place.' She pulls out what looks like a couple of dog harnesses. 'Here they are. Let me go and catch them, won't take a minute.'

Back in the garden, the goats have other ideas. Every time Liberty gets close to them, Mabel runs away and Gladys, unwilling to be parted from her buddy, follows. After ten minutes of chasing them around the garden, Liberty is no closer to catching them. She stops beside Hattie, breathing heavily. 'I guess they really do like those carrots.'

'Can I try something different?' asks Hattie.

'Go ahead,' says Liberty, breathlessly.

Stepping across the lawn towards where the goats are grazing, Hattie swings the lead rope of the halter she's holding, and gets Mabel and Gladys to trot away from her. She doesn't run after them or try to catch them as Liberty had been doing, instead she stays behind them at a distance, and keeps swinging the rope, encouraging the goats to keep moving whenever they look like they're slowing down.

Liberty stands on the patio, watching with a quizzical expression on her face.

Hattie stays focused on the goats. After they've done a few laps of the garden, she notices them starting to look at her as they trot along. When both Mable and Gladys are giving her eye contact, she stops swinging the rope and turns, walking away across the garden in the opposite direction to the goats.

Gladys and Mabel turn and follow her. When she's sure that they're close behind her, Hattie stops and waits. The next moment, Mabel appears on her right and reaches out to nibble at the hem of her t-shirt. Gladys is a couple of steps behind. Hattie loops the rope over Mabel's neck and puts on her headcollar. She turns back to Liberty, who is watching open-mouthed. Nerves flare in her stomach. This is usually the point people accuse her of witchcraft.

Liberty claps her hands together as a smile widens across her face. 'Well damn! That was amazing. How did you—'

Hattie exhales slowly as relief floods through her. 'I used horse whispering. Goats are prey animals rather than predators, just the same as horses. I thought it might work.'

'It's genius,' says Liberty. Walking over to join Hattie, Liberty gives Gladys a rub on her back and then fastens her head collar into place. 'Like reverse psychology – tell them to go away when really you want them to come closer.'

'That's exactly it. Then it's their choice to connect with you. It isn't forced,' Hattie says, feeling a tiny buzz of hope for the first time in months. She smiles at Liberty. 'You know you're the first person in a while that I've used horse whispering in front of who hasn't reacted badly. It's... refreshing.'

As they walk out of Badger's End and back along the lane to Clover Hill House, the goats trot along beside them.

'This is amazing,' says Liberty, gesturing to Mabel and Gladys. 'Usually I have to bribe them with carrots to get them back along the road.'

Hattie smiles. 'It's because they made the choice to come with us.'

She keeps smiling as they walk up the driveway of Clover Hill House and in through the back gate. It's only when they reach the yard that the smile fades. Bill has taken the door off one of the stables and is replacing the hinges. He stops drilling when they get near.

'You got them, then.' Bill sniffs loudly. 'Shame that.'

As if sensing his feelings towards them, Mable spooks at Bill and the door he's working on, jumping backwards into Liberty and Gladys. Gladys bleats pitifully.

'A thank you would be nice,' says Liberty.

Bill scowls. Muttering something under his breath, he starts drilling again.

Gladys leaps forward, scared by the noise. Stroking the little goat's neck, Liberty catches Hattie's eye and shakes her head. They keep walking.

At least Bill has repaired the fencing in the goats' paddock. Letting them loose, Hattie shuts the gate and escorts Liberty along the pathway at the side of the paddocks and back through the garden to the front of the house. It's a longer route back, but preferable to going through the yard and seeing Bill again. 'Thanks again for your help, Liberty. And for being so good about Gladys and Mabel breaking into your garden.'

'It's totally fine.' Liberty laughs. 'Look, I'm having some people over for a barbeque next weekend. Nothing fancy, all very informal. It'd be great if you joined us. I know things can be lonely when you relocate.'

Hattie smiles. It feels like she's made a friend. 'I'd love that, thank you.'

~

Later that evening, Hattie leans on the fence and watches the goats grazing happily. The sun is starting to sink below the horizon, painting the sky in a gold and orange haze. Peanut and Banana are running about, chasing sniffs in the long grass. Hattie takes a long breath in. She feels relaxed. It's so peaceful here now that Bill has left for the day. Maybe this place is starting to feel more like home.

Calling the dogs, she turns back towards the house. As they scamper along the path in front of her, Hattie's mobile vibrates in the pocket of her jeans. Taking it out, she sees the name of someone she hasn't spoken to in many months on the screen: Ryan Donaldson. Ryan works for Blake Mentmore – the horse whisperer she was working for in the States when her mum became ill. She reads the text.

> How you doing? Blake's still holding the job for you. When you coming back? Rx

Hattie stares at the screen. Specifically, she's staring at the kiss beside Ryan's initial, wondering what it means. He shouldn't be sending kisses to her. He's with Jessica now. What she had with him was over a long time ago. He couldn't handle that Blake made her his first rider rather than Ryan and the jealousy-motivated petty sniping and pass-agg comments destroyed what could have been a good thing.

They're better off just colleagues. Definitely. But the job, she did love it, and she was good at it. She helped Blake prepare youngsters on the ground, got onboard as their first rider, and then trained them on. She'd also worked with some of the horses sent to Blake with problems for fixing – with his guidance she'd helped them overcome their fears.

She thinks about Blake. His weather-beaten face and dark eyes, half shielded by the brim of his Stetson pulled down low over his brow. He had a steadiness with which he moved and endless calm and patience with the horses. Those factors combined with the quiet intensity made him a true force of nature. He was a man of few words, but when he took the time to coach you, the improvement in your understanding, and the way your horse responded to you, accelerated beyond anything Hattie had thought possible.

Part of her wants to text back right away and say yes, I'm coming back. But she can't. She signed up to house sit for Robert – the goats and the dogs are depending on her. And, anyway, working in the States isn't what she should do right now. Training her own horse and riding at Badminton Horse Trials is her dream. She'd told Blake that, and he understood. Much as she would love to return to work with him, she can't. It might seem impossible at this moment, but if she doesn't *try* to achieve her dream she'll always regret it. She thinks about Lady Patricia asking her what she was waiting for, and Liberty giving up her life in London and setting up her own business here because life's too short to wait. And knows that they're right.

She taps out a message to Ryan, and presses send before she can reconsider.

> Sorry. Have to stay for foreseeable. Tell Blake I'll never forget what he taught me. H.

There's got to be a way to progress towards her dream. She'll think of something. She has to.

She won't give up.

CHAPTER TWELVE

DANIEL

*H*e's never flown first class before. In fact, he hasn't flown that often at all; his parents loved their exotic holidays overseas, but they didn't appreciate having a child with them, holding them back and spoiling their fun. So Daniel's school holidays were made up of pony club camp and being looked after by the nanny. When he got older and had more horses, he found it hard to take time away. Now he doesn't have a choice but stay put; there hasn't been any money for holidays in years.

He'd been excited about this trip and having the opportunity to view some top horses for sale in Germany and France, but now he's beginning to think it's a mistake. In fact, he's starting to think, in agreeing to Lexi Marchfield-Wright's terms, he's made a huge error.

Lexi insisted they had champagne and caviar in the first-class lounge before boarding the plane, but he'd not been able to stomach much of the caviar. It's never been his thing – he's much more of a beans on toast kind of guy – and with Lexi draping herself over him the whole time, it put him off the food even more. Still, he necked a couple of glasses of champagne, to help take the edge off.

The first-class cabin is something else. As he enters the space, he sees that there are only fourteen spots, and each has its own individual space and privacy screens. He finds his seat – number 14A. The chair is high backed and comes with its own footstool, he's told it converts into a flat bed when needed too, and he has a small side table with a reading light and lampshade above it. It hardly feels like he's on a plane and if it wasn't for the engine noise, it'd be easy enough to forget.

He turns to Lexi, who is behind him. 'This is me.'

'I'm in front of you, in 3A,' she says, slipping her arm around his waist and kissing his neck. 'See you soon, darling.'

Stepping into his space, he puts his overnight bag down on the footstool, and then sinks down into the chair. A blonde cabin crew member offers him a drink and he takes a fresh orange and a glass of champagne, and puts them onto his side table.

He's relieved that Lexi stays in her seat even after take-off. He eats dinner off real china plates with actual silverware while watching the latest *Fast and Furious* film on his flat screen telly. After dinner, Daniel switches the chair into bed mode and settles down for a nap. Damn, it's comfy. The gentle blue backlighting creates a calming feeling and after Lexi's constant attention in the airport it's nice to have a bit of space.

But it doesn't last long.

He wakes with a start. Feels warm breath on his face and a weight holding him down. He opens his mouth to cry out and a hand clamps it closed.

'Shush, darling. It's me.' Lexi pushes her hand under his blanket and rubs her fingers against his dick.

Daniel tries to push her away, but she's stronger than she looks. 'Lexi? Jesus! I—'

'It's time for some fun,' she says, seductively. She bites his earlobe and then murmurs breathily in his ear, 'Let's join the Mile High Club.'

'We can't.' He glances up over the privacy screen; there's a member of cabin crew just a few metres ahead. 'Someone might see.'

Lexi stifles a laugh. 'So what? Let them watch – they might learn something.'

Daniel thinks quickly. Lexi obviously isn't going to be dissuaded. 'No. Not here.'

Lexi narrows her gaze. 'Where then?'

'The loos. That one at the back on the other side of the cabin.' It's the only place he can think of. 'You go first. I'll leave it a minute, then follow.'

'Okay, darling,' Lexi says, running her tongue along his jaw and giving his neck a playful nip. 'Don't be too long, though. I don't like to be kept waiting.'

∽

Two minutes later, he raps softly on the door of the bathroom and holds his breath. He hears the lock disengage and the door opens. That's when he realises Lexi's naked.

He steps inside and slides the door closed, making doubly sure it's locked before he turns to face her. She's already undoing his belt and pushing his jeans down. Her jade-painted fingernails scratch at his skin.

There's not much room, but it's still the biggest airplane toilet Daniel's ever seen. There's a proper vanity unit with a full-size counter-to-ceiling mirror and stainless-steel sink that's partially separated by a half wall from the loo.

Daniel catches a glimpse of his reflection in the mirror over the toilet. His skin looks yellowed in the harsh lighting and there are dark patches beneath his eyes.

Bending over, Lexi grabs hold of the vanity countertop and

shoves her bum back towards him. She meets his glance in the mirror. 'Come on, cowboy. Saddle up.'

He tries to do what she wants. Running his hands over her back, he leans forward and cups her breasts, massaging her nipples. He feels her arch her back beneath him, pressing her body closer into him. He kisses the back of her neck and she moans.

He hears a noise outside the toilet and wishes she'd be quiet. Hopes no one heard her. He's not shy, but this feels so forced. So fake.

'Fuck me,' Lexi says, her voice thick with lust.

Daniel tries to enter her, but his dick isn't playing ball. He's too soft and he can't get it in. He fumbles about, trying again but still no luck.

Lexi looks over her shoulder and frowns. 'Sort yourself out, darling.'

Daniel's never had this problem before but he realises telling Lexi that would be a bad move. He closes his eyes and strokes himself, trying to coax a hard on. He has to be able to perform. The money is already in his bank account, and a big chunk of it has already been used to pay the staff wages, the yard's outstanding debts, and The Rogue's ongoing vet bills. He knew the terms Lexi offered and he agreed to them. He has to deliver.

Finally he manages to thrust into her. As soon as he's inside, she starts with the directions.

'Fuck me like you mean it.' Her tone is strong and commanding. 'And look at me when you fuck me.'

He opens his eyes. Meets her gaze in the mirror.

'Better,' she says. Reaching back, she grabs hold of either side of his arse, digging her nails into his flesh, pulling him deeper. 'Now harder... harder...'

He clenches his jaw. Keeps eye contact. Tries to do as she says. Grabbing her hips, Daniel pulls her closer to him. Thrusts harder.

'That's it,' she says, breathlessly. 'Just like that.'

Daniel wishes she'd shut up. He wishes he'd never signed the contract.

'Come on... put your back into it. Fuck me like you're being given half a million pounds to fuck me. Because, darling...' Letting go of his arse, Lexi reaches between her legs, slides her fingers up his inner thighs and squeezes his balls hard. 'You are.'

CHAPTER THIRTEEN

LEXI

God, Daniel is being so boring. All he cares about is viewing the horses. Four days in Germany and two here in France, and he's instigated nothing fun with her. She has to make the running every time and that's just boring. It's not at all good enough. She didn't pay him half a million just to feel ignored; she can get that feeling from her husband for free.

That's why so far she's refused to sign off on him buying any of the horses he likes. She's stringing him along, of course, because although they're disgusting, smelly creatures, the point of getting them is to win, and Lexi's going to show the dowdy tweed brigade that a winning owner can speak and dress however the hell they want. But Daniel doesn't need to know that she'll buy them just yet; let him sulk and stew a while longer.

And it's good horses mean so much to Daniel because that love of them gives her control over him. That's the most important thing – being the one in control. That way you're never the one getting used or hurt.

Daniel needs to learn how to treat a woman right. In fact, he could learn a few lessons from Jean-Luc Malmond, the owner of one of the horses Daniel is keen to buy. The Frenchman invited her to a business lunch in his suite at Le Grande and it's taken a rather pleasing turn. Stretching out on the grey silk sheets, she looks up at the elegant chiffon draped like a sheer curtain over the frame of the huge oak four-poster, and opens her legs wider.

Lower down the bed, Jean-Luc continues to work his magic.

Lexi clutches at the sheets and lets out a soft moan.

Now this is a man who knows how to go down on a woman. He doesn't look much – wiry, balding and at least an inch shorter than her – but he makes up for that with what he can do with his tongue. He's given her three orgasms in barely twenty minutes and she hasn't had to give him a word of instruction. That hardly ever happens. She's actually impressed.

She looks down at Jean-Luc's shiny bald pate. She's never been one for the bald guys, but the way he's sucking her clit, it's possible he might just convert her. Damn. If he keeps this up, she might even reconsider buying his bloody horse.

CHAPTER FOURTEEN

HATTIE

She wakes with the sun pouring through the gap between the curtains and the dogs lying beside her – Peanut on her left, Banana on her right – making her feel like she's the filling in a hairy kind of sandwich. Sitting up, she reaches for her phone on the bedside table and is surprised to see she's got a text from Robert Babbington.

> Aunt P gone bonkers. Told her not to send the damn thing but she insists. You'll have to handle until I'm back. Get feed etc from Cox & Anvil – put it on my account.

Hattie rereads the message several times and still has no idea what he's referring too. Maybe Patricia has rescued more goats – there's plenty of acreage, after all. She's still trying to puzzle it out when there's a loud knock at the front door.

Immediately alert, Peanut and Banana leap off the bed and scuttle downstairs, barking. Throwing off the duvet, Hattie shoves her phone into the pocket of her pyjamas and follows at a slower pace. It's barely seven-thirty – who would be arriving at this time? It has to be Lady Patricia, maybe with more goats. Although last time she came over she used her own key.

As she approaches the front door, Hattie runs her fingers through her hair and rubs any makeup smudges from beneath her eyes, trying to make herself more presentable. She looks down. There's nothing she can do about her faded *Lion King* pyjamas. Taking a breath, she opens the door.

'Harriet Kimble?' says the flat-cap-wearing delivery driver. He taps his pen against a piece of paper on the clipboard he's holding. 'Livestock delivery.'

'Yes, I'm Hattie Kimble,' says Hattie, her eyes widening as she looks past the guy to the horsebox with 'JDF EQUESTRIAN TRANSPORT' painted in two-foot-high lettering along the side. The lorry is parked nose out, with the ramp end close to the side gate that leads around to the yard and paddocks. 'What kind of livestock?'

'A horse. It's a mare. Chestnut,' says the guy with a grimace. He cocks his head to one side. 'Not what you were expecting? I'll need you to sign before I unload.'

Hattie's heart is pounding so hard it feels as if it's going to burst out of her chest. She wonders if she's still asleep and dreaming. A horse? Not more goats? Robert's text definitely didn't mention a horse.

The driver looks at her quizzically. 'Problem?'

'No, no, it's totally okay,' Hattie says, as inwardly she squeals with excitement. She takes the clipboard from him. 'I'm happy to sign.'

'Well, good,' he says, taking the clipboard back after she's signed the paperwork. 'I'll get her out for you.'

After putting the clipboard into the cab, he walks around to the back of the lorry. Hattie taps the code into the pin-pad beside the gate and opens it wide. If it's already open, it'll make it easier to lead the horse through the unfamiliar surroundings to the yard. She glances up at the ramp of the lorry and then towards the transport guy. 'What can you tell me about her?'

He shrugs. 'It's a chestnut mare. You know how they can be.'

She nods. Chestnut mares traditionally have a bad reputation for being fiery and unpredictable. In Hattie's experience, any horse can be that way if they're treated badly.

'You ready?' asks the guy.

'Yep.'

She watches as he unfastens the ramp. Holds her breath as it starts to lower. There's silence from inside the horsebox. The only sounds are from the birds singing overhead and the creak of the ramp hinges.

The equestrian transport guy steps onto the bottom of the ramp. Next moment, the horsebox starts rocking from side to side. Hattie can hear hooves clattering inside. A horse snorts loudly, twice. There's a thud against the side of the horsebox, then another. The mare's kicking the walls, Hattie realises. She must be extremely stressed.

'Steady, steady,' says the delivery guy, undoing the end doors into the body of the lorry. He slips inside, closing them again behind him and disappearing from view.

The lorry starts to rock more violently. A shrill neigh comes from inside.

'Stand back,' the flat-cap-wearing guy yells. 'This one breathes fire.'

Hattie hears the sound of the inner partition being unfastened. The clattering of hooves gets faster. The lorry rocks more violently. The guy is saying, 'Woah, woah.'

She steps closer to the ramp. 'Are you okay? Can I—?'

There's a loud bang against the end doors, and she hears the man bellow in pain. Moments later, the doors fly open and a chestnut horse gallops down the ramp, her lead rope trailing between her legs. She speeds through the open gate, and away across the gravel and lawn, before disappearing out of sight.

Inside the lorry, the delivery guy is doubled over, sweating and gasping for air. His flat cap lies upside down and trampled halfway down the ramp.

Quickly, Hattie closes the gate. Knowing the horse is safe from getting onto the road now, she turns and hurries up the ramp to check if the man is injured. She puts her hand on his shoulder. 'Are you—?'

'Winded... shoved me against... doors.' He presses his hand against his chest. Takes another gulp of air. 'I'll... okay in a... minute.'

Hattie hears a horse whinny from somewhere over near the paddocks. Moments later Mabel and Gladys start bleating. From her vantage point at the top of the ramp, Hattie can see the horse trotting around the lawn. Her strides are long and even, and so light-footed she almost seems to float above the ground.

The delivery guy coughs a couple of times and then straightens up to standing. He's red-faced and his breathing is heavier than it should be. 'She was easy enough to load for the journey over. The sedative the vet gave her must have worn off.'

Hattie's surprised they'd give a horse a sedative to travel. It doesn't sound safe. 'Are you sure you're—?'

He waves Hattie's concerns away. 'I'm fine. Don't worry.' He gives a rather forced smile, and limps down the ramp, wincing as he bends to pick up his cap. 'It's all part of the service.'

Hattie follows him down and helps him close the ramp. She's not sure if she's supposed to pay or tip him. She clears her throat. 'Erm, do I owe you anything for the delivery service or—?'

'No. It's all sorted.' As he climbs up into the driver's seat, he gestures in the direction the horse went. 'Good luck with that one. She doesn't like humans much.'

∼

Hattie finds the mare on the lawn, munching grass beside the immaculately tended flowerbeds. There are hoof prints in the grass, and huge divots where the turf has been cut up with long skid marks. In the centre of the lawn, a purple lead rope with a frayed end lies as lifeless as a decapitated snake. Hattie sees the first foot of the rope remains clipped to the horse's head collar; she must have trodden on the rope and snapped it while she was cavorting around.

She moves towards the horse. Keeps her breathing steady and her voice gentle. 'Hey, girl.'

The mare jerks up her head and gives a loud snort. She swings around to face Hattie. Her ears are pricked forward. She raises her head higher, the whites of her eyes showing as she eyeballs Hattie. The mare's nostrils flare and she gives another snort.

Staying calm, Hattie remains still, watching the horse. 'It's okay, girl.'

Gradually, as the minutes tick by, the mare relaxes a little. She lowers her head a fraction. Her eyes become less wild.

Hattie takes another step closer.

The horse throws her head up again and lets out a shrill whinny. Spinning a one-eighty, she gallops across the lawn towards the goats' paddock. She doesn't slow down as she reaches the fence, doesn't hesitate. Hattie gasps as the mare springs effortlessly into the air and clears the five-foot post and rail fencing by at least an extra foot.

Landing safely, the mare takes a few strides across the paddock before skidding to a halt. With Mabel and Gladys leaping excitedly around her, she turns and stares at Hattie. Her head is held high. Her ears still pricked. She snorts loudly.

The mare is greyhound thin, wild-eyed, wild-spirited and ready to defend herself. Hattie has never seen a horse more beautiful. Pulling her phone out of the pocket of her pyjamas, she taps a reply to Robert's earlier text.

Don't worry. I've got this.

CHAPTER FIFTEEN

DEXTER

*D*exter has no desire to be here. His chest is tight and he's on edge. Standing still is a real struggle. He tried to get out of it. Told Lexi he wanted to stay behind and work, but no, she insisted he had to come with her, and so here he is, standing next to this arena filled with artificial sand, watching Lexi watch this Daniel Templeton-Smith bloke ride the pink-looking horse over some jumps.

Dexter clenches and unclenches his fists. Jigs his right leg, his heel bouncing up and down a half inch from the ground. Being here is just making things worse. Making him think about all the money they're pouring into these horses as part of Lexi's latest fad. He still can't believe Lexi wanted half a million from him for this – event horses. Actually, scratch that, with the extra horse she insisted on buying on her European shopping trip the cost is going to be higher than a half million. And that's more money than he's got. Dexter rolls his eyes, then checks to see if Lexi noticed. Thankfully, she doesn't seem to have done.

It's a mystery why she's suddenly decided eventing is the sport they should patronise. If he'd had a say in which horse sport to go for, he'd have picked show jumping or even polo – competitions where there's always a good bar and a dry place to observe the competition. But horse trials? Yes, you can go to the VIP enclosure at the biggest competitions, but the rest of it is so *outdoors*.

As the bloke and his horse canter past, Dexter takes his phone from the pocket of his new Barbour and looks at the screen: still nothing.

Lexi nudges him and hisses, 'Put that bloody thing away and at least try to pretend you're interested.'

Dexter supposes he should. He's paid enough for this, after all. So he shows willing and watches the horse jump down the line of four fences without hitting a pole. He claps his hands and shouts, 'Bravo, well done.'

The pink horse scuttles sideways away from where Dexter's standing and the rider, Daniel, shoots him a pissed-off look. 'Please don't clap, he's very sensitive.'

Great, thinks Dexter. That worked well then.

Daniel jumps the horse down the line of fences again. Patting the horse's neck, he calls over to Lexi as the horse eases back from a canter to a walk. 'Can you see how he's improving?'

'Yes, he's looking marvellous, darling.' Lexi turns to Dexter. 'This is the extra horse we bought, the French one. So worth it, don't you think?'

Dexter forces a nod but says nothing. Frankly he has no idea whether the horse is any good, but right now he'd rather they'd have saved the money rather than spent it.

Lexi either doesn't notice or doesn't care.

'Let's do a bit more,' says Daniel, gesturing to the sweet-looking girl in the blue sweatshirt and jeans standing by the gate to the arena. Dexter thinks her name was Bunty. She reminds him of a shy sunflower standing there with her face turned down. 'Pop them up a couple of holes.'

As Bunty walks over to the jumps and raises them a couple of inches higher, Dexter feels his phone vibrate in his pocket. He takes it out again.

Lexi scowls at him, but he ignores her and checks the screen anyway. He's glad that he did. There's a notification from his banking app. He reads the message and feels sweet relief flood through him.

Stanton-Bassett's two million has gone into Dexter's business account. It's happened a week later than planned, and he'd almost given up hope, but it's there. It means the standing orders will go through and the dividend payments should be okay. As the horse canters round to jump the fences again, Dexter does the maths in his head and thinks it'll all work out. He'll run the projections when they get home, but this is a good moment – a good day.

Funds received and cleared.

Thank God.

Finally Dexter feels like he can breathe again.

CHAPTER SIXTEEN

HATTIE

Hattie sits by the water trough in the paddock from ten in the morning until almost four in the afternoon but the horse doesn't come over to her once. The mare stays on the other side of the paddock, snorting every time Hattie moves, and galloping to the furthest corner when she stands up to stretch. The same can't be said about Mabel and Gladys.

The goats love that Hattie's in the paddock with them. Now Mabel is using her back as a scratching post, again, and Gladys is chewing at the toe of her boot. Hattie shuffles away from the pair. 'Will you two pack it in?'

Gladys stares sadly at her. Mabel registers her dissatisfaction at having her scratching post removed by giving Hattie a medium-strength headbutt between the shoulder blades.

'Ouch, that hurt. Will you...' She notices that Peanut and Banana have stopped sniffing about in the long grass and are standing, attention focused in the direction of the yard, on full alert. Standing up, Hattie calls to the dogs, 'What's going on, guys?'

They don't look around. Instead they sprint away in the direction of the yard, barking. Hattie knows what that type of reaction usually means – they've got a visitor. Reluctantly, she follows them across the paddock and out through the gate. As she gets to the archway that leads to the yard, she turns and takes a look back. The mare is at the water trough, drinking. Hattie sighs, disappointed the horse wouldn't drink while she was sitting there. Mare – 1, Hattie – 0. Hattie realises if she's going to connect with this mare, she'll need to up her game.

As she walks under the archway into the yard, Hattie sees why the dogs are making such a racket. 'Lady Patricia?'

'Afternoon.' Lady Patricia raises her hand in hello as she strides over to meet her under the archway. 'And, as I've said before, call me Pat, for God's sake.'

'Yes, sorry,' says Hattie. 'Pat.'

'Much better.' Patricia looks out across the arena to the paddocks. 'Ah, there she is. Now how'd you like my little surprise?'

'She's wonderful.'

'I thought you might like her, and she's had the most God-awful time.' Patricia cocks her head to one side. 'When I heard about her plight, I thought the two of you could be made for each other.'

'I'm very happy to look after her for Robert until he's back.'

Patricia waves away Hattie's words. 'Robert? Nonsense. He'd have no patience with a horse like Mermaid's Gold.'

'She is very sensitive.'

'Yes, she's definitely that, dear. So, you see, she needs someone who truly gets horses.' Patricia looks meaningfully at Hattie. 'You understand?'

'You'd like me to see if I can win her trust?'

'Well, yes of course,' says Patricia. 'But I'd rather thought you might like to see if you can get her back to her old form.'

Hattie frowns. 'I'm not sure I understand what you—'

'Mermaid's Gold is an event horse – a very brave and talented one. But, as I understand it, she's been messed around by certain humans and is now viewed as dangerous and unrideable.'

Hattie remembers the horse's fear as she came down the ramp earlier; how she threw the transport guy around like a ragdoll, and how she hasn't let Hattie get within a half-acre of her all day. 'What happened?'

Patricia puts her hand on Hattie's arm and steers her towards the house. 'Now that, dear, is a conversation that needs a tot of whiskey to accompany it in order to make the sorry tale more palatable. Shall we go inside?'

∼

Ten minutes later, they're sitting at the kitchen table with a single whiskey for Hattie and a double for Patricia. The dogs are snoring contently at their feet having been given cheese. Lady Patricia clinks her glass against Hattie's and starts to tell the story. 'She was a high-potential youngster. Started off in Jonathan Scott's yard, and progressed quickly up the ranks through Novice and Intermediate. Jonathan had high hopes for her, but when she was a seven-year-old, the owner's daughter decided she wanted Mermaid's Gold for herself. The owner, who's a rich, but stupid, man in my opinion' – Patricia gives Hattie a knowing look – 'dotes on his daughter, and so of course the idiot agreed. At first the horse stayed at Jonathan's yard and Jonathan continued to school her and also trained the daughter. But it was clear after a month or so it wasn't going to work out. Jonathan's a hard taskmaster – very particular about the way things are done – and the girl just wasn't up to the level of perfectionism he demanded. Apparently there was a huge row when he told her she wasn't ready for a horse like Mermaid's Gold and she should get herself an older, more experienced schoolmaster and work up the levels in the open classes. It didn't go well. The upshot was that the owner sacked Jonathan Scott and removed Mermaid's Gold along with all his other horses to Greta Wolfe's yard. The daughter lasted even less time with Greta, and moved with Mermaid's Gold to some mixed discipline competition yard. That's when things started to go wrong.'

'Like what?'

'The daughter started competing, and rather than step down a level or two, and start off with a few Intermediate or Open Novice events to get her eye in and build confidence between her and the horse, she went straight in at Advanced.'

Hattie winces. If a top rider tells you you're not ready, you really should believe them.

'They got round the first couple of events unharmed, but Mermaid's Gold is a quick horse and not always careful in the show jumping, and the daughter wasn't skilful enough to get the best from her. They had four or five poles down each round. So they started changing the horse's tack. They added stronger bits to stop her running forward, a grackle noseband to clamp her mouth shut, then a standing martingale when she started throwing her head up in protest at the bits and the noseband constricting her. By that point the poor dear was practically going backwards, so the daughter wore bigger spurs to kick her on.' Patricia shakes her head sadly. 'It was then that the accident happened. They were competing at Tweseldown Horse Trials. According to my sources, the daughter was hanging on tight to the reins while spurring the horse on across the country. The mare was obviously uncomfortable and confused – shaking her head, plunging on the approach to fences, bolting off as soon as the girl gave an inch on the reins. They took a tight turn to a big Trakehner – a telegraph pole suspended 1.15m above a massive ditch – and the daughter yanked on the reins at the wrong moment. The horse lost all her impulsion. Then the girl gave her a boot in the ribs with her spurs and brought the whip down on the mare's bottom. Apparently the mare squealed with rage and took off a stride early. She hit the fence with her forelegs and the pair somersaulted upside down and into the stagnant water at the bottom of the ditch. The mare was shaken but didn't have any lasting damage. The daughter broke her pelvis and an arm. As I understand it, the only way a person has been able to do anything with the horse since is if she's been put under sedation.'

That explains the mare's reaction when the transport guy tried to unload her earlier, and how she ran away and stayed away from Hattie in the paddock. Hattie takes a gulp of whiskey, coughing as it burns the back of her throat.

'Still want to take her on, dear?' asks Patricia. 'Or have I put you off?'

From what Patricia has told her, the mare's trust in people is entirely broken. It won't be easy to connect with her, but humans have failed this horse. Hattie wants to make amends for that. 'I'm not put off.'

'Good,' says Patricia, sloshing another measure into her and Hattie's glasses. 'Drink up then – for Dutch courage. You're going to need it because that little horse is wild.'

'I thought you said you didn't know anything about horses,' says Hattie, narrowing her eyes. She's sure that's what Patricia told her the first time they'd met.

'Well, I don't, dear,' says Patricia, her voice rising an octave. 'But I talked to a few horsey people as I investigated the mare's history, and my memory works well enough.'

Hattie's not entirely convinced, but can't see any reason Patricia would lie about her knowledge of horses. 'So where did you find her?'

Patricia's expression turns serious. 'A lady at one of the animal rescues I support called me. She'd had a tip off from a local vet about Mermaid's Gold. The owners wanted the mare euthanised, but the vet wasn't willing to do it. Apparently the vet went along to the appointment and recognised the horse – she's an eventer herself and had seen Mermaid's Gold fall at Tweseldown. She was shocked at the state she was in, and told the owners so. They gave her some cock and bull story about not being able to get close enough to feed the horse, but the vet suspected all they were after really was the insurance money. She refused to put her down, and called the animal rescue as she drove away to give them a heads-up. She was worried the owners would just call another vet and ask them to do the job.'

Hattie tastes sourness on her tongue. Feels sick. Disgusted that the people would try and kill the horse for insurance money. 'But she's so full of life, so—'

'Yes, indeed,' interrupts Patricia. 'Anyway, long story short, I got my private secretary, Gerald, to call the owners and make them an offer they couldn't refuse. Said I was looking for a broodmare and Mermaid's Gold had the perfect breeding. They pushed the price up a few grand, but it was quickly sorted. Gerald dropped the money off first thing this morning and watched as the vet sedated her and the equestrian transporter picked her up. You know the rest.'

'That poor horse.' Hattie looks down. Her head is spinning. She's not sure if it's the impact of Mermaid's Gold's story or the effects of drinking whiskey on an empty stomach taking hold. She clenches the glass tighter. Anger at what's happened to the mare flares in her belly. She looks back at Patricia. 'I'll do everything I can to make things right.'

Patricia smiles and clinks her glass against Hattie's. 'I know you will, dear.'

~

Later, as the day turns to night and sunlight into darkness, Hattie sits in the paddock with her back pressed up against the water trough. She's left the dogs in the house, worried that they'll chase off after the nocturnal wildlife that follow their nightly hunting paths through the fields. Every now and then, the bug chorus gets drowned out by the rasping call of a fox in heat, or the hooting of the white barn owl that flits like a silent but deadly ghost above the paddocks, looking for its next meal. Hattie has been out here for nearly three hours.

Still the mare keeps her distance.

And so Hattie waits. The first step in building a bond with this horse is to prove she's not a threat, and the only way to do that is to show it. The mare will want a drink of water at some point, and she'll have to come close to Hattie in order to get to the trough. That's enough to start the process – getting in close proximity to each other and for Hattie not to force the horse to do anything. It's just a question of waiting.

Hattie feels her eyelids getting heavier.

∼

She wakes in the hazy light of dawn. Stiff-backed from sleeping propped up against the water trough, she wiggles her toes to try and ease the pins and needles in her legs. Opening her eyes, Hattie's breath catches in her throat. On the grass beside her, Mable and Gladys are stretched out, asleep. A couple of feet away, standing guard over her and the goats, is Mermaid's Gold.

Hattie feels her heartrate accelerate. Moving slowly so as not to spook the horse, she looks up at the mare. 'Hello, girl,' she says softly. Her voice sounds overly loud in the quiet of the early morning.

The mare jerks up her head, and takes a step back. She eyes Hattie with suspicion.

Hattie reaches into the pocket of her jeans and takes out a half-eaten packet of Polos. Removing one, she puts it on the flat palm of her hand. Then slowly raises her hand towards the horse.

Mermaid's Gold lowers her head a fraction.

Hattie feels the horse's warm breath on her hand. She raises her palm a little higher.

The mare leans down and takes the Polo. Hattie stays still and tries to keep her own breathing calm and regular; doesn't want to give the horse cause to spook or hurry away.

It works. Taking a step closer, the mare reaches down and puts her velvet soft muzzle against Hattie's cheek. Her whiskers tickle against Hattie's skin. The horse exhales; it's as if she's saying thank you.

Hattie's eyes start to water and she smiles as the tears run down her cheeks.

For the first time in a long time she feels something like happiness.

CHAPTER SEVENTEEN
DANIEL

The new lorry that Lexi has bought certainly gives Daniel more space and every mod con, but the white leather seats aren't very practical and he misses the familiarity of his old Bedford TK. Looking out of the door to the living area, he can see Eddie screwing spiked studs into Pornstar Martini's hind shoes to give her better grip – just like a footballer's studs – as they gallop round the course. The little lemon-and-white skewbald mare is one of his three new horses. Rather than buy two top eventers, he persuaded Lexi to sign off on three very talented but slightly less experienced horses; she eventually agreed on the condition they were all renamed after her favourite cocktails, therefore he now has horses called Pornstar Martini, Rocket Fuel and Pink Fizz. This is the first time he's running each of them, and it has to go well.

It's odd, because initially Lexi fought his proposal to buy the then-named Petit Chou-fleur, but after lunch with the owner Jean-Luc Malmond she changed her mind. Daniel has no idea what led to the change of heart – he's learnt Lexi rarely backs down on anything – but he's glad it happened this time. Today is the horse's first time at Advanced level and although the mare is bold, Daniel wants to make sure he gives her a happy, confidence-giving ride around the bigger track.

As he changes into his cross-country kit – polo shirt, stock, body-protector, blue silk on his jockey skull cap – Daniel runs through the course in his mind, visualising him and Pornstar Martini jumping their way around. The coffin fence at twelve is tight on the striding; he'll need to make sure he gets the mare steadied up in good time so she doesn't over-jump and end up too close to the ditch. The water at fifteen is fairly straightforward so hopefully they'll manage the direct route. He's halfway through riding the course in his mind's eye when he hears a familiar, grating voice.

'Daniel? Where are you, darling?' calls Lexi.

He clenches his jaw. Concentration broken. He knows trying to focus again will be impossible as long as Lexi is around. Stepping out of the living area and down the steps, Daniel says, 'I'm here.'

'Hey there, Danny-boy,' says Dexter Marchfield-Wright, slapping Daniel on the back as he reaches the ground. 'Good job on Pink Fizz. Third place in the Intermediate – not bad at all.'

'Thanks,' says Daniel, forcing a smile. 'I've still got two more cross-country rounds to do – Pornstar Martini here, and then Rocket Fuel's running towards the end of the class.'

'You using the Waterford snaffle for her?' asks Eddie, who's finished fitting the studs and is now in the process of adjusting the mare's breastplate, designed to stop the saddle from slipping too far.

'Yes, I think so,' says Daniel. Flinching as he hears the pop of a champagne cork. 'I don't want to use anything stronger, and it did a good job stopping her running through the bridle last time.'

'Cool.' Eddie finishes buckling the breastplate, and walks over to the tack locker towards the rear of the lorry to get the bridle.

'Darling, have a glass,' says Lexi, thrusting a champagne flute at him. 'It's divine and we need to toast Pink Fizz's success.'

'Not yet,' says Daniel, waving away the glass. 'Not until I've finished riding.'

Lexi pouts. 'There's no need to be so tetchy.' She hands the flute to her husband and they both down the champagne in one.

Jesus, thinks Daniel. He catches Eddie's eye. Eddie raises his eyes to the heavens.

Thank God for Eddie, thinks Daniel. He focuses on the job in hand and doesn't let the Marchfield-Wrights distract him. Daniel wishes Lexi and her husband would go so he can get ready, but with Lexi now topping up their champagne flutes, and Dexter patting Pornstar Martini's rump with one hand and holding the mobile phone he's now talking into with the other, it seems unlikely. Daniel grits his teeth. This is a bloody nightmare.

Across the lorry park, a loudspeaker splutters into life. 'We're about to get going on the cross-country with the first of the afternoon's starters – Greta Wolfe and her own and Mrs Clifford's Westworlder. This is Westworlder's second outing at Advanced level and they'll be our pathfinder on the new Advanced track here at Tettington Park.'

As the commentator prattles on, Daniel checks his watch – he's due on the course in nineteen minutes. He'll need fifteen minutes to warm up Pornstar Martini and put her over a few of the practice fences, and it's a two- or three-minute ride down to the cross-country start. That gives him a minute to get rid of the Marchfield-Wrights and get onboard the mare.

'She's all set. I just need to do the grease,' says Eddie, as he tightens Pornstar Martini's girth, ignoring the mare's swishing tail as he does so. 'You about ready?'

'In a minute,' says Daniel, gesturing towards the Marchfield-Wrights. 'I need to just…'

'Yeah,' says Eddie, rolling his eyes. He runs his hand through his blond-flecked ginger hair. 'Hard to concentrate, right?'

Daniel nods. Stepping over to Pornstar Martini, he gives the mare's neck a rub as he starts his pre-flight checks – making sure all the tack is in the right place, the girths are tight, and the mare's protective leg boots are properly fastened and taped.

As Daniel double-checks the equipment, Eddie starts applying event grease to the mare's legs. Smeared over the front of the horse's legs from above their boots to the top of the leg, the thick ice cream-like white grease helps a horse slide free of a fence if they misjudge it and hit the obstacle with their leg.

'Oooh that's a lot of lube,' says Lexi, laughing. She moves closer to Eddie and puts a hand on his back. 'Maybe you can do me after.'

Eddie's ears turn red. 'I don't think this is meant for humans,' he says, his tone serious.

'Oh well,' says Lexi, catching Daniel's eye as he repositions the over-girth around the saddle, looping it through the girth strap of the breastplate. 'Some other time perhaps.'

Daniel lets go of the over-girth and it falls to the floor. Pornstar Martini flinches from the sudden movement and moves sideways, almost treading on Eddie. Cursing under his breath, Daniel picks up the over-girth. Lexi is out of order. Eddie wasn't part of the deal. Lexi has no right implying what she's implying.

Before he can reposition the over-girth, Dexter sidles up to him. 'Look, I need you to help me out, mate. I'm looking for some of your equestrian contacts – people who've got a bit of spare cash and fancy a—'

'Sorry, I can't right now,' says Daniel, gesturing to the over-girth. 'I need to get this sorted.'

Dexter looks put out. 'Fine, mate, fine. We'll talk later. We'll do dinner soon, yeah?'

'Okay,' says Daniel, hoping not pandering to Lexi's husband won't result in another black mark against him. Things have been difficult with Lexi since they returned from France and he can't afford any more problems. But right now, he needs the Marchfield-Wrights out of the way so he can finish his final checks, mount up and go down to the cross-country.

He knows Lexi won't leave the horsebox without a fight – she hates to be told what to do and will make a point of doing the exact opposite just to spite him. He doesn't have the energy to argue with her. He needs to think of another way.

What's the expression Grandma used to say – you catch more flies with sugar than you do with vinegar? He figures that's true when it comes to Lexi and grimaces at the thought of the sort of sugar she wants from him.

He waits until Dexter has wandered off around to the other side of the lorry to have a look at the awning that can be attached to the living area pop-out, then moves quickly towards Lexi. She's facing away from him, towards the show jumping arena.

Daniel knows this is his chance.

Taking a breath, he runs his hand down over Lexi's snakeskin print dress and cups her arse. Squeezing hard, he wraps his other arm around her waist and pulls her to him. Biting her neck, he forces his voice to sound as heavily laden with desire as he can fake, and whispers, 'I want to fuck you so hard.'

'Now, darling?' Lexi sounds surprised but not displeased. 'Here?'

'Tonight. My place. In the stables, over a manger.'

'How very biblical,' says Lexi, but her voice is full of lust.

Daniel bites her neck harder. Tries to ignore the pointed stares and raised eyebrows of two riders walking past the lorry on their way to the cross-country. 'It will be.'

The sugar, or the promise of it, works. But as Eddie leads Pornstar Martini over to the steps so Daniel can check over her tack and get on board, and Lexi and her husband walk away towards the owners' tent, the anxiety Daniel was experiencing from them being here is replaced by different emotions.

Now he feels fake and dirty.

CHAPTER EIGHTEEN

HATTIE

Standing in the paddock beside Mermaid's Gold, Hattie tries again. Reaching out with her right hand, she places it onto the horse's wither. The mare flinches.

Hattie tries not to take it personally. She knows winning the horse's trust will take time and patience. A week ago, she couldn't touch her at all; as soon as she moved to put a hand on her, the mare would step away out of reach. This is progress. She just needs to keep on doing it until Mermaid's Gold doesn't find it so worrying.

Slowly, Hattie runs her palm from the wither along the horse's back. She keeps her tone soothing. 'It's okay, girl. It's just me.'

The mare blows out. Some of the tension releases from her body. Hattie lifts her hand and places it back on the horse's wither again. The flinch is smaller this time. She repeats the process over and again. 'Good girl.'

Mermaid's Gold nudges at the pocket of Hattie's jeans with her nose. Asking her for a Polo. Laughing, Hattie removes the packet and feeds her one. 'Fine, I guess you deserve it.'

The mare takes the mint and crunches it happily. Hattie looks at the nylon headcollar with the raggedy piece of lead rope still hanging from it. She's touched the horse's face, but not tried to remove it yet in case the mare spooked when it was half off and galloped away with it still attached. It needs to come off, though; the cheap nylon has rubbed the delicate fur from Mermaid's Gold nose. Who knows how long she's been wearing it.

Hattie runs her hands up the horse's neck and over her face. The mare stays relaxed, so Hattie rubs her fingers along the headcollar noseband, then up the headpiece and over the buckles. Mermaid's Gold doesn't seem to mind.

'Good girl,' says Hattie, as she starts to ease the buckle open. 'Let's get you out of this.'

The buckle is stiff; it must have been on Mermaid's Gold for months. As Hattie works at it, trying to open it, the horse flicks her ear towards Hattie. The white of her eye starts to show and her body tenses. Hattie keep talking to her, telling her it's okay. She needs her to stay calm and let her finish this.

Moments later, the buckle releases and Hattie removes the headcollar. Mermaid's Gold is free. Hattie steps back, assuming the mare will run away.

But she stays. Blowing out, the tension of a moment ago leaves her body and she steps closer to Hattie, nuzzling at her pocket for another Polo. Smiling, Hattie leans against the fence and feeds her the mint. This is definitely progress. The change from the day the mare arrived – bolting away from the horsebox and jumping into the paddock to get away – to this now, choosing to be with her, is really positive. But there's still a long way to go if Hattie's going to get the mare confident enough to let her sit on her back.

They stand together for a long while. It's a lovely day and the sun is warm against Hattie's skin. Mabel and Gladys are sleeping over in the shelter, out of the heat. Mermaid's Gold grazes beside her, the rhythmic chewing of the horse as relaxing as the birdsong overhead.

Then, suddenly, the yard gate clicks as it's unfastened and the peace is shattered. Mermaid's Gold throws up her head, snorting. Mabel and Gladys, as if sensing their friend's fear, spring up and hurtle across the paddock to join her. The three of them stand ears pricked and alert. Mermaid's Gold snorts again. There's tension in every fibre of her being.

Hattie looks round in the direction of the yard. Moments later, Liberty appears beneath the archway. She waves and Hattie beckons her over to join them in the paddock.

As Liberty comes closer, Mermaid's Gold spins around and canters off to the far side of the field, the two goats following close on her heels.

'Something I said?' asks Liberty, looking over at where Mermaid's Gold is hiding behind the field shelter.

'Don't take it personally,' says Hattie. 'She's only just managing to accept me. Other humans are too much at the moment.'

'I understand,' says Liberty. 'I just popped round to remind you about the barbeque later – people are arriving from four onwards. So anytime from then is good.'

Hattie wonders whether to make an excuse and say she can't come. She hates it when she doesn't know people and the only person at the barbeque she'll know is Liberty.

As if reading her mind, Liberty says, 'Oh no, don't you bail on me, girl. You said you'd come.'

Hattie puts her hands up in surrender. 'Okay, okay. I'll be there.'

'Well, good.' Liberty gives Hattie a 'you'd better be' look. 'It'll be fun, and you need to meet people – it's hard when you move to a new area.'

It's true, she's only seen Liberty, Lady Patricia and Bill – if you count Bill, and she prefers not to – since she's moved here. But she's been so focused on Mermaid's Gold, she hasn't really noticed the lack of human company. Generally, animals are more trustworthy than humans anyway. She narrows her eyes. 'How'd you get in? The gate was locked...'

'Well, yes...' Liberty looks out across the fields towards Gladys and Mabel. 'I remembered the code from before.'

Hattie frowns. She's pretty sure Liberty wasn't watching when she'd tapped in the combination when they brought the goats back. 'Before, when?'

'When Robert and I...' Liberty shakes her head. 'Just before.'

Hattie stares at her for a moment, then she remembers how Liberty was taken aback when she told her Robert had gone away for the rest of the year when they first met. She tilts her head to the side. 'Were you and Robert...?'

Liberty laughs. 'Oh my God, no. But he wanted us to be.'

'Ah,' says Hattie. 'Awkward?'

'Complicated,' says Liberty, looking a little sad.

'Really?' says Hattie, noticing Mermaid's Gold and the goats have crept back towards them, as if they wanted to know the gossip too.

Liberty sighs. 'I'll tell you about it, yeah, but you'll need to come to my barbeque and get me really drunk.'

Hattie's intrigued. She wants to know what happened between the two of them. She might not have a love life of her own, but at least this way she can live vicariously through Liberty. 'Deal.'

~

Liberty's barbeque is far more crowded than Hattie imagined. Instead of the small group promised by Liberty, there must be at least thirty people packed into the back garden of Badger's End. Arriving with two packs of Corona under her arms, and wearing her usual jeans and polo shirt combination, Hattie feels very dowdy compared to the colourful and flamboyant crowd. She almost turns around and leaves immediately.

'Hattie, yay, you're here,' calls Liberty from over by the pond, thwarting her chances of sloping away unseen. Barefoot, Liberty is wearing a gorgeous emerald-green maxi dress and has her hair long and straight, cascading down her back to her waist.

Leaving the group of people she's talking to, Liberty hurries across the garden to Hattie. She takes the beers and puts them in buckets of ice on the patio to keep them cool. Then thrusts a cold one into Hattie's hand and takes her other hand, leading her across the garden. 'There are meat-free burgers, vegetable skewers and baked potatoes on the barbeque, plus jackfruit, stuffed peppers and a load of salads, but first let me introduce you to some people.'

Hattie follows her back over to the group by the pond and smiles as Liberty introduces them. She's always rubbish at remembering names, and forgets these ones almost as soon as Liberty says them. After a few minutes, Liberty leaves them to go and greet some new arrivals. Hattie stands politely on the edge of the group, listening to them talking about the best electric plug-in cars on the market, and the new community bookstore that's opened in West Drayton, a neighbouring village. They seem nice enough, but Hattie doesn't feel like she's got much to contribute to the conversation. Moving back a few steps, she wonders if she'll be able to slope away unnoticed after this beer. She takes a sip, and then another. The faster she drinks it, the quicker she can leave.

She's almost done when a pair of young mop-haired blond boys torpedo into her. Tipped off-balance, Hattie drops her drink and steps back, narrowly avoiding slipping into the pond. One of the kids shoves the other, who cries out as he falls towards the water.

Hattie lunges for the child and grabs his t-shirt as he topples backwards, saving him from a ducking. The other boy screeches angrily as he sprints away.

'Bradley!' shouts a curvy woman in a yellow sift dress. Her American-accented voice carries loudly across the garden as the pusher scuttles off towards Liberty's vegetable garden. 'You mustn't push your brother.'

'Are you okay?' Hattie asks the boy. She's still holding onto his shoulders and can feel him trembling beneath her fingers. She wonders if he's steady enough to stand unaided.

He nods but his lower lip is quivering.

The American woman rushes over. 'Chandler, baby.' She pulls the blond boy to her in a fierce hug. Looks up at Hattie. 'Thank you so much. I'm real sorry about my other son. Really, the kid just can't—'

'It's fine. No harm done.' Hattie steps back, letting the woman take over with the child, and picks up her fallen beer. Luckily it landed upright so nothing spilled.

'You alright, Chandler?' A short, friendly-looking guy with rectangular wire glasses, jeans and an oversized Hawaiian shirt puts his hand on the boy's shoulder.

'Yes, Daddy,' says the kid, although he still looks like he's holding back tears. He sniffs loudly. 'Bradley tipped my potato salad into the flower bed.'

'It's okay, honey,' says the woman. 'We'll go clean it up.' She looks up at Hattie. 'He hates waste or mess. Gives him anxiety.'

Poor boy, thinks Hattie, glancing over at the child's brother, who has snuck back over to join them and is now collecting chicken and duck poo from around the pond with his hands. It's obvious the brothers are polar opposites.

The man seems to notice she's looking in horror at the boy. He gives her a rueful smile. 'Anyway, hi, I'm Tony Alton. This is my wife, Willa.' He gestures towards the kids and rolls his eyes. 'And you've already had the pleasure of meeting our beloved offspring – Chandler the angel and Bradley the devil.'

Hattie's not sure if he's serious or joking.

'Pleased to meet you,' says the cherubic-looking Chandler. 'Do you make candles too?'

Hattie shakes her head. 'I don't, but I live next door and I have goats.'

Chandler's eyes widen. 'I love goats.'

'We're neighbours then,' says Tony. 'We live at Palisade Heights just along the lane.'

Hattie remembers back to her first day here – she saw the pink-painted house through the torrential rain as she ran up the hill searching for Clover Hill House. 'Great to meet you.'

'I want proper food, Daddy. The food here is shit,' the kid Tony described as the devil shouts. He punches his father's leg repeatedly, squishing the poo in his hands into his dad's jeans. 'Get me a meat burger.'

'I'm so sorry,' says Tony, looking at Hattie as the child contorts his face into a shape resembling the iconic 'Scream' painting and screeches like a wild banshee. 'Bradley just doesn't understand veganism.'

'I want a burger now!' yells the child, punching Tony in the stomach.

'Honey, please don't do that,' says Willa. She lowers her voice. 'Daddy will make you a meat burger when we get home.'

Bradley crosses his arms and scowls. 'Want. It. Now.'

'Soon, sweetheart,' says Willa in a cooing voice. 'Another half an hour and we'll go.'

'How's Robert doing out in the States?' asks Tony. 'Tell him we're missing him at the golf club.'

'I will,' says Hattie. She hasn't heard from Robert since the texts on the day Mermaid's Gold arrived and is reluctant to instigate a conversation unless it's an emergency.

'How are you liking the house?' asks Willa.

'I love the animals, and I'm looking after the new addition – a rescue horse Robert's aunt bought a few weeks ago,' says Hattie, before taking another sip of beer.

'Exciting,' says Willa. 'What sort of horse?'

'She's thoroughbred. An eventer, but she had an accident cross-country and lost her trust in humans. I'm trying to get it back.'

'Interesting, interesting,' says Willa, nodding. 'And how long do you think it'll take?'

'It's hard to say,' says Hattie. 'You can't really put a timescale on it. It'll take however long it takes.'

'I like that,' Tony says. 'Life isn't always about timescales. I learnt that when I was wooing this woman.'

Willa gives a loud laugh and affectionately punches him on the arm. 'And this from the man who lives for a deadline.'

'Work's work, though. Animals are different. We're into dressage. Got a few horses at our place in different stages of training.' He glances at Willa. 'As well as beautiful, my wife is very talented.'

Willa blushes. 'I'm lucky that my husband is so supportive.' She lowers her voice and leans towards Hattie. 'And so rich.'

'I'm the best at riding,' announces Bradley, loudly, waving his arms at the adults to get attention. Beside him, Chandler makes eye contact with Hattie and shakes his head.

As Willa confides in her, telling her that it's her dream to represent the United States at the Olympics, and talking her through each of her horses and the different levels of dressage training they're working at, Hattie has an idea. Dressage has always been her weakest of the three phases of eventing. Maybe she can get some useful tips from Willa. 'Would you give me some lessons? I really need to work on my dressage skills.'

Willa grins. 'I'd love to. Just let me know when you're ready.'

Thrilled, Hattie clinks her beer bottle against Willa's glass of rosé. 'Thank you.'

They chat a while longer but with Bradley's histrionics getting worse by the second, it's not long before the Altons decide to leave. Young Chandler walks hand in hand with his mum, while Bradley has to be carried, kicking and screaming, by his dad.

Hattie puts her now-empty beer bottle in the bin marked 'recycling' and says her goodbyes to Liberty and the two hipster types she's got helping her at the barbeque. It's only as she arrives back at Clover Hill House that Hattie realises she didn't find out anything more about what happened between Robert and Liberty.

CHAPTER NINETEEN

DEXTER

Dexter knows he's had too much to drink when he goes to recharge their glasses and misses his own by a good half-inch. The red wine splatters down the outside of the glass and seeps into the white tablecloth like a bloodstain. He tries to mop it up with his napkin but only succeeds in worsening the mess. He apologises to the waiter who comes to his aid.

Opposite him, the rider bloke, Daniel, looks even more awkward than he has for the rest of the meal, shuffling in his seat and not making eye contact. Dexter glances to his left at Lexi, expecting her to be annoyed, but no, she's smirking. Amused by his inebriation or his clumsiness, or maybe both.

'Can I get the bill, please?' Dexter asks the waiter.

'Of course, sir,' says the waiter, hurrying off. No doubt happy at the thought of getting rid of them quickly. This is a fancy establishment – Michelin starred, long waiting list, old country house grandeur. They won't want a drunkard lowering the tone.

Dexter can understand that. In truth, he's glad the dinner is almost over. He'd been in high spirits before they came out; today he made all the dividend payments successfully and wanted to celebrate. But this horse bloke has very little personality, and Lexi seems to have spent most of the night talking at them. Still, Dexter reminds himself, the horsey set are a good group to find new investors in and, although a tricky clique to get in with, as an event rider Daniel should be able to get him inside the metaphorical tent. If nothing else good comes from this dinner, at least he can start that ball rolling.

Dexter clears his throat and looks across at the horse bloke. 'Got to be lots of wealthy sorts looking for good investments in your line of business, Danny-boy?'

'I don't know about that,' says Daniel, not making eye contact as he removes his napkin from his lap and puts it on the table. 'I focus on the horses.'

Lexi drains the last of her wine, then cocks her head to the side. Seemingly intrigued by the discussion.

Trying not to be deterred by Daniel's brush off, Dexter ploughs on. This is important. He needs more investors. 'Well, maybe not riders like yourself as much, but the people who own the horses?'

'I don't ask them about their finances.'

The waiter returns with the bill and Dexter glances at the total and hands over his black Amex. He's spending over a thousand quid on this meal so he's damn well going to get what he needs.

Leaning across the table towards Daniel, Dexter presses the point. 'But eventing is a rich man's game, surely. And if you can afford a few horses, you can afford some property investments.'

'A lot of people can barely afford their horses,' says Daniel, pushing his chair back from the table as if about to stand. 'No one with horses will ever be rich.'

'Ah, but that must be nonsense,' says Lexi. 'Think of all the race horse owners; those creatures are worth millions.'

Daniel turns towards her. 'Eventing isn't like—'

'And polo: those ponies change hands at vast sums, and every rider needs, what? At least six ponies, or twelve or something.'

Dexter waves his hands around to emphasise his point. 'The thing is, where there are horses there's money. And those are the people I need to be talking to about these investment opportunities.'

Daniel frowns. 'I don't know what you're—'

Lexi puts her hand on Daniel's arm and strokes the sleeve of his shirt. 'What my husband is trying to say, darling, is that he'd like you to set up some kind of soiree with your other owners.'

Daniel looks uncomfortable. 'Well, I don't know about—'

'It doesn't have to be an evening thing, it could just be a relaxed meet and greet at your yard, so we could all get to know each other.' Lexi smiles at Daniel, clutches at his arm again. 'Nothing big, just little bit of fizz and a few snacks. It'll be so much fun.'

'That would be perfect,' says Dexter. If he can get in front of some of the other event horse owners, he knows he can get them onboard. Once he's had the introduction, he can do the rest.

Daniel looks unconvinced. He glances at Lexi.

Dexter watches a look pass between his wife and the horse bloke. He's too drunk to be able to work out its meaning, but it doesn't matter because a few seconds later Daniel looks over at Dexter as he stands up and says, 'Maybe.'

'Good chap,' says Dexter, rising unsteadily from his seat and clapping Daniel on the back. He exhales, relieved. Stanton-Bassett's two million won't last forever. He needs to leverage the investment he's made in the event horses Lexi wanted, to get the best return he can. To do that, he needs people with deep pockets willing to invest, and plenty of them.

He has to find the best way to milk this.

CHAPTER TWENTY

HATTIE

Mermaid's Gold rears into the air. Eyes wild. Snorting. Her front legs strike out violently. As the horse towers above her, Hattie sees the pale orange of the mare's belly just feet from her face. One blow to the head from the horse's hooves and she'd be dead. But the mare isn't attacking her; she's telling her she's afraid.

'It's okay, girl.' Hattie lowers the white saddlecloth and tucks it against her side.

The mare takes a step towards her. Her head is raised. The muscles in her body are rigid. She eyes Hattie and the saddlecloth suspiciously. Reaching out, Hattie strokes the horse's neck. 'I know you're scared but it'll be okay.'

Gradually the mare starts to relax. The muscles in her neck feel softer now, less like steel. Her clenched jaw relaxes and she starts to nuzzle Hattie's pocket for a Polo.

'In a minute, girl,' says Hattie, slowly moving the saddlecloth towards the mare's shoulder a few inches, then moving it away quickly so as not to scare her. 'Let's see if we can do this first.'

If she's going to have any hope of putting a saddle on Mermaid's Gold, she needs the horse to be comfortable having this lightweight cotton saddlecloth on her back first. She's taken it slowly, using approach and retreat techniques to get her used to it without putting too much pressure on her, but whenever Hattie touches the material against the horse's skin, she seems to find it too much.

Hattie continues moving the saddlecloth towards and away from Mermaid's Gold. The mare seems happier with it now. She rests a hind leg and nudges at Hattie's pocket again. Okay, thinks Hattie, let's try this.

As she moves the saddlecloth closer to the mare's wither, Hattie watches the horse's face; she still looks relaxed. The next time, Hattie touches the saddlecloth against the mare's skin. Mermaid's Gold flinches as the material touches her, but stays standing beside Hattie.

'Good girl,' says Hattie. 'You can do this.'

She continues the same toward and away routine with the saddlecloth, each time leaving it for a moment longer against the horse's skin. The mare cocks her ear back in the direction of the material. She's wary, but seems to be tolerating it, finding the contact bearable so far.

Encouraged, Hattie decides to move to the next stage. She makes sure her breathing is calm and even, tries to keep her heartbeat steady – knowing that horses are so sensitive to body language and tension that Mermaid's Gold will pick up on it immediately if she shows signs of nervousness.

Hattie takes a breath and then places the saddlecloth on the mare's back and then moves her hand away, leaving it sitting there. 'It's okay, girl. It won't hurt you.'

Mermaid's Gold doesn't believe her.

Leaping into the air, she pogos a one-eighty-degree turn and sets off across the paddock like the best bucking horse at a rodeo championship. Divots of turf kick out behind her. The saddlecloth somersaults into the air, landing in a crumpled heap in the dirt. Skidding to a halt, the mare spins around and faces the saddlecloth. She snorts twice, then lowers her head and charges towards it, teeth bared.

Hattie hasn't seen a horse react with such raw fury before. She steps back, towards the paddock fence. Holds her breath.

Squealing, Mermaid's Gold stamps her front feet down on the saddlecloth repeatedly. Even the goats keep their distance, watching from the safety of the field shelter.

On the other side of the paddock fence, Liberty and Willa Alton gasp.

With the saddlecloth now a muddied, torn rag, Mermaid's Gold stops her attack. She stands still, nostrils flared and flanks heaving, as the adrenaline wears off.

Hattie steps towards her. Puts her hand on the mare's neck. 'You okay, girl?'

The horse blows out loudly as if to say that she's all right now. Hattie strokes her neck. Tells her it's okay, that the saddlecloth can't really hurt her. She knows that's not what the mare believes though.

'I'm glad you didn't try her with one of my saddles first,' says Willa.

Hattie's glad too. She can't afford to buy a saddle or bridle but Willa kindly offered to lend her some tack – a basic snaffle bridle and an all-purpose GP saddle. Willa said they're just spares she had in her tack room, but even so Hattie would feel super guilty if they got destroyed like the saddlecloth.

'Well, that was quite the rodeo show,' says Liberty, giving a long whistle. 'But she seems fine now.'

Liberty's right. Mermaid's Gold has relaxed. Now the threat of the saddlecloth has been neutralised, she's back to nuzzling Hattie's pockets for mints. It wouldn't take much to set her off into a panic again, though. Hattie gives the mare a Polo, and leaves her crunching it happily while she goes and retrieves the saddlecloth from the dirt. It's mud-covered and grass-stained, but it's mainly the edging that's been torn. With a good wash and the worst of the ripped edging cut off, it'll probably be useable.

'Are you going to try again?' asks Willa, with a concerned frown.

Walking back towards Willa and Liberty, Hattie shakes her head. 'I'm not sure she's ever going to accept wearing tack. It triggers too much fear in her, and then she goes on the attack.'

'Maybe she'll relax more in time?' says Liberty.

'I don't think so. It's been like this for days,' says Hattie as Mermaid's Gold, seeing the saddlecloth in her hand, turns and canters away across the paddock to join Mabel and Gladys in the field shelter. 'Nothing seems to help.'

Willa is looking thoughtful. 'You know, I don't think she associates you with her bad experience, only the saddlecloth. If tack is what triggers her, maybe you should ride her without it?'

Liberty raises her eyebrows and looks pointedly at the tattered saddlecloth Hattie's holding. 'You don't want to end up looking like that.'

'True,' says Hattie. She thinks about the height of the bucks and the terror in the horse's eyes when the saddlecloth was on her back. If she does that with her onboard bareback, she'll risk serious injury. 'But it's worth a shot.'

Taking the rope halter and lead rope from where she'd left it earlier, looped over the gate, Hattie walks over to Mermaid's Gold. She slips the halter over her head, and ties the knot to fasten it. The mare stays relaxed and happy; she's grown comfortable with the halter. Leading the horse out of the field shelter and into the paddock, she stops.

Trying not to be put off by the worried looks of Willa and Liberty from over at the paddock fence, Hattie thinks about the time she'd watched her mentor, horse whisperer Blake Mentmore, working with wild mustangs. He'd got them used to the halter, then his hands against their body, and then he'd got onto their backs without any tack. She follows the process with

Mermaid's Gold. If the mare can't bring herself to tolerate the tack, Hattie must find a different way to prove to the horse that having a human on her back doesn't have to end badly.

She turns away from the fence, focusing only on Mermaid's Gold. Slowly, she runs her hands over the mare; her neck, her shoulders, her back, her rump. The horse stays relaxed. Her breathing is steady. She adjusts her weight and rests a hind leg.

Encouraged, Hattie leads her across to the fence on the opposite side of the paddock from her friends. Climbing up onto the fence, Hattie repeats the same process, running her hands over Mermaid's Gold, but this time from a higher position – one more equivalent to the height she'd be at if she was sitting on the horse's back.

Mermaid's Gold turns her head, looking closer at what Hattie is doing, but she doesn't tense up. Hattie keeps stroking the mare, runs her fingers through her mane, scratches her on the wither. Mermaid's Gold raises her top lip, enjoying it.

Hattie takes a deep breath. This is it: the moment of truth. Make or break: very possibly literally break if things go wrong and she's thrown from the horse. Holding the lead rope in her left hand, she puts that hand on Mermaid's Gold's neck just in front of her withers. Then, decisively, but gently enough to hopefully not cause the mare to spook, Hattie leans forward from the fence until she's leaning over Mermaid's Gold – her belly across the horse's back, her head and right arm on the horse's off side, and both legs on the left. She keeps her breathing regular, calm. Rubs her right hand on the horse's shoulder. 'It's okay, girl. It's just me. You're doing great.'

Mermaid's Gold blows out hard. She swings her head around to the right, looking closer at Hattie. Reaching out, Hattie strokes the mare's nose. 'Good girl. Great job.'

All her weight is on the mare's back now. Still the horse remains relaxed.

Hattie makes a decision. Calmly, she moves herself so she's

lying more forward on the horse's neck. She keeps talking to her, telling her she's doing great. The mare still seems relaxed so Hattie swings her right leg up and over the horse's rump. Now she's sitting astride.

She feels Mermaid's Gold tense. The mare throws her head up. Hattie sees the whites of her eyes. Can feel the horse's heart rate accelerating. She leans forward and strokes her neck. Keeps her voice calm and even. 'It's okay, girl. It's just me.'

The mare blows out hard. Her heart rate starts to return to normal. Her muscles relax.

Hattie takes a Polo mint from her pocket and leans forward, offering it to Mermaid's Gold on the flat of her palm. The mare turns her head and takes the mint. Relaxed and in harmony, they stand in the paddock – Mermaid's Gold crunching happily on her Polo and Hattie sitting aside her, grinning like a Cheshire Cat. Across the fields on the horizon, the sun slowly begins to set.

Hattie can't think of a more perfect moment.

CHAPTER TWENTY-ONE

LEXI

'Am I hearing this right? You're refusing me?' Lexi stands with her hands on her hips, pouting. She doesn't care that it's pouring with rain and her big red golfing umbrella is making the horse Daniel's sitting on bounce around like a fool. The way he's behaving right now, she hopes the bloody thing throws him off. She narrows her gaze. 'That is *so* not okay.'

'I'm refusing your husband. Surely there's a difference?' says Daniel, stroking the horse's neck and trying to calm it.

There's a whine to his voice that makes Lexi want to punch him. 'No. *I* asked you as well.'

'And I've thought about it and I'm saying no...' The horse, eyeing the umbrella fearfully, jigs on the spot, then bucks. Daniel waits until it's back at a standstill before continuing. 'I'm not hosting a meet and greet here at the yard just so your husband can hard-sell investments to my other owners.'

'But I'm paying you, so—'

'Pimping your husband's business wasn't part of the deal.' Daniel leans closer to her. 'Only pimping myself, and I'm doing that, aren't I?'

'You really are an ungrateful bastard, you know.' Lexi flaps her umbrella, sending spray towards Daniel. The horse, Rocket Fuel, snorts and leaps sideways to avoid it, almost unseating Daniel. Lexi smiles.

'God, you're childish,' he splutters, battling with Rocket Fuel to stop the horse from bolting.

'And you're a dick,' she says, sneering. 'And not a very hard one.'

Even through the cold drizzle she can see him blush. It's a low blow, she has to admit. Daniel's got better in bed, although it has taken some intensive coaching. At least he's consistently getting it up these days. But the way he treats her, and the way he talks to her, it's not right. He seems to be forgetting who's in charge here.

He needs a reminder.

With a second shake of her umbrella that sends the horse into histrionics again, Lexi turns and walks away from the outdoor arena towards the yard.

'Don't you want to see Rocket Fuel jump?' calls Daniel. 'Isn't that what you came here for?'

She doesn't even turn around, just holds up her free hand and gives him the finger.

Daniel's response is muffled by the rain. Lexi doesn't care what he says anyway.

She struts into the yard, her mind set on getting to her Bentley and driving away from here. Maybe she'll go and do some shopping – somewhere high end where the shop assistants will run around picking things out for her while she sips champagne. Yes, that'd be something nice to ease the sting of Daniel's insubordination.

'Are you okay? Would... would you like a coffee?' asks a female voice.

Turning round, Lexi sees the timid mouse-like girl who mucks out the stables for Daniel smiling nervously at her from the tack room. What's her name, thinks Lexi. Brenda or Betty or something plain and boring, it hardly matters. But the mention of a hot drink sounds suddenly attractive. 'Do you have Earl Grey?'

'Of course,' says the mouse-girl.

'Okay then.' Lexi walks across to the tack room and collapses her umbrella. Giving it a good shake, she heads across the room so that she can sit on the bench seat close to the heater. Daniel's black cat is curled up on the only cushion. Lexi picks up the cushion and tips the stupid creature onto the floor. It hisses at her, so she pokes the umbrella at it, pleased when it stalks off into the rain. Settling herself down onto the cushion, she waits for her tea.

The girl takes forever to return. By the time she arrives, Lexi's already shivering. The warmth from the heater in the tack room is pathetic and the room smells of stale sweat and stinky horse. Lexi wishes she'd just left as planned.

'Earl Grey,' says the mouse-girl, holding out a chipped mug with liquid the colour of dishwater inside.

Lexi takes a sip. Grimacing, she spits out the tea. 'That's disgusting. Are you trying to poison me?'

'No, I—'

'Did you put milk in this?'

'Yes, I thought—'

'I take Earl Grey with lemon not milk,' shouts Lexi, throwing the tea at mouse-girl. She doesn't see it coming and cries out as the hot liquid splashes across her face and drenches her ugly sweatshirt. Lexi doesn't care. She keeps shouting. 'Are you so stupid you can't even make a cup of tea?'

'What the hell's going on?' Daniel appears in the doorway. He's drenched, the water dripping off the peak of his riding hat and running down his face. His jacket has soaked the rain up around the shoulders, giving it a darker blue appearance.

Lexi waves her hand dismissively towards the mouse-girl. 'She can't do her job. She's utterly incompetent.'

The mouse-girl looks like she's about to start snivelling. Lexi rolls her eyes – ridiculous attention-seeker.

Daniel's regarding the girl with concern. 'Bunty? You okay?'

'She... she threw her tea at me,' stutters the mouse-girl, dabbing at her face with the sleeve of her sweatshirt.

'Did you?' says Daniel, narrowing his eyes as he turns to Lexi.

Lexi shrugs. 'Don't look at me like that. She put milk in it instead of lemon. Milk in Earl Grey? I mean, come on, it's ridiculous.'

Daniel shakes his head, his expression one of disgust. Turning back to Bunty, he says, 'Go and get dry in the house, okay. I can sort Rocket Fuel out.' He puts a hand on the girl's damp shoulder. 'Did the tea burn you? Do you need to go to A&E?'

The mouse-girl sniffs loudly. Her lower lip is trembling. 'It wasn't that hot. I'm okay... just wet and...'

'Go inside and get dry,' says Daniel. 'But if you need me to drive you to the hospital, just say, okay. It's not a problem.'

The mouse-girl nods and scuttles out of the tack room.

Lexi stands up. It's so cold in here and Daniel hasn't shown any concern for how she's feeling. She hasn't even had a hot drink to warm her up because of that stupid girl. She crosses her arms. Looks at Daniel. 'You need to fire that girl.'

'I'm not doing that,' says Daniel, his tone implying there'll be no negotiation. 'You're the one in the wrong here.'

If she wasn't feeling so pissed off with him, this more masterful Daniel would be quite the turn-on. Instead, she glares at him. How dare he refuse her? She steps closer to Daniel. Their faces are now just inches apart. 'You'll do as I say, or else,' she hisses. 'I pay you to be on my side.'

CHAPTER TWENTY-TWO

HATTIE

*A*s Hattie turns her towards the line of three makeshift jumps, Mermaid's Gold pricks her ears forward and bounds towards the fences. Together they see a good stride for the first jump. At a height of about 1.15m, it's made of a spindly fallen silver birch tree trunk balanced on two towers of vegetable crates borrowed from Liberty. It's an odd-looking construction, but Mermaid's Gold is undeterred and leaps over, powering on towards the second fence.

This one is trickier. It's a single blue plastic barrel; around 1m high but at barely 70cm wide, it's a real test of accurate riding and the honesty of the horse. Hattie uses her weight and legs to steer Mermaid's Gold straight towards the barrel, rather than pulling on the rope that's tied to the halter. The mare responds, lining up with the barrel and maintaining a steady, bouncy canter with lots of impulsion. Again they clear the fence with plenty of height to spare. As they land, Mermaid's Gold is already looking for the next obstacle.

Using her legs and weight to communicate a left-handed turn to her, Hattie sets the mare up for the final fence – a gnarly oak tree trunk that she found in the spinney and hauled out with Robert's quad bike, dragging it into the paddock. It's big. Far bigger than they've jumped before at just over 1.25m, and extremely solid. Hattie feels her heart pounding in her chest. This is their biggest test so far.

Mermaid's Gold isn't worried. Seeing the tree trunk, she bounds forward, accelerating towards it. On the last stride, Hattie, still riding bareback, clutches the horse's flaxen mane between her fingers and clings on tight. Mermaid's Gold doesn't falter. She soars over the obstacle like it's a tiny twig. Hattie is laughing as they land. Leaping off Mermaid's Gold, she throws her arms around the horse's neck. The mare nuzzles her pocket for a Polo mint.

Over by the fence, Liberty and Lady Pat are clapping and cheering. Peanut and Banana are watching Hattie closely, their tails wagging, waiting for the command to be allowed back into the paddock to chase sniffs. Hattie gives them the nod and the pair duck under the post and rail and chase off together.

'That was awesome,' says Liberty, as Hattie and Mermaid's Gold walk over to join them. 'She's come on so much since I last saw you.'

Hattie shakes her head. 'Mermaid's Gold has always been brilliant, I just needed to figure out how to show her I was trustworthy.'

Lady Pat claps her hands. 'Well, dear, you certainly seem to have achieved that. What the pair of you have achieved in just a few weeks is really rather remarkable.'

Hattie strokes the mare's neck and looks back at the fences. 'Did you see how brave she was?'

'She loves to jump, that's obvious,' says Lady Pat, looking thoughtful. 'You know, I've got an idea. High Drayton Horse Trials is coming up in four weeks. It's just up the road. You should enter.'

Hattie frowns. 'I can't. I'm not registered and I can't afford it.

Anyway, the last time I read the rulebook, bridles and saddles were definitely compulsory.'

Lady Pat waves Hattie's words away. 'That's all easily fixable.'

Hattie turns away and undoes Mermaid's Gold's halter. She feeds the mare another two mints and then puts the packet away. 'That's enough for today, girl.'

Mermaid's Gold begs to differ, nudging at Hattie's pocket.

'I checked Mermaid's Gold's record online. She's qualified for a CCI3*,' says Lady Pat. 'If you compete at High Drayton and get the feel of each other, you could do a CCI3* before the end of the season.'

Hattie gives in to the mare's persistent nudges and feeds her two more Polos. 'I don't want to over-face her. You know what happened with her last rider.'

'That was entirely different. They tried to force this sensitive mare with harsh bits and long spurs. You won't do that.' Lady Pat looks fondly at Mermaid's Gold. 'She loves to jump; just remember how she flew over the fences today. Isn't it about time her reputation was restored?'

'It would be amazing,' says Liberty. 'And you might even get to see JaXX.'

'JaXX?' asks Hattie, watching Mermaid's Gold wander off to join the goats on the other side of the paddock.

'He's a singer-songwriter. The front man for the Deciders. You must have heard them?' says Liberty. She waits for Hattie to respond, but when she doesn't she continues. 'He wears big hats? Is good at dancing? No? Well, anyway, he's really reclusive and apparently bought High Drayton because of its land and the high walls all around the perimeter.'

'Sorry, no. I'm not really up with current music.' Hattie smiles to soften the blow. She knows Liberty's just trying to encourage her. 'And I just don't know if we're ready.'

'Nonsense,' says Lady Pat. 'You will be. And don't worry about the registrations or the entry fees, I can take care of that.'

'I don't...' Hattie looks from Lady Pat to Liberty. They both look excited and hopeful. She thinks about the progress she and Mermaid's Gold have made in the past three weeks; from not being ridden to jumping big fences bareback. Could what Lady Pat is asking be possible? Perhaps, thinks Hattie. 'Okay, look, if Mermaid's Gold is willing to have a saddle and bridle on, and if she seems happy wearing them, and I'm a hundred percent sure that we're ready, then I'll compete at High Drayton.'

'Excellent,' says Lady Pat. 'I'll make the arrangements, dear. I believe entries close at the end of this week. But, of course, if you don't think the timing is right, we can withdraw nearer the time. Deal?'

Hattie looks across the paddock at where Mermaid's Gold is grazing happily with Mabel and Gladys alongside her. As if sensing something important is going on, the mare looks up and wickers at Hattie. Hattie smiles. Maybe they can do this together. She looks back at Lady Pat. 'Okay, deal.'

As she walks back towards the house with Lady Pat and Liberty, the full extent of what she's just agreed to starts to sink in. She's going to ride at an affiliated British Eventing competition. It has to go well because she needs to restore Mermaid's Gold's reputation, and prove that using the horse whispering techniques she learnt out in the States really does work.

She's only got four weeks to get the mare comfortable and confident wearing a saddle and a bridle. In Hattie's mind's eye, she relives the moment Mermaid's Gold broncoed around the paddock with the saddlecloth and then, once it had fallen from her back, attacked it, pounding it into the dirt until it was muddied and torn.

Hattie shudders. She's not sure four weeks are going to be enough.

CHAPTER TWENTY-THREE
DANIEL

Daniel rides back into the yard having finished schooling Pink Fizz in the arena. Bunty smiles at him as she leads Rocket Fuel away from Jenny, the vet, and back to his stable. Bunty might be quiet and shy with humans but she's got a great way with the horses. Rocket Fuel can be a real pain in the arse – biting and kicking out with reflexes fast as lightning – but he's a lamb whenever Bunty is handling him.

Despite the fuss Lexi's still making about him refusing to fire Bunty, Daniel knows he's in the right. Bunty is hard working and loyal. Lexi is a bitch, and the way she treated Bunty is inexcusable. If it had been any other owner, Daniel would have asked them to take their horse elsewhere, but Lexi is different – she's paying him ten times what owners usually pay, and he knows she'd never go quietly; she'd do all she could to ruin him.

Having dismounted from Pink Fizz, he walks over to where Jenny is packing her equipment into a canvas kit bag. 'How did it go?'

'All good. I've taken some bloods from Knightime but his vitals are good, so it's probably a low-grade virus and he'll be back to form soon. I'll run some tests and let you know.'

'Thanks.' Daniel swallows hard before asking the question he's most anxious about the answer of. 'And how do you think The Rogue is doing?'

Straightening up, Jenny looks across the yard to where The Rogue is peering out over his stable door. 'He's doing okay. The tendon is healing, but it's a slow process and that's as we expected.' She puts her hand on Daniel's arm. 'Just keep on doing what you're doing and try not to worry.'

Daniel nods. 'Thanks, I appreciate it.'

'No problem.' Jenny holds his gaze. Tilts her head to the side. 'How are you doing, Danny?'

'I'm fine.'

She squints at him, appraising him as if he's one of the horses in her care. 'Really? Because you look tired.'

He doesn't answer her immediately. Jenny's a good friend and he hates lying to her, but how can he tell her the truth about what he signed up to with Lexi, and that the only way he can cope with the stress of it is to pop anti-anxiety pills like they're candy? So he fakes a smile and tries to keep his tone light. 'It's nothing. Just a lot going on, you know?'

Jenny pushes her unruly curls off her forehead. Softens her tone. 'Well, I'm always here if you want to chat.'

'Thanks,' he says, forcing his smile wider. 'You're a pal.'

She holds his gaze for a long moment. In the end it's Daniel who looks away.

'Like I said,' says Jenny, her voice more serious. 'I'm here if you want to talk.'

Before he can answer, Daniel feels his phone vibrate in his pocket. Pulling it out, he sees the name Tyler Jacobs – the owner of one of his promising young horses, Dewberry – is on the screen. He looks back at Jenny and gestures at the phone. 'I'd better take this.'

'No problem,' says Jenny, her voice returning to its usual business-like efficiency. She picks up her kit bag. 'I'll be in touch when I've got the results of Knightime's bloods.'

As Jenny heads off towards her Land Rover Discovery, Daniel answers the call. 'Hello?'

'Daniel? It's Tyler here. Have you got a minute for a chat?'

'Sure.' Walking across to The Rogue's stable, Daniel swaps the phone into his other hand and takes a ginger biscuit from his pocket with the other. It's a bit squashed, but The Rogue doesn't seem to mind – crunching happily and resting his chin on Daniel's shoulder. 'How are you doing?'

'I'm good,' says Tyler. 'Everything under control.'

Daniel frowns. Tyler is an easy owner to deal with – he has a pleasant manner and doesn't interfere – his young granddaughter, Sophia, loves horses; that's why he bought Dewberry. Other than turning up once a month to watch his training and at competitions, they leave Daniel to get on with things. It's an arrangement that works perfectly. But Daniel can tell there's something strange going on from the tightness of his voice. 'So how can I help?'

'Yes, well, you see I was contacted earlier in the week by this chap, Marchfield-Wright, about an investment opportunity. He said that he has some horses with you?'

Daniel feels his stomach start to churn. 'Yes, the Marchfield-Wrights have three horses with me.'

'Good, good. So what can you tell me about him? Is he a trustworthy sort to jump into bed with, as it were?'

'Well... they're prompt in settling their bills,' says Daniel cautiously. The last thing he wants is to be caught in the middle of business deals between any of his owners. This sort of conversation is exactly why he didn't want to host a meet and greet at the yard for Dexter and Lexi. But it seems like Dexter's found a way to target his owners anyway. 'The thing is, they're relatively new owners – just came on board in the last few months – and I tend to interact with Mr Marchfield-Wright's wife on all things relating to their horses so I have little more than a passing acquaintance with him.'

'Ah, yes, I see.' Tyler falls silent. There's a slight wheeze each time he inhales.

'Sorry I can't be more helpful,' says Daniel.

'Not a problem at all,' says Tyler, his voice returning to its usual heartiness. 'I'll put the feelers out and see if anyone at the club has had dealings with him.'

After a brief discussion about Dewberry's progress at BE100 level and the events Daniel's aiming him for in the second half of the season, he ends the call. Tyler seems happy enough but there's a bad taste in Daniel's mouth and his stomach is still churning. After giving The Rogue another ginger biscuit, he reaches into his back pocket and pulls out a blister pack. Popping out a tablet, he puts it in his mouth. The Rogue watches him as he swallows the pill, and Daniel imagines he sees disappointment in the horse's soulful eyes.

Closing his eyes, Daniel takes a few deep breaths while he waits for the medication to kick in and help him relax. If Dexter has started targeting his other owners, Daniel supposes it's just a matter of time before he gets more calls like the one he's just had with Tyler. The thought makes his stomach churn faster. He knows Lexi will expect him to vouch for her husband but he doesn't want to; he knows nothing about their business.

If any more owners call asking about the Marchfield-Wrights, he's going to stick with what he told Tyler – no more, no less.

He hopes it's not a problem.

But he knows that it will be.

CHAPTER TWENTY-FOUR

HATTIE

She's with Mermaid's Gold in the all-weather arena behind the stables. Balanced along the fence are four saddles and three bridles that Lady Pat had sent over from the local saddler – each of them chosen for being lightweight, close contact and as unobtrusive as possible. This is the third day Hattie has taken Mermaid's Gold into the arena with them. The first day, they stayed at the opposite end of the arena, practising their dressage with some pointers from Willa. Yesterday, they moved further along the space so that they passed the tack with each lap of the arena, although Mermaid's Gold was reluctant to get any closer than a metre or so to it. Today, Hattie hopes they'll make more progress.

She rides Mermaid's Gold up to within a couple of metres of where the tack is sitting on the fence and then dismounts. The mare sniffs at the air loudly. Then she stretches her neck, her nose raised, and lifts her top lip. Hattie smiles. This is the flehmen response that many horses have when they're introduced to new smells or tastes. It's a good sign.

The mare steps closer to the tack. She flares her nostrils and takes a deep inhale.

Hattie follows her movement. Keeps the lead rope loose, letting the horse decide when she wants to move towards the saddles and bridles.

Mermaid's Gold moves her head from side to side, eying the saddle nearest to her. She lifts her upper lip again.

'It's working, yeah?' asks Liberty in a stage whisper from the other side of the arena fence.

Hattie nods. It was Liberty who suggested using the lavender oil as a way to intrigue the mare to be curious about the tack and also prompt relaxation.

Mermaid's Gold takes another step forward. She's right in front of the closest saddle now, a pale tan close-contact jumping saddle that Hattie knows costs more than a thousand pounds. She hopes this works. There's no way she can pay back Lady Pat anytime soon if the saddle goes the same way as the white saddle-cloth did a few weeks ago.

The horse stretches her neck, sniffing towards the saddle. Her ears are pricked. Her eyes are bright and interested. She skims her muzzle over the saddle flap.

Hattie realises that she's holding her breath and exhales.

Mermaid's Gold jerks her head away from the saddle and takes a step back.

Shit, thinks Hattie. Annoyed with herself for probably causing the horse to spook by holding her breath and tension in her own body. Horses are so sensitive, they can feel the emotions around them. If she acts like something is scary or a problem, Mermaid's Gold will believe that there's danger and back off; the opposite of what she's hoping will happen. Hattie steadies herself and focuses on her breathing.

Mermaid's Gold steps forward to the saddle again. She presses her muzzle against the seat and licks the pommel, the place where Liberty dabbed a couple of drops of lavender essential oil earlier this morning.

'She does like it,' whispers Liberty, unable to contain the excitement in her voice.

Hattie moves towards the fence. She puts her own hand on the saddle. Mermaid's Gold doesn't mind; she keeps licking the pommel. Slowly, Hattie lifts the saddle off the fence. The mare doesn't spook or seem worried. When Hattie carries it a few strides into the arena, Mermaid's Gold follows. Hope flares in Hattie's chest; this could actually work.

With the mare still nuzzling the saddle, Hattie lifts it so the off-side saddle flap touches Mermaid's Gold's shoulder. The mare doesn't flinch.

Hattie glances across at Liberty, who gives her the thumbs up. This is it: time to see whether the lavender oil really has worked to relax the horse and make her feel happier in close contact with tack.

Keeping her breathing steady and calm, Hattie lifts the saddle up onto Mermaid's Gold's back. As the leather touches the mare's coat, she tenses. 'Good girl. It's okay,' says Hattie, trying to convince her. 'You like this one.'

The mare turns her head around and sniffs towards the saddle. She takes a couple of breaths and then relaxes. Hattie feels relief flood through her. This is real progress.

She steps towards the fence. The mare follows her, seemingly unbothered now by the saddle on her back.

Taking the girth that was lying over the railing beside the saddle Mermaid's Gold picked, Hattie holds it out to the mare. She stays relaxed as she sniffs the leather and then starts to lick the point where Liberty had put a drop of lavender oil.

'Wow, she really does love the lavender,' says Liberty.

'Seems that way,' says Hattie. 'Let's see if she lets me put the girth on.'

Moving around to the off side of the mare, Hattie attaches the girth to the girth straps. The horse turns her head to watch, but doesn't seem bothered.

Encouraged, Hattie moves around to the near side. Steadily, she reaches down under the mare's belly and takes hold of the girth hanging down on the other side. Talking to the horse as she does it, she brings the free end of the girth up to the straps on the near side of the saddle. Mermaid's Gold seems relaxed as she turns her head towards her and inhales deeply.

Hattie fastens the girth this side, gradually tightening the fit until it's snug enough to keep the saddle in place, but not so tight to affect the horse's movement or breathing. Still the mare seems unconcerned.

The final, and biggest, test is moving. Horses are prey animals. In the wild they were hunted by lions and large predators who'd plunge their claws into the horse's withers and leap onto their backs to prevent them running. The reaction to throw a predator from their back is instinctive and strong, even in domesticated horses. Mermaid's Gold might have accepted Hattie as non-threatening, but will she do the same with the saddle? There's only one way to find out.

Moving backwards towards the centre of the arena, Hattie gives Mermaid's Gold the full length of the lead rope and clicks her tongue, asking the horse to walk forward. The mare takes a step, then halts abruptly. She throws her head up. Snorts loudly.

Hattie's heart pounds in her chest. She tries to keep her breathing steady. Keeps walking, hoping the horse will follow. 'It's okay, girl.'

Mermaid's Gold turns her head and sniffs the saddle. Her nostrils flare as she inhales. She straightens her neck and blows out hard. Takes one step forward, and then a second. Her head lowers, and her body relaxes. She trots forward to catch up with Hattie, nuzzling her pocket as she does so. Together they walk around the arena together.

Liberty cheers from the arena fence. Hattie grins. Mermaid's Gold raises her top lip.

It feels like a huge step forward.

Later, Hattie and Liberty sit out on the patio, celebrating with cold beer and cheese on toast. The fading sun is still warm enough to only need jeans and a t-shirt. The climbing roses over the arbour are in full bloom, their scent heavenly. Peanut and Banana sit at their feet, staring hopefully at the food, waiting for a bit of crust or cheese. Across the paddock, Mermaid's Gold grazes happily with Mabel and Gladys at her side.

'Does Robert know about Mermaid's Gold?' says Liberty, taking a gulp of beer.

'He knows she's here and that I'm looking after her,' says Hattie. 'But I haven't mentioned the riding or the plan to take her to High Drayton Horse Trials. After all, she's Lady Pat's horse, not his.'

Liberty looks thoughtful. 'He might not see it that way.'

'You think I should tell him?'

'No,' says Liberty, with caution in her tone. 'That's probably not a good idea.'

Hattie raises her eyebrows. 'What don't I know?'

Liberty doesn't reply immediately. 'Look, it's a complicated family, that's all I'm saying. When the goats arrived, there were all kinds of fireworks, same before when Lady Patricia tried to persuade Robert to have a cat she'd rescued.'

Hattie's confused. 'He got angry about a rescue cat?'

'Not angry, exactly.' Liberty looks conflicted. 'But his mother... when she heard Lady Pat was sending animals his way, she... well, let's just say there was a tragedy in the family many years ago which put a divide between Robert's parents and Lady Pat's side of the family. Robert somehow managed to stay on good terms with Lady Pat but...' Liberty shakes her head. 'I've said too much.'

Hattie can tell she's not going to get more details out of Liberty about this, not now at least. She remembers back to before Liberty's barbeque when she indicated Robert had asked her out. From the way Liberty mentioned it, Hattie assumed Liberty shut him down quickly. Now she's not so sure. 'Seems like you know quite a lot about Robert. You still haven't told me what happened there.'

Liberty looks guilty. 'I rather hoped you'd forgotten I'd mentioned that.'

'Sorry, no,' says Hattie, smiling. 'Now tell me everything.'

CHAPTER TWENTY-FIVE
LEXI

She's sitting at the huge island, her morning grapefruit, fresh squeezed orange juice and coffee set out on the marble countertop, when Dexter comes into the kitchen. He's already put in several hours of work in his study, unlike Lexi who didn't rise from her bed until well after nine. He kisses her on the cheek and puts a small box wrapped in gold tissue paper on the counter beside her coffee.

'What's this?' says Lexi, picking up the box. 'It's not my birthday.'

'You'll see,' says Dexter, pouring himself a coffee from the pot and putting a couple of pieces of bread into the toaster. 'Go ahead and find out.'

Lexi doesn't need to be asked twice. She loves gifts. Ripping off the gold tissue paper, she opens the box. It's beautiful, but still she frowns when she sees what's inside. With a gift from Dexter, there are always strings attached. And the Gucci hearts-and-diamond bracelet nestled inside the jewellery box must have cost him over five grand, which means the string is going to be more like a rope.

'Do you like it?' Dexter says, looking at her with hopeful puppy dog eyes.

'Of course, darling, it's Gucci.' She takes the bracelet out of the box and puts it on. For a moment, she admires how the eighteen-carat white gold contrasts with her tanned wrist, and the way the diamonds catch the light, then she looks at Dexter and says, 'So what do you want?'

He looks crestfallen. 'Why must I want something? Can't I just buy my wife a present?'

'You'd think,' says Lexi, raising an eyebrow. 'But I know you too well.'

Dexter blows out. 'Okay, so look, here's the thing, honey. I've landed a couple of big investors this month, and when I was doing the deals I told them about our little dinner parties, and the fun we have, and they indicated they'd be keen to attend.'

'So you want me to throw a party for them?'

'Just a small one with a handful of new investors and some of our regulars, nothing that's too much trouble.' He takes her hand and strokes the bracelet on her wrist. 'You can wear this, it looks great.'

She says nothing. He's right, after all; it does look great. But she also knows that with Dexter a dinner party is never just a dinner party. Sure there's food and drink, but it's the after-dinner activities that the guests come for. And that takes a lot of preparation.

'Come on, honey,' says Dexter, a wheeling and dealing tone accompanying the charm. 'I know how you enjoy our parties.'

She used to, it's true, when she was younger and Dexter only had eyes for her. But in recent years he's changed from focusing solely on her, or having her and another woman or man, to leaving her to do whatever she wants and him playing with two women, neither of whom are her. He doesn't even act jealous when he watches her shagging the other men anymore. It's taken much of the fun away, if she's honest. 'How many people?'

'Twelve, fifteen, something around that. And invite whoever you like,' says Dexter. His tone is light but he's looking slightly shifty. 'Ask that eventing bloke if you want.'

Lexi narrows her eyes. Dexter's asked quite a few questions about Daniel in recent weeks, and not just related to the money she's spending on the horses. Now she wonders if he's guessed that they're shagging and he's jealous about it. She certainly hopes so. If the party gives her a way to stoke that jealousy, it could be worth it. Smiling, she says, 'That could be fun.'

'Okay,' says Dexter, flinching slightly as he opens the huge Sub Zero fridge and takes out the butter and cheese.

Lexi's smile grows. Daniel's definitely a sore point with her husband. Well, good. This party could be the perfect opportunity to get both men re-focused on her. Dexter has been locking himself away working more than usual and Daniel is becoming increasingly distant. Yes, this could play nicely to her advantage. 'When were you thinking?'

'Next weekend?' says Dexter, setting his coffee cup down on the counter as he butters his toast. 'I've got a couple of big fish potential investors I need to land and, from what I've heard about their preferences, coming to one of our parties could be the thing to clinch the deal.'

'We'll do Saturday,' says Lexi, already planning the theme and décor in her mind. 'And al fresco, I think. It's warm enough. We'll use the spa pool and the hot tub, and I'll have the table laid out on the patio.'

'Perfect,' says Dexter, nodding.

Yes, thinks Lexi, relishing the opportunity to play both men off against each other and in the process get them back fully under her control. It will be.

CHAPTER TWENTY-SIX

HATTIE

Three days later and she's still thinking about what Liberty said. Getting up from her chair at the kitchen table, Hattie rinses her coffee mug and the plate she used for her usual breakfast of toast and Marmite, and sets them on the drainer.

Liberty's surprise towards Robert leaving suddenly makes sense now, as does the fact that she knows a lot about his family. What doesn't make sense is why he'd up and leave for a job in America without telling Liberty. Hattie hadn't realised it at the time, but she was the one to tell her new friend that Robert had left for the US when she turned up on her doorstep apologising that the goats had escaped into her garden. No wonder Liberty was caught off guard.

Liberty confided in Hattie that it had started because of the goats. The first time Bill went round to collect them, things were fine, but after he'd tried to get Liberty to buy animal fat from his friend for her candles and she'd refused, the next time they escaped and he arrived to collect them he'd been snappy and mean. The third time they escaped, Bill wasn't around and Robert took several days to realise they were gone. Eventually, Liberty went over to Clover Hill House to tell him she had his goats and he really should look after them better. They'd argued briefly on his doorstep – Robert hating any form of criticism – but they'd both then hurried to Badger's End. After ages spent chasing after the goats – trying and failing to catch them – they'd ended up laughing. It had been the start of a friendship, Liberty had thought. They'd met up for lunch, gone on long walks together, and enjoyed each other's company. It had been platonic, easy. Until suddenly it wasn't.

Liberty hadn't even realised dinner that night was meant to be a date until they'd arrived at the restaurant – a fancy French place. Robert had seemed different, nervous almost, and Liberty had wondered what the hell was going on. She found out when they got back to Clover Hill House. She'd joined him for a coffee in his kitchen, but when she stood up to go home he grabbed her and tried to shove his tongue down her throat. Caught off guard, Liberty acted on instinct as she brought her knee up and slammed it between Robert's legs.

Hattie thought about the conversation they had. How she asked Liberty. 'Did he try to force you?'

Liberty shook her head. 'Nothing like that, I think he just assumed I wanted him. And my reaction, well, it made it very clear that I wasn't going to consent.'

'So he apologised.'

'No. He looked embarrassed and muttered something about misreading the signs.' Liberty shook her head again. 'I thought we were friends, you know, good mates. I guess he was thinking differently.'

Liberty had left quickly. She'd thought he'd come round the next day and apologise, but he didn't. And Liberty sure as hell wasn't going to instigate the conversation – Robert was the one who'd been out of line; he needed to own that and do the right thing. But one week passed, and then another. The following week, she'd learnt from Hattie that Robert had left for America.

Maybe he was ashamed, Hattie said. Liberty agreed it was possible, but she still didn't understand why he hadn't come and cleared the air before he left. Instead, he'd ghosted her – no calls and no texts. She'd heard of his reputation as a serial shagger but would never have imagined he'd have been that upset just because she wasn't interested in being another notch in his headboard. And that's all she would have been. He'd told her as much.

Liberty said Robert had told her early on in their friendship that he didn't do romantic relationships – said that they never worked out in his family – but although Hattie tried, Liberty wouldn't be drawn on the issues she'd alluded to between Robert's parents and Lady Pat.

Hattie knows all about complicated families. She walks through into the lounge and stops in front of her mother's memory box. It's pushed up against the wall with one of Robert's tasteful cream throws draped over it. Just looking at it makes her heart beat faster. She knows she should open it. It's been nearly six months since her mum died.

Removing the throw to reveal the oak trunk with prancing horses carved into the panels, Hattie twists the iron key in the lock and unfastens the catch. Butterflies flutter and backflip in her stomach. This is the closest she's got to opening it so far.

With trembling fingers, she lifts the lid. It's lighter than she'd imagined and it flies open, banging against the wall and making her flinch. Here's a cream quilt with tiny red rocking horses pictured on it folded over whatever else is inside the trunk. Hattie swallows hard in recognition; the quilt was her baby blanket, her most treasured possession until she got her first proper bed. Mum had told her the quilt was a gift from her daddy; a man she'd never known.

Lying on top of the quilt is an envelope. Hattie's name is on the front, the large, swirling letters written by her mum's hand. She reaches out and touches the envelope. Traces the lines of her mum's handwriting. She feels the pressure building in her chest.

Gulps at the air as if she's drowning. Drops the letter back onto the quilt and slams the lid of the trunk down as the grief crashes over her.

She doesn't hear the back door opening or footsteps coming through the kitchen and along the hallway to the lounge. Hattie jumps when she feels a hand on her shoulder. Spins around. 'What the…?'

'It's me,' says Liberty, taking a step back. 'I called out – didn't you hear me?'

Hattie shakes her head. Turning away, she repositions the cream throw over her mum's trunk and wipes her eyes. 'Sorry, I was miles away.'

Liberty looks at her, concerned. 'You okay?'

'Yeah.' Pushing away the thoughts of her mum, Hattie tries to focus on the reason Liberty's here. She forces a smile. 'Are you ready to do some heavy lifting?'

Liberty grins and holds her arms up in a strong-man pose. 'As ready as I'll ever be.'

'Let's get this done then.'

∼

Two hours later, they've cleared a path through the overgrown spinney that borders the far hedge of Robert's paddocks and built some makeshift cross-country fences. Bill has been sulking about in the garden, pretending to weed the flowerbeds but is really just watching Hattie and Liberty working and being sure to shake his head every chance he has to make eye contact. Hattie doesn't care, though. She needs to practise with Mermaid's Gold over solid fences and making her own is a way to do it for free. She can't afford to hire a purpose-built course and, after how generous Lady Pat has been already, she isn't prepared to ask her to put her hand in her pocket again.

'Are you sure they're not too big?' asks Liberty, frowning as she gazes into the bottom of the ditch between the end of the last paddock and the spinney. 'This is really deep.'

'It's fine,' says Hattie, trying to ignore the nerves fizzing in her stomach. 'If we can't manage these fences, there's no way we'll be ready for High Drayton Horse Trials.'

Liberty keeps looking pensively into the ditch. 'Well, if you're sure.'

'I am,' says Hattie, decisively.

'Good work,' says Lady Pat as she strides over to join them in front of the makeshift Trakehner. Slapping her palm down onto the spindly silver birch trunk that's balanced on towers of Liberty's vegetable-packing crates and angled diagonally over the ditch, she looks at it approvingly. 'This is excellent, dear. Did you get Bill to help?'

'I didn't want to distract him from his gardening,' says Hattie.

Lady Pat frowns. 'He's paid to help with whatever needs doing outside, and if making jumps is the most pressing activity, he should be getting stuck into that.'

Hattie glances across towards the garden where Bill is studiously weeding between the roses. 'Somehow I don't think he'd see it that way.'

∽

Hattie warms up Mermaid's Gold over a couple of small logs they pulled into position along the side of the first paddock. She rides on a loose rein; the mare is willing to wear the bridle and saddle now, but Hattie can tell she's happier with a very light contact to the snaffle bit in her mouth.

Lady Pat stands with her hands on her hips, studying the pair of them. 'She looks ready. What do you think?'

Hattie gives the horse's neck a rub. 'I think so too.'

'On you go then,' says Lady Pat. 'Show us the magic.'

Putting the mare into a steady canter, Hattie guides her in a circle before starting the short course of makeshift jumps. Years earlier, when she was a child riding borrowed ponies, her mum used to make jumps for her to practise over: little logs and sticks piled together in the woods. This course is very similar, just a hell of a lot higher.

'Good luck,' calls Liberty.

Hattie nods but doesn't reply. She turns Mermaid's Gold towards the first fence – the big oak log that they've jumped before. Keen, the horse bounds forward and pops over it like it's nothing. Encouraged, Hattie lines her up with the next jump – a section of the post and rail fencing that will take them into the second paddock.

The post and rail is taller than the log and completely vertical so requires care. If the horse doesn't tuck her front legs tightly, they could both end up on the floor. Hattie takes a light feel on the reins, asking the mare to steady and build her impulsion. Mermaid's Gold responds immediately. Together they spring over the fence.

'Good girl,' says Hattie, stroking the mare's neck as she rides her towards the next obstacle – a bramble hedge that borders the paddock and the spinney. 'You can do this.'

They canter towards the hedge. It's the biggest jump on the course – so tall that Hattie, at five foot four, could barely see over the top when she was standing next to it. It looks a bit smaller from the back of a horse, but not much.

They thunder towards the hedge and fly over it. Mermaid's Gold snorts as she lands and gives a triumphant shake of her head, this time from delight rather than fear. Hattie's thrilled how much the horse is enjoying this.

The next jump is trickier. As Hattie suspected when she saw the geese in the paddocks weeks before, there's a small pond in the spinney and so she and Liberty have managed to craft a water jump. They've made a pile of logs and brush on the edge of a quarter of a metre drop down into the water, then there's a couple of strides through the water and the blue plastic barrel as a narrow 'skinny' fence on the way out.

'Steady, girl,' says Hattie, giving a light touch to the reins as they weave through the recently cleared path between the silver birch and oak trees.

Mermaid's Gold responds immediately, shortening her stride. Ears pricked, focus on the path ahead, Hattie knows she's ready for the next challenge.

As they make the turn into the small clearing and the water is revealed, Mermaid's Gold doesn't hesitate. She jumps enthusiastically over the log pile and down the drop into the water. The power of her leap pitches Hattie forward onto her neck, but the mare raises her head, helping Hattie back into the right position. Water splashes around them as they canter towards the blue barrel. Here in the spinney the barrel looks impossibly narrow; the easiest option is to duck around it. But Mermaid's Gold stays on a straight line. She never falters. They reach the barrel on a perfect stride and soar over.

Hattie feels elated, but the course isn't over; there's one more fence to jump and this is the true test of their relationship. Nerves cause her stomach to flip. This is the make-or-break moment. The last fence is the Trakehner – the silver birch tree trunk balanced diagonally over a huge metre and a half wide ditch. It's a replica of the jump where Mermaid's Gold and her last rider had their accident.

As they make the turn towards the Trakehner, Hattie feels the mare start to slow. Her ears are still pricked, but she's shortening her stride. As they get closer, the mare drops from a canter to a trot. A stride away from the jump, she halts abruptly.

Hattie puts her hand on the mare's neck. 'It's okay.'

Mermaid's Gold doesn't think so. She snorts twice. Then rears, her front legs striking out towards the ditch and rail.

Hattie grabs the horse's mane to help her stay in balance. She strokes Mermaid's Gold's neck with her other hand. Keeps her voice calm. 'It can't hurt you, girl. You're okay.'

Mermaid's Gold doesn't believe her. Coming down from the rear, she recoils from the ditch, pushing all her weight back on her haunches. She doesn't rear again but Hattie can feel her shaking beneath the saddle. Hattie knows she needs to do something to help the mare get over her fear.

Dismounting, Hattie calls over to Lady Pat and Liberty who are in the paddock on the other side of the Trakehner. 'Can you drop one side of the pole down?'

'Sure,' says Liberty, rushing forward to the fence and, with the help of Lady Pat, lifts down one side of the silver birch trunk from the pile of vegetable crates, so that the end of the log is resting in the bottom of the ditch.

'Thanks,' says Hattie. Once Liberty and Lady Pat are clear of the fence, she takes Mermaid's Gold's reins over the horse's head and walks towards the Trakehner. The horse stays where she is, watching her suspiciously.

Undeterred, Hattie slides down into the ditch. She needs to prove to Mermaid's Gold that it won't hurt her again, and the best way to do that is to show her. Standing in the bottom of the ditch, Hattie puts her hand on her pocket.

Mermaid's Gold starts to lick her lips; she knows Hattie keeps a packet of Polos in that pocket. The mare takes a step forward.

'Good girl,' says Hattie, taking the mints from her pocket.

The horse steps forward again. Now she's standing on the edge of the ditch. Her whole body is shaking, but she's focused on the packet. Hattie takes a Polo and offers it to her on the flat of her palm. Slowly, the mare stretches her neck and takes it.

As Mermaid's Gold crunches on her Polo, Hattie pulls herself up onto the bank on the far side of the ditch. Turning to face the horse, she says, 'Come on, girl.'

Hattie doesn't pull at the reins or boss the horse around; she just stands and waits for the mare to make her own decision. It takes less than a minute for Mermaid's Gold to jump the ditch to join her. Hattie feeds the mare another Polo. They've made good progress, but there's a way to go yet. As the mare licks her lips, Hattie climbs back into and out of the ditch. As soon as she's on the other side, the mare jumps across to join her. Hattie repeats the activity again, and this time the mare jumps beside her.

Remounting, Hattie trots and canters a few circles around the paddock before aiming her towards the fence with the silver birch still dropped down at one side. The mare doesn't hesitate – she leaps over easily. As they head into the spinney, Hattie calls, 'Can you put it back up?'

This is the real test. As she asks the mare to turn, she knows Mermaid's Gold is feeling happier; she's stopped shaking, her ears are pricked and she's focused back along the pathway towards the Trakehner. Leaning forward, she strokes the mare's neck. 'You've got this, girl.'

They canter towards the fence. Nerves fizz in Hattie's stomach, but she swallows them down. Concentrates on getting Mermaid's Gold on a good stride to the fence. It's at full height now, a massive Trakehner – the horse's nemesis.

Mermaid's Gold increases her speed as they approach. She feels confident. Happy. Hattie holds her breath on the last stride. Together they fly over the fence.

'Wooohooo,' shouts Liberty, as they land. Beside her, Lady Pat claps her hands.

Jumping off Mermaid's Gold, Hattie throws her arms around the horse's neck. The mare nuzzles at her pocket for a Polo. Laughing, Hattie feeds her several mints at once. 'You deserve all of them.'

'You're ready,' says Lady Pat. 'High Drayton Horse Trials, here we come.'

CHAPTER TWENTY-SEVEN

DEXTER

The horse bloke is the last guest to arrive. Dexter is in the kitchen, checking the catering staff are on track with all the dinner preparations, when he sees Lexi hurry to the front door. There's something about the way she's moving – an urgency that she hasn't shown for any of their previous arrivals – that makes him follow her. As she opens the front door, Dexter hangs back in the doorway from the kitchen to the hallway, watching.

'Well, hello, darling,' purrs Lexi, stepping closer to the new arrival.

Dexter sees the familiarity. The way she presses herself up against Daniel, looking up at him from under her lashes, full of temptation. Dexter remembers when she used to look at him that way. When she didn't only initiate sex when she wanted him to buy her something or to get her way.

He flinches as Lexi kisses Daniel. Holds his breath as it continues on. Clenches his fists tight as if that can help stop the pain of his heart splintering.

Dexter's used to his wife having casual liaisons; it's been that way for a while now and he's tolerated them if that's the price of remaining married. He accepted long ago that he'll never be able to fully satisfy her. That's why he started putting on these parties – to help her feel satiated, and help him keep her. It's an added bonus that the parties are popular with some of his investors too.

But the way Lexi is looking at Daniel, and the way he's looking at her, indicates there's far more here than a casual fling. There's a relationship of sorts, one where Lexi is very much in control. Dexter sees the familiarity and the power dynamic coupled with desire, and it reminds him of his own relationship with Lexi. And that really worries him.

Because he needs his wife. Everything he's done has been for her, because he loves her and because of the life she expects to live. He's built the company, taken risks and decisions that other men would shy away from, all in pursuit of her respect and her affection. Her costly dabble into the world of eventing will break his business if it doesn't deliver new investors and greater income. He can't allow that. As much as his heart is crushed from this evidence of her dalliance, Dexter knows he must use it to his advantage.

As Lexi leads Daniel through the house and out onto the terrace, Dexter waits a brief moment, then follows. He watches as Lexi gets Daniel a drink from one of the waiting staff carrying silver trays of champagne, and then leaves him on the terrace as she moves away to speak with another guest. The horse bloke just stands there, on the terrace beneath the archway of climbing roses, sipping his drink and looking awkward.

This is Dexter's chance. Hurrying across the terrace, he approaches Daniel.

'Lexi told me you were coming,' says Dexter. His voice is gruff with none of its usual bonhomie. 'I trust you found the place easily enough?'

'Erm, yes, thanks, I... lovely evening,' says Daniel, stuttering. He looks shifty, won't meet Dexter's gaze. His eyes are darting from side to side, and he's swapping his weight from one foot to the other. 'You... have a beautiful home.'

Ignoring the compliment, Dexter fixes the younger man with his most steely gaze. 'And a beautiful wife, yes?'

Daniel flushes red, looks down at his champagne. 'I... I don't know what you—'

'Don't play the goddamn innocent with me, Danny-boy. You know *exactly* what I mean.' Dexter steps closer. Their faces are just inches apart now. 'I saw how she *welcomed* you this evening, and I know what that means.'

'I... I don't—'

'My wife has been putting a lot of money into you, Danny-boy, a lot of *my* money. It wasn't my choice, but I'm okay with it as long as you're introducing me to a new clientele group. But remember this is a business arrangement. If I can't bring my clients to watch you compete, or you refuse again to host a meet and greet at your yard, or you stop winning, everything you've got going on here...' He glances towards Lexi and shakes his head slowly. 'Will be done.'

He sees Daniel swallow hard. Knows he's got his message across.

'Sure,' stammers Daniel, nodding vigorously. 'I understand.'

'Good,' says Dexter. 'I expect results. Make sure you deliver.'

CHAPTER TWENTY-EIGHT
DANIEL

Daniel can feel Dexter's eyes burning into his back as he walks across the terrace to the huge table in the centre of the patio beneath the vine-draped pergola. The light is beginning to fade into dusk and the patio is lit by hundreds of candles. Classical music plays from concealed speakers. The table is set for sixteen and decked out in black chinaware, gold cutlery, napkins and candelabras. A huge centrepiece arrangement of roses stretches along its length. The effect is far more decadently dramatic than it is tasteful.

He feels jittery. Shaken by Dexter's words. Dexter saw Lexi kiss him, and it's crystal clear that he isn't happy. Daniel's surprised. That first time she came to look around the yard, didn't Lexi tell him she was in an open marriage? It was one of the reasons he felt able to justify their arrangement. God, the bloody arrangement – he doesn't want Lexi's affections, no matter what her husband might believe.

Daniel glances back towards the pool area. Dexter is still glaring at him. Looking away fast, he realises whatever Lexi said must have been a lie. There's no way her husband is okay with what he just saw.

Walking quickly around the table, reading the placement cards and looking for his seat, Daniel's glad that none of his owners seem to be on the guest list. He finds his seat – he's at the furthest end of the table from Dexter, thankfully, but is sandwiched between Lexi, at the end of the table, and an overly made-up woman on his other side.

As he goes to sit down, the overly made-up woman smiles warmly at him and he feels a little better. Then he feels his mobile vibrate in his pocket. Hopeful it'll give him an excuse to leave, he pulls out the phone.

It's a text from Jenny the vet:

> So? Is it a sex party??!

He taps out a response:

> Not so far! Just dinner.

Jenny's reply is almost immediate:

> That's how it starts… 😉

'No phones at the table,' says Lexi, gesturing towards his mobile. 'Turn it off unless you want to get spanked.'

The bird-like lady opposite giggles.

'Sorry,' says Daniel, powering off the phone and stuffing it back into his pocket. He remembers now that'd been a specific rule on the invitation that had been mailed to him – all mobile phones must be switched off for the duration of the evening.

Over on the far side of the patio, Dexter approaches the chair at the opposite end of the table to Lexi. Throwing his arms out wide, he smiles warmly. 'Welcome, everyone. It's great to have you all here. And rest assured, you're in for a magical evening.'

Everyone claps. The overly made-up lady beside him whoops

and cheers. Looking around the table, Dexter smiles at each of the seated guests. His expression hardens as his eyes meet Daniel's.

Looking away, Daniel swallows hard. He tries to act naturally but his stomach's churning and there's a bitter taste in his mouth. As a waiter fills his wine glass, he grabs it and downs half, holding it out again for a refill.

The bird-like lady seated opposite him chuckles and raises her own glass towards him as if it's a silent toast. 'That's the spirit.'

The moustached man sitting next to her nods approvingly. He's formally dressed in a three-piece suit and he looks the sort to have a bowler hat tucked away in his car just in case.

Daniel just wants to be out of here. When he gets the courage to look back towards the other end of the table, he sees that Dexter is seated and chatting animatedly with two blondes, who look rather like twins, sitting on either side of him. It's a reprieve of sorts, but Daniel wonders how long for.

The three courses pass Daniel by in a blur of alcohol and anxiety. He takes an anti-anxiety pill when he thinks no one is looking, and washes it down with several glasses of the dry white wine. The duck liver starter, lobster and steak main, and mini tarte au citron for afters, are perfectly cooked and presented, but Daniel has zero appetite. All he can think about is Dexter, his words and the look of fury in his eyes.

'This is wonderful, isn't it?' says the overly made-up woman sitting beside him. She gives him a nudge with her elbow. 'You should eat up. It's important to keep up your strength.'

He knows she's just being friendly, but her bright blue eyeshadow matches her dress, and Daniel finds the effect quite disconcerting. Still, he tries to show willing and manages to force down the lobster and half of his steak.

'Atta boy,' says the bird-like lady opposite, with a wink.

From the woman's stare, Daniel feels like he could be next on the menu. Lexi has been swapping seats around the table as guests get up to go to the loo or for smoke breaks. Currently she's talking animatedly to one of the blonde twins and a muscular guy with a shock of white blond hair and an awful mullet.

'So how do you know Dexter and Lexi?' asks the overly made-up woman. Her frosted pink lipstick has rubbed off onto her top teeth. Daniel tries not to stare at it.

'I'm an event rider and they own a couple of horses I ride.'

The lady is gazing at him like he's saying the most interesting thing she's ever heard. 'How wonderful.'

'A rider? That's lovely,' says the bird-like woman opposite.

There's something about the way they're both looking at him that's making him feel even more uncomfortable. He's never been good at small talk, but he tries to show interest. 'What about you both, how do you know the Marchfield-Wrights?'

'Well, honey,' says the lipstick lady, patting him on his arm, 'when my Bernard died a couple of years back, Dexter stepped in to help me with my finances. I was in an awful pickle – Bernard handled all the money, you see – but luckily for me, Dexter came along and sorted everything out and advised me on some investments. He's been a real godsend, and the investments have done awfully well.'

'Oh, me too,' says the bird-like lady, fiddling with the string of pearls around her slender neck. 'When my divorce went through earlier this year, lovely Dexter helped me get my finances in order. I'm so excited to be an investor in White Sands Beach Condos, and when the monthly dividend payments arrive it's like Christmas.'

'Sounds good,' says Daniel. He gestures towards the house. 'Have you been here before?'

'Oh yes,' says the overly made-up lady, grinning. 'I'm a regular. Wouldn't dare miss one of these, you know what I mean?'

'It's my first time,' giggles the bird-like lady. She looks around the table, her eyes widening. 'And let me tell you, I'm very excited to be here.'

Daniel thinks about Jenny's text. The alcohol might have dulled his senses somewhat, but from the over-enthusiastic expressions of the two ladies, he's getting the feeling there *is* more to this dinner party than he's been told.

Along the table, a petite brunette is laughing at something a curvy woman in a plunging black dress is saying. Everyone seems in good spirits – relaxed – but Daniel has an uneasy feeling. Maybe it's the richness of the food, the bottomless wine, or the strong, cloying perfume of the woman seated beside him, but he's feeling increasingly sick. At least the dinner is almost over. He should be able to leave soon.

As the waiters clear away the dessert plates and coffee cups, in their place they leave a shot glass full of clear liquid and a gold half-face mask. The music changes from classical to a fast dance track with a thumping bass. It seems overly loud, but there are no close neighbours – the Marchfield-Wrights' garden must be at least a couple of acres – and the American couple seated further down the table said they lived next door, so he supposes Dexter and Lexi don't have to worry about the music volume.

Frowning, Daniel picks up the mask. It's made of moulded plastic with gold satin and sequins glued onto the front. 'What's this for?'

'Just wait and see,' says Lexi, with a sly smile.

The bird-like lady giggles again. The moustached man joins in with a hearty laugh.

At the far end of the table, Dexter taps his shot glass with a teaspoon. Having got everyone's attention, he stands and slips his mask on, covering the top half of his face. He raises his shot glass. 'Firstly, thank you to my wonderful wife for organising our glorious dinner.' He downs the shot.

Everyone else follows suit. Daniel does the same. It's tequila; his eyes water as it hits the back of his throat.

Dexter wipes his mouth and then looks around the table,

grinning. He puts the shot glass back on the table and opens his arms wide. 'And now, my friends, we play!'

Squealing, the blonde twins on either side of him stand up and pull their shift dresses over their heads. They're wearing nothing underneath.

'Jesus!' says Daniel.

Each of the twins grabs one of Dexter's hands and they lead him over to the hot tub. As they get close, movement-activated fairy lights start to twinkle along the high hedge that screens the hot tub and pool. The muscle guy starts kissing the redhead seated beside him. A petite brunette snogs the moustached man who is casually fondling the large breasts of the woman on the other side of him. There's a shriek followed by a loud splash as several guests jump into the pool in various stages of undress.

The overly made-up lady leans closer to Daniel and scrapes her pink painted fingernails over his thigh. 'So, honey, what's your fantasy?'

'I… I don't…' Daniel recoils. Pushing his chair back to put some space between them, he looks towards Lexi. Her fist is clenched in the bird-like woman's hair as she kisses her, but her eyes are open, watching him through the eyeholes of her gold mask.

When she sees the shock on his face, she laughs and beckons him to come join her. Shaking his head, he can't believe he let himself think this would be a normal dinner party. *Nothing* with Lexi is normal. He's been such an idiot.

The overly made-up woman's fingers are at his belt now. Batting her hands away, Daniel stands up. He steps away from the table, towards the house. He needs to leave.

Breaking away from the bird-lady, Lexi jumps up from her chair and heads him off. Her eyes are wild. Her red, glossy mouth is fixed in a sneer. 'Where the hell do you think you're going?'

'Home. Away from…' He gestures towards the four or five bodies writhing and splashing about naked in the pool, the threesome Dexter has going on with the twins in the hot tub, and the large-breasted woman on the daybed who's giving the muscular guy a blow job while the moustached man pounds into her from behind. '... this!'

Lexi looks at him with disgust. Shaking her head, she runs the cherry-red fingernail of her index finger down his throat to his chest and starts undoing his shirt buttons. 'I never figured you for a prude, darling.'

'I'm not.' Daniel flinches away from her, hurriedly redoing his shirt buttons. 'But this isn't my thing...'

'Oh, how tiresome you are.' Lexi sighs theatrically. Leaning closer, she lowers her voice to a hiss. 'Your thing, darling, is whatever the hell I tell you it is.'

'No. I'm not...' Daniel pushes her away.

Lexi's eyes widen in surprise. She puts her hand to her chest. Then she laughs.

Not sure what to make of her reaction, and definitely not wanting to wait around and find out, Daniel turns and sprints across the patio towards the exit.

His head is fuzzy and his vision is a little hazy. He almost trips on some flower planters, and cannons from side to side along the passageway between the wall and the side of the house. Staggering as the ground underfoot changes from block paving to gravel, he pulls his mobile from his pocket and frantically dials. The call rings seven times before it's answered.

'You alright?' Eddie's voice is muffled and heavy with sleep.

'I need... you to pick me up.' Daniel hurries through the side gate, weaves between the line of cars parked outside the house and out onto the driveway. He starts running, desperate to be away from this place. The gravel crunches rhythmically beneath his feet.

'I thought there was transport—'

'I've left early. I can't...' Daniel thinks he hears a voice. He looks around but there's no one there. Did the voice come from down the phone? 'Is there someone with you?'

Eddie ignores the question. 'Okay, fine, I'll come and get you. You're at the Marchfield-Wrights' place, yeah?'

'No, I've started walking back. I'll be on the lane.'

As the call disconnects, Daniel sprints out of the driveway. Templeton Manor is twenty-four miles over the hills from here. Upping his pace, he runs along the dark lane with just the moon and his phone torch for light. The road is potholed and uneven and as he trips for the fifth time he knows he should slow down, but he won't.

All he can think about is how stupidly naïve he's been.

He can't get home quickly enough.

CHAPTER TWENTY-NINE

HATTIE

It's still early, before six o'clock, as they turn off the lane and drive through the gateway into High Drayton Horse Trials. A blanket of ground mist swirls across the parkland, hiding the grass and giving the place an ethereal feel. Nerves flutter in Hattie's stomach like hyperactive butterflies.

Liberty grins. 'This is so exciting. I've never been to a horse trial before.'

Hattie gives her a nervous smile. Steadily, she drives the hired horsebox across the grass towards the parking steward. Following their directions, she continues along the row of vehicles to the end and parks alongside a huge ten-horse lorry painted in a bright metallic blue.

Hattie glances up at the vast horsebox. It's super fancy and must have cost at least two hundred grand. Beside it, her workmanlike, wooden-sided hired lorry looks like Cinderella before the ball. Hattie's stomach does a flip. She's so far out of her league here, it's ridiculous.

'It's the horse and the partnership that count in this game,' says Lady Pat, as if reading her mind. 'Not how much money you splash out on toys.'

Pat's right. But still it's hard not to feel intimidated. For a moment, she regrets letting Lady Pat talk her into entering, but then Mermaid's Gold whinnies from inside the horse area behind them, and Hattie smiles. Mermaid's Gold is a star. She's going to restore her reputation and show that horse whispering techniques can help; that they're far more than rope-wiggling and pony-patting. Swallowing down her nerves, she looks at Lady Pat. 'I'll just see if Mermaid's Gold wants a drink, and then I'll declare and walk the course.'

∼

Two hours later, Hattie rides Mermaid's Gold towards the warmup area for the dressage. The sun has burnt away the ground mist, and its warmth mingling with the scent of recently cut grass makes it smell like high summer. Mermaid's Gold's coat shimmers like polished copper in the sunlight. Her flaxen mane is plaited and rolled into neat, circular balls along her neck, and her hooves are painted with oil to make them gleam.

'You look so smart,' says Liberty, smiling at Hattie encouragingly. 'And hot; the cut of that jacket is everything.'

'Thanks,' says Hattie. She feels awkward in her new cream breeches, long leather boots, white shirt, cream stock and black jacket. She wishes she'd practised riding in them before today so that she felt less buttoned up and constricted. Only her jockey skullcap remains from her usual riding gear, although it's sporting a new black velvet silk and the aqua tag given to her following its inspection for safety when she declared to ride and collected her competitor number.

They're number 213. She's hoping that thirteen is lucky for them today.

This first phase is being held in a huge field that's adjacent to the lorry parking area. There are six dressage arenas laid out along the far hedge; the white plastic boards that define their rectangular shape glint in the sunlight. At each of the markers – the letters positioned around the arena that serve as the guide to the riders on where to perform the set of predefined movements within the dressage test – is a large flower arrangement. For each arena, there is a judge and a writer, who will write down the marks and comments on each competitor's performance, sitting in a vehicle parked at the 'C' end, facing into the arena and towards the warmup area.

'Good morning,' says a lady with an efficient-sounding voice and eager smile as she bustles over to Hattie wearing a fluorescent tabard. She's brandishing a clipboard and has a large badge with 'dressage steward' pinned to the collar of her Joules polo shirt. 'Number 213? Wonderful. Let me check you off.'

Hattie waits as the steward runs her biro down the long list of competitor numbers and names attached to her clipboard. 'Ah yes, here you are. Harriet Kimble and Mermaid's Gold?'

'Yes, that's us,' says Hattie.

'Excellent,' says the lady, putting a tick against Hattie's number. 'So your arena is number four and it's running to time. You have twenty minutes before you'll be going in.'

'Great, thank you,' says Hattie.

'No problem,' says the tabard-wearing steward cheerfully. 'Have a good test.'

As the steward moves on to speak to the next new arrival, Hattie squints across the field to the arenas. Each one has a number on a stand in front of it and she scans along the line to arena number four. The big bay horse currently doing their test in that arena looks very fresh. As the rider asks them to transition from trot to canter, the horse leaps into the air and lets rip with a succession of fly bucks. Luckily the rider sits them and keeps their composure enough to steer the horse around the end of the arena and continue in a more controlled gait. The bucking will have cost them a lot of marks though. Hattie chews her lip. She hopes it isn't an omen for her own test.

'You'll be just fine,' says Lady Pat, as if reading her mind. 'Don't look at anyone else. Concentrate on yourself and Mermaid's Gold.'

Hattie nods. Lady Pat's right. This is about the two of them, no one else. 'I'm going to go and find a quiet place to warm up.'

'Good idea,' says Lady Pat, nodding. 'We'll let you know when the horse before you is in the arena.'

Their warmup time seems to go past at double speed. Finding an unoccupied space in the far left corner of the field, away from the twenty or so horses and riders also doing their final preparations before their test, Hattie focuses on helping Mermaid's Gold relax and loosening up her muscles at walk, trot and canter.

She tries to concentrate, but it's hard. She can't believe she's here, competing at an affiliated horse trials. Hattie glances across the field towards the other riders. Horses large and small are going through their paces. Bays, greys, chestnuts and roans, all groomed to perfection. Hattie sees Greta Wolfe, stalwart of the German team and recent silver medallist at the Olympics on a floaty-paced grey gelding; Jonathan Scott, the famous Australian rider who's been at the top of the sport for the last ten years calming an athletic black mare; and over in the far distance someone who looks very much like one of the USA squad is cantering perfect ten-metre circles on a well-muscled grey.

It seems crazy. A couple of months ago, Hattie was horse-less and had little hope of even getting to ride a horse anytime soon; now she's riding this super-talented mare at their first competition. Hattie strokes Mermaid's Gold's neck. The mare blows out, and turns her head, asking for a Polo. Laughing, Hattie takes one from the pocket of her breeches and feeds it to her. Mermaid's Gold crunches it happily.

'You're next.' Lady Pat's voice carries across the field, pulling Hattie back to the job in hand.

She turns and sees Liberty and Lady Pat are waving her over towards the dressage arenas.

'This is it, girl,' says Hattie, rubbing the horse's neck. She swallows down the butterflies backflipping in her stomach. Mermaid's Gold springs into a trot and they head towards arena number four. 'It's time to show them what we can do.'

CHAPTER THIRTY

DANIEL

*P*ink Fizz is really full of himself this morning. Squealing under his breath and bouncing along the horse walk towards the dressage arenas, it's all Daniel can do to stop him breaking into a canter every few strides. The horse loves his work, but Daniel thinks that they haven't got his food quite right yet. Riding him today feels like sitting on an unexploded bomb.

He lets the fluorescent-tabarded dressage steward know he's arrived, then walks Pink Fizz around the edge of the warm-up arena, away from the collection of owners and grooms who are waiting on hand to help with any last-minute tack adjustments. He looks for a quiet spot with not many other horses around so he can try and get the gelding to settle. The warm-up is pretty busy. He says hi to the riders he knows as he passes them: Andrew, Greta, Jonathan and Kittie.

Pink Fizz jigs into a trot. Snatches at the reins.

'Steady,' says Daniel, closing his fingers tighter on the reins. The horse responds by striking out with his front feet and throwing his head up.

'That looks fun,' says Greta as she passes him again.

'Yeah,' says Daniel, with a rueful smile, as Pink Fizz skedaddles sideways away from Greta's big grey horse. 'He's a bit of a livewire today.'

He steers Pink Fizz further away from the other horses and starts trotting large circles and figure eights, focusing on the horse's rhythm and relaxation. Gradually, after ten minutes or so, the gelding begins to feel more relaxed. Daniel asks him to canter, and starts repeating the exercise at that pace.

That's when he spots Lexi over by the entrance to the dressage arenas. She's hard to miss, dressed in a bright pink mini dress, knee-high brown boots and a brown leather jacket with fringe on the sleeves. She looks like she should be in a cocktail bar or shopping on Oxford Street rather than in the middle of a field at a horse trials. As if sensing his gaze, she turns towards him. Their eyes meet. She scowls.

His mouth goes dry and his stomach clenches. He hasn't seen Lexi or Dexter since the dinner party fiasco. Hasn't spoken to them either; the only communication they've had has been by text. He hoped she wouldn't come today, but instead it seems as though she's brought an entourage.

Along with Dexter, who is at least more appropriately dressed in a polo shirt and chinos, there are three other men with her. All three are dressed in too-clean cream field trousers and tweed jackets that are stiff and obviously brand new. City people, thinks Daniel, come to play in the country for the day.

He wishes Eddie was here; at least then he'd feel like he had some moral support and could use Eddie as a human shield if necessary, but he's back at the lorry getting Daniel's next ride – Rocket Fuel – ready. He's got all three of the Marchfield-Wrights' horses running today, and that makes the timings between phases and each horse really tight.

Changing direction, Daniel canters Pink Fizz on the other

lead. It's a glorious summer day – not a cloud in the sky and already warm – but now he feels like storm clouds are gathering just out of sight. He tries to put Lexi, Dexter and whoever they've brought with them from his mind so he can focus on Pink Fizz, but it's hard. Lexi's sent him several texts since the dinner party, each making it crystal clear she expects him to apologise to both her and Dexter for running out.

Daniel doesn't want to apologise.

Finishing another canter circle, Daniel asks Pink Fizz to change direction. This time, as he takes the turn towards the dressage arenas, one of the tweed-jacketed men in Lexi's entourage turns towards him. Something twists in Daniel's already clenched stomach as he recognises the man. They've met before. The moustached man meets his gaze and smiles, raises a hand to wave.

Jesus. The last time Daniel saw him, he was pounding into the large-breasted woman from behind. Daniel looks away fast. It isn't an image he wants to relive.

Beneath him, Pink Fizz tenses up. His stride becomes shorter and tighter. He squeals as he throws in a buck, and then another.

'Jesus!' Daniel grabs for the horse's mane plaits and he's almost unseated by a third twisting corkscrew buck. 'Steady, Pinky, steady.'

Pink Fizz plunges forwards, yanking at the reins and throwing in a couple more bucks. Daniel sits them better this time, and brings the horse back to a walk. Takes a breath, and rubs the horse's neck.

'Nice airs above the ground there,' says Jonathan, cantering past on a relaxed and smart-looking black horse with a white blaze down its nose and four knee-high white socks. 'Ever thought about a career in the circus?'

'Yeah right,' says Daniel, forcing a laugh. 'Might be this one's calling.'

As Jonathan canters away, Daniel rubs the horse's neck. He

doesn't punish him; that would make no sense. He knows the incident was his fault. Seeing Lexi and her entourage made him tense and Pink Fizz would have sensed that. When a horse is as full of himself as Pink Fizz is today, he is always going to take advantage of his rider not being one hundred percent focused.

Daniel checks his watch. He's got five minutes before he's due in the arena. What matters now is getting both himself and the horse as relaxed as possible, otherwise they've no hope of doing a decent performance in the dressage.

Checking no one is looking, Daniel pulls the blister pack from his pocket, quickly pops out an anti-anxiety pill and dry swallows it. He tries not to think about how many of the pills he's taken, or the fact that until he met Lexi he hadn't needed the medication for years, not since the aftermath of his parents' deaths. These days the little pills seem to be the only things that are keeping him sane.

'Number 314,' shouts the tabard-wearing steward. 'You're in next.'

Picking up the reins again, he walks Pink Fizz towards the dressage arenas. Purposefully not looking towards where Lexi and her entourage are, he smiles at the dressage steward and thanks her, then puts Pink Fizz into a trot and heads over towards Arena Three.

As they trot around the outside of the arena, waiting for the dressage judge sitting in the Mercedes at the C end to toot their horn for him to start the test, Daniel notices the little chestnut horse and her rider in the arena next door. Watching the pair trot down the centre line and halt perfectly square at X for their final salute, Daniel doesn't think he's ever seen such harmony between a horse and rider.

The judge for his arena toots their horn, and Daniel loops back towards the A end of the arena to make his entrance. As he finishes the turn, he sees the rider of the little chestnut horse jump off as soon as they've left their arena and throw her arms around the horse's neck. She's laughing and telling the horse how amazing she is. Daniel can almost feel the joy coming off her. With a jolt, he realises that's how he used to feel, especially when he was competing on The Rogue.

Right now, he can't imagine ever feeling that happy again.

CHAPTER THIRTY-ONE
DANIEL

Because his horses' running times are all so close together, the show jumping steward lets him jump Pink Fizz out of order in a slightly earlier time slot. After a passable score in the dressage, the roan gelding pulls out the stops in the show jumping with a bouncy and enthusiastic clear round. It's all the more impressive from the young horse as the jumping arena is tight and the course twisty.

As he flies over the last combination, a treble of fences – two blue-and-white uprights to a large square blue-and-white oxer – Daniel grins and gives the horse a couple of big pats on the neck. Pink Fizz, sensing Daniel's centre of gravity is a little further forward than it should be, responds with three big bucks and a corkscrew twist for good measure.

'Shit,' says Daniel, cursing under his breath as he's pitched forward onto the horse's neck. Pink Fizz snorts and speeds across the arena, letting out a loud fart as they pass the spectators.

Wrestling the gelding back to a walk, Daniel's on his guard for more antics from the horse as they head back across the arena to the entrance/exit.

'Well, that was certainly an exuberant round from Pink Fizz and Daniel Templeton-Smith,' says the commentator in his overly plumy accent. He laughs. 'It's not often we see Daniel getting a tad unstuck. But no harm done and they go through to the cross-country on their dressage score.'

Indeed, very exuberant, thinks Daniel, as he tries to stop the gelding from shying away from the commentary box and then nearly getting pitched onto the horse's neck again as he spooks violently at the water trays under one of the fences.

'You've just jumped that,' says Daniel, shaking his head.

Over on the other side of the arena where the spectators are gathered along the white ring ropes, there's a murmur of laughter. Daniel looks towards them. It's lunchtime so the crowd is pretty big: owners, pony clubbers, happy hackers along for a day trip and eventing wannabes all tucking into burgers, falafels, pizza or whatever their favourite food truck fare is as they watch. Playing to the crowd, he smiles and mimes an exaggerated shrug. Pink Fizz pops in another buck and fart. The laughter gets louder.

Finally they reach the exit. Daniel halts Pink Fizz to allow the next horse and rider into the arena first. It takes him a moment to realise the woman riding towards him on a little chestnut is the same one he saw finishing their dressage test earlier.

'Good luck,' he says, holding a plunging Pink Fizz at bay as she trots past.

She smiles; she's got one of those smiles that could light up the greyest of days. 'Thanks,' she says. 'Well done on your clear.'

Then she's gone. The buzzer sounds for her round to start as Daniel exits the arena. Rather than ride straight back to the lorry to swap onto Rocket Fuel as he ought to do, he turns Pink Fizz around so he can watch the little chestnut jump.

It's interesting. The woman rides on a very light contact, too loose really, but it doesn't seem to affect their performance. And although the chestnut mare must be barely fifteen hands high, as they jump round the course they make every fence look easy. The related distance between three and four, the water trays at six and the final combination – nothing puts them off their rhythm. Just like in the dressage, Daniel can't remember a time he watched a horse and rider who were so in sync with one another. The way they jump looks effortless.

'And a jolly good round there from Harriet Kimble and the diminutive Mermaid's Gold,' says the commentator heartily. 'They go forward to the cross-country phase on their dressage score.'

As she exits the arena, the woman is rubbing her horse's neck and telling the mare what an amazing job she did. She halts a few metres from Daniel and pulls a packet of Polos from the pocket of her black competition jacket. The little mare twists her head round, lips smacking together as if asking for a mint. The rider laughs and feeds her a handful.

Daniel smiles. The relationship between the woman and the little horse reminds him so much of how he is with The Rogue. He walks Pink Fizz forward a couple of steps. 'Great job in there. Your round was foot perfect.'

The rider looks over at him. She's grinning. 'Thanks. It's our first event and I wasn't sure how it'd go. Those fences are pretty big.'

'They are,' says Daniel, nodding. 'I reckon they're all pushing maximum height.'

'I'm just so pleased with her,' says the woman, stroking her horse's neck. 'She was brilliant.'

'Well, congrats again,' says Daniel. 'Good luck on the cross-country.'

'Thanks,' says the woman, beaming. 'And you.'

As he turns Pink Fizz back towards the lorry park, Daniel realises he's still smiling. There's something about her – Harriet

Kimble – that makes him want to get to know her better. She's a great rider, yes, and the relationship she has with the little chestnut is obviously fantastic, but there's something more, something happy and bright. Something energising.

For the first time in several months, he feels less anxious.

He feels hope.

CHAPTER THIRTY-TWO

HATTIE

They're three-quarters of the way around the cross-country course and clear so far. Hattie's nerves have vanished, replaced by intense focus on the fences to be jumped. She needs to keep Mermaid's Gold on track, giving her the best setup to each fence and making sure they keep their impulsion and forward momentum.

They shoot out of a wooded area over a large log pile and head downhill to the second water. The going is good – firm, but the old turf has some spring to it – and Mermaid's Gold seems to be enjoying herself. But the water is a tricky, technical fence and although the cross-country has only been running for an hour, it's already caused quite a bit of trouble. Hattie knows Mermaid's Gold doesn't mind water, but she tends towards a faster gallop than is ideal for this combination of fences because the striding is tight between them. The jump into the large pond is over an upturned rowing boat and down a drop into the water. It's big but simple enough; however, the five strides through the water to the step out have been riding short, and the two strides from the top of the step to the 'skinny' triple brush fence, that's barely a metre and a half wide, are riding long. It means she'll need to be collected for the first two fences, then push on to reach the third at the right spot for take-off.

As they reach the bottom of the slope, Hattie takes a light check on the reins. 'Steady, girl.'

Mermaid's Gold shortens her stride. Her ears are pricked on the fence.

They meet the upturned boat on a good stride but rather than popping over it economically, Mermaid's Gold does a huge leap and launches herself far out into the water. Hattie is taken by surprise but she manages to slip her reins and give the horse enough room to use her head and neck to balance as she takes her first stride in the water.

The step out is looming towards them very quickly. As she gathers up her reins, Hattie keeps focused on the skinny brush on the other side of the step. Steering the mare towards it with her legs, they make the distance to the step on four strides rather than five and then manage two good strides to the skinny brush. Mermaid's Gold never wavers from the line and leaps over the narrow fence like a pro.

'Good girl,' says Hattie breathlessly as she pats her neck and they gallop on across the country.

The next two fences – a bullfinch and a table – are big and solid but straightforward, and Mermaid's Gold makes quick work of them. The next jump is a huge Trakehner – a broad oak log suspended over a deep, water-filled ditch. As they gallop across the pastureland towards it, the wind whistles in Hattie's ears, almost drowning out the thunder of Mermaid's Gold's hooves against the ground. She steadies the mare as they turn towards the Trakehner. 'It's okay, girl. Nearly home.'

Mermaid's Gold has her ears pricked. She gallops towards the fence. But three strides out, she falters. Her stride slows. She lowers her head and snorts.

Hattie puts her hand on the mare's neck. 'You've got this. You can do it.'

For a moment, Hattie thinks she's going to refuse to jump. Then Mermaid's Gold accelerates and leaps over the Trakehner with ease.

'Good girl,' says Hattie as they land.

The last jumping effort is in sight: an inviting-looking brush fence. They power across the field, Mermaid's Gold's long stride eating up the distance, and soon they're flying over the last and galloping through the finish flags.

Tears are streaming down Hattie's cheeks. Dropping her reins, Hattie pats Mermaid's Gold's with both hands. As the horse slows to a walk, she jumps off and throws her arms around her neck. She's still crying as she tells the mare over and over what a good girl she is.

'That was so brilliant,' says Liberty, rushing over. 'She was so brave.'

'She's amazing,' says Hattie, loosening the girth and keeping the horse walking as she catches her breath. 'She made it feel easy.'

'Never drop your reins like that at the end of a course,' says Lady Pat, sternly, as she joins them. 'You could have unbalanced her, and if that happens when she's tired she could pull a muscle and injure herself.'

Lady Pat is right, and Hattie feels guilty that in her elation she did something that could have put Mermaid's Gold at risk. But it's not just the guilt that throws her. For someone who says she doesn't know anything about horses, Lady Pat seems very knowledgeable. She turns towards her. 'How do you know—'

'It's something Robert's instructor always used to say to him at the end of practice chukkas,' says Lady Pat. She waves away Hattie's questioning look. 'You pick up these things, don't you?'

Hattie supposes so. Turning her attention back to Mermaid's Gold, she takes the mare's reins over her head and has a quick glance at each of the horse's legs, checking for injuries. She looks fine, and as she strides happily along beside Hattie it looks like she's been out on a stroll rather than just finished a cross-country jumping round.

'Her fitness is good,' says Lady Pat. 'She's hardly blowing.'

'You looked fast as well,' says Liberty. 'You must be within the optimum time?'

'I don't know, maybe,' says Hattie as she feeds Mermaid's Gold a Polo. She doesn't have a stopwatch so has no idea of the time it took them to complete the course. Getting safely round was her goal for today. She looks from Liberty to Lady Pat. 'Let's get her back to the lorry and wash her off.'

∽

They walk back to the lorry and Lady Pat and Liberty ask her for a jump-by-jump account of how the course rode. As she talks them through each fence, it feels like she's in a dream, as if she's describing something that happened to someone else.

Lady Pat puts her hand on Hattie's arm. 'You rode very well, dear. I hope you're proud of yourself.'

Hattie turns to look at Lady Pat. After two clear rounds – one in the show jumping ring and the second on the cross-country – they're finishing on their dressage score. It's a better result than she dared hope for. And a big step closer to her dream.

But there's something missing.

Hattie feels a wave of grief punch her in the chest. Her mum would have loved to be here watching her compete on this amazing horse. She looks towards Mermaid's Gold as tears fill her eyes again. This time they're not happy tears.

She wishes her mum were here.

CHAPTER THIRTY-THREE
LEXI

The prize giving takes place in front of the scoreboards. It's drawn quite a crowd, and along with people queuing at the burger-and-chips food truck a few metres along from the saddlery stand, there must be sixty or so people watching. The chief executive of the event sponsor, Michman Auto, and the owner of High Drayton Manor, the singer-songwriter JaXX, stand in front of the eight-foot-high whiteboards where the scores have been displayed throughout the competition, ready to present the prizes. They make an odd pair, thinks Lexi: the tall, slightly balding CEO, and the diminutive and, as always, be-hatted musician. But from the way they're laughing and joking with the plain girl holding the basket with the rosettes and prizes, they seem to get on well enough.

A moustached man dressed in a tweed suit claps his hands and the crowd falls silent. 'Hi, everyone. I'm Alan Winkler and I'll be MCing the prize giving today. Firstly, I'd like to thank JaXX for kindly allowing us to use his land here at High Drayton Manor. This year, all proceeds are going to the My Last Wish charity which he's patron of, and I'd like to encourage you all to give generously in the yellow collecting buckets you see around the event.'

Applause from the crowd forces Alan Winkler to pause. Lexi crosses her arms and glances at Daniel to her right but he doesn't turn to meet her gaze. Irritated, she looks back at Alan and hopes that he hurries up and gets on with the bloody prize giving.

As the applause dies down, JaXX, dressed in jeans, a green Barbour and a huge fluffy leopard print hat, presses his palms together in a prayer position and says, 'Thanks, it's been great hosting you all.'

Alan Winkler nods and continues with his speech. 'And a big thank you to our event sponsors, Michman Auto, who I'm delighted to say will continue to sponsor the horse trials next year.'

As the CEO of Michman Auto bangs on about how proud they are to be part of the horse trials, Lexi sighs. The smell of the burgers from the nearby food truck is getting to her. She hasn't eaten bread in over a decade, but she's hungry and the meat aroma is making her mouth water; it's very distracting.

Dexter, standing on her left, nudges her with his elbow and whispers, 'That CEO bloke could be a potential investor. I'll try and speak to him once this is done.'

'Fine,' says Lexi. She doesn't care about investors right now. She wants her moment in the spotlight.

Finally the CEO stops droning on and the prize giving can get underway. As the highest-level class running that day, Daniel's will be the first to be announced. The plain girl with the rosette and prize basket steps closer to Alan Winkler. Lexi feels the excitement building inside her.

The CEO clears his throat. 'Okay, ladies and gentleman, the results of Class A are as follows.' He glances at the piece of paper in his hand. 'I'm going to award the owners' prize first, going to the owner of the most successful horses here at the event, and the prize goes to Mr and Mrs Marchfield-Wright for their horses Pink Fizz and Rocket Fuel.'

The crowd starts to clap as Lexi strides across the grass, taking care to keep her weight on the balls of her feet so her fuchsia satin heels don't sink into the dirt. She's the only person here wearing heels, but she doesn't care. When she realised Daniel had won, and Dexter said he thought she should collect the owners' prize alone as she was the one who picked the rider and the horses, she knew boots wouldn't do. The only way to collect a prize is in Jimmy Choos.

'Congratulations,' says Alan Winkler, shaking her hand. 'Two splendid horses you've got there.'

'Thank you,' says Lexi, graciously.

'Well done,' says JaXX, handing her the owners' rosette – a big gold-and-silver affair.

She takes the rosette and thanks him. Then the CEO of Michman Auto hands her a silver trophy of a jumping horse.

'Oh, how lovely,' says Lexi, batting her eyelashes at him as she remembers Dexter's words about wanting to woo him as an investor. 'Thank you so much.'

As the applause continues, and the photographer snaps her picture, Lexi relishes the moment. She's come a long way from the smart but bored girl from an average and ordinary family, who lived in an ordinary three-bed house, in an ordinary suburb of an ordinary town. When she left at eighteen, she promised herself she would never tolerate ordinary and boring again; she would be extra-ordinary. And here she is, the picture of extra. She thinks of all the people who said she'd never make anything of her life and smiles. This is a fuck you to all of them. She is far better, far richer, and far more successful than they are now.

Taking her prizes, she walks back to Dexter and Daniel. Dexter is clapping enthusiastically, as are his investor friends. Daniel isn't; he's looking distracted. When she reaches them, Dexter throws his arms around her in a big hug and kisses her cheek. Daniel gives her a tight smile and nod. She tries not to let him see her disappointment. Keeps the smile in place, because she knows the people around them are watching. Nods back at Daniel graciously while inside her the rage flares.

'And now onto the rider prizes,' says Alan Winkler. 'The winner of Class A is Pink Fizz, owned by Mr and Mrs Marchfield-Wright and ridden by Daniel Templeton-Smith.'

Removing his riding hat, Daniel approaches Alan Winkler and the others as the crowd applauds. JaXX presents him with the winner's red rosette and the CEO of Michman Auto hands him an envelope with the prize money for first place and a voucher for free vehicle servicing at Michman Auto for a year. Daniel thanks them all and shakes each of their hands before taking his place to their left.

'And second place, in what can only be described as a bit of a clean sweep, is Daniel Templeton-Smith again, this time on Mr and Mrs Marchfield-Wright's Rocket Fuel. Rocket Fuel came in just one penalty behind his stablemate Pink Fizz.'

Lexi watches as Daniel receives the prizes for second. Dexter is clapping away, acting the big guy with his investor friends, who seem very impressed. Still irked by Daniel's behaviour towards her, Lexi only claps because she doesn't want to look bad. She's going to have to tell Daniel he needs to step up his game. His behaviour today, after him running out on the party, is just not good enough. He needs to know that if he doesn't perform in all areas as she expects, there will be some serious consequences.

Daniel stands to the left of the prize givers, forming the start of the winning line-up.

'And now to third place, which goes to Harriet Kimble on Lady Babbington's Mermaid's Gold.'

Lexi watches the curvy brunette go to collect her prize. There's something familiar about her, but she can't place it exactly. It's only when the brunette joins the line-up beside Daniel and he leans forward and kisses her on both cheeks that she recognises her: it's the woman she saw Daniel talking to after the show jumping. Rage builds inside Lexi as she watches the pair of them chatting and laughing as the other prize winners are announced and awarded. They're standing too close together. They're looking at each other too much, too intensely. No, no, no. Lexi clenches her fingers tighter around her prizes.

This is *her* moment, and Daniel's ruining it. Even Dexter realised how important this is and said she should receive the owners' prize alone rather than with him, but not Daniel; he doesn't seem to care a damn. All he seems interested in is the brunette.

With all the winners announced, there's a final applause as the photographer takes pictures of the line-up, and then the prize giving is over. The crowd starts to disperse. Some people congratulate Lexi as they walk past and others simply stare.

She revels in it, but the moment is tainted. Of course many eyes are on her, the fuchsia pink mini-dress and shoes stand out among the sea of boring tweed and browns and greens that the horsey set so love to wear, but the eyes that should be on her – Daniel's – aren't. Instead he seems fixated on the distinctly average-looking girl with the straggly brown hair who won third place.

Beside her, Dexter is chatting away but Lexi isn't listening. Instead she watches as Daniel hugs the bloody brunette again before she walks over to join a haughty-looking older woman and a glamorous black-haired woman who is being pulled by an exuberant Labrador and a ratty-looking terrier towards the girl.

As the brunette, Harriet Kimble, walks away with the other two women, Daniel can't take his eyes off her. He seems rooted to the spot, staring. Fury bubbles inside Lexi. How dare he look at another woman like that? Why isn't he paying *her* that much attention? Why is he so bloody ungrateful?

Dexter puts his hand on Lexi's shoulder and she jumps.

'Honey, I'm taking the boys back to the car for some champagne. Are you joining us?'

'Of course, darling,' says Lexi, without taking her gaze from Daniel. 'I'll just say our goodbyes and I'll be right with you.'

As Dexter leads the investors back towards the owners' car park, Lexi strides over to Daniel. Halting next to him, she leans in close and hisses, 'You're mine, not hers.'

He turns to face her. The shock on his face is really quite delicious.

Lexi stands on tiptoes and leans in as if she's going to kiss him, but instead she bites his earlobe hard. As he winces away from her, she glares at him, eyes blazing. 'Don't you ever look at that little bitch again.'

CHAPTER THIRTY-FOUR

HATTIE

Back in the paddock at Clover Hill House, Mermaid's Gold waits for Hattie to remove her halter and give her a mint. Once the mint is eaten, she turns and gallops across the field, neighing her arrival to Mable and Gladys, who are in their shelter. The goats scuttle out to meet her. As Mermaid's Gold stands still, they canter around her, leaping and bleating and giving her a hero's welcome home.

Hattie smiles as she watches them larking about. Raising her phone, she takes a short video of them. Her mum would love to see this. She's about to message it over to her when the grief hits her as she remembers again: Mum's gone.

'Hurry up,' calls Liberty from the garden. 'It's time to celebrate.'

Hattie wipes her eyes and turns. Liberty and Lady Pat have set out a bottle of champagne in an ice bucket and some flutes on the patio table.

Liberty beckons Hattie to come over. 'Come on.'

Smiling, Hattie loops Mermaid's Gold's halter over the gate and takes the path along the side of the paddocks and all-weather arena to the garden. As she gets closer to her friends, Lady Pat pops the cork off the champagne and a plume of fizz arcs into the air.

'Quick, don't waste it,' she says, grabbing the closest flute and using it to catch the champagne as Liberty holds the other two glasses out, trying to catch the spray.

Hattie laughs as she joins them. It might be bittersweet, but this is a good moment and as her mum always said, with horses you have to enjoy the good times when they come because who knows what is around the corner. She swallows hard and tries not to think about her mum's illness, and how she'd not told Hattie until she had so little time left. It's a struggle to fight back the anger at the lost time as it intertwines with the grief.

'Here you go,' says Liberty, passing her a champagne flute. 'Stop looking so serious, girl.'

'I just…' Hattie shakes her head.

'What?' asks Lady Pat.

'Nothing,' says Hattie, forcing a smile. 'I'm just a bit overwhelmed.'

'You were splendid, both of you,' says Pat, smiling. She raises her glass. 'To Mermaid's Gold and Harriet.'

'And to both of you,' says Hattie. 'I couldn't have done it without you supporting me.'

The three of them clink their flutes together and drink.

'So what's next?' asks Liberty.

'I don't know.' And she doesn't. Hattie realises she focused everything on High Drayton without any thoughts as to what's next. She doesn't own Mermaid's Gold, and Lady Pat bought her with the aim of rehabilitating her and getting her confidence back. That job is done. Hattie looks at Lady Pat. 'She's your horse. Do you have any thoughts about what next?'

Lady Pat says nothing. As Hattie watches her drain the last of her champagne, she hopes that she won't sell Mermaid's Gold. She might not own the horse but they're connected, a partnership. She couldn't bear to lose her.

'Kingsland Park International,' says Lady Pat. 'The CCI3*-Short there should be your next event.'

Hattie's relief that she's going to be able to keep Mermaid's Gold is followed fast by the fear that she won't be good enough to do an international level competition. 'I don't know if we'll be ready.'

'But you were great today,' says Liberty as she refills the champagne flutes.

'Exactly, you'll be more than ready,' says Lady Pat. 'Your jumping was foot-perfect and there's four weeks for you to do more fitness work and get your dressage a little more precise. You should both be at your peak at exactly the right time.'

Hattie takes a big mouthful of champagne. From the way she's talking, it's impossible to believe Lady Pat has no real horse knowledge, despite what she claims. The question is why doesn't she want Hattie to know? 'How do you—'

Her phone rings in her pocket, cutting her question short. Pulling it out, she looks at the screen and sees it's a local number, although not one she recognises. She presses answer. 'Hello?'

'Is this Harriet Kimble?' says a guy with a smooth tone and slight North London accent.

'Yes.'

'I'm Gareth Baker from the *Leightonshire Chronicle*. We'd like to do a local interest piece on the winners of High Drayton Horse Trials – you, the winner Daniel Templeton-Smith, and the owner of High Drayton Manor, JaXX. It'll be an interview and photo-shoot for our lifestyle section. Probably take about four hours. We're thinking Wednesday. Is that something you'd be interested in?'

'You want me to be part of a newspaper article?' says Hattie, frowning. 'I've never really…'

Liberty raises her eyebrows. Stage whispers, 'What paper?'

Hattie looks at Liberty and mouths, '*Leightonshire Chronicle*.'

'Yep, a feature,' says Gareth Baker. 'So is that a yes?'

'I don't really...' Hattie looks at Liberty who is nodding frantically. 'Are the others doing it?'

'I've got a confirmed yes from Daniel and JaXX,' says the journalist. 'It would be great to have you on board.'

Hattie doesn't like to draw attention to herself but maybe this is a good way to spread the message that natural horsemanship techniques can be useful in the competition world. And she liked Daniel and enjoyed their conversation at High Drayton; it would be good to see him again. She makes a decision. 'Okay.'

'Great. Give me your email and I'll send the details across.'

Hattie tells him and ends the call. She looks at Lady Pat and Liberty. 'They want to do an article about High Drayton in the *Leightonshire Chronicle*. JaXX, Daniel Templeton-Smith and me.'

'OMG, that's so exciting. Can I come with you?' says Liberty. 'JaXX is so hot. I thought I was going to faint when he was giving out the rosettes at your prize giving. I'd love to meet him, or even just lust after him from across the room.'

Hattie laughs. 'Sure you can come. As long as you don't faint.'

Liberty claps her hands together. 'I'll do my best.'

Lady Pat purses her lips and looks serious. 'You have to be careful with journalists. They have a habit of twisting things around and putting them out of context.'

'He sounded nice, though,' says Hattie, wondering if she's done the right thing in agreeing to the interview.

'They always do,' mutters Lady Pat.

CHAPTER THIRTY-FIVE
DEXTER

The week started well. Two of Lexi's horses won at High Drayton Horse Trials and Dexter sealed the deal with a couple of minor investors he'd taken along to spectate – low five figures apiece on one of his less exclusive investment opportunities, but every penny is welcome right now. Still, Lexi has been in a horrific mood all week – shouting, sulking and spending money even faster than usual. Every time they're in the same room, she snaps at him. Nothing he does is right. So he's doing his utmost to stay out of her way.

Here, now, squirreled away in his minimalist office at the top of the house, is the most calm he's felt all week. That is until the phone rings.

Dexter knows it's a serious investor because the call comes in on the red phone. He has two business phones as well as his personal one, and the red one is the 24/7 line for those clients who deserve the most premium of all premium services. He only gives the number to investors of multiple millions.

He snatches up the phone and answers within two rings. 'Dexter Marchfield-Wright.'

'Dex my boy, George Waterstock here.'

Dexter relaxes. George is his biggest and longest-term investor; whenever he calls, it's to invest more money. 'George, hello. How great to hear from you. How are you doing?'

'I'm good, thanks.'

'And Marcie and the kids?' says Dexter, wondering how much George is thinking of investing this time. Hopefully it's a big wedge, another million at least.

'They're great, all great, Dex, and that's sort of why I'm calling.'

Dexter detects something in George's voice, apprehension perhaps, and it bothers him. 'Okay, how can I help?'

George exhales loudly down the phone. 'So, here's the thing, Dex. I need to pull my money out. Cash in the investments.'

'Pull your money out?' parrots Dexter, staring at the limited-edition Mount Blanc pen on the white notepad beside his laptop. He brought that pen when he first landed George as a client all those years ago and it's still one of his most treasured possessions. Surely he can't have heard George right. 'How do you—'

'The kids left university this summer and they're just starting their first jobs. Hilary is moving to New York next month and joining a big consultancy, and Edwin will be based in Canary Wharf with his accountancy firm. You know how it is with the twins; they have very high standards, and so they're looking to me to set them up, help them on their way, you know what I mean?'

'Sure, George, I get it.' It's easy to have high standards if someone else is paying, thinks Dexter. 'So how much are you thinking?'

'All of it, my boy. Apartments in the city cost a packet if you want to live in anything bigger than a shoebox, and of course the twins need entertaining space, and spare rooms for myself and the wife to come visit.'

'All of it?' Dexter feels a cold sweat beading across his forehead as he tries to work out the total of what George has invested across the years. He struggles to keep a relaxed, charming tone to his voice but knows he must in order to have any chance of talking George into keeping some of the money invested. No one wants to do a deal with a desperate man. 'Now, George, mate, you're sure you don't want to keep a nominal amount in play? The returns have been increasing significantly again this year and I'd hate for you to lose out further down the line because you cashed out early. I'm sure I could work a special deal that'd let you buy the twins their properties and maintain a level of skin in the game.'

George lowers his voice. 'Personally, Dex old boy, I'd keep half of it with you, but the wife is putting her foot down on this. Says the kids need our help, so I'm afraid my hands are tied.' He clears his throat, his tone becoming more business-like. 'I've done my sums. Looks like, with the rate the assets have been appreciating, and give or take a few thousand in partial month dividends, I'm in with you for around nine million.'

'That sounds about right,' says Dexter, picking up the Mount Blanc pen and writing GEORGE – NINE MILLION on the notepad. It's almost a half million too low, but he isn't going to argue George up. There's a bitter taste on his tongue. He feels sick.

'Good, Marcie will be pleased. She's already picked out a London place and there are a few possibilities in New York.'

'Sounds like the apartment hunting is going well then,' says Dexter, trying to keep his tone light, while in his mind he's silently cursing that bitch Marcie and her meddling ways. The phone shakes in his hand as he asks the critical question. 'When do you need the cash?'

On the other end of the line, George inhales, sucking air in through his teeth. 'Well, that's the other thing. You know how these estate agent types are. Damn pushy bastards. They're urging a quick completion and Marcie wants to make it happen. So I'm going to need it by the end of October latest.'

'Right, end of October it is.' Dexter fights to keep his voice calm. Knows he mustn't appear panicked. Reputation is everything in this game. 'The twenty-eighth okay?'

'Perfect,' says George, the relief clear in his voice. 'And thanks for taking it on the chin, Dex my boy. You're a class act.'

'Always,' says Dexter through gritted teeth. 'Love to Marcie.'

Dexter ends the call. His heart is thumping against his chest, accelerating ever faster. It feels like he's trussed up in a straightjacket, the straps around his chest and throat tightening with every second. The phone falls from his hand onto the desk.

Oh God. Nine million will clean him out. He's got a few potential investors he's working on, but they won't bring in enough to pay off George and make all the dividend payments the following month.

He stares at the Mount Blanc pen on his desk as the invisible straightjacket continues to tighten. It feels as if his heart is going to explode. His throat goes dry. He can't catch his breath. Wide-eyed, he gasps for air.

This can't be happening. This *can't* be happening.

Whatever way he looks at it, he's completely and utterly screwed.

CHAPTER THIRTY-SIX

HATTIE

They were told to arrive for two o'clock. Hattie and Daniel Templeton-Smith have been here, waiting, since a few minutes before the hour. JaXX is late, twenty minutes and counting. Hattie thinks it's pretty poor considering the rendezvous location is the reception area of High Drayton Manor. Mind you, the house is seriously impressive. The huge foyer is lit by a chrome-and-crystal chandelier, illuminating the black-and-white marble floor, the wood panelling below tall white walls and the grand sweeping staircase.

In the last twenty minutes, Hattie's learnt that Gareth Baker, the journalist from the *Leightonshire Chronicle*, is fun but incredibly indiscreet. So far he's told her which local actor hit on him during an interview, which singer from the neighbouring county arrived high on coke for a photoshoot, and numerous scandals involving some of the great and the good across the Leightonshire county. Despite her nerves, Hattie can't help but smile.

Daniel, on the other hand, seems twitchy and on edge. He keeps fiddling with the cuff of his riding jacket and avoiding eye contact; he's nothing like the friendly, interesting person she chatted with at High Drayton Horse Trials. Maybe he feels as awkward as she does wearing her full competition outfit in a non-horsey setting. Or maybe he's nervous about the interview too. It's strange, but other than a quick nod and hello, he hasn't spoken to her once. Hattie tries not to let it get to her. She wishes Liberty was here; she'd been so keen to come but Gareth was insistent that only Hattie, Daniel, JaXX, himself and Milo the photographer could be in the house.

Glancing at her watch, she realises it's two twenty-four. She wonders what happens if JaXX doesn't show.

'Don't worry, he'll be here,' says Gareth. 'Trust me, musicians are always late.'

Daniel mutters something under his breath but Hattie doesn't catch it.

Gareth raises an eyebrow but lets it go. 'Now, did I tell you about the time I met...'

JaXX appears at the top of the sweeping staircase. He's wearing black jeans, a grey t-shirt and an oversized houndstooth hat. Hurrying down the stairs, he reaches for each of their hands and shakes them. 'Sorry to be a shit and keep you waiting. I was on the phone to LA about a collab, couldn't get them to shut up, y'know?'

'Sure,' says Hattie. JaXX has a warmth and friendliness that seems genuine.

'Are you ready to jump right in?' asks Gareth.

'Hell yeah,' says JaXX, gesturing for them to follow him across the foyer and into a massive kitchen. 'Let's set ourselves up in here. Less formal, yeah?'

'Great.' Gareth takes a seat at the huge island unit and sets his notepad and smartphone down on the white marble counter.

Hattie glances around the kitchen as she takes a seat opposite Gareth. The black-and-white theme is continued in here with dark grey cabinets and white marble counters. On the far side of the room, bi-fold doors line the whole wall, giving a perfect frame to the terrace and lawned gardens beyond. The view across the garden and out across the open countryside is stunning.

Daniel barely seems to notice. He climbs onto the stool beside Gareth and angles his body to face the journalist.

JaXX hops onto the stool beside Hattie. 'Okay, mate. Shoot.'

'We'll do the interview first, then the photos,' says Gareth. He looks at JaXX. 'So what made you want to host a horse trials at your home?'

'Why shouldn't I?' says JaXX, shrugging. 'The locals were all really welcoming when I moved here and it's a really horsey place. When Alan Winkler approached me, asking if he could use the grounds as a venue for an event – and promised me that he and the rest of the organising team would do all the hard graft – I thought why the hell not.'

Sitting on his right, Hattie is impressed by how relaxed JaXX is. He looks and sounds like he's having a chat with an old friend rather than a journalist. She, on the other hand, is feeling more anxious by the moment. It doesn't help that Daniel hasn't looked at her once; instead, his gaze seems locked onto Gareth. Clenching her hands together, she wishes she'd said no to the interview.

Gareth nods. Checks his notepad. 'And the proceeds are going to charity, is that right?'

'Yep, totally. We made just over ten grand, and I'm doubling it. It's going to the My Last Wish charity, which supports kids with terminal illnesses to tick a big-ticket adventure off their bucket list.' He lowers his voice a notch. 'It's a cause super close to my heart, mate.'

'Of course,' says Gareth. His voice changes, sounding sly. 'You funded the setup of the charity after the death of your daughter, Madison, aged three, isn't that right? I understand your marriage broke up shortly after—'

'I don't talk about my family,' says JaXX, the relaxed tone gone, replaced with one that's granite-hard.

'But your marriage was previously thought of as one of the strongest in—'

'This interview is terminated if you keep going with that question.' JaXX stares at Gareth. Doesn't blink. 'And you'll have to get out.'

For a long moment Gareth stares silently back. Then he nods. 'Cool. No problem. We'll put the details of the charity in the piece.' He turns to Hattie and Daniel. 'As local riders, it must be nice for you to compete on home ground?'

Keen to move them on from the subject of JaXX's family and the tension that caused, Hattie starts talking before she's thought of what to say. 'Yes, well, I—'

'Definitely, it's…' Daniel starts talking too. When he realises they're talking over each other, he stops and gestures towards Hattie but doesn't meet her eye. 'Ladies first.'

It's obvious that Daniel is deliberately trying not to look at her, but she pushes that from her mind. At least the few seconds' pause has given her time to collect her thoughts. 'I moved to the area a few months ago and High Drayton Horse Trials was the first time I've competed on Mermaid's Gold. It was so nice to have such a great event just up the road.' She looks at JaXX. 'Thank you.'

JaXX smiles warmly, the tension from moments earlier gone. His oversized black-and-white houndstooth hat is pulled down low on his brow. Beneath it, his eyes have a real twinkle. Even though he seems laid back, he has a kind of magnetism that draws you into looking at him. Hattie can see why Liberty is so keen on him. 'You're very welcome.'

Daniel's nodding, looking directly at Gareth. 'Yes exactly, having a quality competition on our doorstep is brilliant.'

'And you came in first and second on your horses, Daniel?' says Gareth, consulting his notes. 'That must have been satisfying after what happened at Badminton?'

'It was a really good day. I'm lucky that I've got good owners who support me.' Daniel's cheeks flush. His voice and smile seem a little forced.

'How's The Rogue doing?' asks Gareth.

'He's doing better,' says Daniel, looking less strained. 'He's been resting in his stable as the injury heals and can hopefully be turned out in the field soon to continue his rehab.'

'That's good news.' Gareth turns to look at Hattie. His previously friendly tone changes into something more cynical as he says, 'So I hear that you're rather unconventional in your training methods – is it right that you trained as a horse whisperer?'

A spark of anxiety flares in her chest. Hattie wonders where this line of questioning is going. She's seen how his friendly act can change, like it did with JaXX when he tried to get details of his marriage breakup. She doesn't want him coming after her. 'I spent some time in the States working with a world-renowned horse whisperer.'

'I see,' says Gareth, his tone sceptical. 'And does that help with your eventing?'

Hattie's throat goes dry. She'd naively assumed the journalist would be neutral but his tone makes it sound like he's got an agenda. She thinks back to Lady Pat's words when she agreed to do this interview: how journalists have a habit of twisting your words and putting them out of context. She swallows hard. She has to stand firm in her beliefs. 'It does. The horse I ride had a bad experience with her previous owners and had been labelled dangerous and unrideable before I got her. I used some of the horse whispering techniques I'd learnt out in the States to gain her trust and confidence.'

Gareth narrows his eyes. 'Is that right?'

'Yes, it is,' says Hattie, the irritation starting to show in her voice. 'If it hadn't been for what I'd learnt about horse whispering, I'd never have managed to put a halter on her, let alone get on her back.'

Gareth frowns. 'But surely—'

'I watched Hattie and her horse in action,' says Daniel, cutting off Gareth. 'They are a great partnership, totally in harmony. If that was created through using horse whispering, then I'd say it's a great endorsement that it works. It's not like horse whispering is new, anyway; it's been around for years. It's just not mainstream.'

'So you'd use it yourself?' says Gareth, turning to Daniel.

'If I had a need, yes. The horse world has moved on from blinkered tradition. We're sports people, athletes – both us riders and our horses. It makes sense to use different approaches to get the best performance.'

JaXX is nodding. He tips the brim of his hat back. Hattie realises his hair is dyed blue beneath it. 'Yeah, I totally get that. It's like that with music. You've got to move with the times. You can't ever stay static or the world will pass you by. Innovation, that's the key.'

'Exactly,' says Hattie. 'Every horse is different; you have to innovate and get creative to find the best training methods that work for them.'

'Interesting,' says Gareth, nodding as he scribbles down shorthand notes on his pad. The cynical tone has gone. 'I'm loving the parallels between music and equestrian sport here.'

Hattie isn't sure what just happened – did Gareth have an agenda or was he just being provocative? It's hard to know for sure. She's grateful that JaXX and Daniel had her back, though. She looks across the island at Daniel. He meets her gaze and smiles.

For the first time since arriving, Hattie relaxes.

～

The photoshoot is the weirdest experience of her life. She and Daniel are dressed in their riding gear as instructed: cream breeches, long black riding boots, shirts and stocks under black show jackets, and holding their jockey skull caps. JaXX looks like he's dressed for a different photoshoot – *NME* rather than *Horse & Hound*. He's wearing black denim jeans, studded biker boots, and a grey v-neck t-shirt. He still has his oversized houndstooth hat, and he's added a black leather jacket with red fringe along the arms.

They make a very mismatched grouping. It's fun, though.

As Milo, the photographer, positions them in various weird poses on the staircase, Hattie can't help but smile.

Milo is a cherub-faced man in his forties with a strong sense of drama. 'Serious face, now,' he says. 'Remember, you are fashion.'

Hattie has never 'been fashion' in her life and doubts she ever will be. And the photos are for the lifestyle section of the local magazine, not the cover of *Vogue*. But still, she tries to stay in the position Milo has put her into, even though leaning back over the banister at her current angle is making the muscle over her right hip spasm.

As Milo clicks away, directing them to change from one bizarre pose to another every few shots, Daniel catches Hattie's eye and they both smirk.

An hour later and it's all over.

'The feature will be in the magazine next month,' says Gareth, as Milo packs away his lighting equipment. 'We'll send you all a complimentary copy.'

They say their goodbyes and Hattie follows Daniel towards the door. Before she reaches it, she feels a hand on her shoulder. Turning, she sees it's JaXX.

'I've been meaning to ask,' he says, suddenly looking awkward. 'Can you give me your friend's number – the one you were with at the horse trials?'

Hattie smiles. It seems it isn't just Liberty who was taken with JaXX; he'd noticed her too. She wants to connect them, but needs to warn Liberty first. 'Why don't you give me your number and I'll pass it on to her?'

JaXX looks uncertain and for a moment Hattie thinks he's going to say forget it. She's heard that he's reclusive and values his privacy, so giving out his number could be a big deal.

But then he smiles. 'Okay, deal. You got any paper?'

In her pocket, Hattie finds a scrunched-up receipt. She gives it to JaXX and he writes his number on it and hands it back to her.

'I'll get it to her this evening.'

JaXX touches his hand to the brim of his hat. 'Appreciate it.'

Smiling, Hattie turns towards the exit. Daniel is standing in the now-open doorway, glaring at JaXX. As Hattie walks towards him, their eyes meet. He looks furious. With a shake of his head, Daniel turns and walks away.

CHAPTER THIRTY-SEVEN
DANIEL

The Dog and Duck is a proper village pub – good beer on tap, traditional pub grub and sport playing on the telly in the far corner whatever time of day you visit. It's Saturday night and so busier than usual, but it's still possible to get a seat. When Eddie suggested a yard team night out, Daniel was all for it – this weekend being one of the few he's not competing over the summer – but now he's here, the lively chatter and yesteryear hits playing on the elderly jukebox are grating on him. Even his pint tastes off.

'Come on, Danny,' says Jenny, nudging him with her elbow. 'You've got a right face on you. You need to lighten up – it might never happen.'

'It already did,' he snaps back.

Jenny puts her hand to her mouth. 'Oh, shit, I'm sorry, Danny. I didn't mean to... with The Rogue still not right...' She bites her lip, her cheeks colouring red. 'I didn't mean to imply—'

'It's fine,' says Daniel, holding up his hands. In truth it wasn't The Rogue's latest scan – the one that had shown only minimum improvement in the past six weeks rather than healing at the same good rate as the previous weeks – on his mind right then. It was Harriet – Hattie – Kimble he was thinking about, how she'd given JaXX her number after the photoshoot, and how even if Daniel had asked her first, he knows from Lexi's reaction after the prize giving at High Drayton that she'd be furious. 'I'm just feeling grouchy today.'

'And every day,' mutters Eddie under his breath as he feeds his three-legged rescue dog, McQueen, a pork scratching.

'What's that?' says Daniel.

Eddie looks over at him. 'All I'm saying is you've not been your usual cheery self for a while. We're all worried about Rogue, and I know he's your favourite, but we used to have fun while we got the work done and now...' He shrugs. Looks apologetic. 'I can't remember the last time we laughed.'

Daniel knows he's not been a barrel of laughs but he hadn't realised his mood had affected the team. He turns to Bunty, who's sitting quietly, sipping on her beer. 'Is that what you think too?'

She bites her lip. Looks from Daniel to Eddie and back again. 'Yeah. Sorry, boss.'

Daniel looks down at the table. It's oak and it would have been smart once but now it's pitted from use and ringed from all the drinks that have been put on it without a beermat's protection. That's how he feels right now: battle-scarred and used. It's not the team's fault, though. Without them, things would feel even worse. Exhaling, he looks back at them and forces a smile. 'Okay, so look. I'll try to be less of an arse in future.'

'You're not an arse, boss,' says Bunty, twisting a strand of her hair around her index finger. 'You've just seemed rather preoccupied.'

Daniel can understand that. 'I'll try to be more present then.'

'I'll drink to that,' says Eddie, grinning.

'How's you, anyway?' says Daniel, looking around the team. 'What's new?'

He sees a look pass between Eddie and Jenny.

'Well…' says Jenny, glancing meaningfully at Eddie. 'We have some news.'

'Yeah, we thought we'd put it out there, you know,' he says, grinning. 'Make it official.'

Smiling, Bunty gives a wry shake of her head. 'Like I didn't already know after the other night? You guys are not that quiet. And Eddie's room is right next to mine.'

Jenny blushes.

Eddie reaches across the table and takes Jenny's hand. 'What can I say? I like to please.'

'Ewww. That's disgusting,' says Bunty, wrinkling up her nose.

'Wait. What? You two are together?' says Daniel. He looks at Bunty. 'Am I the only one in the house who didn't know?'

'Looks that way,' says Eddie, feeding his dog another pork scratching and giving the black-and-white collie's ears an affectionate rub. 'Even McQueen here has given us his blessing.'

'Only because I bring him a bag of pork scratchings when I visit.' Jenny laughs.

Eddie nods, a fake serious expression on his face. 'Very true. He relaxed once he realised you weren't there on official vet business and weren't going to inject him or something.'

Daniel remembers how he suspected Eddie wasn't alone when he called late from the Marchfield-Wright party asking him to come and get him. How he guesses Jenny must have been with him although she wasn't at the house when they arrived back. He raises his beer in a toast. 'To the happy couple.'

Jenny pulls a face. 'Bit soon for that.'

'Oh, I don't know,' says Eddie.

Jenny's eyes widen.

Eddie laughs and clinks his glass against hers. 'Joking. Okay?'

'Phew. I can breathe easy again then,' says Jenny.

Daniel smiles but it feels forced. He's happy for Eddie and Jenny, of course, but them being together makes him feel a little more alone. It's ridiculous. He knows that. To compensate, he buys them all another round.

It takes him a while to get served. Mike Reynolds, the jovial owner and chief barman, is quick pulling the pints but the football has just ended so the old boys have moved away from the telly and are getting their drinks in, arguing over the best goal and the worst miss.

When Daniel gets back from the bar, Bunty has been persuaded to play pool by some lads from Church End Farm and from what Daniel can see she's currently winning. He's pleased; a few months ago, she would never have been confident enough to join their game.

Eddie's moved around to join Jenny on the bench seat along the wall, his arm now casually draped over her shoulder. Daniel sits down opposite them and puts the pints, plus another bag of pork scratchings for McQueen, on the table. 'Here you go.'

'Thanks,' says Eddie, taking a long drink and then opening the pork scratchings and tipping them onto the flagstone floor for McQueen.

'Cheers,' says Jenny, finishing the last of her previous pint and pulling the new one over to her. She looks at Daniel and narrows her gaze. 'You alright, Danny?'

He doesn't answer right away; watches McQueen hoover up the pork scratchings as he thinks what to say. He can hardly tell her the truth – that he got so close to running out of money that in order to keep the yard running he took a deal as a paid gigolo. How he swapped not sleeping due to money worries for not sleeping due to the stress of dealing with Lexi Marchfield-Wright and her demands. And he felt the start of a connection with Hattie Kimble at the interview but hadn't the courage to talk to her properly; that he'd been worrying if he did that, Lexi would find out and cause more drama. He runs his hands through his hair. Who's he kidding? It wouldn't have made a difference anyway – he'd seen JaXX swoop in and get Hattie's number at the end of the photoshoot; how could he compete with him? He meets Jenny's gaze. 'I'm okay.'

'Yeah right,' she says. 'This quiet moodiness really isn't like you, I think—'

'I know what'll cheer you up,' says Eddie, rubbing his hands together. 'Local gossip.'

'Oh yeah?' says Daniel, keen to get the pair of them away from him as a subject. 'What's going on?'

Eddie leans closer. 'Well, you might be able to add to what we know, actually.'

'Yes,' says Jenny. 'You kind of know them.'

'I do?' Daniel frowns. He has no idea who they're talking about.

'Well, you know JaXX because you did that photoshoot and interview together, right?' Jenny's eyes are shining. She lowers her voice. 'Apparently, as the village grapevine has it, he's got a new girlfriend.'

Daniel feels like he's been punched in the chest. JaXX is a fast mover, he'll give him that but damn, he only met Hattie a few days ago. He takes a long drink of his beer and tries hard when he replies to keep his tone light. 'Really?'

'Yes, her name's Liberty something. She makes vegan candles, apparently.'

'Liberty?' repeats Daniel. He remembers Hattie mentioning how sad her friend and neighbour, Liberty, had been because she couldn't come along to the photoshoot. 'She's called Liberty?'

'Yes, Lib-er-ty,' says Jenny, raising her eyebrows. 'Am I not speaking clearly enough for you?'

'No, it's just...' Daniel smiles as he works it out. JaXX's number *wasn't* for Hattie. He'd given it to her to pass on to her friend. Suddenly he feels lighter. His smile broadens into a full-on grin. 'So JaXX's new girlfriend is Liberty.'

'That's what I said, and I...' As Jenny continues talking about the rumour and where the new couple have been spotted, Daniel feels his mobile buzz in his pocket.

Pulling out the phone, he reads the name on the screen. His good mood dissolves as quickly as it arrived. 'Shit.'

'What is it?' asks Eddie.

'It's... I...' Daniel rereads the text.

It's from Lexi:

> Where are you?

As he's rereading it, another text appears from her:

> Tell me

Then a few seconds later, another:

> We have to meet now

Cursing under his breath, he reluctantly taps out a reply:

> At the Dog and Duck

Thirty seconds later, she replies:

> On way now. ETA 15 mins. Wait outside

Fourteen minutes later, he's made his excuses to Eddie and Jenny and waved goodbye to Bunty, who is still on a winning streak at the pool table. He's outside in the drizzle waiting for Lexi, just as she instructed. He hates himself for it.

She pulls into the car park with a squeal of tyres, sending puddled rainwater flying up and drenching his trainers and the bottom of his jeans. The electric window glides down and Lexi peers out at him. 'Get in.'

He does as she asks. The inside of the convertible Bentley is warm and dry. Lady Gaga is playing through the speakers. The car smells faintly of eucalyptus. He looks at Lexi. She's wearing a black raincoat and knee-high black suede boots. He forces a smile. 'Hi.'

She says nothing. Reversing back, she turns the car around and then drives to the far end of the pub car park, where it backs on to open fields. Braking to a halt at the fence, she turns off the engine and the lights. Even in the semi-dark, lit only by the full moon, Daniel can see her jaw is clenched and her lips are pursed into a thin line.

'So you wanted to see me?' he says, feeling anxiety twisting in his stomach.

She turns to face him. 'You made me look like a fool at my own party.'

'I didn't—'

She presses her fingers against his mouth. 'Don't deny it, and I don't want to hear excuses.'

'What do you...?' His words are muffled beneath her fingers.

Lexi presses her hand harder against his mouth. 'I said, shut up. You ran from the party and then you ignored me at that prize giving. And don't forget I saw the way you looked at that bloody rider – Harriet Kimble. But you can't have her. We made a deal. You're mine.'

He stays silent.

'Did you hear me?' She removes her hand from his mouth.

'I heard you.'

'Good. Now fuck me, for God's sake,' she says, undoing her raincoat to reveal nothing but a tiny red lace thong underneath. 'It's been forever.'

Daniel does as she asks. He has no choice. As she's just reminded him, it's part of why she pays him. He feels as if he's on autopilot, detached from what he's doing, but thankfully Lexi doesn't seem to notice. It's awkward in the car; the gears and the steering wheel make getting into the right position trickier. But, as he strokes her through the lace of her knickers, he hopes he's learnt enough about what she likes and what she doesn't.

He does his best to please her.

But it isn't good enough.

'What are you doing?' says Lexi, irritation clear in her voice. 'I told you to fuck me.'

'I... I'm...'

Swearing under her breath, she pushes him back against the seat and climbs on top of him. Grabbing his dick, she guides him inside her. Daniel's just thankful that he's managed to get hard this time. As Lexi rides him cowgirl-style, Daniel tries to fake pleasure. He makes the right noises and hopes it'll all soon be over.

It takes a while.

As soon as it's done, Lexi climbs off him. She re-buckles her coat and slides back over to the driver's seat. 'You can leave now.'

It's pouring with rain and it's several miles from home. He checks the time on the dashboard clock – it's well past closing; the team will be long gone. 'I don't have the Land Rover with me.'

'So walk then,' says Lexi as she switches on the car's engine and returns her seat to the upright position. 'I need to go. Dexter will wonder where I am.'

Realising she's serious, Daniel zips himself up and pulls his shirt and coat on. As he goes to open the car door, he looks back at Lexi. Hating himself a bit more, he asks, 'So are we good?'

She ignores him. Keeps staring straight ahead, like earlier. When he realises he's not going to get a response, he gets out of the car and shuts the door. He feels disgusting – no, worse than that, he feels used, weak and trapped. He curses the day he got involved with Lexi Marchfield-Wright. Maybe bankruptcy would have been better than this.

Trudging back across the otherwise empty car park towards the pub that's now in darkness and the road beyond, Daniel reckons it'll take him at least half an hour to get home. The rain's lashing down and the wind has picked up. His lightweight jacket is drenched within seconds. He steps in a puddle and feels the cold water seeping through his trainers and into his socks. He swears under his breath, pulls his collar up and walks faster.

As he reaches the road, Lexi's Bentley draws level with him, the driver's side window glides down and Lexi stares out. She's smiling but it doesn't reach her eyes. 'Remember, you're under contract, Daniel. We have a deal and you've been well paid. So if you so much as look at that girl again, I'll ruin you. I'll take my horses and I'll tell everyone that it's much more than your horse riding skills that are for hire.'

The venom of her words takes him by surprise.

He doesn't doubt she means them.

CHAPTER THIRTY-EIGHT

HATTIE

Hattie thinks she's going to be sick. Kingsland Park International Horse Trials is on a whole other level to High Drayton. From the lorry park filled with top of the range horseboxes, to the teams of grooms attending to the horses, and the owners with their designer clothes, Fortnum & Mason picnic baskets and champagne, everything is scaled up to the max.

And it's not just that. On her walk from the lorry park to the start of the cross-country course, she's passed three Olympic medallists, the winner of last year's Badminton and Kentucky horse trials, and two members of the royal family. Going from jumping makeshift fences in the paddock at home to competing here is a massive stretch. She hopes that they're ready.

Over to her right, the shopping village of tented trade stands is buzzing with people looking for a bargain, but after a week of heavy rain the grassy walkways are already turning to mud. At least the rain has stopped for now. Hattie hopes it'll stay dry for the rest of the competition.

On her left is the cross-country warmup area. It's currently empty – the cross-country phase won't start until tomorrow morning – so this is the perfect time to walk around the course and plan her strategy.

Hattie looks at her watch; it's a few minutes to one o'clock. She's not due in the dressage arena until quarter to five so she's got enough time to walk the course and then go back to prepare for the dressage. Ducking under the white ropes onto the course, she strides towards the first fence.

The course is big and imposing, but as she walks the route Hattie feels increasingly confident that Mermaid's Gold will handle it well. That confidence takes a knock when she arrives at fence fifteen, the water complex.

She stares at the challenge. The direct route has three jumping efforts, and the alternative route has four. The whole area has been given a nautical theme. She walks towards the first element, a maximum height post and rail with white-and-orange lifebuoys roped onto the rails. Going around the fence, she walks the distance from the first fence to the second, an identical post and rail decorated with lifebuoys on the edge of the lake. It's a large drop into the water, and three long strides from one to the other. Mermaid's Gold isn't likely to spook at the water, she's very bold, but the striding from the second fence to the third – an upturned boat painted orange and white that's anchored in the middle of the water – looks tight.

Glad that she wore her wellies, Hattie moves around the second fence and steps down into the water. It's higher than she expected – almost to the top of her boots – and she feels the coldness even through the neoprene lining. The heavy rainfall over the past week must have raised the water level. That's another aspect to consider; the deeper the water, the greater the drag on the horse's legs, and the higher the chance of a stumble or fall. She strides out the distance, converting seven of her own strides to one of Mermaid's Gold's. As she reaches the boat, Hattie's suspicions are confirmed. The distance is tight.

Wading back through the water and up the back to the first

element again, Hattie wishes Lady Pat and Liberty were here. She misses having someone to bounce her thoughts off. But Liberty has a stall at an artisan market in Radwick today, and Lady Pat isn't able to come until tomorrow. Leaning back against the rail of the first element, she looks at the direct and alternative route options, considering each in her mind.

'You decided how you're going to ride it?' The man's voice is familiar.

Turning, Hattie sees Daniel Templeton-Smith. Considering the last time she saw him he had a face like thunder and left without saying goodbye, she's surprised he's speaking to her. 'No, not yet.'

He moves around to join her on the landing side of the first element. 'Me neither.'

They stand together in silence. Hattie doesn't get why Daniel's not walking on. She needs to concentrate on the course, on her route, and it's hard with him standing so close. She tries not to be distracted, but she can't focus. The way he behaved towards her at the interview and photoshoot was so erratic, she can't tell if he likes her or can't stand her. It's confusing, and she doesn't have time for it.

He clears his throat. 'What are you thinking?'

'It's the striding,' says Hattie. 'The short route is the fastest option but tricky with a long three strides to a tight four. The alternative is going to take a lot longer unless you cut in front of the jetty between fences two and three, and that's very risky.'

'Yep.' Daniel walks between the first element and the second element of the direct route, a maximum height fence with a big drop down into the water. 'My horse isn't super keen on water. Might chip in an extra stride here.'

'Mine's more likely to fly it but if we land too far out in the lake it could make the striding to the third element difficult,' says Hattie. 'The water's pretty deep, and I've not jumped a fence in the middle of water before.'

'I saw you at High Drayton and you'll do great with that little horse of yours.' Daniel smiles. 'She's quick and smart, and you ride instinctively – I'd say go the straight route; you'll figure out the distance to the third element just fine.'

Hattie nods. She doesn't want to dwell on the compliment he's just given her, as who knows when he'll switch from being friendly to blanking her. Instead, she makes up her mind about the fences; the direct route is her best option. 'What about you?'

'Depends on my time. If I'm up on the clock at this point, I'll go the alternative route, but if I need to push on I might risk going straight.'

'Makes sense,' says Hattie. She doesn't ride with a stopwatch, unlike most of the other competitors, preferring to go with the speed that feels right to her and Mermaid's Gold rather than chase after the optimum time.

'You want to walk the rest of the course together?' asks Daniel.

Hattie meets his gaze. She wants to say no, he's too distracting, but there's something in his eyes, a hint of… something vulnerable that makes her say, 'Sure.'

As they walk on to the next fence, she hopes that she doesn't regret it.

CHAPTER THIRTY-NINE
DANIEL

Despite the drizzle and strong wind, Rocket Fuel is feeling surprisingly relaxed. The dressage is being held far from the rest of the event, in the deer park, and even though the rain has been relentless the old turf seems to be bearing up well considering.

As Daniel completes his warmup, cantering Rocket Fuel in large circles, he can't help but smile to himself. Meeting Hattie while walking the cross-country was unexpected. She seemed a bit reluctant to talk at first, but after the initial awkwardness they walked the rest of the course together and it was fun, more fun than he's had in a long time.

He feels happier, lighter. Rocket Fuel seems to have picked up on it too, and as Daniel asks the big gelding to go into a collected trot and practise some sideways movements, the horse responds with far more fluidity than usual. He repeats the exercise in canter and then drops the horse down to a walk and lets him have a long rein so he can stretch out his neck.

A dressage steward wearing a headscarf and waxed jacket waves her clipboard towards him and shouts, 'Number 118, you're in arena B now.'

'Thank you,' says Daniel, smiling politely as he turns Rocket Fuel towards the arenas.

They're set out in a row of three along the deer park fence. Along the fence are six white flag poles, the flags alternating between the British Eventing logo and that of the main event sponsor – a luxury car manufacturer. The judges are sitting five metres or so behind the arena boards at the markers for C, M and E. They each have a silver four-by-four with the sponsor's logo and the words 'OFFICIAL VEHICLE' on the doors.

As Daniel trots Rocket Fuel towards the arena, he takes a slightly firmer grip on the reins. The senior judge at the C end toots their horn as soon as he reaches the arena, but rather than start the test straight away, Daniel trots Rocket Fuel around the outside, determined to do a lap before entering. The big gelding can be spooky and with the wind and the flags he doesn't want hijinks to spoil their chance of a decent dressage score. He needs to let the horse see the flags and the judging cars before they begin and there should be enough time. You're allowed forty-five seconds to start after the signal before you get eliminated.

He's glad he used the time. As they get down to the C end of the arena, a gust of wind whips up the flags and they flap loudly. Rocket Fuel jumps forward a couple of strides, snorting.

'It's okay, boy,' says Daniel. 'It's not going to hurt you.'

The horse blows out and settles back into a good trot rhythm. Daniel's relieved the spook happened outside of the arena. Once he starts doing the test, he's not allowed to speak to the horse, and with three judges at different positions around the arena it's hard to get away with breaking that rule without being seen.

Taking a breath, Daniel asks Rocket Fuel to canter and makes the sweeping turn into the arena. He rides straight down the centre line and at X – the middle point – he asks Rocket Fuel to halt. The horse obeys and stands calmly with his ears pricked as Daniel salutes to the judges. Re-gathering his reins, Daniel asks the gelding to proceed in collected trot.

The trot work, with the shoulder-in and half pass, goes smoothly. And the rein-back – a halt followed by four steps backwards – that's so often forward-thinking Rocket Fuel's nemesis, goes much better than usual. As they start the canter movements, usually the gelding's strongest work, and do a great medium canter extension, Daniel is feeling hopeful of a good dressage mark.

That's when the heavens open and it really starts to pour.

Bowing his head a little lower, Rocket Fuel battles on against the driving rain. Daniel asks him to collect – shorten – his canter stride and they start the serpentine movement – three loops across the arena with a flying change across the centre line each time they cross it.

It's hard to imagine worse conditions for the dressage. But then it happens. Hail. Bigger than usual, hammering down. It's bouncing off Rocket Fuel's neck and back and it's all Daniel can do to keep the horse going forward and not twisting his body away from the hailstones. Still, like a trooper, Rocket Fuel maintains the canter and performs the flying changes on point.

Nearing the end of the test, Daniel tries to ignore the icy bullets pelting his face. They finish the canter section and return to a trot. Squinting through the hail as he turns the horse down the centre line for the last time, Daniel hopes the judges can see well enough to mark the movements.

As they halt at L for the final salute, the hail eases and softens into rain. As he salutes to each of the judges, Daniel can feel the water running down his face. His black competition jacket and cream breeches are heavy and sodden. The judge at C and her writer sitting in the car beside her give him a sympathetic smile.

The test over, he loosens his reins and turns Rocket Fuel back towards the exit of the arena. As they exit, he pats the horse's neck. Pleased with the test. 'Well done, boy.'

They head back across the deer park towards the warm-up area and the horse walk back to the lorry park. The rain has reduced to a light drizzle and Rocket Fuel shakes his head and then his whole body like a dog, getting rid of as much water as he can. Daniel wishes he could do the same.

'Well done.'

Daniel's heart leaps as he recognises the voice. Turning, he sees Hattie and her little chestnut mare walking over from checking in with the dressage stewards. 'Hey,' he says. 'You been yet?'

'Not yet,' says Hattie. 'I've just arrived – my test's in half an hour.'

'Hopefully the weather will be kinder to you,' says Daniel with a rueful smile.

'Hopefully,' she says. 'But the hail didn't seem to do you any harm. That was great.'

'Thanks,' says Daniel, giving Rocket Fuel another pat on the neck. 'He did good.'

They sit, their horses standing alongside each other, for a long moment. Daniel wants to keep the conversation going but knows that time is ticking and he's going to need a change of clothes before he goes to the show jumping.

'Well, I—'

'I really should—'

They both speak at the same time, and then stop, laughing.

'Good luck for your test. I'm sure you'll be brilliant.' Daniel gestures to himself. 'I'd better go and dry off.'

'Thanks,' says Hattie. 'See you later.'

'Definitely,' says Daniel. He's smiling as he turns Rocket Fuel back towards the horse walk. They've barely taken a couple of strides when the smile dies on his lips. There, a few metres away, sheltering beneath one of the huge oak trees, stands Lexi.

Arms crossed. Jaw clenched. Gaze narrowed. She's staring right at him.

She looks absolutely furious.

CHAPTER FORTY

HATTIE

The ground in the show jumping arena is as heavy and water-sodden as a bog. The darkening sky, relentless rain and sharp gusts of wind make it feel apocalyptic. But Mermaid's Gold doesn't seem to care. She easily leaps the last show jump – a tall vertical of red-and-white planks – and canters through the finish flags.

They're clear! Hattie can hardly believe it.

A whoop of joy goes up from the side of the ring. Looking over, Hattie sees Liberty jumping up and down, still whooping. Beside her, Lady Pat claps her hands, a broad smile on her face.

Rubbing Mermaid's Gold's neck, Hattie hears the commentator say, 'And that's a clear round for Harriet Kimble and Mermaid's Gold, keeping them on their dressage score and guaranteeing them to go forward to the cross-country in at least fourth place.'

Hattie rides towards the exit, grinning. As she reaches it, Daniel Templeton-Smith enters the arena on his bay gelding. He catches her eye. 'Well done, that was a great round.'

'Thanks.' She pats Mermaid's Gold again. 'Good luck.'

Back in the collecting ring, Lady Pat and Liberty huddle

around her and Mermaid's Gold. Hattie hears the buzzer go for Daniel to start his round. She pulls a packet of Polos from her breeches pocket and feeds a couple to Mermaid's Gold.

'Number 163,' calls the collecting ring steward, a pink florescent tabard draped damply over her waxed jacket. She pushes her rain-sodden trilby off her forehead. 'You've got two minutes before your round.'

There's a shout from the practice jump area. Number 163, a bouncy-looking grey horse with a male rider, jumps the practice fence and puts in a cheeky buck on landing. Behind them, a flushed-looking woman on an unhappy-looking chestnut turns her horse towards the practice fence. The horse plunges around the turn, fighting the woman's hard contact on the reins, then skids to a halt in front of the fence at the last moment, sending all the poles flying. The woman swears loudly and gives the horse two hard whacks on the backside with her stick. The horse bucks, drops its shoulder, and deposits her into the mud. Hattie feels the woman kind of deserved it.

'Super job,' says Lady Pat, patting Hattie's leg. 'You made it look easy.'

'She made it feel easy,' says Hattie, turning away from the collecting ring and stroking Mermaid's Gold's neck. 'How's the cross-country course riding?'

Liberty pulls a face. 'There seem to be a lot of problems.'

'It's the going. It's tiring a lot of horses,' says Lady Pat in a brisk, no-nonsense tone. 'But you'll be fine. Just kick on and this little mare will glide right over the top of it.'

Hattie hopes that she's right. Before she can answer, a cheer goes up from the side of the show jumping arena. Turning in the saddle, she sees a group of unlikely-looking supporters – four men holding golfing umbrellas over their dark suits and brown brogues, and a woman in a zebra print dress, Burberry mac and white Hunter wellies – slapping each other on the back and cheering as Daniel rides out of the arena.

'And that's a clear round for Daniel Templeton-Smith and Rocket Fuel, keeping them on their dressage score and in the lead as they head into the cross-country phase,' says the commentator.

Daniel exits the arena, patting a prancing Rocket Fuel on the neck, and looking rather embarrassed by all the attention. He nods towards the group but doesn't stop. The woman in the zebra print dress trots after him but Daniel doesn't seem to notice and the woman gives up and returns to the others in her group, scowling.

'Who's that?' asks Hattie, gesturing towards the group.

'No idea,' says Lady Pat with a shrug. 'Owners perhaps, but obviously not horse people. Look at what they're wearing; those suits will be ruined before the day is out.'

Lady Pat's right, thinks Hattie. If they are the owners of Daniel's horse, she hopes they don't give him a hard time for not advising them to wear more waterproof clothing.

'You riding back to the lorry park?'

Turning, Hattie sees Daniel and Rocket Fuel halting alongside her. Mermaid's Gold, not impressed with Rocket Fuel standing so close to her, swishes her tail and snaps her teeth at the tall bay gelding.

Hattie smiles. 'Sure.' She looks at Lady Pat and Liberty. 'See you back at the lorry.'

∽

Everyone they pass on the way back to the lorry park has a tale of woe to tell. Hattie tries not to let it get to her, but the butterflies in her stomach are ricocheting around in there as if they've got a death wish.

'It's bad,' says Fergus Bingley. 'After the second refusal, I put up my hand and called it a day. Dodger just wasn't moving across the country right, you know? And two refusals by fence seven – that's a strong message to quit.'

'You couldn't have done anything else,' says Daniel, sympathetically.

Hattie's shocked. Fergus is known for his precise riding and excellence over the more technical fences. If he retired from the competition less than halfway round the cross-country course, things must really be bad.

'Poor Aaron ended up on the floor at seventeen, those double corners,' says Bunnie Andrews, Aaron's Barbour-wearing wife. 'The striding is so hard to get in this going.'

Helga, Greta Wolfe's blonde head groom, joins them. 'It's tough. Greta got round okay. We were lucky she was first on the course before it got churned to hell. But Penelope Stockley was taken off in an ambulance, did you hear? They think it's a fractured ankle.' Helga grimaces. 'It'll put her out for months. Such bad luck. This weather is an asshole.'

'Yeah, it is that,' says Daniel. 'I hope Penelope feels better soon.' He looks at Hattie. 'We'd better go and get ready for battle.'

Hattie nods. The butterflies in her stomach are making her nauseous.

'Be careful out there,' says Heidi, before turning back to Bunnie and Fergus to continue gossiping about those who came a cropper out on the course.

'How are you feeling?' asks Daniel as they near his lorry.

'Nervous.'

'Good. Nerves keep us alert, make our reactions quick.'

Hattie hopes that's the case. She changes the topic. 'Have you decided about the water yet?'

'On this going, after all the rain overnight, I'm going to take the longer route and play it safe.'

'Sounds like a good plan,' says Hattie. 'Good luck.'

He stops Rocket Fuel next to his huge horsebox. It's metallic blue with 'DANIEL TEMPLETON-SMITH EVENT TEAM' along the side in silver. There must be room for at least six horses, and the living area between the cab and the horse area is almost as big as the full length of Hattie's rental lorry. The door into the living area is open and Hattie can see white leather seating and a fitted kitchen made from what looks like walnut. She hates to think how much something like that would cost. She meets Daniel's gaze and smiles. 'And you.'

∼

Back at her hired horsebox, Hattie untacks Mermaid's Gold and gives the mare a fifteen-minute break to relax before she starts to prepare their kit for the cross-country phase. Having offered her a drink, she leaves the horse tied to the outside of the lorry and goes up the steps into the tiny living area.

There's a cool bag with some refreshments on the bunk seating. She grabs a bottle of water. As she takes a long drink, she hears a phone vibrate on the counter. Reaching for it, she reads the text. Her eyes widen. It's from Robert:

> Good luck at Kingsland International today. R.

'What is it?' says Liberty.

'I've had a text from Robert. He's wished me luck for the competition,' says Hattie, frowning.

'Ah, okay.'

'Did you tell Robert you were here with Mermaid's Gold?' asks Lady Pat, her tone suddenly brusque.

'No. Didn't you tell him?'

Lady Pat shakes her head. 'And why would I do that, dear?'

Hattie tries not to let it bother her that he knows; after all, the text is nice enough. Still, someone must have told him. She shudders. Hates the idea that she's being spied on.

It has to be Bill. There's no other person who'd know she's competing here today.

Question is, why does Robert care enough to wish her good

luck?

CHAPTER FORTY-ONE

LEXI

*H*e's disobeyed her. Twice. And she will not stand for it.

Stomping through the muddy lorry park towards the damn expensive horsebox she bought for the ungrateful bastard, Lexi thinks of what she'll say to Daniel, and how she'll say it. She needs to get through to him. He obviously isn't taking her seriously. Because she was very clear before. She explicitly told him not to so much as look at Harriet Kimble again. But he's broken her instruction twice already today, once by the dressage and again at the show jumping. He even had the audacity to ride back to the lorry park with the girl. It's as if he doesn't care. But he will care. Lexi will make sure of that. He'll regret not taking her seriously.

She turns along the row towards the horsebox. The rain is starting again and she curses, frustrated that yet another outfit is going to be ruined with mud and damp before the end of the day. It's all Daniel's fault. The bastard.

Up ahead, she can see the lorry. There's a horse tied up outside it, the brown one; she can't remember its name. The groom is rubbing white lube down the creature's legs.

'Daniel?' Lexi calls. 'We need to talk.'

A man walking a shivering whippet glances at her from beneath his baseball cap. A woman untacking a small grey horse next to a tatty green lorry turns to look at her. Let them look; Lexi doesn't care. She needs Daniel's attention, and she needs it now. These other people can sod off.

As she reaches the lorry, Daniel emerges down the ramp at the back. He's wearing cross-country gear which makes him look like a jockey. When he sees her, a pained expression crosses his face.

'We need to talk – now,' says Lexi, striding across to him.

He dodges past her, towards the horse. 'We're a bit busy at the—'

'I don't give a crap how busy you are.' Lexi turns and follows him, prodding him on the shoulder with her fingers. Jab. Jab. Jab. 'You'll listen to me.'

As she passes the groom, his cheeks flush, but he keeps on with greasing up the horse's legs. Good, thinks Lexi. You're the help. Don't get involved; know your place.

She squares up to Daniel. Looks into his eyes. 'I told you not to speak with that bitch. I said not to even look at her. But you've been with her twice today already.'

'I've been cordial. I can't ignore her.'

'You can and you will.' Lexi leans closer to him, her words coming out in a snarl. 'If you don't, I take the horses away and sue you for breach of contract. And, as I said before, I'll tell everyone in your precious eventing world that you are a gigolo for hire – nothing more than an expensive escort. What will your friends and your precious little Harriet think then?'

She watches as the fear flashes across Daniel's face.

Good. He should fear her. Because she will ruin him if he doesn't do as she says. 'So remember, darling. I own you.'

She sees him swallowing hard. He's turned pale.

Nodding, he says, 'Okay.'

Over by the horse, the groom has finished with the leg grease and is walking the horse round. Lexi wonders if the groom heard any of the conversation. It doesn't matter a jot to her if he has. Victory feels sweet. She smiles at Daniel. 'Good. So stay away from the little bitch and win me this competition. No excuses.'

Daniel holds her gaze a moment longer, then walks over to the big brown horse. Putting his foot into the stirrup, he jumps up onto the horse's back then looks down at Lexi. 'Hattie isn't the bitch.'

Lexi narrows her eyes. 'You're going to wish you hadn't said that.'

Daniel doesn't respond. Doesn't even look at her. Instead, he starts adjusting a strap around the saddle. Talking to the groom as he does so. Ignoring her.

Rage flares inside her. How dare he ignore her? She throws the only thing she has to hand – her Lulu Guinness golfing umbrella. It hits Daniel on the thigh and whacks against the horse's lower belly. The horse scoots sideways, almost dislodging Daniel, and then rears into the air, snorting.

'What the hell...' says Daniel, battling to get the creature under control.

'Don't cross me, darling,' Lexi says, her tone hard as steel. 'Because you will always lose.'

～

She waits with Dexter and his investor friends along the ropes by fence fifteen – the water complex. All their umbrellas are up, but it's still hard not to get wet. The rain is pelting down and the wind gusts around them, sending the rain in every direction. In the last few minutes, the sky seems to have darkened further. Thunder rumbles overhead.

That's when Daniel gallops into view.

He runs along the outer ropes, and then begins to gradually

swing left towards the fences. It's as he starts his turn that their eyes meet. Lexi frowns. Daniel's eyes widen. Next moment he takes a harder pull on the left rein and changes course, switching from the longer, safer route to the direct approach.

The big brown horse, Rocket Fuel, jumps the first of the post and rail fences with orange-and-white lifebuoys strapped to them, and canters on to the second. Lexi is no expert at this stuff, but she overheard the people standing nearby talking and apparently the horse should take three long strides between the first and second fences. But Daniel's horse, Rocket Fuel, does something different. He spooks as he sees the water beyond the second fence, and tries to chip in an extra stride.

There isn't enough room. The creature tries to stop, but his speed carries him forward and he hits the fence with his front legs. Momentum keeps his back end moving, and although the pin releases to drop the rail to the ground, it's too late. Rocket Fuel and Daniel somersault over the fence and down into the water.

The horse is up on its feet quickly, shaking water off itself like a dog. Daniel stays under the water, splashing. The spectators all peer towards the jump, trying to see what's happening. The jump judges, an elderly pair who'd been sitting in their four-by-four out of the rain, open their doors and hurry across the grass towards the water.

Over the loudspeaker, the commentator announces, 'And Daniel Templeton-Smith and Rocket Fuel have fallen at the water complex at fifteen.'

There's a cry from a Joules-clad, headscarf-wearing woman along the ropes. 'His foot's caught.'

The male fence judge has made it to the edge of the water. The horse, spooked by the man, leaps sideways and then takes off across the water, dragging Daniel, whose foot is caught in the offside stirrup. The crowd gasps. The man hurries around the water to the other side to try and head Rocket Fuel off, arms extended, trying to grab the horse's flapping reins.

Rocket Fuel dodges to avoid the jump judge and somehow the movement causes Daniel's foot to become dislodged. He's left sitting in the water, coughing and wheezing, as the horse gallops off up the course towards the finish.

'Damn it,' says Dexter, to Lexi and his investors. 'That's our winning chances screwed. We may as well go and have some drinks in the bar.'

There are murmurs from the crowd: *Is he okay? Did he get hurt? Is he moving okay? That had to hurt.*

'We're waiting for word on Daniel Templeton-Smith,' says the commentator over the loudspeaker. 'But it looks like Rocket Fuel is set on finishing the course riderless.'

As the ambulance slithers through the mud towards where Daniel is still sitting in the water, Lexi stands stock still, watching.

She doesn't rush to help Daniel. And she doesn't run after the horse.

She just smiles to herself and thinks, thank you, karma.

CHAPTER FORTY-TWO

HATTIE

Hattie's next to go on the cross-country. Daniel is already out on the course with Rocket Fuel. She hears the news when she's beside the starting box, just after the starter has given her the one-minute warning.

The commentator's voice comes over the loudspeakers. 'And Daniel Templeton-Smith is eliminated on Rocket Fuel after a fall of horse and rider attempting the direct route at fence fifteen, the water.'

Daniel said he was going to take the longer route. She wonders what made him change his mind. She hopes he's okay. The thought that Daniel or Rocket Fuel might be hurt makes her feel nauseous.

'Forty-five seconds,' says the starter, writing something on his clipboard.

It feels as if the butterflies in her stomach are gnawing at her intestines. Vampire butterflies. She's never felt this nervous before. If Daniel with all his experience has fallen, what hope does she have of getting round? So many top riders have failed to finish the course. Maybe it would be safer, better, to withdraw.

'Don't even think it,' says Lady Pat. 'Mermaid's Gold is a star and you'll be fine.'

'But what if I can't—'

'Snap out of it.' Lady Pat gives Hattie a firm pinch on her thigh. 'Forget about everything else. Concentrate on the fences. Take it steady and listen to the mare. She'll tell you if she's not comfortable and if she tells you that, then you pull up and retire. But don't give up before you've started. Not when you've come so far.'

Hattie knows it makes sense. Nodding, she swallows down her fear.

'Thirty seconds,' says the starter.

'Good luck,' says Lady Pat. 'You can do this.'

'You've got this,' says Liberty, giving her the thumbs up.

'Thanks,' says Hattie through gritted teeth so she doesn't vomit with nerves.

'Ten seconds,' says the starter. 'Nine, eight, seven, six…'

Hattie rides Mermaid's Gold into the start box. Strokes the mare's neck.

'… two, one, good luck.'

And they're off. Mermaid's Gold canters happily towards the first fence. Hattie sits lightly out of the saddle, crouched forward slightly, making sure she's in the optimum position for keeping in balance with the mare. It's the two of them against the fences now.

∼

The rain is coming down in sheets. Hattie can barely see a few strides ahead. But still Mermaid's Gold keeps jumping. They're approaching fence fifteen, the water complex. Heart in her mouth, Hattie turns towards the first element and looks for her line. She's sticking to her original decision and going the direct route.

Mermaid's Gold pops over the first set of rails with the orange-and-white lifebuoys easily. She takes three long strides and leaps over the second fence and down the drop into the water with gusto. Hattie's ready for her enthusiasm this time, and sits back, letting her reins slip through her fingers to the buckle so the mare can use her head and neck to balance as she lands. It's as they take their first stride towards the upturned boat that Hattie realises she has a problem. Her right foot is suddenly unsupported. There's something wrong with the stirrup. But she can't stop to fix it or she'll get penalties for presenting at the fence. She has to keep going. Gripping her leg tight to Mermaid's Gold's belly, she gives the mare her head and hopes she can stay onboard.

The mare sorts out the striding easily, taking a long three strides rather than a tight four, and springs over the upturned boat. As they gallop out of the water, Hattie glances down at her right foot. The stirrup is hanging upside down, the stirrup leather – the strap that connects the stirrup to the saddle – beneath it. Something has gone wrong; the leather could've slipped off the bar that connects it to the saddle or the strap has snapped. Either way, she won't be able to get the stirrup attached before the end of her round. For a moment, Hattie considers whether she should pull up, but Mermaid's Gold is jumping so well and seems so happy, she doesn't want to. So Hattie kicks the stirrup and its flaccid leather off her foot, choosing to ride the rest of the course without it.

They fly over the next few fences. It's harder to balance without the right stirrup but Mermaid's Gold has such a smooth gallop, Hattie is managing to stay in position. They take the direct route at the quarry – jumping up the three big steps cut into the hillside – and gallop on towards the last of the big technical questions – the double corners at fence seventeen which took out Aaron Andrews.

The corners are sited on undulating ground at the top of the hill. This is the most exposed part of the course, and as they ride towards the fences the wind buffets them from the left and the driving rain turns to hail, pelting them hard. The ground up here is worse than lower down, the dips in the undulations have collected the water and turned into quagmires. Heart pounding, Hattie's afraid Mermaid's Gold will slip and fall.

As they prepare to turn towards the corners, Hattie asks the mare to steady. Mermaid's Gold responds, but as they straighten up and Hattie looks for her line between the fences she realises her mistake: she's slowed the horse too much and now they don't have enough impulsion.

The corners loom through the rain, bigger and more solid than she remembers them. Squeezing her legs against the horse's sides, she urges Mermaid's Gold forward. 'Come on, girl.'

The mare tries to accelerate through the boggy ground. With a huge effort, she leaps over the first corner, the suck of the mud loud as they take off, and lands steeply the other side. Hattie pushes her on. Sees that they'll need to put in an extra stride to be safe, and rides the distance accordingly. Mermaid's Gold listens, and they reach the second corner on a better stride. She springs over the fence, clearing it easily. But as they land, she slips badly on the waterlogged turf.

Hattie holds her breath. She sits upright. Doesn't interfere, knowing that Mermaid's Gold is the only one who can stop them falling. She grabs the horse's mane and prays that the mare can recover her balance.

With a grunt, Mermaid's Gold propels herself up and forwards. As they gallop away down the hillside, the mare gives a shake of her head, as if to say, 'Well, that was close.'

Hattie pats her neck and is able to breathe again. 'Thank you.'

The mare blows out like it was no big deal.

Two fences later and Mermaid's Gold is still full of running; it's Hattie who feels like she's hitting a wall. Her right leg is cramping from gripping around the horse's belly without the stirrup and all her muscles are aching from trying to stay up out of the saddle as best she can. At least the rain is starting to ease and they're only one more jump from home.

The final fence is in the shape of a giant horseshoe and painted bright silver. It's a weird-looking fence after so many rustic jumps, and Hattie hopes that Mermaid's Gold won't spook; she doesn't think she has the strength to stay on her if she does.

Hattie doesn't need to worry. Mermaid's Gold leaps over the last fence without hesitation and gallops through the finish flags. Over at the side of the ropes, Liberty and Lady Pat are cheering and hugging each other.

Leaping off Mermaid's Gold, Hattie loosens the mare's girth and throws her arms around her neck. 'You did it, girl. You did it.'

As Lady Pat and Liberty rush over to join her, Hattie feels like she's being watched. She glances back towards the finish and sees the woman in the zebra-print dress and white wellies that she'd last seen in the show jumping collecting ring is standing there motionless. Her fists are clenched. Her posture is rigid. And as their eyes meet, the woman scowls, seemingly furious.

Hattie has no idea why.

CHAPTER FORTY-THREE

HATTIE

Hattie is in shock. They won. They actually won.

It seems unbelievable, like a dream that's happening to someone else. She feels as if she's in a daze as she tucks up Mermaid's Gold for the night. She puts the blue Thermatex rug that Lady Pat bought at one of the trade stands on the mare and checks that her leg bandages, covering the kaolin clay that helps to alleviate any strain or bruising, are in place. Rather than being at home now as planned, the storm has become so violent that Hattie has decided to stay the night at the event in the stabling onsite. She'll drive home tomorrow when the weather forecast is better. Lady Pat and Liberty left a couple of hours ago; they'll feed the goats and the dogs.

It's dark outside, and the wind gusting around the lines of tented stables makes the canvas roof lift and fall in time to its rhythm. Still, the inside feels cosy and Hattie's made Mermaid's Gold a thick bed of wood shavings. The mare seems happy as she munches on her hay. Most of the other riders and grooms have gone back to their lorries for the night, but Hattie wanted some time with Mermaid's Gold alone without the constant banging of stable doors and chatter of people. Now, as the last person besides her leaves, a quiet calm descends on the temporary yard.

Hattie rubs Mermaid's Gold's neck. 'You were amazing. Thank you for looking after me. You deserved to win.'

The mare blows out, as if to say it was nothing.

Hattie smiles. It wasn't nothing; it was incredible. Lady Pat is already talking about Hattie and Mermaid's Gold getting some more experience at this level over the rest of the autumn and the first half of next season, and then aiming for Blenheim International. It sounds good to Hattie, but she can't focus on the future. Right now, she wants to enjoy this moment.

'You did good,' says a Yorkshire-accented male voice.

Hattie flinches. She thought she was alone. Looking round, she sees show jumper turned eventer, Fergus Bingley, as tall and willowy as ever, leaning over the stable door. She smiles. 'Thanks.'

He gestures to Mermaid's Gold. 'If you ever think about selling her, give me a call. She was a real machine out on the cross-country.'

Just the idea of being separated from the horse makes Hattie feel sick. 'Sorry, but she's not for sale.'

'Like I said, give me a heads-up if you change your mind.' Fergus glances over his shoulder. Lowers his voice. 'There's a lot of people with their eye on her after today's performance. Just remember I spoke to you first.'

'Sure.' Frowning, Hattie turns back to the horse and rechecks her rug is in the correct position and the straps fastened with just the right amount of tension to keep it in place but also allow her to move. As she adjusts one of the buckles, her fingers tremble. She can't bear the thought that Mermaid's Gold could be sold.

In the low glow of the temporary lighting, Hattie leans against the mare and puts her arm over her back. She rests her head on the side of Mermaid's Gold's belly and closes her eyes. She inhales the aroma of sweet meadow hay and horse. Listens to

Mermaid's Gold's rhythmic chewing and steady breathing, the canvas roof flapping above them, and the sounds of the other horses in the forty or so other stables eating and resting. Hattie smiles. This is her happy place. Mermaid's Gold and her together.

That's when the realisation hits her.

These past few weeks have been the happiest she's felt in months.

∼

It's a short walk from the temporary stabling to the lorry park, but with the mud sucking at her boots with every step the distance feels longer. At least the rain has finally stopped and the wind is beginning to fall. Hattie takes a right into the row of horseboxes where her rental is parked. Most of the lorries are occupied. There's music coming out from the open door of the four-horse Bedford TK on her left, and a multi-coloured strobe light is visible through the window of the living area. As she walks past, she hears a guy doing a passable karaoke rendition of a Coldplay song.

Continuing on along the row, she sees three people sitting around a picnic table inside the tented awning attached to a huge lorry. They're laughing and joking. Hattie doesn't know who they are – the only lights at the table are a couple of candles so the people are in shadow – but whoever it is, she isn't in the mood for jokes. She's worrying about Fergus's interest in Mermaid's Gold, and what he said about other people wanting to buy her. Head down, she hurries past.

'Hey, Harriet, isn't it?' calls a man as she gets level with the group. 'Come and join us.'

She doesn't want to stop, but she doesn't want to seem rude either. She steps towards them, and in the light of her phone's torch she sees the man who spoke to her is Jonathan Scott, the medal-winning Australian rider. German Olympic medallist

Greta Wolfe is sitting beside him, and the oracle of the eventing world, Daphne Wainscoat, is opposite. If she wasn't so knackered, she'd stay and chat, but right now all she wants to do is get back to the lorry and sleep. 'It's Hattie, actually. I'm just going back to my—'

'Cheer up, kid. You won,' says Jonathan, grinning. 'And that's a bloody good day from where I'm sitting.'

'Ha! Where you sat today was in a muddy ditch at fence eight.' Greta laughs, slapping him on the back.

'Fuck the fuck off,' says Jonathan good-naturedly. 'Mud's good for the skin.'

'Join us for a tipple so we can toast your success,' says Daphne, raising an almost empty sherry glass. While Daphne's attention is on Hattie, Sheridan the terrier jumps up and takes what looks to be the remains of a steak off her plate. Daphne drains the rest of her sherry but doesn't seem to notice her dog is making quick work of her dinner under the table. 'Come on, do have a drink, and tell us all about yourself.'

Hattie thinks Daphne's had more than enough sherry already. 'Thanks, but I need—'

'You must celebrate!' Greta pours some sherry into a glass and thrusts it into Hattie's hand. She clinks her own against it. 'To success and more success.'

'Yes, jolly good work today,' slurs Daphne, holding her glass out for Greta to refill and then tapping it against Hattie's. 'Go on, drink up.'

Hattie takes a sip and grimaces. The sherry is disgusting – thick as cough medicine and far too sweet.

'Sit, dear, sit,' says Daphne, swaying as she gestures to the empty chair between her and Jonathan. 'There's some snacks too, if you fancy them.'

Reluctantly, Hattie sits down. Daphne is pretty much eventing royalty, as are Jonathan Scott and Greta Wolfe. She'll be polite and quickly drink the disgusting sherry, then leg it as soon as she can.

'It's pretty impressive, what you did,' says Jonathan, leaning closer towards Hattie. 'Mermaid's Gold had been totally written off as a dangerous ride and you had her jumping round this bloody awful track like one of the best.'

'She was never dangerous. Just misunderstood.' Hattie takes a gulp of the sherry. Tries not to gag.

Jonathan doesn't seem to notice. There's a mischievous glint in his eye. 'Very true, and I'm glad you understand her. I've always liked that little horse.'

Hattie tenses, sensing he's going to ask her something and fearing he's after buying Mermaid's Gold like Fergus. 'She's not for—'

'So tell me.' He lowers his voice. 'You're a horse whisperer, right?'

Hattie's not sure what to say. The question is unexpected. Suddenly she's aware that Daphne and Greta have stopped their conversation and are waiting for her to answer. She swallows hard. 'I trained out in the US.'

'And did you whisper to Mermaid's Gold?' says Daphne, leaning so close towards her that Hattie can see the whiskers on Daphne's chin and the bloodshot whites of her eyes. 'What did you say to her?'

'You don't actually whisper,' says Hattie. Taking another gulp of the sherry. 'It's more groundwork techniques to gain trust and respect, and then using the horse's instinctive responses to work for you.'

'Interesting,' says Greta, nodding.

Hattie frowns. She's not sure if Greta is taking the piss.

'I have a friend into dressage over in the States. They had a very difficult horse. He was ring shy. A natural horsemanship person fixed it.' Greta nods. 'Was very good. Horse does much better now.'

'How'd you get into eventing?' asks Daphne, her beady eyes peering over glasses that have slid halfway down her nose. 'Do the rest of your family ride?'

Hattie swallows hard as a wave of grief slams into her chest. 'My mum used to work with horses.'

'Aha!' says Daphne, nodding knowingly. 'So it's in the blood. I thought as much. Did your mother—?'

'Stop interrogating the poor girl,' says Jonathan, laughing. He gestures towards the bottle of sherry. 'You don't have to have another glass of that shit. Have something better – wine, beer, whiskey?'

'No, I'm fine, thanks. I need to get back.' Hattie stands up to leave. She can feel the alcohol kicking in, mixing with the grief that's sitting like a brick in the pit of her stomach. Tears prick at her eyes. She wants to shake off the melancholy. Stop thinking about how Mum would have loved to have been here, sharing in the win. And more alcohol isn't going to help.

'Sure?' says Jonathan, giving her a meaningful look. He glances at Greta and back to Hattie. 'Fancy joining us for a nightcap a bit later?'

Hattie's heard the rumours about Jonathan and how partial he is to threesomes. She doesn't have the energy or the inclination. She shakes her head. 'No, I'm okay, thanks.'

Jonathan shrugs, and says affably, 'Got to ask, haven't you. But, look, on the horse front, if you ever want a job, I've got a few tricky youngsters that could do with some of your magic.'

He seems sincere, but he's obviously had quite a bit to drink so Hattie's not sure if the offer of work is real. It's mid-September and after New Year, Robert will return to Clover Hill House and she'll have to move out and find another job. She doesn't want to think about that right now, but she doesn't want to close the door on a job with Jonathan entirely. She smiles. 'Thanks. I'll think about it.'

As she walks back to her rented lorry, happiness and grief wrestle within her.

CHAPTER FORTY-FOUR
DANIEL

He's had a couple of drinks. Okay, maybe more than a couple, but he needed something more than paracetamol to dull the ache in his shoulder and leg from the cross-country fall and the guilt of what an idiot he was to let Lexi's demands affect his decision on the route he took at the water. Poor Rocket Fuel didn't deserve the ducking. Now he's going to be even more reluctant to get his feet wet and Daniel's going to have to put in some serious time regaining the gelding's confidence.

As he sits on the steps to the little wooden-sided lorry's living area, he thinks again about Lexi's hissed warning that he must stay away from Hattie. He takes another sip of beer. Runs his hand through his hair. He's sick of Lexi bossing him about, treating him like a piece of meat and, with several beers inside him, he feels the courage to say 'fuck it' to all her rules. He never should have agreed to her absurd requirements in the first place. He wishes he could go back and do it over again, and this time not entertain the idea for one second.

He wants to feel less whipped. Like he's his own man again.

Maybe that's why he's here, waiting.

It's pretty dark now, and although the rain has finally stopped, the air is damp and the night's getting colder. He's not sure how long he's been sitting here; half an hour, an hour maybe. Most people are in their lorries; there are lights on behind the drawn curtains. Lights off in some cases. It's a close-knit community, the eventing world, and because of that both relationships and friends with benefits are common. Daniel shivers, and hopes he hasn't made a mistake; maybe she's not coming back to her own lorry tonight. Pulling his Puffa tighter around him, he hunkers down and closes his eyes.

'Hey.'

Daniel looks up with a start. He must have fallen asleep. Smiling, he says, 'Hey yourself.'

She looks puzzled. 'Are you…?'

'Waiting for you? Yes.' He clears his throat. Rubs his face to wake himself up. 'I wanted to congratulate you on the win. You did a fantastic round.'

'Thanks. Mermaid's Gold was amazing.' She's smiling at him. Looks happy to see him. 'I'm sorry about your fall. Is Rocket Fuel okay? Are you?'

'He's not injured but I expect he hates the water even more than before.' Daniel gives her a rueful smile. 'And I've never enjoyed falling in water.'

She smiles at his feeble attempt to make light of things. 'I heard you tried the direct route? I thought when we walked it, you decided to go the long way?'

He sighs. 'I made a bad decision. The owner was pressuring me for a win and I stupidly let them influence me.'

'Everyone makes mistakes,' says Hattie. She gestures to the lorry. 'It's cold out here, do you want to come in?'

'Sure.'

He follows her up the steps into the living area. It's about as far from his new lorry's interior as it's possible to be. Instead of white leather seating, a fully-fitted kitchenette and a flat screen

TV with surround sound, Hattie's lorry has a Formica table with a bench seat, a tiny sink and a one-ring travel stove, and a mattress to sleep on in the Luton over the cab.

It's basic, functional, and he much prefers it.

'Coffee? Tea?' asks Hattie, tipping a bottle of still water into the kettle on the single gas ring.

'Coffee, please. One sugar, no milk.'

'That's good because I don't have any milk left.' She turns on the gas to heat the kettle and spoons coffee into two mugs. 'There's some biscuits in the Tupperware container. Feel free to help yourself.'

'Nice place you've got here,' Daniel says.

'It's a rental but it does the job.' Hattie turns to face him. 'One day I aspire to having a lorry like yours.'

He laughs, although it's not a happy sound. 'Fancy lorries aren't always all they're cracked up to be. Some come with a lot of strings attached.'

Hattie raises an eyebrow. 'Owner problems again?'

'Same owner. Always a problem.' He forces a laugh, trying to make light of it, but doesn't quite pull it off. Still, he doesn't want to spend this time with Hattie talking about Lexi. 'They're a necessary evil sometimes. I couldn't run my yard without the support of my owners, and most of them are amazing. But some are higher maintenance than others.'

'Mermaid's owner seems easy-going so far,' says Hattie, turning off the gas as the boiling kettle starts to whistle. 'I guess I should be thankful for that.'

'I didn't realise she wasn't yours,' says Daniel. 'I just assumed...'

'No, Lady Babbington owns her.' Hattie pours the water into the mugs. 'I just got lucky.'

'From seeing the two of you in action together, I'd say you both got lucky. And very few people could have won her trust the way you did. I heard what happened to that horse. The word is that she was unrideable before you worked your magic.'

'My horse whispering magic? Thanks.' Hattie's smile fades into a frown and she stirs sugar into the coffees. 'I worry about losing her sometimes, is that crazy? I don't own her and there are far more experienced riders out there Lady Pat could put her with. I had Fergus Bingley ask whether she's for sale this evening. He said there are others after her too. If they offer a lot of money, then maybe Lady Pat would be tempted.'

Daniel knows it can be hard for owners to resist when other people start offering silly money for a horse. After Mermaid Gold's win today, she will have caught the eye of other people; Fergus Bingley is probably just the tip of the iceberg. But he doesn't want to say that and add to Hattie's worry. 'Do you really think that's likely? Has Lady Babbington said anything?'

Hattie shakes her head. 'No, she seems happy enough and is already talking about the next competition to aim for.'

'Then don't worry,' says Daniel. 'Just enjoy your win.'

'Thanks,' says Hattie, passing him a mug of coffee. 'I'm just… it's all so new and Mermaid really is the horse of a lifetime.'

Daniel cups his hands around the mug, warming his hands. 'That's how I feel about The Rogue.'

'How is he?' asks Hattie, sitting down beside him on the bench seat.

'He's doing better but injuries like his take time to heal.' Daniel's voice breaks as he says the word 'heal'. He looks down at his coffee mug.

'It must be tough,' says Hattie, putting her hand on his arm.

Daniel tries to swallow back the emotion he's feeling, fear and guilt about The Rogue's injury mixing with sparks of electricity from Hattie's touch. He looks back at her. Holds her gaze. 'I bought him as a yearling. He was this big gangly creature, really uncoordinated, but I could tell, even at that age, that he had the biggest, most genuine heart. He's twelve now. We've been through a lot together.'

Hattie nods. 'I bet.'

He doesn't know if Hattie knows what happened – that his parents were killed in a car accident in the Alps eleven years ago. That it wasn't until the will was read that he discovered they'd burned through most of the family money and really all he stood to inherit was the house, yard and a huge set of unpaid debts. The Rogue was the only horse he hadn't sold to pay those debts. He'd stood calmly as Daniel cried into his mane every time another horse or family heirloom was taken away. He'd stood solid as a rock when Daniel confided to him that he thought he wasn't going to make it through, and he'd carried Daniel to victory when a few years later they took the event world by storm. 'Aside from Eddie and Jenny, The Rogue is the only family I have. I just want him back at one hundred percent, or at least well enough to live out his days happily in the fields at home.'

'I get that,' says Hattie, and from the look on her face – intense and thoughtful and kind – Daniel believes that she does understand. 'I know I haven't had her for very long, but that's how I feel about Mermaid's Gold. She's like family.'

They sit in a comfortable silence for a moment. Daniel can't remember the last time he felt this relaxed in the company of a woman he finds attractive. The coffee has sobered him up and the anxiety he's been carrying for so many months seems to have dissolved. He looks over at Hattie. 'Can I ask your advice?'

'Sure.'

'Rocket Fuel's always been reluctant about water, and after falling today I wouldn't blame him if he doesn't want to go anywhere near a water fence. What would you recommend to help him?'

Hattie tilts her head to one side, thinking. 'You need to make it fun for him. I'd take him for some no-pressure play in water. Start him on a long rope first, no tack, and have him go in and out and enjoy it, then gradually work up to stepping and jumping in from there. Do you have a water complex at your place?'

'No, but there's a stream that runs through the bottom of one of the paddocks. I could have that dug out a bit.'

'Then I'd do that, and take him into it every day. Even feed him standing in the water if you feel it helps. Make the water his happy place.' She smiles. 'I hope that's useful.'

'Definitely,' says Daniel. He goes to take another sip of coffee but realises he's finished it.

Hattie stifles a yawn. 'Sorry. Long day.'

'Don't worry, I should be going,' says Daniel, getting up and walking over to the door. He doesn't want to leave but he doesn't want to overstay his welcome either. 'I've got an early start tomorrow.'

'Are you competing again?' asks Hattie, collecting up the two mugs and taking them over to the mini-sink.

'I'm meant to be.' He peers out of the window, but it's too dark to see if it's raining. 'It's so wet I wouldn't be surprised if the ground jury cancel the rest of the classes.'

'Here, let me help you with that; it can be a bit sticky.' Hattie steps over to join him at the door. She fiddles with the latch a few times before it releases, then pushes the door open for him. 'Well, goodnight, and good luck tomorrow.'

'Thanks,' says Daniel, softly. He can't take his eyes off hers. Reaching out, he pushes a tendril of her hair back from her face. His fingers caress her cheek. It feels like there's an electric current pulsing between them.

She leans in and he does the same. Their lips are inches from each other. There's a brief pause and Daniel feels nerves flare in his chest. Then his lips are on hers and they're kissing. Tenderly at first and then stronger, more passionate.

His heart soars. Hattie is kissing him back.

CHAPTER FORTY-FIVE

HATTIE

Something's wrong. Hattie knows it from the moment she turns into the row on her way to give Mermaid's Gold her breakfast. Five stables down, the mare's light blue Thermatex rug is folded neatly over the stable door and her rope halter has been laid over the top of it. Hattie breaks into a run. Dodging around two grooms wheeling barrows piled high towards the muck truck, she hurtles towards Mermaid's Gold's stable.

The bolts on the door are undone.

She looks inside. Her heart punches against her chest. Her stomach lurches.

The stable is empty.

Hattie feels like she's having a panic attack. Her heart's racing. Her breath comes in gasps. Where is Mermaid's Gold? Why isn't she in the stable? Who removed her rug?

'You okay?' asks a German-accented female voice.

Turning, she sees Helga, Greta Wolfe's head groom, peering over the door of the stable opposite, where she's tacking up Greta's first ride of the day – Top Cat. Hattie gestures towards the empty stable. 'My horse should be in here. I don't know where—'

'They collected her half an hour ago,' says Helga, looking confused.

'Collected her?' Hattie frowns. Maybe she's wrong – Mermaid's Gold isn't missing and instead Lady Pat has come back to help get the mare ready for travelling home. But, no, that's not right. They didn't agree that would happen. And, anyway, the timings don't work. Hattie was in the lorry half an hour ago and there was no sign of Lady Pat or the horse. 'Who took her?'

Helga looks concerned. 'You didn't know they were coming? They told me they'd bought her. It was—'

'Are you okay?' Daniel's hurrying towards her.

'Mermaid's Gold is gone.' Hattie feels discombobulated, as if she's looking down on herself. This is like a horror film playing out that she's unable to stop. Her voice breaks as she says the word 'gone'. 'She's been taken. Bought. I don't understand how that can—'

'I'm so sorry.' Daniel looks stricken. His eyes can barely meet hers. 'I don't know what to—'

'Hold on,' says Hattie as her phone buzzes in her pocket. Yanking it out, she reads the message.

It's from Robert Babbington: *Good result with the horse. I guess that horse whispering stuff works! Had a top offer = sold. They're collecting this morning. Early.*

Hattie stares at the message. Anger courses through her. She fires off a reply: *How can you sell her? You don't own her?*

Robert responds almost instantly: *Auntie Pat gifts me all the useless creatures she dumps at Clover Hill House ergo horse is mine. It's the first thing of any value. Maybe we should get you another horse to fix? Make more profit. Be a team.*

The fury builds inside Hattie. She sends another message: *I don't want another horse only Mermaid's Gold.*

She stares at the phone, waiting for Robert's response. The message has been read, but there are no three dots showing that he's typing. No message. Nothing. He isn't even sorry.

Hattie can't believe it. Lady Pat didn't say she'd gifted Robert Mermaid's Gold and from the way she was talking last night it didn't seem she'd had any plans to sell her. Hattie clenches her fists. Whatever Robert says, Hattie doesn't think Lady Pat will be happy about him selling Mermaid's Gold.

Flicking through her contacts, she calls Lady Pat's number. She only has a landline – Lady Pat thinks mobile phones are more hindrance than help – and it rings until the answerphone kicks in. 'Lady Patricia, it's me – Hattie. Someone has bought Mermaid's Gold. Robert sold her last night and she's already been taken. Did you know? Can you call me back as soon as you get this? Please.'

It isn't until she's ended the call that Hattie realises the woman who was watching Daniel in the show jumping yesterday is now standing beside him. She's wearing a Burberry mac over a scarlet jumpsuit tucked into black Hunter wellies and has a triumphant expression on her face.

The woman smiles at Hattie in a way that makes her skin crawl. The woman looks at Daniel and puts her hand on his arm. 'Aren't you going to introduce us, darling?'

Daniel seems uncomfortable. 'Hattie, this is my owner, Lexi Marchfield-Wright.'

'*Your* owner, exactly,' says Lexi, nodding, giving Daniel's arm a hard squeeze.

Hattie doesn't have time for this. And she's getting a really bad vibe from this woman. 'Sorry... I can't... my horse has—'

'*My* horse actually, darling,' says Lexi with a sly smile.

Realisation hits Hattie. Her stomach flips. 'You bought Mermaid's Gold?'

The woman, Lexi, gives a little, joyless laugh. 'Well, obviously.'

Hattie looks from Lexi to Daniel. 'But I—'

'We thought you'd like your rug and halter back, didn't we, darling?' says Lexi, squeezing Daniel's arm again, her red-painted talons digging into his skin as she pulls him closer to her. 'We don't need them; we have our own team colours.'

Hattie stares back at her. Lexi would be beautiful if it wasn't for the bitchy sneer and the deadness behind her eyes. Hattie can't bear the thought of Mermaid's Gold being owned by this woman. 'Can't we work something out to—'

'No.' Lexi thrusts her hand palm out towards Hattie, reinforcing her words. 'The deal is done. The horse is mine. Daniel needs the best, and your horse proved yesterday that she is the best. So Daniel had to have her.'

'Daniel...?' Hattie looks at him, hoping he'll say he doesn't want the ride, that Hattie should stay the rider of Mermaid's Gold.

He says nothing. Shuffles his weight from one foot to the other. His eyes briefly meet Hattie's gaze, then he looks down at the ground.

Daniel's reaction feels like a roundhouse kick to the chest after she's already been sucker-punched. He listened last night as she shared her fears about people wanting to buy Mermaid's Gold. He understood, and told her it'd be okay. He bloody well kissed her. And then he had one of his owners buy Mermaid's Gold for himself.

'You arsehole,' says Hattie. Her voice is louder than she intended, her anger amplifying her words. 'What you've done... it's shitty. Really shitty.'

He meets her gaze. 'You have to understand, I didn't...'

'Get lost.' Hattie steps back away from him. 'Just leave me the hell alone.'

Daniel reaches for her. 'But, I—'

'No!' Hattie shoves him away. She's shouting now. 'Fuck off.'

All the grooms and riders in the row of stables are watching them.

Beside Daniel, Lexi is smirking. Obviously enjoying the show. She grabs his arm again. 'Come on, darling.'

'I...' He looks at Hattie.

She shakes her head at him, disgusted. Can't bring herself to say another word to him. He's a total and utter arsehole. Not even man enough to look her fully in the eye. She can't believe she actually liked him. That she thought they had a connection.

As Daniel and Lexi walk away, the activity starts up again. Grooms carry on mucking out and preparing horses for competition. Two riders start gossiping about what's just happened, their stage whispers easy to hear.

Hattie ignores them all. She steps inside the stable and closes the door behind her. The stable still smells like Mermaid's Gold. The mare's bandages and kaolin wraps are piled neatly beside the door. The water bucket is half full.

In the corner of the stable, Hattie sinks to the ground. Wrapping her arms around herself, she tries to hold back the tears. Mermaid's Gold trusted her. Now she's been taken.

She never even got to say goodbye.

CHAPTER FORTY-SIX

DANIEL

The squealing from the stable gets louder as Daniel approaches. He hears two bangs against the wooden kickboards and Eddie calling out for the horse to stop. Breaking into a run, Daniel rushes to the stable. He peers over the door. 'What's going on?'

'She doesn't like the saddle. She pulled away from the tie ring when I tried to put it on her back and chased me over here.' Red-faced and sweating, Eddie, his usually unflappable head groom, is trapped on the far side of the stable against the corner manger. Mermaid's Gold is facing him, the rope from her head collar hanging loose rather than being tied up to the ring at the front of the stable. Her ears are back and she's grinding her teeth. Every few seconds, the mare turns her head, eyeing something behind her.

Following her gaze, Daniel sees there are two hoof-shaped holes splintered in the wooden kickboards over by the automatic waterer. A few feet away, there's over a thousand pounds worth of top-quality saddle lying upside down on the wood shavings. There's a horseshoe print on the seat, as if the saddle has been trodden on, and a large tear in one of the flaps. Shit, thinks Daniel. It's probably ruined.

He looks over at Eddie. 'Can you move this way?'

Mermaid's Gold swivels an ear towards Daniel but doesn't take her eyes off Eddie. She looks as tense as a coiled spring and a million times more powerful.

'I'll try.' Eddie takes a step towards Daniel.

The mare moves fast. Pinning her ears back, she bares her teeth and lunges forward at Eddie, snapping. He jumps back to the manger. Swears under his breath. 'I guess that's a no.'

It's obvious the saddle has provoked the mare's flight or fight response. As long as the saddle is in the stable, Daniel doubts she's going to calm down. 'Okay, stay where you are,' he says to Eddie. 'I'm going to try and remove the saddle.'

'Be careful. She freaked when I carried it towards her.'

Undoing the bolt, Daniel opens the stable door and slips inside. The mare swings around to face him. Throwing up her head and showing the whites of her eyes, she snorts twice.

'Steady, girl,' says Daniel. 'I'm just going to get rid of the nasty saddle, okay?'

Moving slowly but deliberately, he moves along the inside wall of the stable towards the fallen saddle. The mare's focus is on him now so, as he moves, he beckons Eddie to go towards the door.

As he gets closer to the saddle, he sees the damage is worse than he thought. The kick mark on the seat has ripped the leather and the metal tree inside that gives the saddle its structure looks buckled. The mare must have stomped on it hard.

'Good, girl,' he says, in as soothing a tone as he can while reaching down for the saddle. 'Let me get rid of this for you.'

The mare's nostrils flare. She throws her head up.

Daniel picks up the saddle. He takes a step back towards the door. Keeps his eyes on Mermaid's Gold.

She snorts loudly. Swishes her tail.

'Steady, girl,' he says, holding out his free hand towards her. 'It's okay, I'm—'

Mermaid's Gold rears up on her hind legs. Towering over him, her front legs strike out towards his head.

'Woah, girl, woah.'

She ignores him. Squealing in anger, the mare steps towards him on her hind legs.

Eddie freezes halfway between the manger and the door. They're both in a dangerous situation. Daniel knows they need to get out fast and take the saddle with them. Raising it in front of him like a shield, Daniel looks over to Eddie and shouts, 'Move.'

He does as Daniel says and sprints for the door.

The sudden movement attracts the mare. Spinning round, she lunges for Eddie, but he's fast and her snapping teeth miss him by inches. Snorting, tail swishing violently, the mare swings back to face Daniel.

Shit. He's still a few feet from the door.

The mare strikes out at him with her front feet. Her eyes are wild. Her breath laboured.

She's blocking his exit. Glaring at the saddle.

Daniel knows what he has to do. Glancing towards the door, he judges the distance and then swings his arm out and throws the saddle over the door. It's not a clean shot, the cantle clips the top of the door, but it falls outside onto the concrete yard with a thud.

The mare, spooked by the flying saddle, leaps away from the door. Racing to the back of the stable, she stands against the manger, shaking. Her nostrils are pink and flared.

'You okay?' calls Eddie from outside.

'Yeah,' says Daniel. Keeping his eyes on the horse, he steps towards her. He keeps his voice gentle, calm. 'It's okay, girl. It's gone now, okay? The saddle is gone.'

The mare watches him. Her eyes are still wild, but she's blinking, coming down off the adrenaline of her flight or fight response. Her flanks are quivering. Sweat has darkened her coat, turning the bright golden red colour more burnished.

Daniel moves closer to her. Stretches out his hand and touches the mare's forehead. Massages the spot in the middle where the hair whorls in all directions. 'It's okay, girl. We won't do that again. You're safe.'

The mare blows out. The tension is starting to leave her.

When Daniel turns and walks towards the door, the mare follows him. He gives her a rub on her neck and then exits the stable, bolting it behind him.

'That horse is Doctor Jekyll and Mrs Hyde,' says Eddie, gesturing to Mermaid's Gold, who's now nudging at Daniel's pocket, asking for a treat. 'A couple of minutes ago she wanted to kill you.'

'She was afraid and she wanted to kill the saddle,' says Daniel. 'There's a difference.'

'True,' says Eddie, walking over to the saddle and picking it up. 'But, Jesus…. what the hell got into her?'

Daniel runs his hand over his jaw. Remembers what Hattie told him about what the mare had been through and how long it took to gain her trust. The horse shouldn't be here; she should be with Hattie. He has to get Lexi to see sense. 'It sparked a bad memory.'

'Must have. She was sweet as anything when we fed and mucked her out. Everything was fine until I took the saddle in, then it's like she got possessed. Once I dropped it, and she pinned me in the corner, she went back and attacked the saddle – biting, stamping.' Eddie shakes his head. 'I've never seen anything like it.'

Daniel runs his hand through his hair. 'She's still traumatised by what happened to her. The only person she really trusts is Hattie.'

'I can't see that changing anytime soon.'

'Me neither,' says Daniel. 'I didn't want Lexi to buy her. She should be with Hattie.'

'Then tell the Marchfield-Wrights to send her back,' says Eddie. He gives Daniel a thoughtful look. 'Have you spoken to Hattie?'

Daniel's stomach churns and he tastes sour bile on his tongue as Hattie's words to him at Kingsland International echo in his mind: that he's an arsehole, that he's really shit, that she wants him to leave her the hell alone. He wants to call her, but he knows he can't make up for what Lexi did, and there's no way Hattie will ever believe he didn't know about her buying Mermaid's Gold until it was already too late. He shudders as he recalls the look of anger and hatred on Hattie's face as she realised Lexi had bought the mare. He shakes his head. 'I can't. This situation is so bad, and she was so mad at me and I... it's better to give her time.'

Eddie looks sceptical. 'I'm not sure it is. She's going to be going out of her mind with worry about the mare. If you called her, you could tell her how things happened, that you didn't know—'

'She won't listen. It'll just make things worse.'

'Then, as I said, get Lexi to send her back,' says Eddie. 'Be very persuasive.'

Daniel searches Eddie's expression for a hint that he's implying anything more than negotiation, but he sees no innuendo or smirk in his friend's gaze. 'Yeah.'

He's thinking about how to play it when he hears dance music, getting louder. Glancing towards the driveway, he sees a magenta Bentley come haring around the side of the house to the parking area, some music thumping from the sound system.

Eddie looks at Daniel. Frowns. 'Great. Speak of the devil.'

Shit. This is all he needs. 'Can you get Pink Fizz and Rocket Fuel tacked up quickly and take them out with Bunty? After what happened with her and Lexi, I don't want her put in a difficult position.'

'Sure,' says Eddie. 'On it now.'

'Thanks,' says Daniel.

As Eddie heads towards the tack room and calls for Bunty to come and tack up, Daniel walks across to meet Lexi at the yard entrance.

'I thought I'd come and see our new star,' says Lexi, climbing out of the Bentley. She's dressed in a short black sequined dress with a pink fake fur gilet and matching UGG boots. Daniel can't think of a worse outfit to wear to a horse yard. 'I thought you could ride her for me.'

'Yeah, about that…' Daniel's words trail off as he sees Lexi's expression change. 'It seems Mermaid's Gold is a one-rider type horse.'

Lexi wrinkles up her nose. 'A what?'

'She's a horse that goes well for one person, but it's hard to replicate that success with another rider.'

'So what you're telling me is that I've bought a dud?' Lexi's voice is getting louder with every word. 'That I've spent all that money and the creature is useless?'

'No. She's a good horse. She's just not the right horse for me.'

Lexi frowns. She goes to reply but stops as Bunty and Eddie ride past on Pink Fizz and Rocket Fuel. Scowling as she sees Bunty.

'We'll do the long block,' says Eddie, looking at Daniel. 'Back in an hour.'

'Great, thanks,' says Daniel. He hopes Bunty doesn't see the way Lexi is glaring at her. And he hopes Lexi doesn't bring up firing Bunty again. He's not going to do it.

'You're a top rider. Surely you can ride anything?' says Lexi, once Eddie and Bunty are out of earshot. 'After all, a horse is a horse, right?'

'Well, yes and no.'

'No? I hate "no",' says Lexi. She turns towards the stables and gestures to Mermaid's Gold. 'It looks quiet enough, surely?'

She's got a point, thinks Daniel. Right now, Mermaid's Gold is looking out over her stable door as she munches happily on her hay. The chestnut mare looks like an angel, not the half-crazed wild thing she was earlier. 'That's because we're not trying to put tack on her or ride her. When we get the tack out, it's a very different story.' He gestures towards the knackered saddle that's sitting over the door of the stable one along from Mermaid's Gold's. 'She attacked that saddle and pinned Eddie to the wall. Someone could have been seriously injured.'

Lexi huffs dramatically. 'Look, you said you wanted the best horses, and that animal won Kingsland International, making her one of the best horses, so I bought her. But if it's not working out then fine, I'll handle it.'

Relieved that Lexi's listening, Daniel feels the knot in his stomach loosen a notch. Things could work out okay. If Mermaid's Gold goes back to Hattie, he can explain exactly what happened. Maybe she'll believe him, forgive him even. 'Yes, you should sell her back to Lady Babbington. Let Hattie have the ride on—'

'No.' Lexi's voice is raised. She raises her hands palms out towards him. 'There's no way that's happening. If Eddie can't even get a saddle on the creature, then there must be something seriously wrong with it. It's a hassle, of course, but she's fully insured. She'll just have to be shot so I can claim back her full value.'

Daniel stares at Lexi, open mouthed. 'She *is* saddleable and rideable. By Hattie.'

'No, darling, don't be so foolish. If she goes back to that girl, then we're helping the competition. They beat you at Kingsland International. We need to be smart here – stack the deck in our favour.'

'Not by killing the mare.'

Lexi shrugs. 'I really don't understand why you're getting so upset. It's just a horse and if it's not going to—'

'I'll work it out,' says Daniel quickly. He can't let Lexi shoot the mare. He has to find another way to fix this. Gritting his teeth, he slides his arm around Lexi's waist. 'Look, I'm overreacting. The mare probably just needs a bit more time to settle in. Give me a few more weeks and I'm sure we'll be getting on great.'

Lexi looks at him suspiciously. 'Really? You seemed so certain a moment ago that she's unrideable?'

Backtracking, he tries to make light of it. 'I was being overdramatic. Ignore it. I'll have Mermaid's Gold working well in no time.'

'Okay then,' says Lexi, cautiously. 'If you say so, but I want a full report on progress each week.'

'Of course.' It's a reprieve for now, but Daniel knows he needs to do more to get Lexi on side. He glances towards the house. Raises his eyebrows. 'We've got an hour before the others get back.'

'I have to go. There's a ladies' lunch at Branigans. I can't be late.'

'You enjoy torturing me.' The words feel forced as he tries not to let his relief show.

'Darling, this is hardly torture.' Kissing him hard, she runs her fingers from his face, down his chest to his crotch. She strokes him through his breeches. 'You just need a little patience.'

It's all Daniel can do not to recoil from her touch. He makes himself press into it. Groans in fake pleasure. Tries to sound turned on. 'Next time, then.'

'You can be sure of that, darling,' says Lexi, airily, as she struts back to her Bentley.

Daniel can guess how much Lexi loves it that she's leaving him hanging. Their arrangement isn't about desire or even sex, not really; it's about her wanting power over him.

Giving him a little wave, Lexi starts the car and accelerates away down the drive. Daniel watches until she's out of sight, then turns back towards the stables. Mermaid's Gold is still munching on her hay. Ears forward, the horse looks like she hasn't a care in the world.

Daniel shakes his head. Lexi buying Mermaid's Gold is just another power play. She didn't want the horse for him to ride, she just wanted to drive a wedge between him and Hattie and realised buying the mare and making it look like he was in on it was the quickest way to make that happen. She'd even warned him to stay away from Hattie.

God, he's been such an idiot. There's no way Mermaid's Gold is going to let him ride her. And there's no way he's going to let Lexi have the mare shot. He *has* to work out a way to get the mare safely back to Hattie.

He clenches his fists.

Whatever it takes, he's going to make this right.

CHAPTER FORTY-SEVEN

HATTIE

It's been nearly two weeks and Clover Hill House still seems empty without Mermaid's Gold. She's tried to keep busy – long walks with the dogs, cleaning out the goats' field shelter, and helping Liberty with her online shop and artisan markets – but nothing helps lift the gloom.

Pulling on her trainers, Hattie opens the back door. As the dogs hurtle outside and as Hattie follows them, her spirits sink further. There's no chestnut mare waiting expectantly at the fence. No Mermaid's Gold whinnying for her breakfast.

With Banana and Peanut scampering along in front, Hattie walks over to feed the goats. Mable and Gladys seem to feel the loss of Mermaid's Gold as much as she does. Their usually joyful bleats sound melancholy, and Mable, who has always hoovered up her food as quickly as she can, just nibbles at her breakfast, barely eating a couple of mouthfuls.

She's pining for Mermaid's Gold as much as me, thinks Hattie with a sigh.

For the umpteenth time since she returned without Mermaid's Gold, Hattie wonders how much longer she can bear to stay here. She feels no loyalty to Robert after what he did, but the dogs have been good companions and she can't leave the goats to Bill's uncaring indifference.

Heading back inside, she feeds the dogs and makes herself a mug of coffee. She's putting the spoon into the sink when the back door flies open and Liberty storms into the kitchen, waving a magazine like it's on fire. 'Tell me you've seen this?'

'What?' says Hattie, taking the copy of the *Leightonshire Chronicle* from her.

'This here,' says Liberty, jabbing a fingernail against the photo in a double page spread.

Hattie's eyes widen. Staring back is her own image. It's the picture that was taken on the staircase at High Drayton Manor. JaXX is in the foreground, Hattie and that arsehole, Daniel, are together a little higher up the stairs. 'I haven't—'

'Well, it's not surprising really,' says Liberty, raising her eyebrow in the direction of a towering stack of post on the end of the kitchen table. 'But anyway, firstly, you look amazing. And secondly, you look *really* amazing.'

Hattie forces a smile. She knows Liberty's just trying to cheer her up and deflect the attention from Daniel, but it's not working. 'Thanks.'

'Oh no, don't give me that fobbing off "thanks" bullshit. This is me, yeah? And you look great.' Liberty frowns, appraising her friend. 'Mind you, you're looking on the skinny side now. Are you eating okay? If that fucker—'

'I'm fine.'

Liberty raises both eyebrows. 'Fine? Oh jeez, you're doing worse than I thought.' She softens her tone. 'Has Lady Pat had any luck yet?'

Hattie shakes her head. 'It seems legally the animals do belong to Robert. Apparently, he had Lady Pat sign some papers way back that gave him ownership of any animals that live at his animal sanctuary.'

Liberty cocks her head to the side. 'His *animal sanctuary*?'

'It's so he can get some sort of tax break or something. Lady Pat said it was the one condition he had if she was going to put animals here. She never thought he wanted to own them, just thought it was a money thing.'

'I guess it was, given he sold Mermaid's Gold without even being respectful enough to talk to Lady Pat first.'

'I guess so. Lady Pat's still trying to get her back – she's got the lawyers looking for any technicalities she can use – but it's looking less and less likely. And she's made offers to buy her back – more than doubling the amount the Marchfield-Wrights paid Robert – but they won't sell.' Hattie sighs. She doesn't want to talk about this anymore – it just makes her feel even sadder. Picking up the magazine, she hands it back to Liberty. 'Anyway, I should be getting on with—'

'Keep it,' says Liberty, putting the magazine back on the kitchen table. She looks at Hattie for a long moment. 'Okay, I'm going to say something now and you might not want to hear it but it's for your own good, yeah?'

'Okay,' says Hattie. 'What?'

'You need to stop all the moaning and moping and get on with life,' says Liberty. 'Yeah, yeah, I know it sounds harsh, but you've *got* to get out of this rut you're wedged in – otherwise you're just going to be stuck forever.'

Hattie knows Liberty is right. 'I just hate that that bloody awful woman owns Mermaid's Gold, and that Daniel went behind my back and got one of his owners to buy her.' She takes a breath. 'I thought I could trust him but—'

'Ha! You can *never* trust a man,' says Liberty. 'They all screw you over one way or another – that I know from bitter experience – and they're certainly not worth giving up your dreams for.' Liberty looks at the picture and licks her lips. 'Mind you, JaXX might just be the exception to the rule, you know?'

Hattie's glad her friend is having fun with JaXX but there's a lot of truth in what she's said about trust and men. Certainly the men in her life so far haven't given her much respect. Ryan's behaviour changed when Blake Mentmore picked her as his first rider, and now Daniel's stolen her horse at his first opportunity. Whenever she's had something good happen and she feels like she's on the up, there's been a man who's tried to knock her back down. She's had enough. She has to fight this. 'You're right.'

Liberty grins. 'There's my girl. So what are you going to do?'

'I don't know but I'll think of something.'

CHAPTER FORTY-EIGHT

LEXI

She doesn't go to Branigans in Mayfair because there is no ladies' lunch today. Instead, she drives the Bentley into central London, past St Martin-in-the-Fields and along the Strand. Daniel might look like a Roman God but he's about as sexual as a Roman statue, and Dexter has been locking himself away in his study all the bloody time, ignoring her.

Lexi needs more. She deserves more. And she's sure as hell going to get it.

The London traffic is awful as usual and, even though she uses the bus lane wherever she can, she's almost half an hour late as she indicates right and makes the turn into Savoy Court and pulls up on the right behind a silver Rolls Royce.

As she gets out of the car, a doorman hurries over to her. 'Good morning, ma'am, welcome to the Savoy.'

Lexi tilts her head to the side. The doorman's really rather cute in his top hat and black suit. The gold edging and buttons on the overcoat are to die for. She smiles. After all, who can resist a man in uniform? And says, 'I'm joining a friend for lunch.'

'Perfect,' says the doorman. He clicks his fingers and a

younger man, again in uniform, hurries over. 'Take the Bentley to the parking garage, Davidson.'

Lexi hands him her car key. 'I'll only be a few hours.'

'Very good, ma'am,' says the doorman. 'Enjoy your lunch.'

'Oh, I certainly will,' says Lexi, smiling wolfishly. 'I'm very hungry.'

As the valet drives her car off to the parking garage, Lexi walks towards the entrance of the hotel. She's always loved the Savoy with its unapologetic opulence and in-your-face glamour. There's no understated chic here and that's obvious before you're even inside the building. The name 'SAVOY' screams 'I'm here' at you in high lettering over the entrance, and the golden accents and flags flying above make it impossible to miss. Just like her.

She goes through the revolving door and into the foyer. Another liveried doorman doffs his hat. Lexi doesn't acknowledge him, but his attention does make her strut across the black-and-white tiled floor a little more pronounced. She does so love to make an entrance.

She stops at the concierge desk. Made of mahogany, with green leather inset into the desktop and a vase of yellow roses to one side, like the rest of the foyer it looks elegant and expensive. There are two uniformed men sitting behind laptops at the desk. Their hair is slicked back neatly and they're both dressed in dark grey three-piece suits with gold ties. They look up at her attentively. 'I'm meeting a friend for lunch in the Royal Suite.'

'Of course, ma'am,' says the concierge with the darker hair and glasses. 'Your butler is waiting to escort you.'

~

They take the private elevator to the Royal Suite. The butler is polite but his stiff aloofness feels judgemental and she finds it extremely irritating. Lexi narrows her eyes, watching as he positions himself on the opposite side of the elevator car to her and remains remarkably still on the ride up. Even though she watches him carefully, he doesn't once glance in her direction.

As the elevator stops, the doors open into a hallway. The butler steps out before the doors are fully open and strides across to the mahogany double doors on the other side of the hallway. 'This way, please, ma'am. Monsieur Malmond is waiting in the lounge.'

'Is he now?' says Lexi, raising an eyebrow at the butler as she walks through the double doors and into the suite. Surely a butler should be seen and not heard. She's late, yes, but it's not the help's place to point it out. She puts an added edge of boss bitch into her voice as she says, 'How nice.'

'Lexi, finally,' says Jean-Luc, standing up from where he's sitting on the turquoise velvet sofa and moving across the antique rug to meet her. He kisses her on both cheeks and then looks over her shoulder at the butler. 'Thank you, James, you can go ahead and have them set up lunch now my guest has arrived.'

'As you wish,' says James the butler, backing out through the double doors and closing them behind him.

Jean-Luc turns back to Lexi and taps his gold Cartier watch. 'You are a very naughty girl to have kept me waiting so long.'

'Traffic was bad,' she says, shrugging. She looks away from him through the huge windows and out across the river. 'And I'm worth the wait.'

'I'm sure you are,' says Jean-Luc. 'But I prefer punctuality.'

She laughs and bats her lashes. She steps closer, so close that her breasts are almost touching his chest. 'Well then, maybe you should spank me.'

'Perhaps I will,' he says, holding her gaze with an intensity that's almost animalistic, like a lion hunting a gazelle. 'But first we eat.'

Lexi pouts. She doesn't want to eat now; she prefers sexual pleasure before food.

Jean-Luc notices and laughs. 'I see that perhaps the wait will be your punishment, no? You must learn to love the build-up, and the anticipation, ma chérie. It will make the climax even more powerful.'

Putting his hand lightly against the small of her back, Jean-Luc guides her out of the lounge and into the dining room. After the bold colours of the lounge, Lexi finds this room a disappointment with wood-panelled walls painted in muted colours. The only colour comes from the forest of green plants and a few pictures. Still, the walnut dining table is nice enough, she supposes, laid for two with green flower-painted china, the food concealed by silver domes.

As they take their seats, James the butler appears from behind a hidden door in the panelling on the rear wall. 'May I serve you?' he asks, looking at Jean-Luc.

'We'll serve ourselves, James, but thank you,' says Jean-Luc. 'You can be excused. I'll call if we need anything further.'

'Very good, sir,' says James, nodding at Jean-Luc and exiting back through the door in the panelling.

Lexi shakes her head. 'What is it with that man? He won't even look at me.'

'I suspect that you are scaring him, chérie,' says Jean-Luc. 'You are a very beautiful woman, no?'

She smiles. She *is* beautiful. And men *should* be afraid. 'You're not scared though, are you, darling?'

Jean-Luc holds her gaze. There's a fiery intensity in his eyes. 'No, I am not.'

Lexi says nothing, but she thinks to herself, maybe you should be.

They eat. The food is exquisite and the wine even better. Afterwards, finally, Jean-Luc takes her hand and leads her to the bedroom. The room is vast and luxurious. Decorated with green-and-pink flowered wallpaper and furnished with black lacquered pieces and a huge four-poster bed. But it's not the interior decoration that interests Lexi.

Letting go of her hand, Jean-Luc takes a seat on the dusky pink chaise longue opposite the bed, but when Lexi moves to join him he puts his hand out to stop her. 'No, stay there and let me look at you.'

Lexi stands in front of him, glad that she swapped the UGGs for her highest Louboutins after leaving Daniel's yard. The short black sequined dress clings to her body in just the right way. She knows she looks great. Still, she's not used to this, being inspected by a man. Usually she's the one doing the inspecting, and finding the man come up short. Somehow Jean-Luc has switched their roles without her realising.

After what must be at least half a minute of silent observation, Jean-Luc gets to his feet. Slowly, he walks around her, appraising her with his gaze, his expression unreadable.

Lexi doesn't like this. She needs to take control. As he draws level with her front, she reaches out and slides her hand around his neck. Moving closer, she presses herself against him. 'Darling, we need to—'

'Not yet,' says Jean-Luc, removing her hand and stepping back to put distance between them. 'Not until I say so.'

Lexi pouts. Men don't say no to her, they just don't. She's about to tell him that when he presses a finger against his lips.

'Take off your dress, chérie.'

She wants to tell him to go to hell, but she doesn't. He's not much to look at – wiry and balding doesn't really turn her on, but there's something about the intensity of his stare, or the dominance of his command, or the sexiness of his French accent that gets her and is making her hornier by the second. So, despite herself, she decides to play along and slowly removes her dress.

She's naked underneath. All she's wearing are the Louboutins.

Jean-Luc walks around her, continuing his inspection.

Lexi stands tall. She's proud of her assets.

He might say he wants to take it slow but she can see the impressive length of his erection through his trousers, so she knows she's having the right effect. She suppresses a smile. She's never met a man who can resist her for long, no matter how much they might want to. It's her superpower. She doubts Jean-Luc will be any different.

The first time he touches her, she feels as if she's going to explode.

'It's all about the anticipation, no?' he says as his fingers press into her. Two fingers. Then three. His thumb circles her clit.

Lexi nods, enjoying the sensation. Now this is a man who knows what he's doing and enjoys his work. It's such a stark contrast to Daniel's lacklustre performances.

'Good, chérie, trés bien,' says Jean-Luc, dropping down to one knee and pressing his mouth to her.

She remembers the wonders he can perform with his tongue from their encounter in Paris. It's the reason she agreed to meet today when he called to say he was in London for a couple of days on business. And he doesn't disappoint. As she widens her legs, Lexi closes her eyes and lets the vibrations flood through her.

He brings her to the brink twice, but pulls away as she's getting there for a third time.

She frowns. 'Why are you…?'

He kisses away her words, then positions her face-down on the four-poster bed so she's lying beneath him, her legs together and her belly pressing against the white bedspread. She can feel him behind her, his legs stranding hers.

The wait is killing her. She hasn't been this wet in years.

She cums again as he enters her.

Smiling, Jean-Luc takes a bottle of oil from the corner of the bed. Continuing to thrust into her, he squeezes oil over her bottom and starts to massage it in. Leaning closer, he whispers, 'Tell me what you want next, chérie.'

She pushes back against him, still riding the ripples of orgasm. 'Fuck my arse, Jean-Luc. Fuck me…'

'Trés bien.' His voice is heavy with desire. 'This I will do.'

He starts off slow, teasingly slow, opening her gradually as he eases himself into her, waiting for her body to yield. It's driving her crazy and she reaches back, trying to pull him into her faster.

Grabbing her hands, he pushes them down onto the bed so she can't interfere with what he's doing. He's in charge. 'Patience, chérie, patience.'

She needs him now. Can't wait a moment longer. She shifts her weight back, feeling him deeper inside her. Hears him groan with longing.

'Fuck me,' she orders him.

Jean-Luc obeys and Lexi cries out as he thrusts hard into her. Sending shockwaves of pleasure and pain ricocheting through her body, delicious and excruciating.

He's speaking rapid French. Thrusting faster. Losing all control. He might think he has the power, but he's exactly where she wants him.

She's the one in charge now.

'Harder,' Lexi shouts, smacking her palms against Jean-Luc's buttocks. Smiling as he continues to obey her. She clenches the bedspread between her fingers to brace herself, and commands him again. 'Fuck. Me. Harder.'

CHAPTER FORTY-NINE

HATTIE

Sitting in the lounge after Liberty has gone home, Hattie stares at her mum's wooden trunk. If Mum were here, she'd have given her some wise words; not telling Hattie what to do, she never did that, but pointing out some options and helping her consider them. Instead, she has to figure this out on her own.

She picks up the *Leightonshire Chronicle* and flicks through to the article about High Drayton Horse Trials. JaXX, Daniel and her own image look back at her. Rage flares inside her as she looks at Daniel. And although she doesn't like to admit it, she feels a smidgeon of sadness too. She liked him. It felt like they had a connection. But he screwed her over anyway.

Folding back the page so she doesn't have to look at his face, she reads the article about the competition. It feels as if it happened a lifetime ago.

Harriet Kimble stands out from the usual eventing crowd. Finishing in third place, she wowed judges and spectators alike with a harmonious and stylish performance in all three phases. This was even more impressive as the horse she rode – Mermaid's Gold, a diminutive chestnut mare – had been labelled dangerous and unrideable after a horrific fall with her previous rider left her with significant behavioural issues.

Using horse whispering techniques that work with the horse's natural instincts, Kimble was able to gain the horse's trust and cure her issues. These two make a formidable team and are already getting tipped by Leightonshire local and long-serving advisor to the selection committee Daphne Wainscoat as ones to watch for future British teams.

Emotions fight inside her. The journalist, Gareth Baker, has given her horse whispering a positive write-up. It feels good – like she's made a difference, demonstrating the ways the techniques can be beneficial in sport. She wants to help people and horses.

The article has reminded her she's come a long way in these past few months. She's not starting back at square one, not entirely.

Hattie clenches her fingers tighter on the magazine. Feels determination surge through her. She won't give up. However long it takes, she *will* get Mermaid's Gold back. And in the meantime, she'll use her skills to help other horses who are having problems.

Before she changes her mind, Hattie picks up her phone and flicks through her contacts until she finds the number Jonathan Scott gave her.

It's answered after four rings. 'Yep, hello?'

There's a lot of background noise; it sounds like he's driving. 'Hi, it's Hattie Kimble. We met at Kingsland International.'

'Sure, I remember.' He sounds pleased to hear from her. 'You know, it's a travesty that little mare got taken from you.'

'Thanks.' Hattie swallows hard. She mustn't let emotion overwhelm her – this is business. She clears her throat. 'That work you mentioned with your tricky youngsters – is it still available?'

CHAPTER FIFTY

DEXTER

*I*t's all about damage control. Whatever way Dexter runs the numbers, they refuse to add up to the right amount. He's in the kitchen, having a fourth coffee, when Lexi arrives home and straight away hands him the monthly invoice from the eventing bloke.

Taking it, he runs his gaze down the itemised bill. Frowns. 'This is wrong.'

She turns, all innocent, wide eyes as she sips on a green juice. 'Is it? Looked fine to me.'

Dexter sets the invoice down on the countertop and taps the multiplier against the livery and training costs. 'It says four rather than three. You need to get that Daniel to do it right.'

He takes another mouthful of coffee while Lexi comes over to have a look at the invoice. He's already working out how to move their money around so he can pay the invoice once it's been reduced.

Lexi looks back at him, gesturing to the invoice. 'It's right. We have four horses now.'

Dexter nearly spits out his coffee. 'How do we...?'

Lexi gives a little shrug. 'I bought another one. It wasn't that expensive.'

'But we didn't discuss this.' Dexter feels adrenaline fire into his bloodstream. How can she have bought another horse without even talking to him? Even if she is carrying on with that bloody event rider, *he's* her bloody husband, for God's sake. 'We agreed two horses, and you pushed that to three, but now it's four and that isn't okay.'

Frowning, Lexi slams her green juice down onto the countertop, sending globules of green gunk across the marble. 'Since when did you become my boss?'

'I'm not your boss, but I do run our finances, and we can't afford a fourth horse.'

Lexi laughs. 'Don't be ridiculous, of course we can.'

'I'm serious. I've had some problems with investors and things are tight. You're going to have to sell one of the horses.'

Lexi folds her arms. Pouts. 'No.'

'I mean it, Lexi,' says Dexter, snatching up the invoice and rereading the total amount. Jesus.

'And so do I. This isn't about money, is it? It's because you're jealous of Daniel.'

Dexter feels like he's taken a blow to stomach. 'What about Daniel?'

'Because he's young and hot and athletic.' She stares pointedly at Dexter's slight paunch. 'Everything you're not.'

Dexter says nothing. It's a low blow and it hits him right where he's the least secure.

'What?' Lexi stands with her hands on her hips as if challenging him to deny what she's said is true. 'Cat got your tongue?'

Dexter shakes his head. There's no reasoning with Lexi, there never has been. She isn't going to help him get out of the nightmare he's in, and if he pushes this further she'll only make it worse. He looks into her eyes and tries to see past the make-up, surgery and designer clothes to the fun-loving, kind girl he first met all those years ago. 'I love you, honey.'

Lexi tosses her hair in his direction and rolls her eyes. 'Then buy me something bloody expensive to prove it.'

As she turns on her seven-inch Louboutin heels and struts out of the kitchen, Dexter knows what he's worried about for many sleepless nights is now certain.

He's doomed.

CHAPTER FIFTY-ONE

HATTIE

November brings with it the end of the event season and the first frost of winter. It's been almost two months since she started working with Jonathan Scott's trickier horses – two youngsters and an older horse who'd become difficult to load into the lorry.

Today in the gel-track indoor arena, she's working with Tiktac – a huge four-year-old bay gelding who's very sensitive and didn't respond well to the saddle. It's taken time and patience to get him confident enough to have things on his back but now he's doing well and Jonathan has high hopes for him next season.

Hattie smiles as she canters a large twenty-metre circle. A few weeks ago, every other stride would have been a buck or a leap with Tiktac snorting and snatching at the reins. Now he covers the ground with an easy lope on a loose rein, relaxed and as balanced as a horse with much more experience under saddle.

'He's looking good,' Jonathan calls from the door into the arena. He's just back from hacking out, and his Ariat jacket and woolly jockey skull cap cover are covered in a fine, icy sheen.

Bringing Tiktac back to a walk, Hattie turns towards the

entrance and rides over to Jonathan. Her breath plumes in the air as she speaks. 'He's feeling much happier.'

'Great. Do you think he's ready to be turned away?'

Hattie thinks about it. It's a good idea to turn youngsters out in the fields for a few months of rest once they've reached a level of basic training – the time off lets them finish growing and maturing. She'll be sad not to work with him any longer but it's not about what's right for her, it's about what's best for the horse. 'I reckon so.'

'Excellent. Pippy and Doc are getting turned out today. He can go in the same field.'

'You're not keeping any horses in stables over the winter?'

Jonathan shakes his head. 'I like them all to have a good rest, and it gives the yard staff an easier month or so before we start gearing up for next season towards the end of January.'

Dismounting from Tiktac, Hattie runs the stirrups up and loosens his girth. The horse stands still as a rock – a far cry from the trembling, biting stress-head he'd been when she first began working with him.

Jonathan blows on his hands and rubs them together. 'What are you doing next Sunday night?'

Hattie takes Tiktac's reins over his head and leads him towards the exit. She hesitates before she answers Jonathan. He's not propositioned her about a threesome since that first time at Kingsland International, but she's well aware of his reputation.

He puts his hands up. As if reading her mind, he says, 'It's nothing like *that*. Come on, you can't have forgotten I'm hosting the Event Riders' Winter Ball this year? And of course you must know that anyone who is anyone in the eventing world will be there. But strangely I'm told you haven't RSVPed yet?'

Hattie bites her lip. She was hoping she'd managed to fly under the radar with the ball. She doesn't want to go. 'I'm not sure that—'

'Oh no, don't tell me you're worried about bumping into Daniel Templeton-Smith and that awful owner of his who looks like a *Real Housewives* knock-off?' says Jonathan as he opens the doors to the arena to let Hattie and Tiktac out. 'You know, word is she owns more than just his horses, if you know what I mean?'

Hattie flushes red. Just the thought of Daniel and Lexi having Mermaid's Gold makes her want to scream, and she tries not to think about Lexi with Daniel. He can screw whoever he wants; it's nothing to her. But she still feels a traitorous ache deep in her chest as she leads Tiktac out of the indoor arena and back towards the stables.

Walking alongside her, Jonathan puts his hand on her shoulder and gives it a squeeze. 'Come on, Hats, you can't hide away forever. You've got a plus one on your invite – I recommend you bring that gorgeous friend of yours and come and get smashed. It's free food and booze, after all.'

'Perhaps,' says Hattie. She knows Lady Pat is going, and if Liberty comes as her plus one maybe it'd be fun.

'No, "perhaps" isn't good enough. Make it a yes and then I'll stop badgering you.' He raises his eyebrows. 'How about I make your invite plus two, and your friend can bring her famous boyfriend?'

Hattie shakes her head. As they reach the beautiful red brick Victorian stable yard, Hattie marvels at the perfectness of the place; twenty stables along with a feed room, hay barn, tack room, wash room and horse solarium are arranged around the four sides of the square yard. The cobbles have been salted to prevent slips on the ice that formed overnight and the slate roof is frosted white. On the dovecote high above the tack room is a weathervane of an eventer jumping a hedge. She's going to miss her daily trips here. Jonathan's been good to her and she's enjoyed working with his horses.

'So?' asks Jonathan in a playful tone as he gives her a nudge with his elbow. 'Will Cinderella and her friends come to the ball or will the wicked Lexi and dastardly Daniel keep her away?'

Hattie can't help but smile. She makes her decision. Jonathan's right; she can't hide forever. Why should *she* miss out when it was Daniel who acted like a dick?

Turning towards Jonathan, she nods. 'Okay, fine. I'll be there.'

CHAPTER FIFTY-TWO

DANIEL

Jonathan Scott's place is really something. The quarter-of-a-mile driveway winds through the mature pastureland and sweeps around in a turning circle in front of the imposing three-storey mansion. Floodlights from within the flowerbeds project light at the house, showing off the striking red bricks and white pointing. The light bounces off the sash windows and glitters in the reflection from the fountain in the middle of the turning circle. In the centre of the house, the double-height portico with four pillars that frames the entrance adds to the grandeur.

'Bloody hell,' says Eddie, whistling. 'JS must be minted.'

'Family money,' says Jenny. 'His great-great-grandfather was some kind of explorer, apparently.'

Eddie nods. Daniel says nothing. He's heard it before and he's trying hard not to feel bitter, but it's not like Jonathan Scott ever had to sell himself in order to pay his team's wages.

'Can you pick us up at midnight?' Jenny asks as she pays the taxi driver.

'Sure, no problem,' says the driver, calling it into the cab office. 'Have a good night.'

Eddie's already got out and is talking to a couple of people who've just arrived in the car in front. Daniel feels his adrenaline spike. Hattie is probably going to be here tonight. He needs to speak to her but he doesn't know what to say, or how to approach her.

'Daniel? Did you hear me?' Jenny is looking at him. 'I said, are you all set?'

'Yeah, sure,' says Daniel. He knows he can't stay in here forever. He swallows down the anxiety and waits for Jenny to get out of the cab. Then takes a breath to calm his nerves and opens the door.

The cold air hits him like a slap in the face after the warmth of the cab. Shivering, he hurries after Jenny and Eddie. They follow a torch-lit path along a red carpeted walkway, through a gateway and up to a huge white marquee. The thing is massive – at least the size of a ballroom. At the entrance, there are waiting staff dressed in black with trays of champagne, handing flutes to each guest as they go inside. Daniel's only been to Jonathan Scott's yard once before, and it's hard to recognise the layout in the dark, but he thinks the marquee might have been erected on the tennis courts.

He feels awkward in his dinner jacket. The invite said black tie, and in the past he's quite enjoyed the end of season party, but when he got his tuxedo out of the wardrobe he was shocked at how badly it fitted. He's lost far more weight over the past few months than he realised. So much so, he had to get an emergency tailoring job done to take the tuxedo in by several inches. Even though it was taken in barely a fortnight ago, the trouser waistband is now too big and his collar too loose again. He has to fix things. He can't carry on this way. Taking a glass of champagne, he thanks the waiter and goes into the marquee, looking for Hattie.

It's loud inside; people are laughing and talking, raising their voices to be heard over the string quartet playing just inside the entrance. Daniel searches for Hattie. He sees plenty of faces he knows, from the old guard to the young bloods, the selectors to the trainers and the owners. But none of them are her.

He pushes his way through the throng. The Event Riders' Winter Ball is always a glamorous affair, but this year it's even more Hollywood than usual. The bar on the other side of the space is bookended by life-size rearing horse ice sculptures and hanging from the tented ceiling above the round dinner tables and their silver-and-white place settings is a vast floral display of winter foliage, berries and flowers. At the other end of the marquee is a huge dance floor. It looks as if the stage is set up for a live band.

There must be well over a hundred and fifty people here already milling about around the bar and the tables. Daniel checks his watch – it's almost eight o'clock. The dinner is scheduled to start at eight so he doesn't have long. He knows Lexi and Dexter are going to arrive a little late and he needs to talk to Hattie; he has to explain. If he doesn't do it now, he might not get the chance.

He scans the marquee. He sees JaXX over at the bar, his arm around Liberty, Hattie's friend, but she isn't with them. Moving through the crowd, he says hello to Greta and Fergus but doesn't stop. Tyler Jacobs asks him a question, but Daniel makes his apologies, saying he'll find him later, and keeps moving. He reaches the bar, but there's still no sign of Hattie. Turning, he looks back across the space.

That's when he sees her. She's over by the tables, walking from group to group, chatting a few moments and then moving on. Her hair is styled in loose waves, and her long red dress is perfect for the ball. She looks stunning. And she's arm in arm with Jonathan Scott. Jealousy flares inside Daniel. He knows the rumours about Jonathan Scott, and from what he's heard they're mostly under-exaggerated.

He clenches his fists. Moves to head them off.

'Not so hasty, dear.' The woman's voice comes from his right, a cut-glass accent with a tone that implies she's always obeyed. Her satin-gloved fingers grasp his arm, and she says, 'I wouldn't do it if I were you.'

He spins round, ready to tell the woman to back off, that he must talk to Hattie. The words fall silent on his lips as he sees who it is. She looks different to when he last saw her at Kingsland International; her hair is slicked back, and she's wearing a burgundy velvet tuxedo complete with a black bow tie. 'Lady Babbington.'

Before she can answer, a waiter approaches them. He holds out a silver tray with canapés towards them. 'Quail egg and caviar,' he says, gesturing to one side of the tray. 'And duck breast and plum jam.'

'Good man, I'm absolutely ravenous,' says Lady Pat. She takes two duck canapés and winks at the waiter. 'I'll double up on this one. I can't abide caviar. Revolting stuff.'

'Sir?' The waiter moves the tray closer to him.

Daniel shakes his head. 'No, I'm—'

'Nonsense,' says Lady Pat, gesturing towards the tray. 'There's nothing left of you, Daniel. You're skin and bone. Get a few of those down you pronto.'

He's sick with nerves about speaking to Hattie so eating is the last thing on his mind, but Lady Babbington is a formidable character and he doesn't think she'd take well to him refusing so he takes a napkin and a couple of canapés. A little way to his left, he sees Daphne Wainscoat chatting with some of the recent medallists. She's been allowed to bring her terrier, Sheridan, who is looking very dapper in a dog tuxedo. Daniel watches as Daphne helps herself to two helpings from each tray and eats one herself and feeds the other to her dog. Daniel looks at the canapés in his hand; maybe Sheridan would like them too.

'Now eat, and leave Hattie be,' says Lady Pat.

Daniel watches Hattie move from one table to a group standing on the edge of the dance floor. He recognises one of the members of the British team selection committee and a couple of other regular supporters. The dinner gong sounds and the people at the bar start to move towards the tables. The dinner must be about to start. He's running out of time. 'I need to see her. I can't not apologise—'

'I said stay away.' Lady Pat steps into his path. She looks at him sternly. 'You've done that young woman quite enough damage as it is. That horse was everything to her. You broke her heart.'

'I… didn't want… Mermaid's Gold,' Daniel says, nerves making his words come out stilted and awkward. He takes a breath. 'Look, I know Hattie thinks I was behind it, but I wasn't. Lexi bought the mare without my knowledge. The first I knew of it was when Eddie said he'd been told to send my old lorry to Kingsland International at the crack of dawn to collect a new horse.'

Lady Pat narrows her gaze. 'Is that so?'

He holds her eye contact. Won't look away. He *has* to convince her. 'Yes, it is.'

Lady Pat gives a curt nod. 'Even if that was the case, you should have sent the horse back.'

'I know,' says Daniel, his anxiety and his tone rising. Hattie is moving over to a table in the centre of the space. Once she sits down, it'll be too late. He needs to move, but he can't leave Lady Babbington without putting her straight on the situation. 'Lexi refused. I told her I couldn't ride the mare – I couldn't even get a saddle near her – but it made no difference.' He looks down. 'I've been fobbing her off since then, telling her things are fine and now the season is over the mare is turned out on a break.' He looks back at Lady Pat. 'The truth is, Mermaid's Gold has been turned away in the field with The Rogue this whole time. It's okay for now, but come the new year I'll need a new plan because

Lexi will expect results. I have to get the horse back to Hattie before then.'

'So do it.'

'I...' He watches as Jonathan Scott pulls out a chair and Hattie sits down. Jonathan takes the seat next to her. Daniel's taken too long. Shit. He looks at Lady Pat. Rubs his forehead. 'It's not that simple.'

Lady Pat shrugs. Her voice is brusque. 'Ridiculous! Why ever not? You can't ride the horse. Hattie can. It's obvious.'

Daniel exhales hard. He has to tell her the worst of it. 'Lexi said she'd have the mare shot rather than let Hattie have her back.'

'Shoot her? That's preposterous! She can't bloody well shoot her!' Lady Pat's voice booms loud. The people closest to them look round, but luckily the room is so noisy with chatter that her words are lost before they reach Hattie.

'*I* know that, but Lexi doesn't care about horses or, well, anything other than power.'

Lady Pat raises her eyebrow. 'Where's the power in shooting a horse she's just paid a fortune for and I would pay to have returned? She's your owner. Surely she'd want the money to get another horse?'

'Yeah,' says Daniel, ruefully. 'She owns me. And if I don't do what she wants, she'll ruin me.'

'Owns *you?*' Lady Pat moves closer. 'Ruin you how? Tell me everything.'

And so he does. He tells her about the arrangement, the horses and all of Lexi's demands. He even tells her about the dinner-turned-sex-party and how he legged it away. He finishes with the latest issue. 'I found out today that she hasn't paid her monthly owner fee for the horses and training. She's always been on time before, but this month, nothing. When I called her, she told me her husband was having some cashflow issues but she'd be able to pay me next week. There was something in the way she said it, though. I didn't believe her.'

Lady Pat listens without interrupting. Now he's finished, she has a determined look in her eye. 'Don't worry. We're going to fix this.'

'I just want to get Hattie her horse back and end the contract with Lexi Marchfield-Wright.' Daniel looks from Lady Pat across the marquee to where Hattie is sitting beside Jonathan Scott. 'I should tell her—'

'No. Not yet, and not here.' Lady Pat taps him on the arm. 'I'm saving you from yourself, you realise? The green-eyed monster is never a good look in these situations, and if what you're telling me is true, we need to act fast.' Lady Pat's expression turns stony. '*I* need to act fast.'

'And what do I do?'

'For now, Daniel, you need to go and take a seat at the appropriate table and eat dinner.' She pats his arm again. 'Leave the rest with me. I have a plan.'

The gong sounds again, calling the stragglers to take their seats for the last time. Daniel walks over to table nineteen. Jenny and Eddie are already seated. Daniel takes his place beside Jenny and says hello to Pippa Fields, the ex-British team stalwart who is now retired and teaching the best cross-country clinics around. The wine waiter pours him a glass of chilled sauvignon blanc while a team of waiting staff serve the starter of scallops, pink grapefruit and lemon verbena.

'This is great,' says Eddie, gesturing at his plate with his fork as he tucks into his scallop.

'Divine,' says Pippa Fields.

'Ditto,' says Jenny. 'Totally orgasmic.'

They make quick work of the starters. Daniel has a few bites and it tastes sensational, but he's too preoccupied to enjoy it. The chatter around the table is jolly and fun but Daniel finds it hard to join in. He's thinking about ending the contract with Lexi and getting Mermaid's Gold back to Hattie. He'll tell Lexi the contract is void due to non-payment, he decides. He'll ask his parents' old lawyers to send the letter, but he won't do it until Lady Pat's plan to get Mermaid's Gold back has worked. Until then, he has to keep the mare safe.

Daniel takes another mouthful of wine and glances over towards table twenty-two where Lady Pat is deep in conversation with Hugh Stewkley and Tyler Jacobs. None of them have touched their starters. Daniel feels his stomach twist with anxiety. He hopes she's not telling them what he told her about the arrangement with Lexi. If what he's done gets out, he'll be ruined, forever known as the subject of scandalous gossip. No one will take him seriously again.

As he watches, trying to lip-read but failing, Lady Pat looks up and meets his gaze. She holds his eye contact for a long moment, and then raises her glass to him and nods.

He wishes he knew what it meant.

CHAPTER FIFTY-THREE
LEXI

She's standing beside Dexter when the shouting starts. It's after dinner and while the band plays and the more energetic-feeling ball-goers show off their dance moves, they've adjourned to the bar area of the marquee. They're having a drink with Dexter's latest potential investor, Aaron Andrews, and his wonderfully gossipy wife, Bunnie, who's telling them all about a new scandal in the young rider team. That's when Hugh Stewkley interrupts.

'I've got a bone to pick with you, Marchfield-Wright,' says Hugh, jabbing his finger at Dexter's chest. 'You've got a lot of explaining to do.'

Dexter, despite being twice the size of the older man, looks like he's worried and Lexi wonders why. A fearful man is certainly not a turn-on. Hugh Stewkley, on the other hand, looks really quite dashing with his quiffed white hair and exquisitely cut tuxedo. In his early eighties and still chairman of the board at his company, Compass Electronics, he's the embodiment of wealth personified, thinks Lexi, and there's nothing that's a more powerful aphrodisiac than that. Dexter told her only a month or so ago that Hugh had invested half a million in his latest property scheme and if it went well he'd be looking to invest at least eight figures in the new year. She puts her hand on Hugh's arm. 'Hugh, darling, there must be some mistake.'

'I sincerely hope you're right,' says Hugh, icily, as he removes her hand from his arm without taking his eyes off Dexter. 'You led me to believe dividend payments were made on the second of the month, is that correct?'

'It is,' says Dexter, fiddling with the napkin in his hand. 'Each month, on the second, just as I was telling Mr Andrews here.'

Aaron Andrews nods uncomfortably. Bunnie, his wife, takes his elbow and persuades him to take a step away from Dexter and Hugh. Lexi bites her lip. This is really rather embarrassing.

Hugh raises an eyebrow. 'Then why, seeing as this is the fifth, have I not received mine?'

Lexi stays silent as she watches the conversation. Dexter appears calm at first glance but it's fake; she can see in his body language and darting eyes that he's becoming agitated. Her mind is whirring. When Daniel told her the payment for the horses hadn't gone through, she asked Dexter about it and he said he'd been moving money between accounts and it'd affected the payment but it was nothing to worry about. He told her it would be paid within a couple of days. But now Hugh is claiming he hasn't received his dividend payment and Dexter is increasingly uncomfortable. Something odd is going on.

Dexter shakes his head. 'I've no idea, Hugh. It would have been sent to the bank with all the other payments. It's odd you haven't received yours – it must be an anomaly. I'll check with my office tomorrow and—'

'It's not an anomaly,' says Tyler Jacobs, moving over from a group by the bar to stand beside Hugh. 'I haven't received any dividends either. Not for my investments in White Sands Beech Condos or the Sunset Horizon Apartments. What's going on, Dexter?'

Another investor with a late payment; this is totally embarrassing. What the hell is Dexter playing at? thinks Lexi, clutching her champagne flute tighter.

Dexter looks from Hugh to Tyler and opens his arms out wide. 'Gentleman, there's an explanation, I'm sure, an error of some kind. Perhaps we could move somewhere a little more—'

'No. We'll discuss this right here,' says Hugh, drawing himself up taller. 'What's the problem?'

'There's no problem at all.' Dexter smiles. It's more tooth than warmth and makes him look like a used car salesman. 'The luxury rental market is as hot as ever, and the properties you've invested in are increasing in value all the time. They're great assets, and the rental income is significant. Trust me, there's nothing for you to worry about.'

'Well, that's the problem,' says Hugh, fixing Dexter with a steely gaze. 'I don't bloody well trust you. Not one jot. You see, I had a friend do some digging into the property developments you said my money had been invested into and—'

'Well I don't think that was at all necessary,' interrupts Dexter. 'The payments are only a couple of—'

'My friend is a private investigator,' says Hugh, talking over him. 'She's extremely experienced at what she does and she found a big problem.'

'As I already said, there's no problem,' says Dexter, his tone falsely jovial. 'I don't know what you're talking about but your friend is obviously mistaken.'

'You're a fraudster, aren't you, Marchfield-Wright?' says Hugh. He turns and raises his voice so all the people close by can hear. 'That's right, I said you are a fraudster.'

The conversations around them fall silent. All eyes are on Dexter and Hugh. Lexi remembers how Dexter told her they couldn't afford a fourth horse. She thought it was a ruse to stop her spending more money on Daniel, but now it seems she was wrong. She's never had anything to do with her husband's business activities, but she knows what he is and how his so-called investment schemes work.

From the way Dexter's body has suddenly gone rigid, his complexion has turned blotchy, and his left hand has started to tremble, it's obvious he fears Hugh has proof of the truth. A cold realisation grips her. If Dexter is exposed as a con man, they'll lose all their money and she'll be dragged down with him. She can't have that. She can't lose the money. She refuses to go back to an ordinary life.

Dexter clasps Hugh by the shoulder and tries to turn him away from the bar and the people surrounding them who have gathered to witness the exchange. 'Please, quiet down, Hugh. Don't be so—'

'Do not try to shush me, Marchfield-Wright,' says Hugh, his voice rising to a shout as he shoves Dexter away. 'I will *not* be shushed. Tell me, do *any* of the properties we've invested in actually exist?'

Dexter shakes his head. He looks from Hugh to Aaron and then Tyler. 'That's not—'

'You're saying the investments aren't real?' says Aaron, looking confused. 'But he's spent half the night telling me what a great opportunity this new place in Borneo is.'

'It likely doesn't exist but, if it does, it's not his,' says Hugh, dismissively.

William Stanton-Bassett steps over from the group he's been chatting with near the dance floor. He sniffs loudly and smooths down his moustache. 'What's this I hear about a problem with investments? Is that why my dividends are late this month?'

'You as well?' Tyler curses under his breath. He puts his finger under his bowtie, loosening the knot, and looks at Hugh. 'What's happened to the money we invested?'

'Gone, I expect.' Hugh points at Dexter. 'My private investigator friend said there's no connection whatsoever between this man's investment company and any property developments. She said his company has no overseas assets and no shares or ownership of any condos or apartments.'

Tyler's ashen-faced. 'But the company records, I checked them and they seemed above board.'

'Faked,' says Hugh. 'Clever fakes, I'll give you, but still lies.'

'What's this you're saying? It's all gone?' roars Stanten-Bassett. 'I gave this man two million pounds and you're telling me it's just vanished?'

Dexter looks like he's going to be sick. His hands are shaking. The game's clearly up.

This is bad. Lexi's heart rate accelerates. She can't stay here. Needs to get out. She takes a step back, away from the men, towards the bar, a plan already forming in her mind.

'What about my two million? What about the projected annual growth of twelve or fifteen percent?' Stanten-Bassett clenches his fists, his face reddening as he steps closer to Dexter. 'Where the hell is my money?'

Dexter looks around the group. His eyes are wild, like a cornered animal. 'Look, there's no need to be concerned, this is all just a—'

'No more bullshit,' shouts Hugh, jabbing his finger at Dexter. 'Tell us the truth.'

'There's… I…' stammers Dexter, stepping away from him.

'You disgusting man! You said investing with you would grow our grandchildren's university fund,' says Bunnie, throwing her drink in Dexter's face.

The temporarily blinded Dexter staggers sideways into Stanton-Bassett.

'Get off me, you rogue,' shouts Stanton-Bassett, shoving Dexter roughly away. 'Tell us what you've done with our money.'

Blinking heavily, Dexter lunges at Stanton-Bassett, his fist connecting with the older man's jaw, then turns to run. Aaron and Tyler block his path. They grab for his arms and pin them behind his back. He thrashes wildly, trying to shake them off.

Stanton-Bassett, who like everyone else has been taking advantage of the bottomless table wine and free bar, drops like a stone. He falls awkwardly, catching the side of his head on a table. There's a sickening thump.

Tyler shouts, 'Someone call an ambulance.'

'And the police,' adds Hugh.

Dexter stops struggling against Aaron and Tyler's grip and stands staring at the injured man at his feet. With all eyes on Stanton-Bassett, Lexi takes her chance. She moves backwards again. She's level with the ice sculpture now. A few more paces and she can duck around the bar and out of the marquee through the tradesperson access behind. So far no one seems to have noticed she's missing.

Dazed, and bleeding heavily from the gash on his head, Stanton-Bassett tries to stand, but needs to be helped up by Hugh and Bunnie. They lift him into a chair and Hugh uses his handkerchief to apply pressure to the head wound. Dexter, still restrained by Aaron and Tyler, stands there motionless.

As people crowd around them, all eyes on Stanton-Bassett and Dexter, Lexi reaches the tradesperson access. She pauses for a moment and takes one last look at the man she married. He looks beaten, broke, nothing like the proud, ambitious man she wanted as a husband. Exhaling hard, she turns and steps out through the doorway in the marquee and disappears into the night.

She doesn't look back.

CHAPTER FIFTY-FOUR

HATTIE

Hattie wakes with her head pounding and a persistent ringing in her ears. She's so groggy, it takes her a minute to realise the ringing isn't in her head but is coming from her mobile phone. Groping for it on the bedside table, she opens her eyes and swears under her breath as the sunlight assaults her vision. Blinking, she sits up and answers the call.

'Hello,' she croaks. 'Why are you calling me so early?'

'Well, hello yourself,' says Liberty. 'It's hardly early. How are you feeling?'

Hattie thinks her friend sounds far too perky for someone who must have single-handedly drunk the majority of two bottles of fizz last night. 'Pretty shit.'

'Well, you need to get yourself together fast. A whole load of stuff's been going down and you're never going to believe—'

'Why are you whispering?' asks Hattie, rubbing her forehead to try and ease the throbbing pain in her head. Through the fog in her mind, she thinks back to the last time she saw Liberty; she was slow dancing with JaXX before the fight broke out and the police arrived. 'Where are you?'

'Erm... I...'

'Are you with JaXX?' asks Hattie, smiling.

There's a pause, then Liberty says, 'Where I am isn't important right now. What you need to know is that Dexter Marchfield-Wright was arrested and charged this morning.'

Hattie remembers all the drama of the fight, and the police storming into the party to break it up. The officers carted off a few people including Dexter Marchfield-Wright. 'How do you—?'

'It's on the WhatsApp group chat.'

'But I haven't even seen...' Hattie looks at the screen of her phone. She's shocked to see it's gone eleven o'clock. She's not slept this late in years. Further down the bed, Peanut and Banana are still snoring happily. They don't seem in any hurry to get up.

'A *lot* has happened this morning,' continues Liberty. 'The word is they're seizing the Marchfield-Wrights' assets including their event horses while they build the prosecution case.'

'Jesus.' Hattie swallows hard, trying to keep the nausea at bay as she toggles across to WhatsApp. Sure enough, there are forty-two unread messages on the Winter Ball chat, all discussing the arrest of Dexter Marchfield-Wright. She tries to think through what it means for Mermaid's Gold if the horses are seized as part of the investigation, but her brain is frustratingly sluggish. 'Where are the horses now?'

'They haven't said.' Liberty breathes out hard. 'You could—'

'Sorry, Lib, I have to go. Thanks for the heads-up. I'll call you later.' Hattie hangs up and immediately dials again. The number is Daniel's; she's almost deleted it many times from her contacts but now she's relieved she didn't.

'Come on, come on,' she says as the phone continues to ring.

She swears as the answerphone kicks in.

∼

Having rattled her old Ford Focus along the back lanes at breakneck speed, she arrives at Daniel's home, Templeton Manor, in twelve minutes. Racing up the potholed driveway as fast as she can, the car's suspension groans and creaks from the strain. Hattie doesn't care about the car, though – all she can think about is Mermaid's Gold.

The drive ends in a wide gravel parking area in front of the big, crumbling manor house. Half covered in a veil of ivy, the house looks like it's peeping out from behind an overgrown fringe.

Skidding the Focus to a halt in a shower of gravel, Hattie leaps out. Around the side of the house, towards what Hattie assumes is the entrance to the yard, is a parked horsebox. It's not Daniel's – Hattie remembers that his has his name painted along the side. With her heart banging in her chest, she sprints towards it.

As she hurtles around the side of the lorry, she sees two men at the back, closing up the ramp. 'Stop, stop!'

Startled, the men turn towards her. One she recognises as Daniel's head groom, Eddie. The other is a stocky man in a plaid lumberjack shirt and jeans.

'You can't take Mermaid's Gold,' gasps Hattie, out of breath from running.

The plaid-shirted guy frowns. Taking a piece of paper out of his shirt pocket, he scans the words. 'Don't have a horse of that name on here.'

'Aren't these the Marchfield-Wrights' horses then?'

'They are,' says Eddie. 'But Mermaid's Gold isn't with them.'

Hattie looks from Eddie to the other man. Her head's pounding and she feels like she's about to vomit. 'Where is she then? I don't believe you.'

Hurrying to the door at the side of the lorry, she flips the steps down and opens the door into the living area. Rushing up the steps, she opens the door between the living and the horse area.

She hears a gentle wicker. Three inquisitive faces turn towards her. There's a bright bay with a white stripe down his nose, a lemon-and-white skewbald with a wide blaze, and a roan gelding. Hattie recognises them – the bay is Rocket Fuel, the skewbald is Pornstar Martini and the roan Pink Fizz.

Mermaid's Gold isn't here.

Defeated, Hattie climbs out of the lorry.

'You done now?' says the plaid-shirted guy dismissively. He looks at Eddie. 'Thanks for your help, mate.'

The guy goes around to the cab. Moments later, the lorry's engine fires into life and the horsebox pulls away down the drive.

Hattie turns to Eddie, unable to disguise the hope in her voice. 'So she's still here?'

Eddie gives her a sad smile and shakes his head. 'They collected her earlier.'

Hattie bites her lip. Doesn't want to cry in front of Eddie. If only she hadn't drunk so much last night. If only she'd woken up at her usual time. If only she'd come here earlier. If only, if only, if only. 'Who took her? Why didn't she go with the others?'

'I don't know, I'm sorry. It was a commercial transport company. They wouldn't tell me where they were taking her.' Eddie runs his hand through his hair and looks troubled. 'Maybe the Marchfield-Wrights managed to keep her somehow…?'

That doesn't make it any better. Mermaid's Gold could be anywhere. 'Will Daniel know where she is?'

Eddie shakes his head again. 'He was gone before I came out to start doing the yard this morning. Said he needed to get answers, I assume from the Marchfield-Wrights. He doesn't even know the horses have been taken yet.'

'What's the latest on Mr Marchfield-Wright? Is there any chance this is all some kind of alcohol-fuelled misunderstanding?'

'It seems pretty serious. Word is that he's been running a Ponzi scam for years, getting people to invest in luxury overseas developments that don't actually exist. A lot of people around here invested significant amounts and it looks like they've lost their money.'

'But surely people would know pretty quickly if the properties weren't real. Wouldn't they want to use them for holidays?'

'They were all meant to be long-term rental or sale properties – the investors got regular payments back as "profit" but in reality that profit was just Dexter Marchfield-Wright repurposing new investors' money as "dividends" in order to maintain the illusion. From what I've heard, it sounds like the number of investors and "profit" payments became unsustainable. Rumour has it the outstanding debts are well into the tens of millions.'

Hattie can barely take it in: her beloved Mermaid's Gold is owned by criminal fraudsters. Who knows where they've taken her. Her headache intensifies from the stress. 'I have to find Mermaid's Gold. Can you tell Daniel to call me as soon as he's back? The least he can do is give me any information he has that could help me track her down.'

'Will do,' says Eddie.

'Thanks.' Hattie turns and starts walking back towards her car.

'You know, he never rode her, Mermaid's Gold,' calls Eddie. 'She wouldn't let anyone put a saddle on her back and Daniel said she was your horse, not his.'

Hattie spins round. 'Then why the hell did he keep her?'

'Lexi Marchfield-Wright threatened to have the mare shot if Daniel didn't ride her. Said he'd have to fake an accident or lame her so she could cash in on the insurance. He was stringing Lexi along, pretending things were going okay.' Eddie shakes his head. 'But he never wanted the horse in the first place. He told Lexi to give her back.'

Fear flares inside Hattie. Her hands start to tremble. 'What if Lexi suspected and that's why Mermaid's Gold was taken away separately? What if she's sent her to the knacker?'

Eddie frowns. Hattie can tell that he hadn't considered that.

'She wouldn't do that, surely?'

Hattie doesn't share Eddie's half-arsed conviction. She's seen the dead look behind Lexi Marchfield-Wright's eyes. That woman is capable of anything.

CHAPTER FIFTY-FIVE

HATTIE

*T*here are two slaughterhouses within a fifty-mile radius, but neither have had a horse of Mermaid's Gold's description delivered to them that morning. Feeling despondent, and not knowing where next to search, Hattie decides to return to Clover Hill House and wait for Daniel to get in touch.

Turning into the driveway, Hattie sees a red horsebox with 'JDF EQUESTRIAN TRANSPORT' written in two-foot-high lettering along the side. Beside it, a familiar-looking flat-cap-wearing man in a red polo shirt appears to be arguing with Lady Pat.

Hattie's stomach flips.

Braking to a halt, she kills the engine and leaps out of the car. 'Lady Pat?'

She hears a horse whinny and hooves stamping inside the horsebox. The lorry begins to rock.

The man clutches at his flat cap. 'Oh Jesus, not again. I tell you this horse isn't safe to handle without the tranquiliser. You need a vet.'

Lady Pat ignores him and turns to greet Hattie. 'There you

are, dear. I wondered where you'd got to. We've been waiting for—'

'Is she here?' Hattie rushes towards the lorry. 'Is Mermaid's Gold in there?'

'Of course, dear. Who else would it be?'

Flipping down the steps, Hattie opens the door to the living area and rushes inside. The whinnying gets louder. With quivering fingers, she undoes the door between the living and the horse area and yanks it open.

Mermaid's Gold stares back at her. Wickers.

'Hello, girl,' says Hattie, her lower lip trembling. 'It's so good to see you.'

Stepping into the horse area, Hattie puts her arms around the mare's neck and hugs her tight. Mermaid's Gold is still for a long moment, then nuzzles the pocket of Hattie's jeans, asking for a Polo. Hattie laughs and pulls the packet out. As she feeds the horse several mints, she strokes her velvety nose. 'You can have as many as you want.'

～

Later, once Mermaid's Gold has been reunited in the paddock with her goat friends, Mabel and Gladys, Hattie and Lady Pat head into the house.

'I should message Liberty and tell her to come over,' says Hattie, taking two clean mugs out of the cupboard. 'We need to celebrate.'

'We do,' says Lady Pat, her tone suddenly serious. 'But there's something else we need to discuss first, just the two of us.'

'Okay,' says Hattie as she switches the kettle on. She glances at Lady Pat, who is looking rather grim-faced. Hattie dreads what she might be about to tell her. Is she selling Mermaid's Gold again? Is there a problem with the mare staying here? Is Robert going to keep fighting for ownership? 'Is it about Mermaid's Gold?'

'Not exactly,' says Lady Pat, sitting down at the kitchen table. She gestures at the kettle. 'We're both going to need something stronger than that. Dig out that whiskey, dear. Dutch courage and all that.'

Hattie's mouth goes dry. She feels a wave of nausea rising, part hangover and part fear. She's not sure she can stomach more alcohol but she fetches the whiskey from the drinks cupboard and pours a generous measure into each of the mugs. Putting them down on the table, she sits opposite Lady Pat. 'What's going on?'

'First of all, I want you to know that my legal team found a flaw in the document Robert had me sign. The sale of Mermaid's Gold to Lexi Marchfield-Wright is null and void, and therefore Mermaid's Gold has been returned to my ownership. Robert, rather reluctantly it has to be said, understands he has no claim on the horse or indeed the goats.' Lady Pat reaches into the inside pocket of her Barbour that's draped over the back of the chair, and pulls out a rather crumpled envelope. She hands it to Hattie. 'This is for you.'

Hattie takes the envelope. 'What is it?'

'I suggest you look for yourself.'

Opening the envelope, Hattie removes the sheet of paper inside and scans the text. The blood rushes to her cheeks. She feels suddenly light-headed. Looking back at Lady Pat, she asks, 'Is this for real?'

Lady Pat smiles. 'Absolutely.'

'But why would you do this?'

'Well that, dear, is rather a long story.' Lady Pat looks down at her whiskey.

Hattie rereads the legal document she's holding but it still doesn't seem real. The letter states that Lady Patricia Babbington has signed over the ownership and all rights related to the event horse Mermaid's Gold to Harriet Kimble. Mermaid's Gold now belongs to her. 'Thank you. This is amazing but I don't understand why—'

'No, of course you don't,' Lady Pat says. 'So I'll start at the beginning and try to explain, things are often easier that way.'

Hattie takes a sip of her whiskey. From the expression on Lady Pat's face, she thinks she's going to need it.

'I always knew my husband, Sir Harry, was unfaithful. We had an understanding, what you young people would call an open relationship these days. I had my own special friend and Sir Harry had plenty of other ladies he entertained but was always discreet. As far as I knew, his extracurricular dalliances never lasted long.' Lady Pat takes a gulp of whiskey. Looks Hattie in the eye. 'It was only after his death I learnt that he'd continued one of those relationships for over thirty years and that they'd a child together.'

Hattie doesn't know what to say, so she stays silent and tries to look sympathetic.

Lady Pat holds her gaze. 'The woman he had a child with was Melanie Kimble.'

Hattie stares at Lady Pat as she realises what that means. 'My mum and your husband were together?'

Lady Pat nods. 'My husband is your father. You see, your mother was an instructor at pony club camp, and our son, Bartholomew, was a pony club member then. That year was actually his last camp.' Lady Pat purses her lips. She looks away as she dabs at her eyes with a tissue, then turns back to face Hattie. Her tone becomes brusquer. 'Anyway, all the parents helped out if they could and Sir Harry always volunteered to be one of the fathers of the night who oversaw the security of the children's camping area. It seems that year he and your mother had something of a romantic tryst.'

'But my mum told me she didn't know where my dad was, that she'd had a wild one-night stand and didn't even know the guy's name. I never felt the need to try and look for...' Hattie shakes her head. She can't believe her mum lied to her for all these years. That she wasn't *ever* going to tell her. 'If your husband didn't tell you he was my dad, how do you know?'

'I found the paternity test – it's conclusive. And there are letters from your mother to Sir Harry. They include photos of you growing up, school reports, that sort of thing.' Lady Pat takes another gulp of whiskey. 'They kept in contact right up until he died last year.'

'But why didn't they tell me?' Hattie's voice is louder than she intended, anger rising inside her at the realisation of having found and lost her father in the same moment. 'If they were in touch, why couldn't I have met him? Why hide it from me?'

'I don't know, dear,' says Lady Pat. 'I'm sorry.'

They sit together in silence. Hattie can't believe it. Her mum kept her dad from her and now they're both dead and gone. She lied about who her dad was – made her believe there was no way to find him, that he didn't know she existed. Questions about her mum and dad's decision race through Hattie's mind, questions that can never be answered now. She massages her temples, trying to ease the headache that's intensifying with every minute.

Eventually, Lady Pat says, 'I'll happily give you the letters, the photos, and everything. Maybe they'll give you some answers.'

Hattie can't bring herself to speak. All her life, she and her mum shared everything. They were more like sisters than mother and daughter. Now it feels like their relationship was a lie.

'I know it's a lot to take in,' says Lady Pat. There's concern in her eyes. 'But I thought you should know the truth.'

Hattie swallows down the sickness she feels. She meets Lady Pat's gaze. 'Is this why you got Robert to offer me the job here?'

Lady Pat nods. 'I wanted to help you out. I felt a responsibility to look out for you; you're family, after all.'

'But I'm not *your* family, am I?' says Hattie, angrily. She runs her hand through her hair. It feels like her brain is going to explode. 'Is all this the reason why you bought Mermaid's Gold and pretended to know nothing about horses? Why you helped me?'

'Guilty as charged.' Lady Pat looks a little embarrassed. 'I thought you needed a project and we could get to know each other better until I worked up the courage to tell you about your father.'

Hattie clenches her fists. Snaps a response. 'So you lied?'

'I didn't lie, dear, I just delayed telling you the full truth.' Lady Pat exhales hard. 'I was grieving just as you're grieving. I didn't want to jump straight into it. So when I heard about Mermaid's Gold's plight, I thought it could be perfect – get her out of a bad situation and give you an unexpected gift.'

Hattie looks at the document on the table in front of her that gives her ownership of Mermaid's Gold. She might not like what Lady Pat has told her but she can't blame her for what her mum and Sir Harry did. Lady Pat has been nothing but decent. In fact, she's gone way over and above decent. Hattie takes a long breath in. Tells herself not to act like a petulant child. She looks back at Lady Pat. 'Thank you for telling me. I'd like to see the letters and everything.'

'Of course, dear. They're in my car,' says Lady Pat, relief clearly visible in her expression. 'I'll get them.'

As Lady Pat stands, Hattie thinks back to the party the previous night and how she saw her deep in conversation with Hugh Stewkley before the drama started. 'Your special friend, is it Hugh Stewkley?'

Lady Pat's neck and cheeks flush red. 'Maybe.'

Hattie narrows her gaze and cocks her head to one side. 'Did you have something to do with Hugh confronting Dexter Marchfield-Wright and the police being called last night?'

'Perhaps I did,' says Lady Pat, giving a mysterious smile and tapping the side of her nose. 'But a lady never reveals *all* her secrets.'

CHAPTER FIFTY-SIX

DANIEL

*I*t's time to decide the future.

Daniel's called a team meeting and, having finished morning feeds, they're sitting around the kitchen table, Eddie, Bunty and himself, drinking coffee and eating custard creams to warm up. Gertrude the cat is curled on a chair, her cushion a stack of old *Horse & Hound* magazines, purring loudly as Bunty strokes her. McQueen, the three-legged collie, is lying at Eddie's feet, looking up hopefully at the packet of biscuits.

Daniel takes a sip of coffee. He's relieved that neither Eddie or Bunty have asked him about the extra duties he performed as an unwritten part of his contract with Lexi. He can't imagine that they didn't know – Lexi was hardly subtle – but their discretion and loyalty has meant a lot to him. He's not heard any rumours about him through the eventing gossip mill either, so Lady Pat must have kept what he told her quiet; again, that's something for which he'll always be eternally grateful. Now it's only right that he fills the team in on what he's thinking. 'So, given everything that's happened, I thought we should talk about the yard and next season.'

Eddie nods solemnly as he breaks off a piece of custard cream and throws it to McQueen. The collie catches it, then drops it onto the flagstone floor and sniffs it before looking up at Eddie as if to ask: 'Where are the pork scratchings?' Eddie shakes his head. McQueen watches him a moment longer before wolfing down the biscuit.

'Will we be okay?' asks Bunty. She's clinging onto her mug with both hands and there's a tremble in her voice.

Daniel thinks about the question for a moment. In the last couple of weeks, everything has changed. Lexi is gone, literally disappeared, and no one knows where. Her phone is disconnected. Her house is abandoned. Rumour has it that before her husband's assets were frozen, she withdrew all the money from her accounts, the joint account and maxed out every credit card she had. According to the press, Dexter still won't say a bad word about her. He's taking personal responsibility for defrauding multiple investors to the tune of more than forty million pounds over the past ten years and has made it known he'll plead guilty when his case comes to court. His lawyer has requested an early court date, and the financial forensics have been completed in record time. Daniel's glad Dexter is holding his hands up and admitting to his crimes, but letting Lexi walk away free? On that, he thinks the man is a fool.

'Boss?' says Bunty, her expression one of extreme concern. 'Will we?'

'Yeah, sorry,' says Daniel, looking down at the printout on the table in front of him – the accounts and bank statements for the yard. 'We can get through this. The Marchfield-Wrights paid us generously for their horses and so I managed to save a chunk of that money over these past months. It means I've got enough to keep us going through the winter and the first half of next season. If I can get some jumping clinics up and running in the new year, and our other owners continue to keep their horses with us, we should be okay.'

'Thank God,' says Bunty, smiling. 'I was really worried there.'

'So was I,' says Daniel, and it's true. His first thought when the Marchfield-Wright horses were taken was that he'd go under without the regular income from them. But that's not the case; his accounts are looking healthier than they have in a long time.

'It is a relief,' says Eddie. 'But we need to think about other ways to bring in money.' He looks thoughtful. 'This would be a great place for overseas riders to base themselves when they come over for the main season. It's close to a lot of events and there's easy access to the main motorways. Plus our facilities are good.'

Daniel nods. 'It's worth exploring. We do need to think about more income generation.'

'What about looking for some more owners? We could even start a syndicate for ownership, I've heard they're becoming popular,' says Eddie, throwing another piece of custard cream to McQueen. 'We've got twenty stables, so there's plenty of space.'

Daniel's thought about that. They've got eleven horses at the moment: a few youngsters early on in their careers, some good Intermediate horses, and The Rogue. 'I'm going to keep things small for now. A couple of the Intermediates will step up to Advanced next year, and if I can I'd like to try and buy Pink Fizz back, but I don't know how long that might take.'

'I guess nothing can happen with the Marchfield-Wright horses until the court case has been heard,' says Eddie.

'True,' Daniel says. He really liked the little roan, Pink Fizz. They clicked instantly and although quite a livewire, the horse has a lot of talent. 'We'll just have to wait and see what happens.'

Eddie clears his throat. Looks a bit nervous. 'What about if you had a couple of horses come as liveries?'

Daniel takes another sip of coffee while he considers it. Doing clinics and hosting overseas riders is one thing, but having liveries could be a lot more hassle. This is his home and the idea of random people showing up at any time makes him feel uneasy.

'I don't know, if we get more people in then it'll turn into a competition yard and I—'

'What if it was just one person, and they also lodged with us?' There's intensity to Eddie's gaze.

'Lodged with us?' Daniel frowns. He doesn't want some random living in his house, but Eddie looks so nervous about asking, it must be important to him. Daniel just doesn't get why. Then the penny drops and he grins. 'You want Jenny to come and live here?'

Eddie's cheeks flush red. 'The lease on her cottage is almost up, and we'd like to live together but obviously I need to be here so... and she'd need to bring her horse Dinky, and maybe a second horse.'

'Brilliant,' says Daniel, slapping Eddie on the back. He looks at Bunty. 'How would you feel about that?'

'Jenny's ace,' says Bunty, smiling. 'And it would be nice to have another woman in the house.'

'It's settled then,' says Daniel. 'Jenny is our new housemate.'

As Eddie phones Jenny to tell her the news and Bunty heads back out to the yard to start mucking out the few stables they have horses in, Daniel gathers up the mugs and stacks them in the dishwasher. He's pleased the conversation went well. They've got a plan for the winter and the next season, and everyone seems onboard with it.

He might have lost his main source of income and three of his most experienced horses, but he feels lighter, happier, than he has in months. He's not needed to take an anti-anxiety pill since Lexi Marchfield-Wright left his life. And the best thing is that The Rogue has been given the all-clear and has started light work. If things continue to go well, he'll be back in proper work after Christmas and could aim for Badminton in the spring.

Things are on the up, and Daniel's grateful for it. There's just one thing that he hasn't managed to fix yet: his relationship with Hattie. He can't leave things the way they are.

And he can't get her out of his mind.

CHAPTER FIFTY-SEVEN

HATTIE

*W*ith Banana and Peanut with her for moral support, Hattie sits on the floor in the lounge next to her mum's memory trunk. Beside her is the stack of letters Lady Pat gave her – the letters that her mum sent Sir Harry. In front of her, the lid of the trunk is open and her old baby blanket with the little rocking horses on it is folded over the rest of the contents. Only one other item inside is visible. The envelope with Hattie's name written in her mum's handwriting is sitting on top of the blanket.

She can't put this off any longer.

Taking a deep breath, Hattie opens the envelope and starts to read.

Dearest Hattie

You are a wonderful, strong and kind woman. I know you will do brilliantly in life, but I'm sorry I can't be there to see all your successes. I will always be with you. Watching over you. But there are things I've not told you that you have a right to know.

I'm sorry it's taken me this long. I hope you will come to understand why.

I told you, back when you asked me, that I didn't know who your father was, and they didn't know about you. That wasn't the truth. Your father is Sir Harry Babbington and he loved you very much. I say loved, because Harry died last year. You didn't know, but he has always been in your life. In this trunk you'll find his letters and the details of the savings account he set up in your name and contributed to on each of your birthdays and every Christmas. He wrote you a letter on each of your birthdays and asked me to keep them to give to you after he died. I know that must sound strange, but there is a reason, so please let me explain...

'Oh my God,' says Hattie, as she reads about what happened. Sir Harry and Lady Pat's nine-year-old son, Bartholomew, died in a freak snorkelling accident in the Caribbean just a couple of months after Hattie's mum fell pregnant. He'd been exploring with Robert and Robert's parents at the time and got trapped in an underwater cave. Robert was the one to find Bartholomew – his parents having snorkelled on ahead, not keeping a close watch on the boys.

The tragic loss of a child is something no parent should ever have to bear. Lady Pat sank into a deep depression and Sir Harry couldn't bring himself to add to his wife's burden by telling her that he'd got someone else pregnant. He'd meant to tell her eventually, Hattie's mum says in her letter, but as the years passed it seemed harder and harder to break the news. So he decided never to tell his wife, and to stay in the background, hidden from Hattie. He loved her and he supported her, her mum says, but always from a distance.

Hattie's fingers grasp the letter tighter. She doesn't agree with Sir Harry's decision – if he'd told Lady Pat a few years later, she would have understood, Hattie's sure of it – but she respects the reason he made it. He was trying to protect Lady Pat.

It's clear that her mum had wanted her to know the truth, but she'd kept Sir Harry's secret for over thirty years. Hattie shakes her head. She wishes her mum had been able to tell her about this when she was alive; that they could have discussed it, and she could have asked questions. She knows it must have been hard for her mum to conceal the truth.

Hattie rereads the last paragraph of the letter. Her hands begin to shake.

...I know you're probably angry with me now, but I hope over time that anger passes. I love you always, my dear Hattie. Please don't ever forget that.

Mum x

Tears pour down Hattie's cheeks. Huge sobs convulse through her. She feels as if she's drowning in her grief. She cries for the lost relationship she could have had with her dad and the strain it must have caused her mum not to tell her the truth. She cries from the sadness she feels that they'll never have the chance to be a family. And because she'll never be able to tell her mum she isn't angry with her and that she understands. She cries because she'll never get to hug her again and tell her that she loves her.

Hours later, after she's read every letter, looked at every picture, and held every one of the keepsakes her mum stored in the trunk, Hattie is feeling drained but strangely also kind of okay. She's all cried out but she has closure.

She knows where she comes from, who her dad was and that

she had a half-brother who died when he was little. The pain of losing her mum is still there, but she's able to breathe into that pain and that's making it feel a little more manageable. She's lost her immediate family, but she's found family too.

Hattie thinks about Lady Pat and the loss she's endured. She didn't have to make contact with Hattie and she certainly didn't have to help her or encourage her to follow her dreams. It says a lot about Lady Pat's character and the kindness hidden within her rather bossy, eccentric exterior. She might not be a blood relative, but it feels to Hattie as if she is – like an aunt, perhaps? Yes, thinks Hattie, that's exactly what she feels like – Aunt Pat.

One by one, Hattie puts the letters, pictures and keepsakes back into the trunk. She smiles as she looks again at some of the photographs. There's Mum and her grinning as they eat ice creams on a windy, grey day on a beach in north Wales. Her aged about five sitting aside a dumpy grey pony and holding up a yellow fourth-place rosette – on the back of the picture, her mum's writing says: *Hattie's first gymkhana – 4th place in sack race*. And her favourite of all the pictures: Mum and her smiling for the camera as they sit on the hallowed Badminton turf in front of the famous Vicarage Vee – the huge ditch stretching out behind them and the thick oak rail above. On the back of the photo, her mum has written: *Hattie says she'll win the Badminton trophy for me one day. I know she will*

Wiping her eyes, Hattie tucks the last few pictures safely into the trunk and covers them with her old baby blanket. There's only one more thing to look at.

She opens the folder marked 'savings account'. In it are printed annual statements. As she flicks through them, Hattie's mouth opens. Her throat goes dry. She stares at the most recent one, printed off a couple of weeks before her mum died. The balance of the account is over seven hundred thousand pounds.

Heart racing, Hattie rereads the statement. She's never seen so much money.

Carefully, with trembling fingers, she puts the statements back into the folder, and places the folder back into the trunk along with all the letters, photos and keepsakes. Closing the lid, she turns and rests her back against the carved wooden sides of the trunk.

She's in shock.

So much has happened today – being reunited with Mermaid's Gold, learning about her dad, going through her mum's memory box, and Lady Pat gifting her ownership of Mermaid's Gold. Hattie feels like she needs time for it all to sink in and for her to decide what next. But there's one thing she's sure of: she's going to make the most of the opportunity she's been given and cherish the friends she's made.

And she's going to make good on her promise and make her mum proud.

CHAPTER FIFTY-EIGHT

LEXI

Dexter was right about one thing: Mauritius really is rather wonderful. As she lies back on the lounger in her two-person beech cabana, Lexi turns the page of the Daily Mail and settles in to read the full story. 'FAKE TOFF FLOGS FAKE CONDOS!' screams the headline. 'The rise and epic fail of multi-million-pound con artist Dexter Marchfield-Wright.' It's a two-page spread with pictures. She's glad of that at least; if you're going to do something you may as well go large.

And Dexter certainly did. His Ponzi property schemes are being heralded as the biggest ever seen in the UK, and so she supposes he deserves a little credit. But he's caught now, and from what it says in the paper, he's unlikely to get less than twenty years in jail for what he's done. He's been locked up without bail, and all his assets have been seized. When he does finally get out, he'll be penniless. Penniless and ordinary, thinks Lexi. She shudders. That has absolutely no appeal.

She looks at the pictures. There's a few of Dexter at the ball – one by the bar before the drama started, and two more taken during the fight. There's a smaller group shot of them seated at the table earlier in the evening, but the picture looks like it was taken on a phone and is grainy from the low light. Lexi's in it, but she's not too worried. With her changed hair colour and the little surgical adjustments she's just had, she doubts anyone would look at her and guess she's the woman in the paper. For starters, she looks at least ten years younger.

The newspaper article says that they're looking for her. The police are appealing for her to come forward as a witness. Well, they can appeal all they like but it's never going to happen. She's seen crime dramas, she knows how these things work; first they ask for you to come forward as a witness and then, once you have, they arrest you and lock you up. No. She won't be coming forward. Ever.

Because, although she'd never admit it, of course she knew what Dexter was doing – how he was conning all those people out of their money. And even if she wasn't charged or convicted with anything, she'd still be a social outcast – shunned and dirtied by association to her fraudster husband. Penniless too. And that she just couldn't stomach.

And now she doesn't have to.

The intensity of the sun is increasing as time marches on towards midday. Her feet are starting to burn, so she tucks her legs up out of the direct rays. She thinks back to the night of the ball. Hugh Stewkley did her a real favour challenging Dexter in public like he did, because it gave her a heads-up of what was coming. It gave her the chance to escape. She had to move fast to make it happen. Always looking over her shoulder, checking she wasn't being watched. But she succeeded.

First she took a cab from Jonathan Scott's place to her house. She electronically transferred all the funds from the joint account she had with Dexter into one of her secret offshore bank accounts, the ones Dexter knew nothing about. Then she did the same with her credit cards, maxing out the 'convert to cash' limits and transferring that money to the offshore account too. Once all the money was in the single offshore account, she split the total into four, and transferred three of those quarters into three other offshore accounts. The banks she used were all famous for their absolute discretion. She hopes their reputation is deserved.

Next she packed as many of her clothes as she could into her two Luis Vuitton suitcases and put all of her jewellery and valuables in her oversized travel bag. She left for the airport less than thirty minutes after arriving home.

She took the first long haul flight out of Heathrow she could get on, even roughing it in business class rather than first to get away faster. Once she landed, she paid cash to travel by yacht to the destination she had in mind. It took a while, and the sea had been choppy at times, but it had been worthwhile. She looks over the top of the newspaper at the azure ocean, the waves lapping gently at the white sand shore. Yes, it was most certainly worth it.

And all those boring tweedy horse people, wouldn't they just love to know where she is and how she pulled it off? It makes her chuckle to think of them all baffled and cold in stupid, damp England, while she's here on this beautiful private beach, with a bucks fizz cocktail, and a handsome and extremely gifted in the bedroom thirty-two-year-old Italian. To be honest, he's a very refreshing upgrade from Daniel, and free as well; he says that he adores her. And although she doesn't care for love, she'll take adoration any day of the week.

Reaching across to the little table between the loungers, Lexi picks up her bucks fizz and takes a sip. She glances at the other lounger. Marco is stretched out, reading a book and eating grapes from the bunch like a decadent god. Bronzed and muscled, he really is in peak athletic condition. And that face? Gorgeous. Lexi licks her lips. His short dark hair frames his features just right, and the dark stubble across his chin is wonderfully masculine.

She wants to lick him all over. Again. He really is delicious.

As if sensing her watching him, Marco looks over at Lexi and removes his shades, revealing those sexy brown eyes of his. 'Erika, you okay?'

'Of course, darling,' says Lexi. Folding the newspaper, she puts it down on the table. She'll get rid of it later. She smiles at Marco. And she *is* okay, because she's Erika now. She has a new passport – it's a fake but a good one – new credit cards and a new life. Lexi Marchfield-Wright no longer exists but Erika Strome is very much alive. 'I was just thinking I should probably put on a little more oil.'

'Let me help,' says Marco, in his sexy Italian accent. He sits up and swings his legs around so he's facing her.

'Thank you,' she says, passing him the tanning oil and turning over onto her stomach.

He pours the oil over her back and gets to work massaging it into her skin. Lexi shivers in anticipation.

Starting from nothing isn't so hard; she's done it before and this time she's starting with a whole lot more – nearly two million pounds. It'll tide her over until she finds her next husband, if she chooses to find one. Because who knows, maybe she'll stay free and single for a while longer.

As Marco slides his fingers under her bikini bottoms, Lexi lets out a satisfied moan and smiles. The bachelor life certainly has its attractions.

CHAPTER FIFTY-NINE

HATTIE

It's the week before Christmas and an overnight frost has hardened the ground and turned the grass white and brittle. It's still early and the frosted landscape glistens in the pale morning light. Hattie and Mermaid's Gold hack along the woodland track towards the all-weather gallops at Turner Racing – a flat racing yard that lets local event riders use the gallops as long as they're off the track before the first racehorse string arrives at eight o'clock.

Both Hattie's and Mermaid's Gold's warm breaths plume like steam into the frigid air. Hattie's glad she put her thermals on under her breeches today.

Mermaid's Gold jigs into a trot, keen to get to the all-weather gallops. Hattie rubs her neck as she persuades her back to a walk. 'Nearly there now, girl.'

Overhead, the birds are in full song as Hattie opens the gate in the fence, and manoeuvres Mermaid's Gold through it and onto the gallops.

'Hold the gate,' calls a male voice from behind her.

A horse wickers. Mermaid's Gold whinnies in reply.

Hattie swings round, surprised. She thought she was alone but through the open gateway she sees Daniel Templeton-Smith trotting up the path towards her on a big bay horse. For a moment she thinks about letting the gate slam shut before Daniel reaches it, but then she remembers how Daniel's head groom, Eddie, told her Daniel had tried to convince Lexi Marchfield-Wright to return Mermaid's Gold to her, and that he'd not been behind the awful woman buying her. So she waits, holding the gate open, but she doesn't smile.

'Thanks,' says Daniel, slowing his bay horse to a walk as they reach the gate and come through. 'Appreciate it.'

Frowning, Hattie closes the gate. She's not sure what to say. She liked Daniel. They had a connection, she thought, but then Lexi took Mermaid's Gold and he didn't return any of Hattie's phone calls. Since then, she's done her best to put him out of her mind. But he's here now, right in front of her. And still she doesn't know what to say, so she says nothing.

The silence lingers. The birds sing louder in the trees. The horses stand, waiting for the signal to move off the grass and onto the all-weather gallop track.

Daniel looks unsure. He's not meeting her gaze. This silence is just stupid and awkward, thinks Hattie. She's going to say something and then get out of here.

She takes a breath. When she does speak, they both talk at once.

'Look, I never—'

'I suppose I should—'

They both stop. Hattie shakes her head. Daniel's cheeks flush.

Damn, this is awkward.

'Go ahead,' says Hattie, gesturing for him to continue.

Daniel flushes redder. Stutters a bit. 'Oh, I, yes, okay. So, the thing is, I wanted to say sorry, basically. I didn't know Lexi was going to buy your horse out from under you. When I found out, I told her to give her back but she was adamant she wouldn't and then she kept threatening to have her shot if I didn't—'

'Eddie told me,' Hattie says, interrupting him. 'But if you weren't behind it, why didn't you contact me and say that?'

'I felt terrible. Embarrassed. And Lexi was so hard to deal with, so I...' Daniel shrugs, a defeated look on his face. His horse blows out loudly as if echoing his rider's feelings.

Hattie feels the anger and hurt of the whole incident bubbling inside her. She can't disguise the fury from her tone. 'After everything I'd told you that night at Kingsland International, how do you think *I* felt when I saw Mermaid's Gold was gone and your owner was behind it?'

Daniel shakes his head. 'Like I was a lying arsehole.'

'Yeah. Exactly.' Hattie clenches the reins tighter, causing Mermaid's Gold to throw her head up in protest. 'Sorry, girl,' she says, immediately releasing the tension on the reins and stroking the mare's neck in apology. She glares back at Daniel. 'I wanted to know why you'd let it happen, and if you'd been behind it. But most of all I was desperate to find out how my horse was – to check she was okay. But you wouldn't even return my calls.'

'I knew you must hate me and I couldn't face you telling me that.' Daniel meets her gaze. They hold eye contact for what seems like forever. 'I really am sorry it happened. I should never have agreed to having the Marchfield-Wrights as owners.' He exhales loudly again. 'It was a bad deal from the start. Lexi wanted far more than I was willing to give and... well, let's just say I've learnt the hard way that not everything is for sale.'

'That woman could have had Mermaid's Gold killed,' says Hattie, rubbing the mare's neck. 'Eddie told me you tried to fake things – pretending you were getting on fine with her even though she wouldn't let you onboard.'

'I was trying to work out a way to get her back to you.' He maintains eye contact. There's grit in his voice as he says, 'I would *never* have let her harm your horse.'

Hattie believes him. Despite the situation, she feels her stomach flip. There's something about Daniel that seems so genuine; it's hard to keep feeling angry with him. 'I'm glad Lady Pat's lawyers found the legal loophole that solved the problem.'

'Me too,' says Daniel. 'So what's your plan now?'

'Well, we're aiming for Windsor and Blenheim next season, then Badminton the year after.' She pauses as Mermaid's Gold gives a big snort, as if to say she can't wait to go to Badminton. 'But first I need to find a place to live because Robert Babbington is due home in two weeks and so he won't need a house sitter anymore. I'd like to stay around here but there's not much on the market at the moment.'

Daniel looks thoughtful. 'There's room at my place if you don't mind sharing and mucking in with the rest of the team?'

'That's kind, but I've got a bed at Liberty's house if I need it, especially as she's practically moved in with her boyfriend so the place is empty most of the time. Robert's said I can keep Mermaid's Gold in his paddocks as long as I want. I think he's ashamed about selling her and wants to make amends.' Hattie doesn't add that since Robert found out she's his cousin, he's become a lot friendlier towards her. She's starting to feel the connection to Daniel again, but she's not ready to share something that personal just yet.

'Liberty and JaXX are getting on well then?' says Daniel with a smirk.

Hattie raises her eyebrows. 'You know about that?'

Daniel laughs. 'This is a small village – Liberty and JaXX are *the* big gossip. There's even a book open in the pub on when he'll propose and they'll get married.'

Hattie grins. 'Maybe I should get in on that action.'

'Maybe you should,' replies Daniel. 'In fact, how about coming out for a drink there with me this Friday? We can grab some food and you can check out the odds?'

Hattie thinks for a moment. Friday is Christmas Eve. On Christmas Day, Hattie is looking forward to celebrating with Lady Pat, Liberty and JaXX but she doesn't need to be at High Drayton Manor until lunchtime, so there'll be plenty of time to feed Mermaid's Gold and the goats even if she's got a hangover and oversleeps. She tilts her head. 'Okay, you're on.'

They smile at each other. This is nice, thinks Hattie. She's glad to be on speaking terms with Daniel again, and that they're going on a sort-of date in the Dog and Duck on Christmas Eve. 'So how are things for you now the Marchfield-Wright horses have gone? It must have been tough.'

'To be totally honest it was a relief to be free of Lexi. I knew I couldn't keep working with her unreasonable demands and frequent histrionics – what she did with Mermaid's Gold was the last straw. I was sad to see the horses go, though, they were good sorts, but now Dexter's trial is done I've managed to buy Pink Fizz from the liquidators and I've got a couple of good youngsters and some Intermediates coming through for my other owners.' He gives his big bay horse a pat on the neck. 'The best thing is The Rogue being back in work.'

Hattie recognises the horse now. He was the one who'd had an accident on the cross-country at Badminton back in May. 'How's he doing?'

'Really great,' says Daniel, smiling. 'We're slowly building up, just straight lines and basic walk, trot and canter at the moment. He's got a scan at the end of January and if things are looking good we can start proper work then.'

'I'm so glad he's okay,' says Hattie, meaning it. She can see how much the horse means to Daniel. 'It'd be great if you can have another shot at the big time with him.'

Daniel has a wistful look in his eyes. 'Winning Badminton together has always been the dream.'

'I hope it happens for you,' says Hattie. She glances at her watch and is shocked how time has passed. As if to emphasise the point, Mermaid's Gold lifts her off foreleg and starts pawing the ground impatiently. 'Look, I should start my first run; I don't want Mermaid's Gold getting cold and we've only got half an hour left before the first racehorse string arrives.'

'Sure, no problem,' says Daniel. He hesitates a moment, then asks, 'Do you mind if I ride along with you?'

'I don't mind at all,' says Hattie. She gestures at Mermaid's Gold. 'But she won't be too impressed if she's not allowed to lead.'

Daniel laughs. 'Duly noted, but don't worry. They were field buddies for a few months while she was at my place, The Rogue knows she's the boss.'

The all-weather gallops stretch for eight furlongs, starting along the flat of the field and then curving right and climbing all the way up the long hill from Lower Leighton to Upper Leighton. Mermaid's Gold jigs as they walk off the grass and onto the track, anticipating what comes next. Beside her, The Rogue sticks out his long neck and pokes the mare's neck with his muzzle. She squeals indignantly. Hattie laughs. So does Daniel.

'You ready?' says Hattie. 'Hand canter?'

Daniel nods. 'Let's do it.'

They canter, side by side and stride for stride, along the flat towards the turn. The conditions are perfect underfoot, the all-weather gallops being resistant to frost and sub-zero temperatures. As they glide around the curve and start their assent, Hattie sees the sun peeping over the crest of the hill on the horizon. On both sides of the track, steam rises from the frosted grass as the sunlight hits it.

Hattie's fingers are stiff with cold, and her cheeks are flushed from the icy air, but she can't think of anything more beautiful. Mermaid's Gold is relaxed and happy, and seems rather taken with The Rogue, although as his nose gets a fraction ahead of hers she takes hold of one of his reins and gives it a pull, making sure the big bay gelding stays slightly behind.

Daniel and Hattie laugh. As they near the top of the hill, Hattie glances at Daniel – takes in his kind eyes, that sexy but bashful smile of his, and the sympathetic way he rides The Rogue. He holds her gaze and her stomach flips again. She grins and he grins back.

It feels like a perfect start to the day.

AFTERWORD

Firstly, I'd like to thank you, the reader, for reading this book. I really hope you enjoyed it as much as I enjoyed writing it. Please let me know your thoughts by posting a review on Amazon; it would really mean a lot.

Getting a book prepared for publication takes a brilliant team. I'd like to say a huge thank you to the brilliant author Ed James for mentoring me through the process, to John Rickards, top copyediting guru, to Victoria Goldman, excellent eagle-eyed proofreader, and the brilliantly creative Louise Brown for the cover design – you are all awesome. A big shout out to my family and friends for all your support and encouragement – and massive thanks to those of you who read the early drafts.

If you'd like to find out more about me, you can hop over to my website at joniharperwriter.com and check out my socials via Instagram @joniharperwriter or Facebook @joniharperwriter – it's always great to connect.

You can also stay up to date on my book news by signing up to my Readers Club – turn the page to find out more!

Until next time…

Joni x

THE CHASE

A FREE LEIGHTONSHIRE LOVERS SHORT STORY

Join the Joni Harper Readers Club and get access to THE CHASE – a free short story set in and around Leightonshire and the equestrian world.

I've also included a bonus short story along with it – THE TROT UP.

As a member of the Readers Club you'll receive book and writing news updates and have the opportunity to enter exclusive giveaways. It's all completely free and you can opt out at any time.

To join, follow this link **joniharperwriter.com** and click on **Join My Readers' Club**.

ENVY & ELEGANCE

LEIGHTONSHIRE LOVERS SERIES BOOK TWO

Event riders Hattie Kimble and Daniel Templeton-Smith are falling for each other, but Hattie is hiding a secret from Daniel and as the weeks pass telling him the truth seems to get harder than ever. As the eventing season throws them challenge after challenge, will Hattie and Daniel's relationship grow stronger or is it going to break apart?

Farrier Wayne Jefferies is living the dream. Fresh from his appearance in the Rural Pleasures charity calendar, he's had more one-night stands than he can count, but when he meets aspiring dressage rider Megan Taylor he starts to experience something he's never felt before – love. If only she felt the same way.

Megan Taylor can barely make ends meet, so when her tack is stolen and she can't afford to replace it, she starts a side-hustle on OnlyFans. The money starts pouring in, but it's not long before she's attracting unwanted attention that threatens to destroy her job, her friendships and her budding equestrian career. The one man she's interested in seems to have friend-zoned her. Can she get him to change his mind?

Dressage diva Jem Baulman-Carter becomes an Instagram sensation when she posts a video of herself crying after her tack room is burgled. But when Daniel Templeton-Smith turns down her romantic advances, she vows to get her revenge on him.

ENVY & ELEGANCE is a spicy, adrenaline-fuelled equestrian sports romance set in the rural idyl of Leightonshire county and the interconnected worlds of eventing and dressage.

https://mybook.to/SI6Uuqz

TINSEL & TEMPTATION

LEIGHTONSHIRE LOVERS SERIES BOOK THREE

It's December and event rider Daniel Templeton-Smith has been invited to jump in the Eventers vs Showjumpers competition at the London International Horse Show. With his top horses and girlfriend, fellow eventer Hattie Kimble, he sets off in the horsebox for a fun week in London. Little does he know that his nemesis from the past is also heading for London, and they're out for revenge.

Up and coming show jumper Maisy Cooper has qualified for her first London International but the pressure is getting to her. When she shows up drunk to walk the course on the first day, it looks as if her dream of competing might be over before she's even set foot in the arena. Then she meets show jumping heart-throb Joe Broughton and everything gets a *lot* more complicated.

Wayne Jefferies is thrilled to be one of the on-site farriers at the London International this year. Loved-up with his girlfriend, the model Megan Taylor, he's hoping the week in London can be a romantic getaway too. He's got a special secret planned, if only the crowds would stop besieging Megan everywhere they go.

TINSEL & TEMPTATION is a spicy, adrenaline-fuelled equestrian sports romance set in the heart of London at the glamorous week-long

London International Horse Show. Trophies are won and dreams are shattered, lovers are made and enemies are out for vengeance, and on the final night of the horse show tensions reach fever pitch, climaxing as the fairy tale Christmas finale takes place and the commentator wishes the audience a Merry Christmas.

Coming Winter 2024...

ABOUT THE AUTHOR

Joni Harper began riding horses almost as soon as she could walk and started her competitive horse riding career aged six years old. She was a keen member of the Pony Club and as an adult rode successfully for many years in British Eventing competitions. She's been a Pony Club instructor in the UK, a Riding Counsellor in the USA, and has mucked out more stables than she can possibly count. She also trained as a horse whisperer. Joni has an MA in Creative Writing and loves to write about horses, the countryside and goings on in rural communities.